"One of the best [books] I've read about the   obsession one needs to keep going under tough odds . . . trying to stay true to himself, and his struggle against the odds makes for a compelling read."

—*Village Voice*

"Not since Henry Miller has a writer so successfully captured the trials and tribulations of a struggling artist. . . . Once again, Nersesian focuses on urban life, and here he has created a masterly image."

—*Library Journal* (starred review)

"[Nersesian] has a talent for dark comedy and witty dialogue. . . . [His] prose is often direct and unapologetic, but contains within its flow much subtlety and artistry. . . . Woven throughout are gems of observational brilliance. . . . Nersesian has taken us on a vivid tour throughout Village life."

—*American Book Review*

"Magnificent. . . . Nersesian's story of a man on a search for authenticity won't leave you hungry. . . . Nersesian is this generation's Mark Twain and the East River is his Mississippi."

—Jennifer Belle, author of *Going Down* and *High Maintenance*

"Finding the key glimmer of hope in the face of humiliation is the Nersesian trademark, present in all his books from *The Fuck-Up* to *Chinese Takeout*, which are set against a New York backdrop that seems to disappear almost as fast as Nersesian can get it on the page. He's an original."

—Thomas Beller, editor of *Before and After: Stories from New York*

"*Chinese Takeout* thoroughly validates Nersesian's rep as one of the wittiest and most perceptive literary chroniclers of downtown life. . . . In addition to deconstructing the backbiting gallery scene, Nersesian's narrative incorporates a highly amusing ethnography of Washington Square Park booksellers. Anyone who lives below Fourteenth Street will be impressed with the writer's sharp eye for physical detail."   —*Time Out* (New York)

For *The Fuck-Up*

"[A] terrific novel. . . . The charm and grit of Nersesian's voice is immediately enveloping, as the down-and-out but oddly up narrator of his terrific novel, *The Fuck-Up*, slinks through Alphabet City and guttural utterances of love."

—*Village Voice*

"Nersesian creates a charming everyman whose candor and surefooted description of his physical surroundings and emotional framework help his tale flow naturally and therefore believably."

—*Paper*

"Nersesian has a knack for making a descent into homelessness suspenseful. It's hard to stop reading."

—*Time Out* (New York)

"Nersesian's *Fuck-Up* is a *Trainspotting* without drugs, New York–style."

—Hal Sirowitz, author of *Mother Said*

"Combining moments of brilliant black humor with flashes of devastating pain, [it] reads like a roller coaster ride. . . . A wonderful book."

—*Alternative Press*

"Read it and howl. And be glad it didn't happen to you."

—Bruce Benderson, author of *User*

For *Manhattan Loverboy*

"Best Book for the Beach, Summer 2000."

—*Jane* magazine

"Best Indie Novel of 2000."

—*Montreal Mirror*

"MLB is paranoid fantasy and fantastic comedy in the service of social realism. . . . [It] assays the grittiest, funkiest urban-magic-realism yet, creating a satirical fiction avidly in search of the truth it's all too aware is even stranger than itself."

—Phil Leggiere, *Downtown*

"MLB sits somewhere between Kafka, DeLillo, and Lovecraft—a terribly frightening, funny and all too possible place."

—*Literary Review of Canada*

"Funny and darkly surreal."

—*New York Press*

Delphi Basilicato

About the Author

ARTHUR NERSESIAN's other novels include *The Fuck-Up*, *Manhattan Loverboy*, *dogrun*, *Suicide Casanova*, and *Chinese Takeout*. He has also written three books of poems and a book of plays. Nersesian was the managing editor of the literary magazine *The Portable Lower East Side* and was an English teacher at Hostos Community College, City University of New York, in the South Bronx. He was born and raised in New York City.

Also by Arthur Nersesian

The Fuck-Up
Manhattan Loverboy
dogrun,
Suicide Casanova
Chinese Takeout

UNLUBRICATED

A NOVEL

ARTHUR NERSESIAN

Perennial

An Imprint of HarperCollins*Publishers*

The text for the play *Unlubricated* on page 210 is based on the play *East Village Writer's Bloc* by Arthur Nersesian.

HarperCollins books may be purchased for educational, business, or sales promotional use. For information please write: Special Markets Department, HarperCollins Publishers Inc., 10 East 53rd Street, New York, NY 10022.

FIRST EDITION

Designed by Elias Haslanger

Library of Congress Cataloging-in-Publication Data

Nersesian, Arthur.
    Unlubricated : a novel—1st ed.
        p.   cm.
    ISBN 0-06-073411-6
    1. Off-Broadway theater—Fiction. 2. New York (N.Y.)—Fiction. 3. Theater—Fiction. I. Title.

PS3564.E67U54 2004
813'.54—dc22

2004044657

06 07 08 ❖/RRD 10 9 8 7 6 5 4 3

To Sasha Kahn

Eliminate men and women will shape up.
—Valerie Solanas, *SCUM Manifesto*

UNLUBRICATED

1

The Industry Bash

Int. ANTONIO's office—day.
ANTONIO's office is a large, seductive space, defined
by retro furniture, hi-tech equipment, pastel-colored
walls, a leather couch.

> ANTONIO
> Look, Virginia, I really have no time for this.
>
> VIRGINIA
> No time for what?
>
> ANTONIO
> You've always got something up your sleeve.
>
> VIRGINIA
> Then I'll remove my sleeve.
> (*VIRGINIA takes off her shirt.*)
>
> ANTONIO
> (*Smiling*) You've always got something in your bra.
> (*VIRGINIA removes her bra. . . . .*)

The screenplay went on like that. They all did.

Lately, the real trick to auditioning was keeping my face from cracking in two and betraying my revulsion for these idiotic little characterizations. I had gone to forty-eight auditions during the first nine months of that year—most of them tiny, forgettable roles. Of those forty-eight awful tryouts, I had gotten nine callbacks, and though I was made several offers, none of them were paying jobs. This script was actually one of the best shots I had—three measly scenes in an indie film. The audition was in one week, and I could only wonder how many other actresses I had to go up against.

Because I didn't want others in Starbucks to hear us, and probably due to the fact that my lecherous rehearsal partner, Noah, was using the script as fodder for some upcoming shower fantasy, we moved closer and closer together. When I finally felt his bad breath on my face, I jerked my chair back.

"You don't seem very in the moment, Hannah," Noah said.

"I'm just a little distracted." Aside from the fact that I didn't like the screenplay, in my handbag were two other scripts that I couldn't wait to get to.

"I'm in the new Coen Brothers film," he mentioned. "You want to catch it with me tonight?"

"I can't."

Over the past year or so, he had been paid to be a body in the background of seven Hollywood films. To sit next to him as he frantically searched the screen for himself and yelled out remarks like, "I was right next to that guy!" was just too sad. In the four movies that had come out since he began extra-ing, he had not survived the final edit.

I thanked him for his time and watched as he straightened his shirt and zipped up his jacket.

"By the way," I said as we headed outside, "I might have something for you soon."

"In Stein's film?" he kidded as we walked north. Stein was the director of the indie film I was auditioning for. Shooting was tentatively scheduled for late fall.

"No, something else, but I don't want to jinx it." I was referring to one of my possible handbag projects, a film that my girlfriend, Christy, was hoping to shoot. Though the latest incarnation of her script was done, I knew it was going to be a mess. I still hadn't yet mustered up the strength to read it.

"Just because you and Christy are lovers . . . I don't get those kinds of opportunities . . . I might not be sexy but that doesn't mean . . ." I only made out occasional phrases that Noah was saying. The Midtown cacophony—horns, bus engines, jackhammers, a bike messenger muttering a profane rap—drowned out all his soft words.

Also my hearing was still impaired from the night before, when Christy and I had attended a noisy industry bash at the Union Square Ballroom. It was a backer's ball for Franklin Stein's upcoming movie, *Success!* Christy had immediately started ordering Bloody Marys, chatting with her old friends at the bar. Excluded from her conversation and finding it difficult to breathe, I went out for air. That was when a handsome guy asked how I was involved in the project.

"I'm not. I don't know anything about it."

He filled me in, seeming to know everything about it, as well as everyone else there. He finally introduced himself as director Franklin Stein. The bash was being thrown for his upcoming film.

I told him I was there with Christy Saffers, who had been invited by his producer, Manny Greene. Franklin said he had seen her first film and loved it.

"She's really talented."

"So what are you? Her producer?"

I told him that I was dating Christy.

"Well, my wife is one of my producers, technically."

"What do you mean, technically?" I asked, unsure if he was coming on to me.

"Just that we're parting ways romantically. We're getting a divorce." A clear sexual vibe was bouncing back.

"Sorry to hear it." I then told the up-and-coming director that I also worked as an actress.

"You look familiar," he said. "What were you in?"

"I've done a lot of downtown theater," I replied, since I had no real résumé. "And I'm starring in Christy's next project about a Central American maid."

"Sure, that's the one Manny's interested in," he recalled.

"Well, it's still in the talking stages."

"You know," he said, I have a supporting actress role in *Success!* that might be good for you."

"Really?"

"Yeah, we were thinking of finding some TV talent, but I want this to be racy, so I'll give you an audition if you want to try out. It's going to require a bit of nudity."

"Is it integral to the role?" I tried to sound sincere.

"Of course," he said without a hint of sarcasm. "I detest gratuitous sex scenes."

"Well, I can't commit to anything until I see the whole script," I said, instead of the thank you, thank you, thank you that was running through my mind.

He asked where I resided so he could drop off the pages of his script for my audition.

"I live with Christy in Tribeca," I said to extinguish any hopes of a homebound romance.

"How long have you lived together?"

"Longer than I intended. It was supposed to be temporary, but the housing situation is impossible."

"I just heard of a place that should be opening up in a few months," he said. That was when my cellular chimed Beethoven's "Ode to Joy." I let it go to voice mail.

"An affordable place?" I asked as I checked the caller ID. Christy was calling me from inside the party.

"Oh, yeah, this actress, Thelma, had lived there a while. It's a studio on Forty-fifth, available sometime soon."

"How much does affordable mean?"

"Around five hundred."

At that moment some assistant raced up to him and urgently muttered something in his ear.

"Shit! It's my wife," he said as the underling raced away. "Do you have a number or something? I have to dash."

I gave him my business card, he gave me his card, and stepping forward—without warning, 'cause I never would've allowed it—he kissed me gently on the lips.

Thoroughly ventilated and buoyed by the prospect of a decent audition, I returned into the fray of party people, where I struggled to get a drink. I finally got a glass of white wine only to stand uncomfortably on the sidelines looking for Christy. Among a million deal makers screaming back and forth, some guy was standing right behind me, murmuring frantically. That technological breakthrough of modern rudeness—the cell phone—was his accomplice: "Yes, I brought the play with me, but the whole thing was a stupid fucking idea . . . 'cause technically *Unlubricated* doesn't even exist . . . Yes, he's here, I'm looking right at him. No! . . . 'cause he'll try to take control of it. Money's not as important as control. It's a great work of art. This play is the only chance I have of ever trying to parlay myself into a serious acting career. . . ."

The young Martin Scorseses, David Lynches, and Spike Lees of the upcoming generation as well as half a dozen of the last generation's more obscure directors, along with various agents and producers, were circulating. I should have been trying to hobnob with them. Miramax people were sipping near the bar. The hot young film producer Barbara Suffolk, who was wearing the exact same outfit as I, was right next to me. Yet none of them seemed nearly as intriguing as this cellular soliloquy behind me:

". . . because she's hot right now . . . Oh really? Just go to any bookstore in the country and look at her book. It's selling off the shelf. Her play was the hottest ticket in town! No! The book is *Bull Session*. Her play is *Coprophagia*, you idiot! . . . Yeah, the book just came out. Yeah, check out the foreword. This fucking play is listed as a lost masterpiece, and I'm holding it in my hand!" Turning around, I realized I knew the hoarse whisperer.

"There you are!" Christy drunkenly yelled before I could approach him. "I'm a little tipsy, help me into a cab."

"Where are we going?" I asked as I walked her up the stairs and out the door.

"I'm spending a couple of nights uptown with Ma so don't forget to water the garbage," she said as we walked north along the west side of Union Square.

"You mean water the plants and take out the garbage," I corrected as I hailed a cab barreling down Broadway.

It screeched to a halt on Seventeenth Street. She was about to get in when she suddenly stopped herself. "Oh, wait! I've been meaning to give this to you."

She frantically searched through her bag and located her screenplay, something she had just had printed at the local Kinko's. She gave me a kiss, slammed the cab door, and the yellow vehicle was gone. I flipped through the pages of her much-anticipated script. In the passionate throes of our relationship, she had promised to cast me in the lead once it was produced.

Since I was half a block from the Barnes & Noble megastore, I dashed inside, located the New Releases Nonfiction shelf and instantly saw it, a copy of *Bull Session: The Unsuspected Writings of Lilly Bull*.

Lillian Bullonus, aka Lilly Bull, was a bona fide psycho who wrote two odd works. Her first piece was a weird man-hating tract called *C.O.C.K.*, done back in the '60s. Her second was a burlesque comedy entitled *Coprophagia*. After shooting and very nearly killing an experimental downtown musician named Gary Ganghole, she was committed to an institution for the criminally insane. When she was released, she worked for a while as a prostitute to subsidize her writings. Soon after that, sometime in the early '90s, broke and alone, she died of pneumonia. Only last year was her comedy finally produced. It had enjoyed a lengthy run in San Francisco. On the cover of *Bull Session* was a photograph of Lilly Bull peeking out of a coffin. Finally, in death, she achieved the downtown icon status she wanted in life.

I flipped through the foreword written by Cathy Pollita, the editor, who described how the executor of Bull's estate, Estelle Bullonus, Lilly's aunt, accepted a collect call late one night from a lady named Eva Bryan who managed the Salinas Valley Hotel Bull had stayed in during the late '80s. Bryan explained that she possessed a crate of Bull's writing and in exchange for two months of unpaid back rent she would be glad to ship her the crate. *Bull Session* was edited from the work in that box. The foreword explained that Bull's notebooks list a variety of pieces that either were not yet written or were lost to posterity, among them "a full-length play, entitled *Unlubricated*." I quickly perused the pages of notes that meticulously described the plot and characters of this "lost masterpiece."

I purchased the book, officially maxing out my credit card, and skimmed through its entries. *Unlubricated* was written during the period Bull spent in the Creedless Institution for the Criminally Insane after shooting Ganghole. According to the foreword, Bull had suspected him of composing tunes designed to control her thoughts. In revenge, she purchased a cheap .22 caliber handgun, and shot him three times without killing him.

I made it back to Stein's ball roughly twenty minutes later, and the party was still in full swing.

"Excuse me, are you Hannah Cohn?" asked the assistant who had ended my impromptu meeting with Franklin.

"Yeah."

He suddenly handed me a bound script. To my delight I realized it was the entire screenplay of *Success!* On the list of characters, someone had placed a star next to my prospective role, "Virginia R."

"Did Franklin leave?"

"Yep." I thanked him and he vanished.

I hunted down the cellular hoarse whisperer—Bree Silverburn. During my first semester at Yale, I had a one-night stand with the drunken captain of the tennis team. After a miserable opening volley he passed out. I tried to sleep but couldn't get past a disgusting gurgling noise coming from the roommate-shared bathroom. There I found a handsome youth lying on his back, sniveling, spasming and aspirating on his own vomit. He was so thoroughly drugged-out he couldn't even flop over. I rolled him onto his side, made sure his air passage was cleared, and went back to bed. About a week later, I saw him tooting happily around on campus. I made the mistake of introducing myself and letting him know that I had saved his happy-go-lucky life—that was Bree Silverburn.

He was standing near the bar in front of a line of empty wineglasses.

"Bree, how are you?"

"Fine. Oh, it's not what you think." He caught himself, and pointing to the glasses he said, "These were ginger ale."

"Oh, then you're still . . . unlubricated." I held up the copy of *Bull Session* that I had just purchased.

"What the hell are you doing with that?" He instantly sobered up.

"I know you got it."

"Wait a sec"—he looked at my dress—"I thought you were someone else."

"What do you mean?"

"Nothing, who told you about *Unlubricated*?"

"Relax. I was just wondering if you were looking to show it to Manny Greene?" He was the bigwig producer who was hosting the shindig.

"No, but I do have plans."

"Who owns it?"

"I've secured the rights."

"Are you putting it up?"

"No, but I got someone else lined up to option it."

"Who?"

"No comment." He sipped his ginger ale.

"Well, let's assume they don't option it," I said, knowing that 99 percent of all deals in this business fall apart.

"You want an option on the option?" he joked. "Truth of the matter is, I just want to perform in it."

"Sounds reasonable."

"But that's not the way these guys work, is it? They buy the rights, turn on the steamroller and that's the last you see of them."

"So you're looking for someone you can trust?"

"Someone I can trust with the clout to get the play up." When he silently waved to the bartender and was served a glass of white wine, I knew that he had been lying, and that all the other empty glasses were also liquor. He leaned toward me a little too close and intimated, "I was actually thinking of approaching a smaller company, but it would have to be of some note in the theatrical community."

"Like Disaffected Artist Types," I suggested, referring to the company I was a part of at Yale.

"Well, frankly, I think I can do better," he said candidly, "but we'll see."

"What will we see?" I asked.

"We'll see if other companies of greater prestige pass."

"But you're not ruling us out?"

"I'm not ruling anything out," he replied, and took a sip from his glass. "Frankly, I want a small company. I want the production to grow slowly but I also want it to be able to go the entire distance, Off-Broadway, Broadway, Hollywood."

"You know we're preparing our upcoming season and we're looking for some new exciting works."

"You guys have cash?"

"Not a lot, but enough."

"Intriguing," he said, with a trace of sarcasm.

"So may I see the play?" I asked, noticing a manila envelope folded into his jacket pocket.

"I do have a spare copy, but I really shouldn't," he toyed.

"What have you got to lose?"

"Frankly, I feel it's cruel to tease you, but I guess I owe you one. I'll let you read it, provided you show it to no one and you accept the fact that you probably ain't getting it."

"'Probably' still gives me some hope."

"Hope is the scum on the pond of failure. There's no skimming it off, it just replenishes. But the fact is, I have some pretty big guns lined up for this and they're probably going to grab it."

"I understand."

"Understand this without a doubt. If circumstances do ordain that you produce this work, I will act the role of Reggie on stage, on screen, and in mime, understand?"

"I understand."

He took the large envelope out of his pocket and handed it to me. We chatted a bit more, drank a bit more, and soon he was fully drunk and I was thoroughly bored. We exited together. He headed north and I went south. By the time I got home, I was too exhausted to look at either Christy's screenplay or Bree's play. I only had enough sense to call Noah, who agreed to read Stein's pages with me at Starbucks in the morning. I fell asleep as soon as I hit the bed.

Late the next morning, after my mini-rehearsal at Starbucks with Noah, I took my seat at the reception desk. I had been working for two weeks at the headquarters of SHW Cable, where I was supposed to field calls, but most of the messages were caught in the voice-mail net. The place was fairly typical of all the offices I had worked in——dark olive carpets, powder-blue walls, and a tinted southern exposure of Midtown Manhattan from roughly three hundred and twenty feet in the air——the thirty-second floor. I'm not sure if it was the fluorescent lights or Noah's bad breath that morning, but I had a throbbing headache. So the only time I actually picked up the phone that morning was to call my acupuncturist, Dr. Wang.

"Can you come in Thursday evening?" he asked.

"Can't you make it any sooner?"

"The only other appointment I have is tomorrow morning at nine."

"That'd be great, I can stop in before work."

As I rummaged through my bag looking for a Motrin I spotted Bree's highly sensitive envelope. I really expected very little. Most plays were crappy. I knew that the key attraction to this entire menagerie was the fact that its dead author, Lilly Bull, would get instant audience recognition.

I opened it up and saw a Xerox of webbed and crinkled pages. By the crooked fonts, I could see the lettering was from an old typewriter.

Handwritten notes were carroted in between the lines and scribbled sideways along the margins. The original title, *Getting It Both Ways*, was crossed out. A new title was boldly written over it—*Unlubricated*.

As I sped through the work, I found myself laughing aloud, deliciously engaged. Without even noticing it, my headache had vanished. The play was a solid two-act dramatic comedy about the last night of a dysfunctional, nonproductive writers' group, complete with mildly effete dilettantes and somewhat buffoonish dabblers. Each character read some minor literary effort, then they critiqued each other's works. But personalities and private entanglements kept bleeding into their opinions. Old issues and dynamics filtered through, stifling the purpose of the group while revealing a gallery of characters along with their complex relationships.

The denouement occurs when it is discovered that one member of the group, a strung-out writer who claims to have the world's worst case of writer's block, has secretly written a monumental epic.

Upon learning this secret, the other writers in the group freak out, each in their own way and for their own particular reason: A would-be playwright, Miles, goes psycho out of envy. A gay poet, Lenny, flames his rage because of his own unrequited love for the strung-out, blocked-up writer, whose name is Waldo. A third wordsmith, named Reggie, misinterprets Waldo's secret epic as a sexual confessional. And, because they both slept with the only female in the group, Reggie fears he might've been circuitously exposed to the HIV virus. When all turn against Waldo, the one woman in the writing circle, Samantha, sticks up for him. It was a juicy role. If the play was ever produced I'd love to play her. Another female writer, Lucy, who only appears in flashbacks, craves male affirmation, in contrast with Samantha's stalwart feminism. But even if Bree let me have the rights to produce it, I didn't really have a production company.

My old college repertory group that I had mentioned to Bree no longer existed. During our senior year at Yale, we were all eager to fatten up our acting résumés in order to get into the prestigious graduate program. Unfortunately none of us did, so we dissolved Disaffected Artist Types. Now Belinda St. John, who initially founded the company, wanted to start it up again. I had all but turned her down. This was probably because we were rivals, always going after the same type of roles, but if that wasn't enough, I had always suspected her of having an affair with my boyfriend. It was one of the reasons I broke up with him, before dating Christy—my only female lover.

After finishing *Unlubricated*, feeling incredibly energized, I tried to read Christy's script. Yet, as the pages and minutes slowly passed, I felt depressed. Even though she had a producer and a real shot at getting a film up, the opening pages were clearly bad. I spent the rest of the day and most of the evening trying to make sense of just the first act. Back at Christy's that night, after cooking myself some organic soup from a can, I finally fell asleep on page nineteen.

2

An Appointment in Chinatown

THE·NEXT·MORNING, I stumbled out of Christy's Tribeca apartment around eight. Tiredly I showered and quickly dressed. A beautiful summer day was wasted on me as I stumbled around the corner and
passed a short line of people outside a public school. It was the may-
oral primary, but I wasn't even registered in the city.

I considered boarding a crosstown bus, but Canal was always the
most traffic-jammed street in the city. Instead I decided to take the A
train. I was hoping to change to the F at West Fourth and go to East
Broadway. To my luck, one was waiting in the station. No sooner did
the doors slide shut than I realized I had accidentally boarded the
downtown A.

I got off at the next stop, Park Place, where I decided to just walk
east to Chinatown. Tiredly climbing the steps of the Park Place station, I was awakened by a hectic swirl of sirens, yells and screams.
Some people were racing north, some headed down the flight of subway stairs.

I trotted a block south to see what all the trouble was about.

From my eighty-degree-angle view up the front of the north tower, I barely saw smoke, let alone flames. Smoldering debris was scattered along the front of the building about a block and a half away. As I looked southeasterly from Church across the concourse, I felt like I had slipped into some strange time paradox—slow motion within high speed. Thousands of office workers were pushing out and dashing eastward. I only had a split second to figure out what the large smoldering chunks of metal were. Things were falling from the top of the building. As I began to wonder if maybe part of the antenna had blown up, I heard someone scream that a plane had crashed into the building.

Before I could return to the subway, I was swept up with others rushing east down the middle of Vesey Street. In an instant, I was locked solidly into a crowd, but it wasn't a crush. Bodies weren't pushed against bodies. I could smell a mix of deodorants, colognes and perfumes. All the while there was a veneer of civility. We were close enough so that if my knees buckled I'd have this great stampede of office workers knocking me down. Without thinking, I extended my hands slightly out front as I couldn't see beyond the back of the five or six people dashing just a few inches around me. When I almost stumbled, it was on a small handbag. Some woman must've dropped it in the run. Feeling mildly claustrophobic, I just focused on moving quickly in this weird, measured step. A stride that was not too far, and a pace neither too fast nor too slow. We were moving at roughly five and a half miles an hour.

"Did you see the plaza!" I heard one lady whispering tensely to another. "Did you see them?"

"Oh God!"

"I never saw anything like—"

"Shush," said the other woman.

It seemed as though most of the people in the crowd knew each other. They moved inside each other's personal spaces. There was a lot of thoughtless touches, a kind of human net in motion. Fingers sprawled above backs. Hands gently grazing alongside forearms, rubbing against cars and emergency vehicles that were frozen in the street. Some of the cops or firemen were yelling, "Make way!" but there wasn't any room. One delicate elbow nudged into my kidney, while another repeatedly grazed along my ribs. About a third of the way up the block, when the crowd suddenly slowed, I accidentally crushed down on the back of the guy's shoe in front of me. That was when the lady behind me kicked the pointy tip of her dress shoe under my heel and I accidentally crunched down on her toes.

"Hey!" yelled an older man off to my right, but it wasn't 'cause of me. Another young woman mysteriously shouted out, "Oww!"

Where the street met the curb, the crowd came to a complete halt. One of those metal coffee stands had caused a bottleneck. Since we slowed, I was finally able to just look around. Next to me, a lady in her fifties, who wore a gray business suit with perfect hair, had a deep cut down her forehead. A young guy was wearing a torn T-shirt that was speckled with blood. A lot of the guys were just in white shirts and ties. They must've left their jackets on the backs of their swivel chairs. A lady who was dressed as a waitress complete with a name tag that said "Lorna" had three wet drops of blood on her light blue shirt, just enough to ruin it. I saw others splotched with blood, but I didn't actually see wounds. Inasmuch as they didn't seem any slower than the rest, I didn't think it was their blood. It was probably from those who were deposited into the ambulances parked along Church. One guy who was dressed like an executive had the shoulder of his expensive suit and shirt torn down, so I could see a bloody gash that he was compressing with his other hand. Something very sharp must have fallen on him.

This awoke me to the fact that I was only witnessing the final scene of a much larger drama. Some of these people must have seen casualties from the accident. What else would compel such a controlled pandemonium? I knew that a plane had hit the World Trade Center, but I also remembered that decades ago, another plane had struck the Empire State Building. It was a much narrower building and it had safely withstood that crash. Looking behind me, at the northern tower, I still couldn't see any flames, so I thought all would be fine.

The notion that I had gotten up early, jumped on a train and got locked into this slow-moving crowd as if it were the first thing on my to-do list, along with the collective tension of the group, actually made me a little giddy. I figured that at the next block, once I was free of all this, I could dash northeast and just be a little late for my acupuncturist's appointment. As the pace of the crowd started picking up again, I found myself running in tight formation.

About twenty feet forward, a little to my right, I saw a pair of arms shoot up from the crowd suddenly. A tall woman tripped, blurting out, "Fuck, my shoe!"

She tried to go back and retrieve it, but there were just too many people pushing her forward.

"Watch it!" someone said.

Only because of the density of human mass she didn't go down, yet she hadn't immediately regained her balance either. She wasn't dressed like the others around us. Like me, she must've just been swept up the street with the office workers. People behind parted around her, allowing her to slow down. I found an opening to my right where she had been walking. As I approached the spot where she tripped, I saw her shoe. Briskly stooping, I snatched it up. After several more minutes, I spotted her limping slowly along the sidewalk. When space opened to my right, I sidled over and handed her the footwear.

"Thanks, so much," she said, pulling it on. "Can you imagine losing your shoe and not being able to . . ."

The crowd pulled us apart. A moment later, though, the crowd jostled me sideways back to her. Together we kept moving. We were almost on Broadway, where the narrow corridor of street opened into a wide expanse.

"How the fuck can a pilot not see the World Trade Center on a gorgeous day like this?" she asked loudly. I felt embarrassed that others were listening so I just smiled. "I mean, the guy's got to be drunk or on cra—"

An unbelievable piercing turned into a high-pitched grinding sound that instantly drowned out everything. From behind the Transportation Building I caught sight of a gigantic airplane as it soared into the south tower. The explosion caused a collective shiver. The massive fireball was so hot that even blocks away and from hundreds of feet below, I could actually feel its flash on my face. Everyone let out a gasp and the slight modicum of control that had set the tone suddenly fell away. These were not accidents. We were under attack.

Who the fuck would do this? was my first thought. Then I realized it wasn't over. More must be on the way. Missiles were probably en route to us.

The flight instinct hit everyone at once as we all broke free and ran in different directions. I dashed across to the southwest border of City Hall Park, where I pulled out my cell phone and tried speed-dialing my parents. If this was my last call I wanted to try to say good-bye. But I couldn't get through. All phones were out. Office workers raced around me locked in a frantic evacuation mode. Circling along the south side of City Hall Park with a clear view westward behind the Transportation Building of the towers, I drifted up Park Row walking backward numbly, not fully digesting all that was happening.

"Get in here!" an older guy shouted over to me. He was standing in front of J&R Music on the far side of the street. When I raced over, I realized he was talking to someone behind me. Emergency vehicles had crowded into all the immediate streets surrounding the towers. The crush of people compelled other emergency vehicles to converge on Broadway and in City Hall Park. I spotted a group of people getting triaged: Office workers with difficulties walking, breathing, or covered in blood were being assisted by paramedics. For an instant the crowd seemed to dissipate, then it thickened again. I imagined these final stragglers as the last from the north tower and the first evacuees from the south tower.

One odd thing that caught my eye was a short guy who looked Central American. The entire time he stood on the intersection across from the park. Despite all that was happening, he continued passing out leaflets. A surprising amount of people who were exiting City Hall Park still grabbed them on autopilot. Finally he ran out of flyers and took off toward the Brooklyn Bridge. The air was full with sirens. Fire engines were pulling up along with cop cars and ambulances, parking along Broadway and Park Row, right on the sidewalk. One cop car narrowly careened to a halt in front of me.

"Get the fuck out of my way!" the cop yelled frantically. I jumped.

"Hey you! Come here." It was the shoeless lady from the crowd. She was in front of the Starbucks on the corner of Beekman and Park Row, holding a cup of coffee.

"It's like a fucking movie," I said, not intending to sound trite, but the enormity of it was remarkable. People were pouring from the southwest and heading northeast over the bridge or streaming up Centre Street.

"Want a cup of coffee?" she offered.

"Yeah, I think I need it." We went in and I ordered my usual: grande, with soy milk, and a chocolate additive.

I felt strangely safe inside the Starbucks, ordering my usual. For an instant it felt like a normal morning, even with all the sirens blaring and people running away. Perhaps they even had Starbucks in hell.

I could see a thick black smoke pouring out of the upper tenth of the northern building, as well as from a lower section of the southern building.

"So were you in the south tower?" she asked.

"I was just going to my acupuncturist, but I got on the wrong train," I explained as we waited for my drink.

"Where?"

I told her that he was up on East Broadway.

"You're only about six blocks from there." She pointed northeast. "I'm heading up that way too."

In another moment I had my coffee and we joined the slow-moving crowd northward, up Centre Street beyond the Brooklyn Bridge, past the Municipal Building, where a cop was directing traffic.

The woman introduced herself as Patricia Harrows. She was in her mid-forties and it turned out she came to New York City in the late '70s to be an actress.

"Was it any easier back then?"

"No, it was the same awful situation as it is today."

"So what did you do?"

She described how she studied under some famous acting guru named Leopold Samyoff whom I had never heard of. Her husband was still involved in the company, but she stopped going to open calls about ten years ago.

"You didn't get any work at all?"

"No, I got some. I did some soaps and small theater roles." She said she even snagged an agent who got her some film auditions, but very quickly she stopped getting calls.

"You completely quit?"

"No, I'm still involved in a local repertory group," she said, "but I mainly do administrative work." The blaring sirens forced us into silence for a minute, then she shouted, "The business doesn't kill you, it just wears you down forever."

That will never happen to me, I thought, since the idea of giving up the only thing I was passionate about was unthinkable. But I had to know why she walked away from it all. Where did her life go wrong? We passed the shiny black marble sword of justice sculpture and drifted up Thomas Paine Park, across from the courthouse where they were always filming *Law & Order*.

"Please evacuate to north of Canal Street," a police megaphone announced as it passed. Throughout our walk, we'd intermittently look back at the towers burning overhead.

"If you could do it all over again, would you?" I asked.

"Sure, you got to. The worst thing at the end of your life isn't failing, it's regretting that you didn't even try." She slurped down the last of her coffee. "All I'm saying is a thousand people are all trying their hardest for that finishing line. The odds are tremendously stacked against you."

This was the refrain I always heard from my parents: The chances of making it in this god-awful profession are so ridiculously small that talent didn't even matter. To avoid showing my sour expression, I looked up at the towers. The thick black smoke which at first seemed concentrated to the sides of impact was now pouring out of more and more floors.

"I really do believe that life compensates you in some ways if you just let it," she said, and then told about how her parents loaned her the money to buy an apartment that she first thought of as "a tiny space on an empty street." It turned out to be a huge loft in Tribeca.

With the crowd, we crossed Foley Square, across from 26 Federal Plaza. "Though I never achieved the success I was looking for," she said, "after a lot of weird sacrifices some really good things just sort of came my way."

Looking back through the veil of smoke, I thought I saw the southern tower slip imperceptibly inward, as though it were folding into itself. "Is the building . . ." I squinted my eyes. "The building's not . . ." Pieces of the tower seemed to be popping out of the side.

"Oh shit!" she yelled. As the building came down it was like watching a landslide. The ground rumbled and we saw a massive wave of grayness billow up Park Row and roll down Centre Street toward us. I dropped my coffee cup and we both dashed out into Centre Street, running north between the bumper-to-bumper traffic. As it passed over, I could feel a hot granular blast like a sandstorm. The sunny day instantly turned dark then milky. I held my breath as long as possible.

When I inhaled through my nose, I sucked in dust and smoke. Coughing and gagging, I pulled my shirt up over my face to breathe through it, and just thought, no, no, this can't be happening.

"This way," Patricia yelled as it cleared, pointing up toward Canal Street.

Though some were racing, we still outpaced most. Following Patricia, I wasn't looking where I was going and dashed right into an older man who was struggling up Centre all alone. He looked to be in his mid-sixties, wearing a dust-covered gray flannel suit. He was nearly convulsing with raspy coughs. I kept running for several seconds.

Then, looking back at him, I felt myself coming to a dead stop.

"Hurry!" Patricia called.

"You go ahead," I yelled to her.

"Where are you going?!"

"I think I know that guy," I lied.

"Good luck!" Patricia replied and resumed dashing.

I turned and ran the half block back, bumping into people along the way. The older man was leaning against a car with his eyes closed, just breathing and gagging into his hand.

"Come on!" I yelled over the piercing alarms and grabbed his arm.

He followed blindly, coughing as I led him a quarter way down the block into the Louis J. Lefkowitz State Office Building.

Once inside, where the air was clearer, he gasped for breath. A security guard brought him a chair. Someone else gave him a cup of water. Periodically, others rushed inside. After a few more minutes of deep, slow breaths, he thanked me, and pulling out his wallet, he took out a twenty.

"No, thanks," I said, knowing that he didn't mean to be insulting.

I waited a while until the air cleared a bit, then I exited. Christy's apartment, where I started out that beautiful morning, was just a few blocks west. I wanted to go home.

As I walked across Worth Street, I was amazed by the sea of papers that were scattered everywhere. Many sheets were still twirling in the air, as though the building was a hundred-story filing cabinet. Office items and pink building insulation were hooked in tree branches. Various things, clothes, venetian blinds and papers, were caught up against cars, trapped in trees, against traffic posts, parking meters, traffic lights, or just blown into doorways. Several firemen with oxygen tanks were putting out little flames that had scattered all over the place. The field of debris seemed to cover the entire city. I couldn't imagine it ever getting cleaned up. It was like a natural phenomenon, as though a volcano had erupted on Wall Street, or a hot powdery snowstorm had struck in summer, complete with a forest of autumn leaves composed of papers. My hair and clothes were totally ruined with that white dust. Visibility was about fifty feet. Everyone was covering their mouths with their shirts, coughing as they ran.

By the time I reached Broadway my eyes were burning and my throat felt completely raw. I kept sneezing and tearing. Though Christy's apartment was due west, I headed north with the crowd just trying to get away from that noxious cloud.

Looking down from Leonard Street I could make out the single remaining World Trade tower with its thick black scarf of smoke. It looked odd, and sad, a twin that had lost its mate.

Thousands of people—had been evacuated all at once. Many were stumbling through in quiet shock. Some people were crying softly to themselves. Others were bleeding, and had been quickly bandaged. Even though sirens were blaring, alarms were piercing, and horns were honking, nothing was moving. Vehicular traffic was at a complete standstill by the time I reached Canal. Nothing was going uptown, over the bridge, or through the tunnel to Jersey.

People had flooded the sidewalk, moving between parked and blocked cars in the streets. I crossed Canal and crept along the inside of Broadway, angling between storefronts where Asian shop owners were watching their portable TVs, and the bulk of the shuffling crowd.

"Oh my God!" a guy said, staring at one of the small TVs. Turning to look at it, I saw the big antenna—the highest point in New York City—was starting to come down. The unthinkable was happening again. Everyone stopped. Looking in the southern sky, I watched as the second tower came crashing down. Even at that distance, the ground trembled again like a series of large dump trucks were rumbling by. Where the first collapse was absolutely terrifying, with this one I felt strangely different. Maybe because I was half expecting it, or perhaps because it was impossible to estimate in terms of human suffering, but watching that incredible structure coming down struck me as one of the most phenomenal things I'd ever witness. It was like watching a page from the Bible come to life. Another fresh cloud of dust rose over us like a gaseous Red Sea. Because I was farther away, it was much more dissipated than the first.

"It was Arab terrorists!" someone yelled. "They just hit the Pentagon!"

"We should just start nuking from the Indian Ocean to the Mediterranean. We have the warheads. We can kill every fucking Arab cocksucker and make Asia into a fucking parking lot!"

"Muslims are fucking evil and they should be wiped off the face of the earth!"

Seeing a subway entrance, I was about to slip down the steps just to get away when I heard someone say the trains weren't running. As I proceeded north through the slow-moving, packed streets, I heard some people weeping. A couple in front of me were talking:

"We got to get the kids and get out of town. More is on the way," the guy said.

"Do you think so?" the female asked tensely.

"Oh yeah. It isn't going to end here," he assured her.

I already felt like a part of Napoleon's army, all dressed in business suits, evacuating from downtown Moscow. I began to wonder if more attacks really were on their way. I had to break free of this angry crowd, these mourning masses. After a moment it occurred to me that Christy lived in the other direction. When I finally circled around and arrived at her place, I discovered her phone was still working so I dialed my parents. My mother answered.

"Is Dad okay?" I asked nervously. Though he was retired, he was in the World Trade Center in 1993 when the bomb went off in the parking garage.

"He's glued to the TV. Where are you?"

"I was at work in Midtown."

"Thank God." I knew she'd freak out if I told her I was down there. "Why don't you come home for a few days?"

"I'm fine."

"But this might not be the end of it," she replied.

"If more was going to happen it would've happened by now."

"That's probably what those people in the buildings thought," she said, though the remark didn't make much sense. "You just don't know."

"Have they announced any casualties?"

"Giuliani said thousands and thousands. And that includes hundreds of firefighters."

When she said that I felt a huge lump in my already raw throat. While I walked and chatted about the adversities of the acting world with Patricia, all those fire trucks and cop cars had been pouring into the area. I had assumed they were hastily extracting the last of the office workers. At the time it seemed like more than enough time to empty all life from the massive towers.

Obviously that was not the case. After hanging up the phone, I pulled off my clothes and shoved them into a plastic bag, then showered. Noticing the thick dust around the frames, I taped all the windows shut. Christy managed to get home from her mother's around three in the afternoon with a bag of food. The entire time we were fixed to the TV. That was when we first learned the names of Osama bin Laden and al-Qaeda. When Giuliani said that more had died than we could bear, we found ourselves crying in each other's arms. Christy and I prayed for the recovery of more survivors, but we were braced for additional attacks. Early that evening, after Building Seven collapsed, we heard a convoy of army vehicles rumble into the area.

The next morning, Christy and I awoke to find that Lower Manhattan had become one big militarized zone. Just getting below Fourteenth Street involved showing ID. The National Guard, kids with rifles, were on patrol everywhere. For a while electricity and then water was turned off in Tribeca, and since neither of us had come out to our parents, we decided it would be easier to just retreat back to our homes for a while than to explain that we'd rather be with our significant others. I stayed in Long Island while Christy moved in with her mother uptown.

My father, who had worked in Tower Two for nearly thirty years, knew twelve people who had been killed. The entire time I was out there, he simply sat on the patio in a daze, staring at the smoke rising in the far distance. I didn't know anyone directly. Yet everyone knew people who knew people. At work, I learned a coworker's brother was killed. From the neighborhood I learned that a girl who I went to high school with had lost her father.

After the first week, they moved the militarized line south, down to Houston Street. Entering the Financial District and the businesses below Canal was nearly impossible. By the second week of Long Island commuting, I started going batty with my parents, so Christy faxed me a formal letter stating that I was her official tenant. I had to show the document to cops and National Guardsmen as soon as I got off the subway, and every time I walked to her house. One evening, when Christy went out to get some food, she suddenly realized she had forgotten her ID and was forced to run like a fugitive from doorway to doorway in order to get back home.

The once-bustling World Trade Center became a smoldering Ground Zero. Underneath six stories of rubble, the fire burned on for months, placing a permanent white cloud over Lower Manhattan. Christy's nose was always running, and the irritants made my eyes perpetually tear. She applied for a FEMA grant to pay for the vent ducts of her loft to be cleaned out.

That constant exhaust of dust and smoke passed over the river, falling upon Brooklyn Heights, Cobble Hill, Park Slope, and all points east. EPA trucks were out everywhere doing constant tests. The smoke could be smelled throughout the remainder of fall through winter, even into the spring of 2002. Though some said it was the odor of incinerated body parts, I thought it was a metallic aroma, like tempered steel from those many massive girders.

Every corner mailbox and lamppost became a taped-up memorial with the radiant faces of "the missing." Despite the fact that New York became a patriotic, even heroic city, tourists avoided it. There seemed to be a lot more American flags than people. The financial area was off-limits. Tribeca was empty.

DOWN AND OUT

THOUGH·I·STILL·WENT to my temp job, all acting auditions ceased, all except for Franklin Stein's film, *Success!* Since he had already booked a studio space in Midtown and made arrangements for the audition before September 11, he held them on September 25. I went in with pages in hand and sat in a reception area with a dozen other actresses who all looked in their teens. At twenty-two, I felt as though I were nearing acting menopause.

"Hannah Cohn?" a receptionist called out. "Go ahead."

In a boxy room, while Franklin, a casting director and an assistant looked on, I did a quick yet competent read-through.

"Do me a favor," Franklin asked, "read it again more slowly. Make it less Meg Ryan perky and more Sharon Stone sultry."

Ignoring his name specifications since I did poor imitations, I tried to slow it down and tease it up.

"Not bad," Franklin said when I finished. "So, are you still looking for an apartment?"

"Yeah, if I can afford it," I replied. Even though I liked living with Christy, the air downtown was difficult to breathe.

"I might just have one for you."

"Really? Is there a fee? Brokers' commissions weren't cheap.

"There's always a small fee," he replied with a smile. How are things with Christy Sapphos?" He made a joke out of her name.

"Fine," I replied with a smile. Two other men sat alongside him across the table from me.

"We'll call you, Miss Cohn," the matter-of-fact casting director said. Franklin smiled with a lusty twinkle in his bedroom eyes. I thanked them all and headed back downtown.

I loved Christy, but at times I sensed a slight competition with her, so I didn't feel compelled to be forthcoming about every little thing. I certainly didn't think my slight flirtation to get a break constituted cheating. The odds of getting the role were minuscule, and because Christy was insecure enough about being unable to get produced, I saw little reason to trouble her about the whole audition. The next few days passed pretty quickly. That Thursday, Christy and I decided to do our patriotic duty by dining out in Little Italy that night, making a modest contribution to the destitute local economy.

"I can't believe all this is happening," I told her, referring to the fact that we were sitting in a completely empty restaurant on Mott Street at seven P.M.

"It's a bad dream," she replied, fidgeting, "but you know what else bothers me, the fact that you've had my script for more than two weeks now and still haven't read it."

I explained that due to the recent catastrophic events I had found it hard to concentrate. She said she understood, but I knew she didn't. Her career had been stalling a lot longer than September 11th.

"It's just that Manny Greene is waiting for this manuscript and he's not going to wait forever."

I promised her that I would finish reading it as soon as we got home.

Christy watched that night as I flipped through the pages. As I scribbled constructive notes in the margins, she would respond with nasty comments just below the range of hearing.

Finally, around eleven, she watched me flip the last page of her sacred work. Just as I thought, the script was a mess. Her dialogue was sappy ("Jesusita: In my country what we feel here [puts hand on arm] we feel here [puts hand over heart].") She couldn't draw characters for shit, and her story just didn't go anywhere. I let out a big sigh.

"So you didn't like it." She caught right on.

As I began to diplomatically choose my words and detail the larger problems with her script, the phone started ringing. Since this was one of the most painful discussions we had ever had, we let the machine catch it. I could hear Franklin Stein's voice clearly. As I softly explained that her heroine was unlikable and the supporting characters weren't sympathetic, Stein's voice grew lively on the machine. When I detailed that her scenes lacked tension and didn't build, Franklin congratulated me for getting a small but important role in his hot new film.

"What the fuck is this!" she stopped me, referring to his ongoing message.

"Nothing, really, just nonsense." I stepped toward the answering machine to turn it off.

"Shush up!" she replied, pulling me away from the phone.

". . . so if you really are looking to get away from Ms. Sapphos, I'd be glad to tell you about this apartment that's opening up."

"Ms. Sapphos! What the fuck is he talking about!" She immediately directed her anger at his rambling message.

"I auditioned the other day for a tiny role in his film and I guess I got the part," I said, embarrassed.

"He's not talking about parts, he's talking about apartments!"

"We had a long talk . . . ," I explained.

"When?"

"At his party."

"You mean the backer's party? With Manny and all?"

"Yeah."

"I didn't see you talking to him," she replied.

"We talked out front."

"Wait a second," she remembered, "this was during the half-hour period when you vanished and I tried to call you but you didn't pick up?"

"You were slightly intoxicated and talking to a bunch of your friends, so I went out for some air."

"Slightly intoxicated, huh?" she replied, grinning. "So let me get this straight. While I was drinking my woes away you were outside hustling this young hotshot."

"I'm an actress," I replied. "In case you didn't notice I've spent the entire year struggling to get a break in the hardest business in the world."

"You are truly amazing," she countered. "By day you beg and labor for roles no one else would want, and by night you martyr yourself helping burnt-out drunks like me."

"Christy, can we just stop this now?"

"I just want to understand this for a minute," she replied, then closing her eyes she pieced together the facts: "I was invited by Manny Greene to his backer's party, and since you're my girlfriend I invited you. And what did you do, you ran off with the hotshot guest of honor, and what exactly did you do with him?"

"I talked with him."

"Don't lie to me," she shot back. "You did a hell of a lot more than just talk. What'd you do—blow him?"

"No, he kissed me good night," I told her honestly. "That's all, I swear it."

"On the lips?"

"It was just a peck."

"On the lips?"

"Yes."

"Then he gave you this role?"

"No, I had to audition, just like the other fifty roles I tried out for this year."

"And how many of those directors did you kiss?" I didn't reply. "You know what, I believe that you more than just kissed him, and I can forgive that if that were all. But how do you think that makes me look when Franklin reports to his buddy, Manny, that he just made out with his lesbian director's lipstick lover?"

"Oh, please, we didn't make out! He just kissed me good night. Big deal. This whole thing is your issue, and I don't know if it's because he's a guy or because he's your rival, but—"

"Did you hear what he left on my machine or do I have to replay it. He called me *Ms. Sapphos* on my own answering machine."

"He was making a dumb joke, I'm sorry. . . ."

She stormed into the bathroom and slammed the door behind her.

"I'm really sorry," I called out again, but to no avail. I heard her turn on the shower and imagined her crying.

I sat there, rereading her script, looking desperately for something nice to say about it. When the door finally opened, she flipped off the lights and jumped into bed. It was almost midnight, so I quietly joined her.

She slept silently with her back to me. I knew better than to reach out. She wanted to be alone.

The next morning, I got up before Christy. Silently I went out and purchased a bundle of roses. I also got her a specialty coffee and an almond brioche, which she always loved. I awoke her with a kiss. As she opened her eyes slowly, I told her I was wrong and truly sorry and begged her to forgive me.

"You know, the fact that you kissed him really hurts, but that's not the real damage here," she replied. "That you jeopardized my standing with the only producer who showed any interest in my future is the real crime."

I had flirted with someone to try to catch a break, and though I knew that I was wrong—I had thoughtlessly committed a minor infidelity—I hardly thought I had jeopardized her career. I was already late for work, so instead of arguing or apologizing, I simply said we'd talk about it later.

Several times I tried calling her from SHW, but I kept getting her voice mail. After work I considered getting her another gift, but I didn't want to appear to be begging. I bought a nice red wine and figured that maybe if we had a romantic dinner together she might begin to forgive me. When I came home that night, though, she wasn't there. A note was on the dining room table.

Hannah,
I'm going away for a few days. I know you're sorry for what you did, but I simply don't know if I can get over this. If I can, I'll call you. Otherwise, I hope we can still remain friends.
Christy

That was how my first and only relationship with a woman ended. Brokenhearted, I packed my bags and made the long and awful trip back to my parents' house in Long Island. As I passed that stretch of northern Queens I considered what Christy had meant to me. On a bad day, love seemed to simply be the suspension of a great and constant loneliness—the numbing fear that life was just a freak biochemical accident that was meaningless and unshareable and ended in death. Christy alleviated the chronic pain that accompanied life. Aside from being sexy, she was courageous and creative.

Long before the Sundance Festival and the rise of independent films, Christina Saffers was a hot young filmmaker who made what was then referred to as "an art house film" entitled *Seven Figure Deal*. Because she was strikingly beautiful, she was on the cover of the *SoHo Weekly News* and various other downtown magazines, where she was touted as a hot young director, someone to watch in the '80s. That year she frequented all the hip clubs and partied with names that were bold-faced in gossip columns. *Seven Figure Deal* was generally regarded as a flawed masterpiece about the early Reagan Yuppies and their vapid values. It won some film awards and made her some money.

Probably because of all that youthful validation, she overconfidently rushed into her second project, *Two Fingers of Scotch*. It was a sober rumination on her drinking problem. In the same way that the first film brought out her humor, sexiness, and visual insight, this second film was moody, obsessive, and self-pitying—a straight-to-video bomb.

The elevator that brought her to the penthouse free-fell to the basement. She lost all self-confidence and took to itinerant teaching. She eventually landed at Yale, where I wound up enrolled in her class.

Christy's contract with Yale had ended roughly a year and a half ago, and when she moved back into her Tribeca loft, she invited me to join her. I eagerly accepted. During our first night together, she excitedly showed me a property that she thought would make a great film. It was an article from *Mademoiselle* or *Elle* magazine, a fluff piece really about a love triangle between an attractive Yuppie couple and their sexy Central American maid, who Christy symbolically renamed Jesusita. I got excited just reading it. I knew that with its mix of hot nude scenes and Christy's whole P.C. bullshit, it would be taken seriously and enjoyed sensuously. "This poor undocumented alien has to make love with these two uptight whites and live in an uptown town house because she is afraid of being deported to her fascist country. . . ."

Until I told her her screenplay sucked, Christy kept assuring me I'd play the lead and be the next hot indie star.

When I first said I wasn't sure I could play an ethnic Latina, she had replied, "If Marisa Tomei can play a Cuban, and Meryl Streep can be any-body, you can damn well slather on some body makeup and play a Latina."

We both expected great things in working together. Yet it would have been far better if we were in different professions. That way there would have been no ambiguity between love and loyalty. The next day when I called to thank Franklin Stein for the role, he sounded distant and aloof.

"Is everything okay?" I asked, nervous that Christy had yelled at him for the Sapphos remark.

"Everything will be okay," he said and told me that some of his vital backers had just backed out. His production, *Success!*, was going to be indefinitely on hold.

"Unbelievable."

"We'll get it back on track."

"Did you say you knew of a cheap apartment opening up?" I asked.

"Oh! After I hung up, I realized I probably shouldn't've made that comment about Christy on her answering machine," he said. "I hope she didn't mind."

"Not at all," I lied pleasantly, instead of thanking him for destroying my relationship. "But I left you my cell phone number. How'd you get me there?"

"Oh, I lost your card, so I got Christy's number from Manny."

"Smart thinking," I said. No matter how many precautions you take, fate always screws you in the end.

"Anyway, I'll check the sublet thing out and get back to you."

The next day and week passed without his response. When I wasn't at work, I'd think about Christy, hoping for a phone call that would never come. My appetite and sleep seemed to vanish. I lost more weight that season than I ever did while on the Atkins diet. While going through my things, I found the Lilly Bull manuscript, *Unlubricated*. When I called Bree to see what had become of the project, he simply said, "It's about to be produced. Thanks anyway."

Staying at my parents' house didn't help at all. When my father wasn't avoiding me, he'd make obnoxious remarks about "my chosen profession." My mother kept asking if I had given any thought to going to law or business school.

"Yes, I gave it thought. No and no" was my standard reply.

One day, while sitting at my ever-changing desk at the SHW office, looking out the window at a view I had come to enjoy, I saw a plane over New Jersey and suddenly experienced an overwhelming fear. I had to get out immediately. I grabbed my purse and coat and walked around the block. When I got back and stood in the lobby, I found myself sweating and realized that I just couldn't go back up there. I called upstairs and told my supervisor that I felt a sudden nausea from something I ate.

"There isn't much to do anyway," she said. "Take the rest of the day off."

It was the first time I ever experienced a panic attack. But it didn't return the next day.

After several weeks of commuting from Long Island and looking for an affordable place, I was just about to sublet a toxic studio in Battery Park City when Franklin finally called back. He said his friend's sublet in Hell's Kitchen had finally opened up and asked if I was still looking.

"Absolutely."

"It's on Forty-fifth and Ninth. I have the keys if you want to take a look at it."

When we met up late that day, Franklin looked as though he hadn't slept in months. Probably due to the fact that his film was indefinitely on hold, he was clearly depressed. There was no longer anything slick about him. In fact, he seemed drained of small talk, so we met outside the apartment building, and he showed me the place.

With a garbage-strewn backyard view and a nonworking fireplace, it was much more than I could've hoped for. Although it was a four-floor walk-up, I needed the exercise and found I could dash down the stairs as though they were a water slide. It was more than he first quoted, but at six hundred and thirty dollars a month it was dramatically below market value.

Thelma Derchoch was the legal tenant. Apparently she had followed her acting dream to L.A. Before leaving she had paid up until February thinking that she was going to come back then. For reasons unknown, she decided not to return. The deal was simple—the landlord was supposedly noninquisitive. Franklin explained that I'd have to compensate Thelma up front for the two months of advance rent. After that, if I just slipped a cash envelope under his door with Thelma's apartment number on it, the landlord wouldn't catch on.

"Isn't there any way I could get my name on the lease?"

"If you can think of a way be my guest. But I'd be careful."

It was the one boom in a season of bust. I thanked him, and since I was now officially single, I asked if he wanted to hang out. He simply said he had no time. He was overwhelmed trying to salvage *Success!*

After I moved in, I called a Landlord-Tenant lawyer to see if I could somehow get on the lease.

"This new landlord is supposedly inattentive," I explained to him.

"Well, it's always a risk." he explained over his speaker phone. "You could take what's behind curtain number one, play it safe and keep paying cash in the original tenant's name. Or if the landlord really is derelict, you can choose curtain number two and try putting your name on the check. If he accepts three months of rent, pass go, the place is yours. If he contests it, though, lose a turn, you'll be evicted."

I didn't care for the mixed Monopoly–*Let's Make a Deal* motif but I always was the gambling type. I mailed out the two months of rent to Thelma. And decided to send a check to the landlord when it was time.

Franklin vanished about that time, taking a lot of meetings on the far coast to get "first monies" to fill in for those investors who had pulled out after September 11.

4

THE WANNABE

"I'M SORRY, BUT I couldn't help hearing that you were a theater producer." That was the very first thing Sheldon Redfield said to
me during the last depressing week of December in a dark, empty
SoHo bar. As my eyes adjusted to the darkness, I made out a young,
well-groomed Russell Croweish–looking guy holding a long-stemmed
glass of red wine, sitting at an adjacent table.

"What about it?" I replied defensively.

"Well, it's none of my business, I'm just always amazed, even a little envious, by people in the arts," he said timidly and took a sip of his
drink.

"I'm actually an actress," I clarified. I had just suffered an excruciating meeting with blow-up doll Belinda. Since all New York theater
was at a standstill, she was meeting with all the old members of
Disaffected Artist Types pitching the idea of a vanity production. After
avoiding her calls for several weeks, I had finally and pitifully decided
to meet with her to find out what she had to offer. For two grand
apiece, she wanted us to all put up a showcase of the patriotic musical

1776—ugh! I was too broke and depressed to put up with any

"You really have my admiration," the hulk said.

"You've never seen me act," I said, holding my wine glass. "How you know I deserve any admiration?"

"I recently read an article that described how difficult it is being an actress nowadays. And it just makes me realize how lucky I am."

"How exactly are you lucky?" I still hadn't decided if I liked where he was heading or not.

"I'm a dentist, which isn't always easy, but all I have to do is hang my shingle, and I earn more than ninety percent of all actresses."

"So you're saying that . . ."

"It just seems unfair that even if you're a talented actress that that isn't enough," he kept talking. "To me it seems cruel. And the fact that you're willing to persevere under those conditions strikes me as admirable, even if you're not talented."

"Sounds like you're reaching a bit, but okay."

"When you consider other arts," he continued, "painters or writers, they can do their work regardless of others and still get discovered after they die, like van Gogh or Kafka. How many great actresses are there that never even made it onto the screen or stage?"

"Gee, when you put it that way," I said, "now I definitely want to kill myself." He made me think of poor Lilly Bull, the writer who died in obscurity and left the terrific play that Bree the druggy was now having produced.

"When you look at the overwhelming odds we're all facing," I said to the dentist, "maybe we're all just pathologically naive, ever think of that?"

"I think you're hopeful of your own talent, and I don't think hopefulness is bad."

"Isn't there a point when hopefulness is just foolish?" I asked, offering my father's argument.

"But who knows exactly where that point is? How many wonderful things came out of extreme hopefulness. I for one think we need more hope in the world."

"Boy, I wish I could introduce you to my parents."

"Better yet, we should get married," he said earnestly. "I mean, artist and business types should mate. We have the money to support culture."

"I'm skeptical about subsidy."

"Did you ever hear about the Federal Theatre, back in the thirties? It was part of the WPA. All these wonderful projects were produced. I wonder why they ended it."

"Actually I studied it in college—a congressman from Texas was responsible for ruining it."

We both bantered more about public and private grants while swilling down more drinks, until out of the blue he took my hand in his and kissed the back of it. It wasn't hard or icky, just a gentle peck.

"What was that?" I asked, just a smidgen indignant.

"That was thank you for sitting here and talking to someone like me."

"It's okay." He really was good-looking.

He paid for both our drinks and we stumbled outside together. In the light drizzle we kissed. Sneakily, he hailed a cab behind my back and shoved me in. He was so good at it and I was so intoxicated that I just kept kissing him as he gave the driver the address to his apartment on the Upper West Side.

Hot and sweet as Sheldon was, I couldn't just give myself over to him. I was still in mourning over the loss of Christy. He gave me his business card. When the cab pulled up at a red light on Forty-fifth Street, I flipped open the door, wished him a good night and walked to my new apartment.

5

In Turnaround

MERCENARY · AS · IT · SOUNDED, after I broke up with Christy, I was sort of expecting to get closer to Franklin Stein. He wasn't bad looking and he had gotten me my first New York apartment. But his real gift was casting me in his film, even though it had become another casualty of September 11.

That polar cap of time—January—I was rutted in a severe mind-numbing depression. Waiting for the injured city to heal and restart was like being stuck in the top car of a Ferris wheel. That was the main reason I finally called the somewhat geeky yet handsome Sheldon Redfield, DDS. I always had problems with men. It was why my most successful relationship to date had been with Christy. In college, I dated a guy who periodically cheated on me, so I placed a premium on honesty, which, if nothing else, Sheldon seemed to have in abundance.

During our first date, when he casually mentioned that he voted for George W. Bush, I tried to keep an open mind. On the second date, though, when he invited me back to his place, I started seeing the tacky signs of true upper-middle-class superficiality.

Large, splashy paintings of New York clichés—horses and buggies in Central Park, Times Square on New Year's Eve, Tall Ships in the Harbor—all done in bright garish colors, covered the walls, giving the impression of cost without much taste. Little trinkets like old cigarette lighters and glass figurines covered end tables and sundry ledges. Although the lobby and elevators all were large and shiny, the three little rooms that made up his place reminded me that he was living in just another tiny New York cubbyhole. Also his musical taste was frozen in the '70s. He put on a CD from Electric Light Orchestra. I also spotted the musical musings of Air Supply and Journey.

We sat down and he asked me about my career, my family, my oral history, the dental hygiene of ex-lovers. In fact, he asked me more questions than anybody had ever asked me in my entire life. Though I never tired of talking about myself, I kept wondering if he had read some Get-Laid-Quick book that said the more questions you ask chicks the more they'll dig you.

Finally, during a breather, I casually said, "So tell me a little about yourself."

Words started pouring out. He confessed that he briefly wrestled with the idea of becoming an orthodontist, but explained "he felt a greater orthodoxy" to the religion of tooth care. He talked proudly about some of the harder cases he had tackled, like impacted wisdoms and other tricky extractions.

"It's not all drill and fill," he said. "Some days I feel more like a tooth sculptor."

As he started going into the history of amalgams used to fill cavities, I kissed his oral cavity just to shut him up. I never understood people who talked in monologues. Still it was difficult not finding his innocence sexy. Of course, personality is no indication of what awaits in the bedroom. In a way, I was half hoping he'd be a disappointment so I could quickly push the ejection button and move on to the next.

Unfortunately that night, I discovered that this was not the case—the man was a sexual chimera: part suction eel, part millipede and part stallion. That first ball game of the season, I rounded the bases five times to his one.

His key problem was his chronic goofiness, which grew worse over time. He was one of those people who couldn't really modulate his voice, or for that matter edit his content. This, combined with wild hand gesticulation left me deaf and constantly fearful of being smacked.

Although I was grateful that he didn't spit, the man had a laugh that was right off the scale. It simply couldn't be parodied. Admittedly I am hypersensitive to those around me in a public space, so whenever Sheldon guffawed, I'd find myself feeling totally embarrassed. Subsequently, like a young curmudgeon, I tried to discourage humor while we were outside.

One evening out, over dessert, I gave my assessment of the leading actors and actresses of the day. Then I made the mistake of asking him his opinion.

"I have to confess," he said while spooning crème brûlée into his gullet, "I really can't tell most actors apart. I mean I know their names and all, but I really don't see why one actor is regarded as good and another is considered crappy."

"You can't see why Brando or Olivier are regarded as great and—"

"I see that some are more thoughtful or have better pronunciation than others and stuff, and some movies are really touching and all, I'm just saying that none of them really move me emotionally more than any other. To me they're all more or less interchangeable."

"Wait a second," I said, seizing his hand before he could spoon more of the pudding into his mouth. Carefully I asked him, "You're telling me you don't feel more affected by . . . say, Juliette Binoche, or Ralph Fiennes than any other actor?"

"Not really, no," he said innocently.

What he was saying in effect was that my career, my chosen path in life was meaningless.

"Actually," he caught himself, perhaps hearing my silent scream, "I do feel deeply moved by . . . well . . ." The barbarian couldn't finish the crucial sentence.

"Who? Who the fuck moves you?"

"Well, not really who," he said earnestly, "I feel deeply touched by extremely attractive teenage girls. When they say something sad, I find it really touching, and when they say something funny, I just can't stop laughing."

I stared at him dumbfounded as he clicked and scraped his spoon against the ramekin and licked the last of the custard.

"I really have a weakness for the WB." He put the cherry on the whip cream.

When my brain finally unfroze, I set a breakup date—a Friday—and a place—the lobby of the MoMA. I even picked my excuse ("I still love my girlfriend and am going back to her").

Soon after I made this decision, though, I went for an appointment with my healer to ask for help with my acutely slumping mood.

Dr. Wang was a Chinese herbologist-acupuncturist who I started seeing early last year. Immediately, he impressed me with his sensitivity and his unorthodox prescriptions. But it was more than that. Just going down to Chinatown was a transporting experience.

The faint steamy odors and unplaceable aromas that rose from steamer plates and sewer grates, the cacophony of Asian tongues, the tight fortune-cookie faces of the people, all moving in the same rhythm—just walking through it all was like a latter-day hike up some thin-aired Nepalese mountain peak. When this short mystery man with his ten thousand years of holistic wisdom finally diagnosed the complications of my modern cyber-plugged, satellite-zapped body, I firmly believed I was very close to some great and ancient secret.

The last time I saw him, while heading down the narrow hallway to his office, I accidentally kicked over a sacrificial bowl of shriveled oranges and dusty pomegranates placed on the ground below a small plastic Buddha. He forgave me, but I should have known from that that some serious bad luck lay ahead. He politely led me into his tiny space. Above his desk was a handwritten sign that read HAPPY HAPPY! To hell with diplomas and certifications.

When he opened his mouth, I knew he wanted me to do the same.

He looked briefly at the ruts and potholes of my tongue then gazed deeply into my face as he held on to my wrists. Drawing a conclusion, he let out a pensive "Hmmmm."

"You don't want to see more?"

"Not necessary."

"But don't you want to know—"

"Not necessary," he repeated and issued his prognosis in broken and figurative English, "Your earth is cold."

"Excuse me?"

"You no been with friend. No long time. No warmth. No intercellularity." How could Dr. Wang divine so much from just a simple pulse and tongue-tread inspection? I had been with Sheldon for about a month, and my heart felt no warmer.

"Actually," I deemed to correct, "I do have a friend, but I was about to end it."

He said something in his native tongue.

"Excuse me?"

"I say—no!" Then I think he said, "You need to work body. Beat heart. Push high. Stretch small, mid-muscles." He mumbled something else in Mandarin or Cantonese that I didn't understand, but from his jazz riff of Chinese words I caught the phrase "a lie-down man."

To eliminate any ambiguities he did this profane pelvic gyration that made my jaw drop, but he went right on in strange multisyllables: "Low interphysicality. Low intergenerationality. Low efficiency."

"Aren't there pills or something?"

"Herbs. I give you herbs." He led me back out to his hallway filled with tiny drawers, reminiscent of the screws-and-bolts shelves in an old hardware store. From each one he took out ingredients that he weighed in a shiny brass hand scale. These contents looked like the flotsam that washed up on a beach or the discarded tidbits that were filtered out of ashtrays. He sorted everything into little cellophane bags. Each bag was to be boiled in a gallon of water, strained, and the tea was supposed to be drunk down over an entire week.

"You boil herbs." He made a universal boiling gesture and added, "You boil self. Sleep well. Eat well. Be happy. Raise perspicacity." How the hell did he know about perspicacity? "And do a lie-down man."

"A lie-down man?" I confirmed.

"You need lie-down man to stay well." And again he did a low pelvic sexual thrust. From what I understood, the acupuncturist was literally prescribing a sexual partner.

"You mean I should . . . ?" I did a quick yet tasteful gesture with my fingers that implied heterosexual intimacy.

He confirmed with a chuckle. Upon doctor's orders, I put up with Sheldon's gawkiness in exchange for more intercellularity and perspicacity than money could buy.

That night I weakened and made my first phone call to Christy, who curtly explained that she was dating another one of her former students. To my surprise it was a guy, her very first heterosexual relationship. Probably to get back at me she specified that it was the best sex she ever had. I tried to act as calm and cool about it, but didn't tell her that I too had been dating.

"Isn't it weird after a lifetime of women?" I asked.

"I slept with men back in the seventies," she corrected. "He's kind of a soft male. It almost feels like I'm with some post-op tranny."

By February, in accordance with my doctor's orders, I was still with the handsome voidoid, Sheldon. Though I felt somewhat better, it was probably because I sent my first rent check to the landlord and he didn't return it. Soon, though, I fell in an even deeper funk. That was when I realized that I should have more carefully considered Belinda's suggestion. The only time I felt really happy was when I was acting. But there was no work anywhere. Still, the idea of dropping two grand for some lame production of the lame-o *1776*, to be a Dolley Madison dancing around with Ben Franklin, sounded terrifying. Even I wouldn't go see it.

Life restarted late one night in that first week of February. After a monotonous day of work and during an evening of crappy TV reruns, I drifted off to sleep. When the phone rang, I thought it was late, but it was only eleven.

"So what's going on?" a male voice asked.

"Who is this, please?" I replied, fearing it was the landlord.

"Bree," he said. Rock music was playing in the background.

"Who?"

"It's me," he replied. "You saved my life in college."

"Oh, yeah." It was Bree Silverburn. "What's up?"

"You read the Bull play. You were interested in producing it, remember?"

I pulled myself up, took a sip of water and thought back a lifetime ago to last summer.

"I thought you already had producers lined up," I replied.

"They fell through."

"Refresh my memory a minute. You have an unpublished play by Lilly Bull."

"A lost masterpiece."

"And you have a permission statement to produce it?"

"Would I be talking to you if I didn't?" he asked. I didn't tell him, but I hardly remembered the work.

"Well, it's been a while," I said, flipping through a stack of magazines at my bedside, "but I remember liking it." There at the bottom of the stack was the Xeroxed manuscript, *Unlubricated*. I never threw anything out.

"Is your company still willing to produce it?" he asked.

" 'Course," I lied as I flipped through its pages to bring myself up to speed, "but you said not to show it to them."

"All right, I'm giving you a free twenty-four-hour option to—"

"Hold it, I don't know if you heard but since September things have sort of been on hold. Some of company aren't even in town," I replied. In fact I hadn't even seen three of the members in months. For all I knew they could be dead.

"All right, I'll give you seventy-two hours, but get on the ball," he lunged right in, "just show them the work and tell them that I'll be playing Reggie and Svetlana is stage managing."

"Svetlana Palas?" There was another obscure name from my unillustrious past.

"Yeah, I said this the first time we met, Svetlana and I were attached to the production."

"You never mentioned Svetlana."

"Look, I'm going to be generous. You have one week," he said, ignoring my response. I felt as if he were holding someone hostage and I had three days to come up with the ransom money. After he hung up, I reread the play and remembered why I was excited by the work. It really leapt off the page. The language crackled, the characters kicked. And the playwright had a following eager to see it.

With my heart beating, and my mind going a million miles a minute, I suddenly realized that for the first time in a while I actually looked forward to something.

6

THE COMPANY

ALTHOUGH·THE·IDEA of putting up a vanity production was Belinda's, she simply had the wrong rocket on the launch pad. *Unlubricated* was worth investing in. If it were someone else's production not only would I go to see it, most of my impoverished ilk would probably catch it. In a small space it would get reviewed and with little effort it could get enough backing to move upward.

The next morning, I got a walk-in appointment with my acupuncturist. He kept me waiting in his office while he filled out someone else's prescription. Finally, as he poked me with pins, I tried to distract myself by studying a Chart of Meridians and Points. It looked as though a human body were converted into a subway map. Two parallel lines, one red and another blue, ran up and down the east and west side of the body, making stops at all the key nerve centers. When the acupuncturist put a needle in my West Ninety-sixth Street station and another one in my East Fifty-ninth Street stop, my rush hour seemed to vanish and I felt a wonderful calm.

After being rekindled further with needles and herbs, I headed to work, eager to track down the three missing members of my defunct company, Disaffected Artist Types. I only had Belinda and Noah's numbers, but figured Noah knew how to reach the others. Unfortunately he had lost his phone book. Through a web of old college buddies, I finally traced the last two members, Edith Rothchild and Mike Mildone. I called and left messages on their machines: "This is Hannah, call me if you want the biggest break you'll ever get in acting."

Finally came the dreaded call to Belinda. Aside from the fact that I always suspected her of having had a fling with my boyfriend, there were only two female roles in this play. Edith was the best actress, yet Belinda was the founder. She also had a monster-size ego, which I knew would be immediately resistant when I pitched back an improved version of her own idea.

I dialed her home number. Nervously I listened to her phone ringing and finally I heard the message: "This is Belinda, I will be on the West Coast for an indefinite length of time. If you need me I can be reached at . . ." I was about to put the phone down, but at the last moment I succinctly stated, "Belinda, it's Hannah, give me a call."

This was bound to happen. Long before September 11, whenever Belinda felt that her career was stalling, that roles perfect for her were being snatched up by underage underwear models, she would peruse priceline.com and consider the cheapest tickets out to L.A., only to finally decide that it was probably tougher to get any parts out there. This time, thank God, she actually took the flight.

Later that day, when Mike and Edith returned my call, I asked them to meet me at my place that night at seven o'clock.

During the afternoon lull at work I made four copies of *Unlubricated* as well as Xeroxes of the foreword of *Bull Session*. On the way home, I stopped at the corner store and picked up some basic staples likes roach spray and baking soda for the prewar fridge. Industrial drums of diet Coke were on sale so I bought one for the meeting. Before I took my coat off, the doorbell rang. Edith arrived early as usual.

With her black frame glasses, square jaw and cleanly plucked eyebrows, Edith had a geometric magnetism that kept earning her audition calls for geeky girl roles. Though she probably could have gone out to L.A., grabbed some dumb TV show and just stayed with it, she was actually the most dedicated theater actress I knew. I once saw her do an *Antigone* with a group of geriatrics in Bayonne that was both exhilarating and heartbreaking.

Her performance style reminded me of Catherine Keener's or Billy Crudup's. Edith's eyes, face, and tone were in constant motion, occasionally at odds. Sometimes watching her onstage nearly gave me vertigo. With this extraordinary talent, she was on a personal mission to conquer every key female role in the major plays of Western literature, no matter how small or abstract the production.

"Nice place you got here," she started politely. The downstairs doorbell rang and I buzzed in the next actor.

Mike Mildone, the eternal student, came stomping up the steps. At the Neighborhood Playhouse, Stella Adler Conservatory and other schools around town he had taken master classes with the likes of Louise Lasser, Tony Randall and other important TV stars of the '70s. Although he was tall and lean, his face had a boyish softness that kept him from making too deep an impression on casting agents. The one benefit to this was his eternally youthful looks.

While still in my filthy hallway, Mike asked, "Is this the apartment that one of your many suitors got you?"

I shushed him. It was an illegal sublet. The neighbors were not supposed to know that.

"So what's going on?" Edith asked as Mike stepped inside.

They were both starving for good news and apparently anything to eat. Mike tramped through my little living room and into my kitchenette, where he opened the fridge. Edith followed him. Seeing only the monster bottle of soda, he unscrewed the white plastic top as Edith put down three glasses that had been left behind by the former tenant.

Determined to make my pitch only once, I told them I just wanted to catch up and see how everyone was doing.

"We were attacked by a camel-fucking, long-bearded, trust-funded brat and now we can't get temp work. Aside from that we're fine," Mike replied as he poured the soda. "What else do you want to know?"

"Okay, just be patient." They knew I was sitting on something and played along, catching up on the recent misfortunes of old friends. At one point, when Mike opened a window, he said, "You can't smell it up here."

He was referring to World Trade Center fumes. He lived downtown and had applied for a grant from the Federal Emergency Management Agency. He wound up getting some dinky little air purifier.

"Hannah almost got a sublet right next to the bathtub," Edith repeated what I had told her earlier. That was what people began calling Ground Zero.

"Do yourself a favor and stay away," he warned. "The place is asbestos city and the government's not helping."

"They gave you some money, didn't they?" I asked him.

"It's all so haphazard," he replied after putting down his soda. "Fucking FEMA gives my neighbor twenty-five thousand dollars for a new roof deck, and they won't even give me a penny toward my rent."

"Where were you guys when the buildings went down?" Edith asked.

"I was uptown," Mike said.

"I was at my parents'," I lied, not wanting to go into it.

"You know what kill's me the most," Edith said, "the missing flyers. I swear I can't walk by them without stopping, and when I read them I can't stop crying."

"I hate those flyers," Mike declared. "I mean, they're all over the place. What the hell do they think, that all those people are just sitting in a Starbucks and they forgot to go home? They're not missing— they're dead!"

"You fucking moron," I shot back angrily, "if you were in one of those buildings and your parents never saw you again . . ."

But by his expression, I could see that Mike already regretted saying it. He later mentioned that he made it a point to read all "A Nation in Mourning" obituaries in the *New York Times*. Like all of us, he was on overload.

"I'd never give up hope if someone I loved was in one of those buildings. I'd always want to believe that they were out there somewhere," Edith said calmly, then added, "The poster that always kills me is of the two sisters—they remind me of my sisters."

"For me it's the guy with his kids on his shoulders," I replied.

"I always find myself walking by firehouses whenever I see them," Mike said, after a pause. We all just silently sipped soda for a few minutes.

Eventually Noah Rampoh stumbled in; he was always late. He joked that he wanted to do industrials but he wasn't industrious. Because he was last, there was nowhere for him to sit.

"Something's off with this soda," he stated, after we had all finished ours.

"So what are we doing here anyway?" Noah asked, looking out my window. "Why aren't we all home having cybersex?"

I handed out the copies of the foreword of the Bull book. Everyone read the excerpt quietly.

"What are you telling us?" Noah said before finishing. "You've shot a musician?"

"Give her a break," Edith said mercifully.

"I was approached by someone with a pretty terrific offer," I began.

"Yeah, a role in a film for a roll in the hay," Noah finished.

"And an apartment," Mike whispered.

"A friend," I ignored them, "stumbled across a copy of this lost play *Unlubricated* by Lilly Bull. No one else has it."

"Go on," Edith prompted before they could make a joke.

"He suggested that I might be able to produce the work. It's a great play for a small stage and a low budget. And considering its author, it'll definitely get noticed," I added. It was one of those moments when all you could hear were garbage trucks rumbling down Ninth Avenue.

"So what's the catch?" Edith asked.

"We have to put up the cash."

"Wait a second, Belinda approached me with a similar proposal a few months ago," Mike replied.

"Me too," Noah said.

"This is not *1776*," I replied, "this thing is ready to go. It has elements that would be perfect for these times. Surviving crisis, loyalty, processing anger, and grief. . . . Just look at it."

"Even if it is hot," Edith asked, "don't you think it's too soon? A bunch of shows have just closed on Broadway because of September eleventh."

"I know, but there are also signs that things will be picking up, and it might actually be a real opportunity if we're the first ones out there. Reviewers have to review something. And eventually people will follow."

"Is there something for all of us?" Mike asked.

"It has six roles," I went on. "Two girls and four guys."

"Perfect if Belinda doesn't return," Noah inserted.

"I left a message for her to call me," I said honestly.

"Really? You told her you were putting this up, because I'd be surprised that she wouldn't dash back here for this." Noah immediately started picking.

"You think this play will fly?" Mike asked.

"Absolutely, this play will push to the front of the pack, guaranteed."

"How exactly would we get it up?" the ever-practical Edith asked.

"By doing exactly what Belinda pitched—two grand per person. We can bring it to a small venue. Get some reviews. Look for investors. I know some producers. We can try taking it to a larger space."

"When can we read this smoking script?" asked Noah.

I pointed to the small stack of manuscripts on the coffee table before him. "There are four copies."

They all snatched one. Mike flipped through a couple pages of it before saying, "I'm free for the next hour or so, why don't we do a reading of it right now?"

"I agree," Noah chirped in. "Let's see how it flies."

"Let me make a phone call and cancel my date," Edith said, heading toward the bathroom with her cellular. She was dating a copy editor at *Us* magazine.

"We're two guys short," Mike pointed out.

"We can double up," Noah said.

So we went through the cast: Mike wanted to play both the flaming gay, Lenny, and the suspected bisexual, Waldo. Noah was Miles, a Vietnam veteran, and Reggie, the drunkard. I made it quite clear that I was born for the role of Samantha, the tough writer. Edith thought it was challenging to go against her usual strong type and play Lucy, the insecures young lover who reads her work throughout different bedroom scenes with Reggie.

7

THE COLD READING

MOST OF UNLUBRICATED takes place over one night, juxtaposed with a series of flashbacks all heading toward an unraveling of youthful hopes and pipe dreams—slightly *Iceman Cometh*. We didn't break for the intermission and only read basic stage directions. There was a terrorist joke and a reference to the movie *Towering Inferno*, both of which we agreed had to be deleted. But after only an hour, we all knew this was the real thing. This was why we suffered through all the little humiliations and frustrations of being actors. Because every so often, if we were lucky, we'd chance upon a script that made our adrenaline run. All our insecurities and deprivations would vanish, and for an instant an electrical charge would pass through all the actors onstage and zap out to the audience seated in front.

"It was great," Mike said. "A cold reading and it was funny, sad, suspenseful . . ."

"This could be just the thing," Noah concluded.

"I heard *Coprophagia* was a mess," Edith said, referring to Bull's first play. "What does the title mean anyway?"

"Eating shit," Mike defined.

"Well, it might eat shit," I pointed out, "but I checked it out online and *Coprophagia* got decent reviews and had a successful two-year run."

"And the fact that this is the last, unproduced play by Bull will really get noticed," Noah jumped in. "We'll get every kook and lesbo in the tri-state area."

"Am I supposed to do a nude scene?" Edith asked mischievously, in keeping with her character's seductive nature.

"I think your character would want that," Noah said, pulling a stinky wooden pipe out of his jacket pocket and slipping it into his big red cow lips. While playing Sherlock Holmes, he had picked up the nasty habit of "social" pipe smoking. If he tried firing it up, I was prepared to extinguish it with the bottle of industrial soda.

Since they were in agreement, now was the time to bring up Bree. Slowly, nervously pondering how to phrase this last entanglement, I stroked my arm and felt a slightly sensitive bump under my right tricep. I dismissed it, believing it to be a bruise. I decided short and to the point would be best. "That brings up the one minor detail. If we do this play, we have to include the guy who brought me the property."

"Huh?"

"And he wants the part of Reggie," I said to Noah, who obviously relished the role.

"No fucking way!" he exclaimed, biting the chewed-up mouthpiece of his old pipe.

"Who is this mystery actor?" Edith asked, cutting to the chase.

"I'll tell you, but I want you to keep open-minded, really open-minded," I said, and at the same time realized that was the wrong way to introduce him.

"Who is it?" Mike asked fearfully.

"He's actually not that bad," I said, trying to relax them.

"Will you please just—"

"Bree Silverburn," I blurted.

"Dopehead Sideburns! He was the biggest druggy at Yale!" Mike exclaimed for all the world.

"How the hell did you come up with this deal?" Noah roared.

"I bumped into him at a party," I said, not wanting to divulge that it was another industry party I hadn't invited him to.

"Wait a sec," Edith finally broke the silence, "wasn't he that mercurial Mercutio who vanished during a production of *Romeo and Juliet*?"

"Look," I said, "everything comes with a price."

"I am not paying two thousand dollars to play second fiddle to some junkie!" Noah rose to his feet, shoved his pipe back into his pocket, and grabbed for his jacket. Mike and Edith were nodding in common indignation.

"All right, all right, calm down, everyone!" I said. "Right now we are all desperately looking for a break and this play could be it. Now we can all go home and each return to our own oblivion, or we can pony up a relatively modest sum and take a gamble toward some modicum of success."

"It's not a bad bet," Mike replied, "but is this Bree guy willing to cough up two grand?"

"Actually, no."

"Fuck!" Noah shouted, stomping the floor. He took his pipe back out of his pocket as though it were a weapon.

"Well, if he can buy narcotics," Edith said, "he would certainly have to put in his share for us to even consider him."

"I won't remain in this production unless I can play Reggie!" Noah stated. "He'll have to take one of the smaller parts."

"All the roles are more or less the same size," I said.

"I don't care. . . ."

"All right," I compromised, "he can play Waldo, but he's not putting any money into the production. He brought us a hot script. That more than compensates for his share."

"Waldo's one of the most difficult roles," Noah said, apparently feeling gypped no matter which way Bree was cast. All sat silent for a while.

"You know what would be a perfect clincher to getting this production up?" Edith said. Her eyes darted around the room, seeing if anyone could guess what she was thinking. "Does anybody know what big theater director loves downtown cultural artifacts like this?"

Silence.

"Oh my God," Noah said with an awed grin, "fucking Baxter—yeah!"

"No way!" I shouted. With his charming British accent and sparkling smile, Huey was all things to most students—director, guru, seer and feeler. He was alleged to have been a part of the Angry Young Men, a movement that included the likes of Pinter, Orton, Osborne and Stoppard. Now, left behind in obscurity, underneath the cute veneer, he was just an angry old man.

"If Baxter directed this play, we'd be a shoo-in," Mike hollered, ignoring me.

"Yeah, a shoe in our asses!" I responded in horror.

"And he's in town, you know. He's putting together some kind of project at the Roustabout." Noah and the others completely ignored my despair.

"Huey Baxter is a no-talent fraud!" I yelled. "He hasn't directed a show in twenty years! And given the slightest authority he becomes a total monster!"

"That's not true," Mike said. "He directed a piece at Lincoln Center in the mid-eighties, and he did something at the Public in the early nineties."

"But no one remembers what they were," I replied, "because they were awful."

"In college I watched him shape and give rise to a million intricate and highly original scenes," Noah stated.

This was true. Baxter was competent with miniatures, but I calmly retorted that a scene was not a whole play.

"He also is one of the most buzzed-about theater directors around," Edith replied.

"He's the shit," Noah added, "and you get along so well with directors."

"Keep it up," I warned him.

"I'm sorry. That just slipped out."

"He does know everyone and everyone loves him," Mike added.

"That's only because he's a gossipmongering lush who has gone to every party that ever had an open bar." He attended all the big theatrical openings, award ceremonies and charity balls. Like someone who defied drowning, his name was always bobbing up in columns, where he could regularly be seen posing in group shots with real celebrities and black-tie society types. He must have had a publicist on his payroll.

"If he were to do this play, I would invest three thousand dollars," Mike stated confidently.

"Me too," Edith said. Noah agreed, and with that all eyes flipped back to me.

"Just hear me out," I countered. "I gave this a lot of thought and I know an excellent downtown director—Thom Morrison."

"Who the hell is that?" Mike asked, expressing everyone's sentiment.

"He did *Marla & Ivana: The Loves of Donald Trump*," I said, suddenly aware that they'd shoot me down.

"Give us a break!" Noah retorted.

"Okay," I caught myself, "here's another." I paused for dramatic effect. "Greg Gainsworth? He just directed *John Wilkes Booth the Musical*, at Lincoln Center. We have a friend in common."

"I am not putting up a cent unless we get someone who is smoking," Noah replied, fitting his unsanitary pipe back in his oversize mouth. "And Huey Baxter is *hot*."

"All right, who wants to approach him?" I asked.

Noah whispered something into Mike's ear.

"Didn't you and Belinda have an affair with him?" Mike asked.

"Yuck no," I lied.

"I think Belinda might have been intimate with him," Edith retorted.

"Very possibly," I replied, not hiding my general contempt.

"We should probably get her to approach him," Noah replied, unfailingly ruffling me with everything that came out of his large nicotine-stained hole. The dumb son of a bitch wasn't completely dumb; Noah knew that if he notified Belinda and told her we had some hot property, she would certainly be on the next flight back, and that would be the end of my cherished role in the play.

Short of medication, this production was my only real chance to shake my growing depression, and if they would only do it with Baxter then I had to succumb.

"Okay," I surrendered, and putting the industrial soda away, I said, "I'll do it."

Not only did I hate Huey Baxter, but now I was expected to hunt down and persuade this two-bit charlatan to direct my freshly discovered masterpiece.

THE ONE-HIT WONDER

AFTER · EVERYONE · LEFT that night, Sheldon made a rare appearance at my apartment ("Oh my God, is that a cockroach?") and we made frantic, fantastic love. While waiting for his second act to start, Sheldon talked softly to me: "In college I once slept with another guy."

"Really?"

"Yeah, but don't worry, I tested negative."

"Thank God for that," I replied, and watching him stare at me, I realized he wanted me to unlock lurid details of my kinky past. "I slept with a guy in college too."

"How many guys, if you don't mind me asking?"

"Not many," I demurred. I wasn't inclined to kiss and tell.

"You know you don't have to be worried. I mean, I'm not judging you or anything."

"Well . . ."

"What I'm trying to say is I really like you a lot. . . ."

"That's nice but—"

"See, there are some things I haven't told you, and you may not believe this, but I don't date many girls."

"You don't say," I replied tiredly. I didn't want him saying something like I love you. That would only make me feel awful.

"The last girl I dated, her name was Irene and we—"

"Look, you don't need to tell me."

"See, that's what I love about you. You're so cool about everything. You're nothing like her. You're so much hipper and cooler than most girls I've been with."

Just before I was about to recommend speed dating, he blurted out, "I want to know everything about you."

"All right." I finally decided to try to tell him something that would humanize the great goddess that was Hannah Cohn. "While I was in college, I slept with two of my professors."

"Get out!" he blurted, as if it were the last taboo.

"I'm serious."

"God, I never dated anyone who . . ." He looked at me with a twinkle in his eyes.

"I wish I didn't."

"Jeez Louise." He pulled next to me as though we were sharing seats on a roller coaster. "Slept with two guys, two professors, at the same exact time!" He made it sound like an emeritus orgy.

"It wasn't at the same time," I corrected him. "And one of those guys was actually a sexy, youthful woman."

"Hold it! No!" He jumped up as though he had just kissed a third rail. "You were . . . you and another . . . ! You are fucking kidding me!"

"Nope."

"You are so fucking fearless! So who was she?"

"A beautiful blonde lecturer who taught 'Intro to Film Production.' "

"Were you the guy or the chick?"

"We were both chicks. What are you talking about?"

"Who was she?"

"No one," I replied, not wanting to have a whole talk about Christy. His pole immediately rose under the circus tent–colored quilt.

"Did she have pubic hair?"

"No, she had feathers. What do you think?"

"I mean, was she shaved like a little girl?"

Sheldon the goof was gone. In his place was an erection with bated breath, and I couldn't resist playing with him. "How'd you know she was shaved?"

"You . . . I mean, she and you wouldn't . . . you wouldn't consider doing a three-way . . ."

"You know, I'd love to. I think she would too, but the dominatrix who now owns her would never unleash her for a night."

He made this involuntarily trembling sound. Then, probably because of the lesbian fantasy, he submerged to periscope depth and insisted on torpedoing me with his tongue. Unfortunately it was clear that he had never really done this before. Fortunately he was good at taking instruction, and soon he was pearl diving with the best of them.

I leaned back and found myself fantasizing that it was Christy.

Sheldon finally emerged from under the covers and tiredly asked if I had climaxed yet—something Christy would never dream of doing.

"Sure, a couple times," I replied, seeing that I had tuckered out his second appendage in less than an hour.

After wiping off his face and catching his breath, he asked, "Are you sure the other teacher wasn't also a woman?"

I wanted to say yes, if only to give him more fuel, but I told him the truth. "Christy was the first, last and only time I ever fell for another woman."

"So who was this other teacher?" Sheldon asked, narrowing his eyes incisively.

"Huey Baxter. He's primarily a director, but he was my acting teacher in college and—"

"Was he into anything kinky?"

"No."

Sheldon smiled like a child who had just tired of his latest toy. Jumping out of bed, he headed for the shower.

Ten minutes later Sheldon got out of the bathroom, and as he toweled himself off, he said, "Okay, you can tell me about the old guy, but try to keep it sexy."

"He wasn't that old," I replied.

I told him how during that same semester, while taking Christy's classes in the mornings, I had an acting workshop with Huey in the afternoons. Slowly I was pulled into his weird and dashing vortex of wry quips and affected airs.

"Skip to the sex," he pushed forward, not needing any backstory or environment.

"One evening I found myself alone with Baxter at this bar off campus where we talked and drank. Then we went to his place and had sex. Good night."

"Slow down," he said. "Tell me slowly how he conned you into performing the various . . . acts."

Huey kept talking about "my promise" as an actress and how I had to get more out of myself if I was going to seriously compete in the hodgepodge of the big city.

"Hold on," Sheldon said, as though he were hitting the Pause button on a VCR, "try to be a little more detailed and sensual."

"Like how?"

"You know, did he make you lick his balls while he was on the phone to his wife?"

"Oh, that's right," I replied, "I always forget about the balls."

"Come on, where's the eroticism here?" It was truly like watching a child frustrated with his X-rated playthings.

"I honestly don't remember," I replied tiredly.

"You must remember something?"

What I did remember was that Huey gave me an A+, while Christy only gave me a B-. Nonetheless it was she who I ended up g the torrid affair with.

When Sheldon realized that I was all out of erotic ini wished me good night, held me in his arms and went to sle

It took two days after that first meeting with Edith, Noah and Mike before I finally got up the nerve to call Huey's office at Yale. The secretary of the Drama Department said Huey Baxter was on an indefinite leave and gave me a cellular number where he could be reached. I left a message on his voice mail: "Hi, Huey, this is Hannah Cohn. I might have a business proposal for you."

I left my number. I also called Sheldon but only got his machine.

Just as I got into a hot bath my phone rang.

"Hannah, this is Franklin Stein. I want to apologize."

"For what?" I asked, dripping all over my living room floor. "You got me a great apartment."

"Cynthia Pumilla forgot to call you."

"Who? About what?"

"Well, don't get angry, but we began shooting *Success!* about a week ago."

"What? But I thought . . ." The last time I spoke to him he was still searching for new investors. "You replaced me?"

"No, not at all. But we had to trim some of the budget so we didn't invite everyone back. I just realized that Virginia's scene was coming up."

"I can't believe that you didn't call me."

"Hey, I'm incredibly overwhelmed and underbudgeted. I'm calling you now. Do you want the role or not?"

"I want it!" I had nearly given up hope that his film would ever get made. In fact, I wouldn't have undertaken the production of *Unlubricated* if I'd known this was coming up. At least I wouldn't have attempted it until after the film was done.

"You still have the script?" he asked.

"I think so." The last time I read it was right before I went to the audition. "Should I come over right now or what?"

"Just sit and look the script over. I'll stop by in a couple days and we'll talk about it."

My call-waiting the other call beeped just as he said good-bye. I switched over to

"Hannah, darling, I can't believe this is really you." It was the despicable Huey Baxter. He was calling from some noisy hellhole.

"So I hear you're no longer teaching," I said calmly.

"I took a furlough this spring. The whole nine-eleven thing compelled me to review my life. And I was offered a little project down here, so I'm taking some meetings."

"What's the project?"

"It's a revival of *The Playboy of the Western World* for the Roustabout Theater. Rupert Everett asked me to direct him."

"Wow," I replied, rubbing my hand over my arm.

"But listen, I still want to hear what you've got. I'm looking at my Palm Pilot, and the only possible time would be in three days."

Even though I doubted he had a Palm Pilot, I told him that'd be fine. "When in three days, and where can we meet?" I asked, as I suddenly felt it.

"Time Café, eight o'clock," he filled in.

As I hung up I realized that the bump on my arm was not a bruise as I first thought, but a lump. I had to show it to Dr. Wang. The man could heal anything with a pulse.

The next day, after six hours of office attitudinizing, phone reception, filings and Xeroxing, I met with Noah again at Starbucks. I agreed to buy him anything up to ten dollars in exchange for a line-by-line refreshment of Franklin's clichéd script. I would've preferred to rehearse with almost anyone else, but he was always available.

Seeing a newspaper headline about the latest developments of the war in Afghanistan, Noah said, "You know I voted against Bush, but in a way, I'm glad he's in office now."

"Why?"

"Because I don't think a Democrat would've invaded Afghanistan."

"That's ridiculous, Gore supported Bush's action. And, just for the record, Gore went to Vietnam while Bush was doing coke lines and tequila shots in the Texas National Guard. I'm sure he would'
the same thing."

"I just can't see a Democrat doing something like that."

I asked if we could not talk about politics.

"The only shortcoming you'll face with this part," Noah said, referring to the seduction scene in my film role, "is that you haven't had any physical rehearsal."

"Don't you worry about that."

"What's the name of this film again?"

"*Success!*"

"See, that's the problem with my career. I can't meet anyone important," he declared, then asked, "Where the hell did you meet Franklin Stein?"

"I don't know—around." I didn't want to talk anymore, I just wanted to go home. As I rose I gave him a word of advice, "Go to industry parties and try not to annoy people."

"Parties, yeah," he replied, ignoring the second half of my advice. As we left the ever-expanding coffee franchise, I remembered the woman I had coffee with on September 11 and hoped she was okay.

9

THE INDIE DIRECTOR

THAT·NIGHT·AFTER a quick dinner, Sheldon agreed to come back to my apartment for the second time, which I misread as a sign of progress. While he was in the bathroom, making snide remarks about "slumming it," I checked my answering machine.

"I was going to be in the area tomorrow morning and was hoping to stop by and talk about your role," Franklin's recorded voice played.

"Who the heck is that?" Sheldon asked, only hearing the end of the young director's voice as the toilet was flushing.

"Good news," I announced, and told him that I had landed a small role in Franklin Stein's latest film.

"Congratulations," he said, "I didn't even know you went for an audition."

I explained that I had been cast in it six months earlier and that for the obvious reason it had been delayed until now.

"You didn't sleep with him for the role?" Sheldon asked, probably trying to squirrel away more foreplay anecdotes for later.

"What a stupid thing to say. Of course not," I snapped back.

"Take it easy! I was just kidding. So where'd you meet Franklin Stein?" Annoying questions didn't die, they kept returning in the mouth of other people.

"At a party that another director I was working with brought me to."

"Who was this other director?" he pressed.

"Christy Saffers."

"The female teacher with the shaved pubes who you went down on for a good grade!" he shot back. If you simply toss in one pornographic detail, a guy would remember anything for life.

"We actually had an adult relationship," I clarified, to discourage his juvenile X-rated imagination.

"So you were in a relationship with her when you went to this party and met Franklin."

"What are you asking me?"

"I guess I was just wondering if you were cheating." He chuckled moronically.

"We didn't do anything," I said with a sigh.

"Your nose just grew three inches."

"Are you kidding me!" It was the exact reason I had broken up with Christy.

"Sorry," he suddenly backpedaled. "Let's just forget it."

I just glared at him. Gently he reached over and started rubbing my arm.

"I got a better idea, let's forget any possibility of sex ever again." I got into bed and rolled away from him.

While he watched TV, I pretended to be asleep, while actually feeling shitty about Christy. I still didn't think I did anything wrong. Christy was a short-tempered, unforgiving asshole. Unlike Goofy, she never had any romanticized or pornographic notions of me, she simply knew me better than anyone else. And that was a big part of love.

Early the next morning, while Sheldon dressed, he apologized and asked if he could make up for last night's faux pas. I actually wanted to break up once and for all, but I didn't want to do it painfully, so I told him, fine, we could talk later. He kissed my cheek and left. While watching the morning news, my downstairs doorbell rang. I buzzed Stein in, and a moment later the boy director was at my apartment door holding a bottle of Australian wine.

"I only have half an hour before I have to be back on set." He sounded like a true professional and proceeded to unbuckle his belt. "Nice apartment."

"What do you think you're doing?"

"I'm sorry, these pants are just too tight. Mind if I take them off?" he asked as he did.

"I guess not." It was such a brash move, I actually couldn't believe he was expecting to get anywhere. I put the wine in the fridge. It was too early to drink.

Instead I retrieved the industrial-size bottle of funny-tasting diet soda and a box of old crackers, which I put on a plate. When I returned, he was sitting on my sofa in his boxers and socks in the middle of a power call on his cell. As he talked about lighting equipment, he made a strange hand-to-mouth gesture, which I interpreted as a thinly repressed desire for a blow job.

As he snapped his phone closed, Franklin asked if Cynthia Pumilla had called me.

"No."

"Be at the Chelsea Piers, Silver Screen, Level Two, Pier Sixty-one tomorrow at noon."

"But I'm supposed to temp all day tomorrow."

"Not if you want to be in the film—report to her." As I scribbled down everything he had quickly said, he sipped the strange soda and nibbled crackers, then he started kissing my neck.

"Can we not do . . . that."

"I just needed a little something to go with the crackers," he said, trying to rub my back.

"Call me old-fashioned," I said, "but I don't respond well when a guy just wants to hit and run."

He looked at his wristwatch. "I guess we'll just have to have our great moment some other time then."

"You can always make some time," I said, not wanting to hurt his feelings.

He kissed me on the cheek, then pulled his pants back on and zipped up. Before heading back to his film shoot, he asked, "Are you going to be ready with your role tomorrow?"

"Barring catastrophic acts of terrorism, I'll be there." I wasn't entirely kidding. Some vague terrorist alert had been announced the night before.

After a frustrating and demeaning day with a bunch of asshole corporate attorneys, I headed up to the dentist's place. On the one hand I could certainly use an evening of kindness. On the other hand, it was high time for a breakup. As soon as I got to his apartment, I immediately sensed that something was wrong; his eyes looked red and he was a little drunk. As he poured me a glass of wine, I asked him if everything was okay. Suddenly I realized tears were coming from his eyes. At that instant, he looked like a sad little boy.

"What's the matter, hon?" I took his sad little head in my hands.

"I lost a tooth today," he said dismally.

"The tooth fairy gives money for those," I said in a playful voice.

"No, it was one of my patients'," he explained. "I pulled it and then I realized I didn't have to."

"Oh, I'm sorry," I said, unsure of how to react.

He held me close, kissed me hard, and whispered, "It was an important tooth, a molar, with a deep, strong root. Why didn't I just leave well enough alone!"

He looked like such a helpless little boy that I opted not to break up with him. In another moment, he was weeping furiously. I led him into the bedroom, where he soon regained control. In another moment he was turning all his professional grief into eros, and before we could even shake off our clothes we were having mile-a-minute sex. Afterward, we lay still a while, just holding each other.

"Last night, there was a reason I was asking you about Franklin Stein," he said just as I was beginning to think he wasn't that bad.

"Let's just skip it." I was nervous about my performance tomorrow and didn't want to be pissed off.

Sheldon reached over me to the end table, where a small slip of paper was sitting. It was a clipping from some tabloid magazine. Under a photo of Franklin Stein and his wife, Helen, it read, "Franklin Stein and his wife Helen."

It was the same raw wound where Christy had mauled me.

"First of all I'm not involved with him, but that brings us to the real reason I came here tonight. You're a nice, handsome, financially comfortable guy. And I'm a struggling actress, and you could find a hundred girls in this city who'd be great for you, but we are not going to work out, and there's little point in staying together."

"Hold it," he jumped in. "Why? What did I do?"

I took a deep breath and realized I was being no better than Christy. The poor guy didn't have a clue. "I'm sorry, Shel, you didn't do anything. You really are nice. I know this sounds like bullshit, but you really do deserve better. I mean, look at me, I'm already involved—in me."

"I like that about you. You got a life."

"Well, I like you too, but this has got to stop here. It really does."

"Well, can't we at least remain friends?"

"Of course."

As I finished dressing, he sulked. I softly wished him a good night, kissed him and cabbed it home.

The next morning I called in sick at SHW, then I showered, dressed and headed to Chelsea Piers. Among a crew of hundreds, I searched out Cynthia Pumilla. All walkie-talkies led to her. As I silently walked down a long hallway, I was aware of someone shadowing me. When I finally reached Cynthia's locked office door, I spun around to find an incredibly cute, lean guy, who I instantly recognized. "You're Hamlet."

"Actually I was Laertes." We had been briefly introduced after the show, a Public Parking Lot production of *Hamlet*, which had been exquisitely staged on the oil-slick concrete of a municipal garage downtown. That was about a year ago, but I couldn't remember his name.

"Hamlet was sick that day," he said, "so I filled in."

"Well, you were great." Neither a parry nor a pentameter missed.

We commiserated about the scarcity of acting jobs until Cynthia Pumilla appeared and let us in her office. I introduced myself, as did the parking-lot Hamlet—his name was Jonah Baye. Cynthia was a harried blond with a telephone headset, a clipboard and a mix-and-match clothing style. Because she was busily reading forms and notes, she barely made eye contact when she spoke. While she informed us of the adversities of this low-budget production, I was never certain if she was addressing me, Jonah or someone on her headset.

"You've got some forms to fill out," she explained and led us to another office, during which she juggled two or more headset conversations.

Intermittently people dashed up to her with short, frantic questions. She answered as she continued walking. Finally, at a small fold-down desk, she had Jonah and me sign multipage contracts, which she notarized herself. She also explained how much money we'd be getting—I was getting roughly two grand for a week's worth of work—when we were getting it, and how much was going to be deducted for SAG as well as other sundry expenses.

"More forms will come in the mail," she explained.

It was difficult to imagine that this woman ever slept, but I was immediately attracted to her, or more particularly to her unpretentious style, considering the boundless knowledge and power she seemed to wield. She gave me a call sheet—a work schedule that broke down the combination of characters in different scenes, as well as the times and places we were filming. Jonah's call sheet was not yet ready. My three scenes were shot in opposite order to how they appeared in the script.

Cynthia explained that our new SAG cards would come in the mail. All the principals had changing rooms in the complex, but I had to share a closet with two other actresses.

Finally Jonah said good-bye and dashed out just as three newly enlisted soldiers entered this makeshift film army. Cynthia quickly introduced me to a bulging-eyed intern named Joey, who was to bring me to Gilda, the wardrobe mistress.

From a clipboard the frizzy-haired, chain-smoking Gilda read that my wardrobe consisted of a shiny pair of black heels, a black leather miniskirt, fishnet stockings and a bright red, lacy garter belt with matching bra and panties. Each item was on a wire hanger sheathed in plastic.

"They shouldn't require any alterations or adjustments," Gilda explained. "When you're done see Harriet, she'll do your face."

After changing into someone who I would neither like nor be, I was led to Harriet, who garishly painted my face. When I argued that I didn't have to look this tacky, she said that Franklin specifically requested it. Probably revenge for his unrelieved sexual tension from the day before. Then I waited for nearly four hours rereading the same news items in the three different daily newspapers and trying not to freeze. I asked my pet P.A., Joey, why it was taking so damn long before my scheduled shot. He explained that actor Ronnie Bridges, sex icon of the '70s who was to play the ethically conflicted producer, had arrived late from L.A., so the entire schedule had been pushed back two hours.

"I should have told you earlier," Joey confessed with an embarrassed giggle.

"I've been waiting a lot longer than two hours!"

"Oh," he remembered glibly, "during this morning's shoot the lighting was too hot. They decided to reshoot it."

"Why the fuck didn't you tell me when I first arrived! I could've come back two hours later."

He shrugged. This little larva didn't mind wasting my time. That's what his entire career would amount to once he got his union card. Finally, around seven o'clock, Cynthia came and informed me that there was no way they were going to shoot my scene today so I might as well go home.

"How does that affect the overall shooting schedule?" I asked.

"We'll just schedule everything back a day and work overtime on Saturday."

"So I have to come in tomorrow?" I clarified since she didn't.

"I'm sorry, yes. At noon," she replied tiredly.

I got home, showered quickly, and opened the fridge. The only exciting find was the bottle of Australian wine that Franklin had brought over. I uncorked it, got a glass, slumped into a soft chair and poured. Before I could drown my sorrows I suddenly remembered that within thirty minutes I was supposed to meet Huey Baxter for the big pitch to direct *Unlubricated*. I pulled clothes on like I was on fire, grabbed my copy of *Bull Session* and dashed downstairs. To make matters worse, I struggled long and hard to find a cab.

When I arrived at the Time Café, fifteen minutes late, Huey was sitting alone at a table wearing tight denim jeans, a beige leather jacket, and a bright crew-neck sweater—the clothes for a man thirty years his junior, contrasting sharply with his unexercised body and ashen skin. As I approached the table, he rose and leaned forward for a sophisticated peck. I expected it on my cheek but shouldn't have been surprised when it hit along my parted lips. Franklin must've taught him that one.

As soon as we sat, a hyper-accommodating waiter came over with a too-tight smile and a partition-size menu. "Would you like a drink?"

"Water, please."

"Bottled or—"

"Unfiltered New York tap, thanks."

"A refill of this," Huey added, touching his not even half-finished goblet. "And get the lady a Bloody Mary. That was your poison, wasn't it, love?"

"Sure," I said politely, but that was Christy's drink, I only borrowed it. He knew full well I would have to pick up the check, and though the price of a drink here was the same as an entire meal at the catty-corner diner, I didn't want to demonstrate that I was broke at my pitch meeting.

"So what have you been up to in this time of war?" he pressed on.

"Auditions, casting calls, endurance."

"You know, I don't know if I ever told you this," Huey said, pressing close, "but I always saw a very real something in you."

"You don't say," I remarked. Pretty lame flattery for him.

"I know that sounds like a crock. Everything I say must sound like a crock at this late date," he said, taking a sip of his drink.

" 'Course not," I lied.

"Come on, don't tickle my giblet, I've been around too long. Well, that's why I'm down here. September eleventh was a day of personal inventory for me." He took another sip of his drink. "Were you down here then?"

"No, I was out in Long Island," I replied, not wanting to share, especially with him.

"Well, I've watched all my contemporaries step up for their Tonys, Obies, and Oliviers, I figure it's my time to do likewise."

"So you're here for work?"

"That I am, and don't think I've forgotten about all my little Yale urchins. I've got your headshots and résumés filed right up here." He tapped his receding hairline. He was half hamming it up and half drunk. He lit up a cigarette with a wonderful bravado.

"Huey, a group of us are thinking of producing a play and we're looking for a director," I blurted out tiredly.

"Intriguing," he said, fascinated with his cigarette. "Well, I know a few younger chaps I can veer your way." He took such a deep drag on his smoke, I could hear the tiny snaps of his burning tobacco.

"We were hoping that you might consider directing it," I explained.

"That's probably out of the question," he responded quickly. "I mean, I'd like to help and all, but I just haven't the time."

In an effort to give it my best shot, I asked, "What exactly would it take to get you to agree to do this production?"

"There's about four or five big balls I have to juggle before I step into a project," Huey launched as if he were speaking to a team from the Nederlander Organization. "I can go short on some of them if I get more of the others."

"Go ahead." This was good, I'd be able to give the group a specific list of reasons he rejected us. Then I could tell my coproducers that it was simply out of my hands.

"First, I would require a healthy budget for the play and a competitive fee." He took another sip of his drink. "Second, I'd absolutely require creative carte blanche." He paused to see if I was still with him. When I didn't protest, he resumed. "Third would be the script. I'd have to believe in the work." Again he paused. "I don't do hip remakes of Puccini, or colorful musicals adapted from the minor works of T. S. Eliot, or for that matter Victor Hugo. Next is the venue. Are we talking Broadway or Off-Broadway, I don't recognize Off-Off. And lastly the actors, specifically star power." He made an up-in-lights hand gesture. "Give me someone from the triple-A-list and I'm immediately on board. A couple from the B-list, maybe."

As I listened to his list of insane demands, I realized that if this clod really had this clout, he wouldn't even be having drinks with me—an unemployed temp in a rainstorm. At best, I would've had to submit a letter to his agent's assistant.

After sitting on my ass in whore's makeup all day I was not in the mood for this pompous drunk's ego spill. Even if he was giving me the rejection that I wanted, I resented having to suffer his steaming platter of overinflated bullshit. As the waiter put my Bloody Mary on a colorful coaster, I quietly asked for the check. Although it was way too spicy, I gulped it down slowly until I completely finished it.

"Wow!" Huey exclaimed as I slowly rose.

"Well, it was good to see you, Huey," I said. "We wish you good luck in future endeavors."

"Hold on now." His accent seemed to diminish.

"I don't mean to be brusque," I said, taking two twenties from my purse, "but if I get home right now and go right to bed, I might just be able to fit in five hours of sleep."

"Why don't you tell me what you got?" he said sympathetically.

"Of the four things you mentioned, I only got one," I said as I pulled on my jacket.

"What one?"

Sheer vanity compelled me to take out the book, *Bull Session*. I flipped to the foreword, and turning it around, I slid it before him. He read the pages, clearly fascinated, and before he could ask, I proudly explained, "I got the script and rights."

"To what, exactly?"

"*Unlubricated* by Lilly Bull. But let me tell you what I don't have," I said loud enough for a crowd of dandies at an adjacent table to hear. "I don't have any grand theater on the Great White Way, no chart-topping matinee idols attached, and only a meager starting budget that doesn't include enough for your magnificent salary."

"Obviously I seem to have disturbed you, and I'm truly sorry. I didn't mean to piss you off, but I am feeling a little undervalued. Perhaps subconsciously I took it out on you."

I felt as though I had called his bluff and he had just folded. But I didn't want to win.

"So, what exactly do you have?" he asked.

"Nothing really. I mean, in addition to the script, I have three alumni who pressured me into asking you to direct."

"Are we talking Equity?" he asked.

"Absolutely not," I struggled to unsell the project, "it's just a nonunion production."

"Oh God, nonunion. What exactly are you putting up, some show-case?"

"I think we'll have to get a waiver," I replied, fearful of getting caught in a lie. "The actors aren't Equity, but it will probably only be a mini-contract situation."

"What's your budget?" he asked, cutting to the chase.

"About ten grand." Again I exaggerated downward.

"A low-budget, nonunion—"

"Look, Huey, I really appreciate your time and . . ." I rose to escape.

"What theater do you have?"

"See, we don't even have that yet," I said, as if to prove his point of our amateurishness.

"Well, I suppose you know that I saw *Coprophagia* when I was out west."

"No, I didn't know."

"Yes, and I knew Gary Ganghole in his heyday. I remember thirty years ago when Bull shot the son of a bitch. I had seen him just a week earlier. I was kind of hoping that he'd die." I nodded silently. A shame Lilly Bull didn't come a week earlier and bring an extra bullet for Huey.

"Actually, the way he finally died wasn't too pleasant. Although it was listed as a suicide, Ganghole accidentally hung himself during an autoerotic act." Huey smirked, paused and continued with his important smoking.

"I have to admit I find this whole sordid tale rather intriguing, but the simple fact is I'm probably going to be directing *Playboy* over the next few months."

"I fully understand." There it was: he had a prior commitment. Baxter was unavailable. Thank God.

"Tell you what," he finally said, "let me look the play over and see if there's any time in my schedule." At least he didn't pronounce it shed-ule.

I tiredly took the manila envelope holding the script and placed it on the tabletop. He took it out and flipped through the fresh Xerox of the creased and marked-up draft.

"My Lord," he said as he flipped through its pages. "Where in God's name did you unearth this fossil?"

"All I'm allowed to disclose is that it came from one of the cast members."

He made a hush-hush gesture as the waiter put the check down. I counted out my change as Baxter finished his drink. Then he scooped up the manuscript, and together we walked out the door. He hailed a cab going uptown. Fearing that he would get out first and I'd be stuck with the fare, I bid him adieu and walked down to Broadway-Lafayette to the subway. As I waited on the platform, I had ample time to hate myself for mishandling the occasion. He had all but rejected me and stupidly I pulled him back in.

"Excuse me." A young woman was suddenly before me. When I turned to look at her, I could see that she was an amalgam of bad skin and poor bone structure.

"Are you okay?"

"Why?" There was always an ulterior motive.

"Well"—she pulled out some piece of literature—"these are just such hard times and I just thought perhaps you could take comfort in Our Lord. . . ."

"You're talking about the World Trade Center tragedy, aren't you?"

"Yes, events that make us question—"

"You know, the faith of those hijackers who flew those planes into the towers was probably greater than anyone I know. They truly thought that by doing those awful deeds they'd go right to heaven."

"I know, but even Islamic clerics will tell you that they didn't represent the Islamic culture."

"But I'm sure some Christians don't feel you represent their culture either. The point is that some people worship silently, while for others their devotion leads them to hijack planes, lobby for legislation, or pamphleteer on subway platforms."

Usually I didn't argue with religious types, and I was surprised at my composure, but I was waiting for the train anyway, and found it annoying that one group of God worshippers were capitalizing on the acts of another group of God worshippers.

"The only thing I'm trying to say is that God can offer some peace of mind," she replied.

"Well, I don't need a god to get peace of mind, or for that matter to lead a good and decent life."

No sooner did I say this than the V train—the younger cousin of the F train—poured into the station. I hopped on, and she turned around and dashed off.

10

THE STAND-IN

THE·NEXT·MORNING, while my voice was still gruff with sleep, I called the shift supervisor at SHW and in a falsely nasal tone informed her that for the second day in a row, I was still too congested to come in.

"You know we can really use you," she said in the meekest of tones.

"If I feel better, I swear I'll hop in a cab and be right there."

I dressed, this time a little less attractively than the day before, and headed down to Chelsea Piers for the reshoot. There I again met with Joey the bug, who, with an irritating buzz of eagerness, swore that today everything was going according to schedule.

"That's good because I'm risking my job by taking off a second day in a row."

He muttered something over his walkie-talkie and said, "They should be ready for you in studio six in about twenty minutes." He suggested I get into costume.

I tried to recite my lines as Gilda helped me on with the dress. Then Harriet rolled on the war paint. As I raced over to studio six, I took a Kleenex and gingerly blotted the gunk off my eyes and lips.

Everyone was again waiting for the great Ron Bridges when I entered the set.

I went over and greeted Franklin. He didn't so much as shake my hand, and nearby talking to one of the techies I saw Helen, his macho, allegedly soon-to-be-ex-wife. He was on his best little hubby behavior.

"Know your lines?"

"Them and nothing else."

"We still have about a half an hour before Bridges gets his fat ass on set, but we have his stand-in, Lionel."

"So," he said and turned to me, "why don't we begin with you."

In a moment a middle-aged, auburn-maned man in a suit and tie appeared. Cynthia introduced us as Franklin talked to the internationally esteemed director of photography, Serge Forte.

"Pleased to meet you," said Lionel, who was a watered-down version of Ron Bridges. We shook hands.

"Guys, when you're ready," Philip, the assistant director, said, ushering us over to Franklin and Serge.

"Okay, Lionel," Stein said, walking him through it, since the stand-in knew neither the story nor the dialogue. "This is really Hannah's scene. You're a producer and you just had a major blowout with a director. You're conflicted over the decision of whether or not to make his art film. So you're exhausted. She's here to comfort you, so just play along. Let Hannah do all the work. You're on autopilot."

"Autopilot," he replied, "my favorite motivation."

"Hannah, when you hear Lionel at the door, you're going to get up, grab him, walk him over to the couch—"

"Franklin," interrupted the short cinematographer as he inspected the scene through a fancy monocle. He spoke through a stubby, thick, unlit cigar clipped in his jagged, brown teeth. "If she walks him this way, we can get that wonderful background into the camera." He pointed down the Hudson toward eastern New Jersey.

"That's fine, but I don't want any accidental views of Lower Manhattan," Stein replied.

The cameraman was shooting perilously close to where the towers once loomed. Film editors the world over were clipping any views of the World Trade Center out of their films. If no one saw the towers it was as if they didn't fall, as if no one ever died.

Serge assured Franklin that there would be no hint of the mass grave that was Lower Manhattan.

"All right," Franklin said to me, "Serge wants you to walk this way. Then you begin your lines."

"Fine," I replied.

"Harry," the director addressed some P.A. offstage, "during the scene, I want you to read Sam's lines with Hannah since Lionel doesn't know them."

"Gotcha," replied Harry, a hairless P.A. who was just sitting out of frame with a script in hand.

"Hannah, you're standing in the wrong place. Serge wants you to begin here," Franklin said, pointing two feet from where I was. He then walked me through my blocking. The producer was supposed to enter my studio apartment, where I was to greet him.

"You're going to walk up to him. Give him a big wet one and bring him over to your couch. You're going to subtly try to convince him that the other film project is better. It's more commercial. It'll assure his future in the company."

"I remember," I replied, having read the scene.

"You'll undo his tie, unbutton his shirt, and start gently massaging his chest. Then cut."

"Fine."

We did our first walk-through without the camera running. Franklin gave me some notes, and along with Serge he reblocked it a bit. He wanted to "cheat the angle" somehow and we walked through it again. Then the cameraman slightly relit the scene and refocused the massive camera. Harriet retouched the makeup on my face as well as places on my body that betrayed any trace of imperfections. The lights came on, another P.A. clapped it, and we did our first take. Considering that the stand-in moved like a living mannequin and I read my lines against hairless Harry, it went without a hitch. Franklin talked to Serge for a bit, then slightly refocused the camera. The makeup girl fixed me up again and another one touched up part of the stand-in's back. Then, action. We read our lines and didn't bump into the furniture.

While we were nearing completion of my close-ups, the great Ron Bridges showed up, interrupting everything with a gluttonous self-assurance that he alone misread as charm. With the face- and neck-lifts, hair plugs, probable liposuction, nips, tucks, and countless other unsung therapies and surgical procedures, Bridges looked like a study in conflict. He was the irresistible force of age struggling with the unmovable ego of man's desire to stay sexy.

Naked Lionel, the sweet and egoless substitute, faded away and twenty minutes later, after bringing the great prima don up to speed on script and blocking, we were doing the same scene again.

"I don't mean to be rude," Ron asked, just as Franklin opened his mouth to say Action, "but would I really just allow this girl to seduce me like this?"

"She seduces you every day. Why would today be any different?"

"May I make a tiny suggestion," he replied, which caused everyone to cringe a bit. "I think instead of just letting myself get dragged through this, I might be a bit more aggressive. After all, I've known more than my share of horny-toad producers."

"Let's try it as written," Franklin said with delicate restraint.

"If I can just show you what I have in mind, I'm sure you'll agree with me," Ron replied with annoying gallantry.

"You're not changing the text are you?" Franklin asked after a sigh.

"Hell no," Ron said, making the sign of the cross, "the text is sacred."

"Go ahead," Franklin conceded, seeing no way around him.

At the door, instead of me meeting Ron and leading him through the scene, he grabbed me. As we both did our lines, he briskly rubbed his hand over my shirt, which was immensely distracting. I had to fight my own instinct to shove him away. This alone made my character seem significantly dumber since only a bimbo would allow such conduct. My sole defense was keeping the lines up at a furious pace, hoping he'd either forget his own or that Franklin would call cut. But the old fool had a great memory and played right along with me. Before we got to the couch, he slipped his fingers along my thigh. When his hand reached up under my miniskirt, I shoved him off of me.

"What!" Bridges shouted.

"Cut!" Franklin called out.

"All I'm trying to do here," said Ron, "is put a little umph! into this scene."

"Keep your umph! in your fucking pants," I fired back.

"Ron, I like the concept," Franklin interrupted, "but the thing is, your character is an ethical colonoscope struggling to locate the polyps of corruption in the bowels of the system. He's not some dirty old reprobate."

"Ahh," the pathetic old actor let out some brain gas.

"Remember, the Academy likes moral characters. This is going to be the role that snags you that Oscar you so richly deserve." Bridges silently took a stiff drink from an opaque glass. "In this scene Virginia is the fiend," Franklin continued, "she's trying to sway a good man who is weakened in his artistic integrity."

"Gotcha," Bridges said.

When we started the scene again, I could smell booze on his breath. Three takes later we were on to the seduction scene. We both stripped and I was sitting on him in my tight red panties and bra. Neither he nor his character wasted the opportunity to paw at my boobs, tug at my cheeks, or try to stick his rotting tongue down my esophagus. All his authentic, method-acting details, which nauseated me, totally eluded the camera.

If this wasn't bad enough, the director of photography restaged the same damn scene first in the bathroom and then in the kitchen. By the day's end, with my body bruised by his clutching and groping, I began to wonder if the old actor hadn't slipped Serge the cash he saved that night on low-priced call girls. Fortunately, the entire time I still managed to keep my bra and panties. We were done by one o'clock that morning.

I cringed at the thought that in two weeks I was scheduled to perform in my first bona fide nude scene. Franklin took me outside, told me I did a tremendous job in light of great adversity and asked if he could drop by later.

"Later tonight?" I asked, dazed.

"Is that okay?" he asked preciously. "I thought we might finally be able to have that slow romantic evening we were waiting for." He was obviously horny. Ron Bridges's cheap feels must have got him going, but wrestling with the older actor had completely exhausted me.

I wanted to get to know Franklin, and possibly get closer, but I wasn't planning on giving anything away, at least not that night.

"I really am looking forward to our honeymoon date," I said tenderly, "and I don't mean to be a tease, but I barely have energy left to shower and crawl into bed. And I have to be at work early tomorrow."

He nodded stiffly. I thought he was angry, but then I realized Helen had just rolled into the vicinity and he had to make a clean break.

As I dressed, I went over some details with bug-eyed Joey regarding the next shoot in two weeks. When I finally stepped outside, it was past two on the desolation of the West Side Highway. Waist-high concrete barricades divided the lanes. Cars were few. Cabs seemed to be extinct.

Across the street, I spotted a pair of late-middle-aged transsexual hookers leaning against cars parked at the light. Looking up at the sky, it was as if God had accidentally placed his greasy hand on the heavenly dome, then quickly wiped it away, forgetting one mark—a thumbprint moon.

I turned to go back inside and ask Joey to call me a private car when a horn started honking. Someone was yelling something at me. A shiny Lincoln Town Car with an American flag on the antenna pulled up before me and the dark-tinted passenger window slowly rolled down. The auburn mane of Ronnie Bridges popped out.

"Can I give you a lift, me lady?" fopped the gallant old lecher.

Ten minutes of his halitosis seemed an acceptable price for a late-night ride home. I got in. It turned out he was going south to the SoHo Grand on West Broadway.

"What do you say we dash across the street for a quick drink?" he asked, pointing to the club Lot 61. I politely declined and he suddenly became pressed for time. He explained that the driver was going to take him home first, then the car could loop north and take me to Hell's Kitchen. Fine, whatever. I threw my head back, closed my eyes and tried to nap. We sped along for a few blocks, then—boom! A massive blast as the rear of the car was lifted slightly in the air.

"I think al-Qaeda just got us!" Ronnie shouted through his polite stupor.

"No, no!" the driver replied. "We had a flat is all." The car coasted to the side of the road. Getting out, the driver kicked the tire, then popped open the trunk and stared down into it with all the bewilderment of a caveman gazing up at the stars.

"Need help?" I called out, trying not to sound patronizing.

"Lady, I know how to fix a flat," he replied. "What do you do when the spare is flat?"

I apologized for my impatience and suggested that perhaps he could radio for another car, which he did. Numbers and locations were exchanged in Spanish and the driver replied, "A car can be here in forty-five minutes."

"Thanks, but I can just hop a cab," I replied tiredly and opened the door.

Fetching a hefty shoulder bag, Ronnie got out with me and we both discovered a fine rain was falling. We were on the corner of Nineteenth Street and nowhere. For ten minutes we stood like statues on the West Side Highway, faced with the same problem as before, no cabs in sight.

"What are those?" Ronnie asked, pointing across to several plastic bottles lined along the curb across the street. They were filled with a golden liquid.

"Piss."

"Why in God's name would anyone piss in all those bottles?" he asked.

"See that place?" I pointed to a closed establishment on the corner. "On weekends that's a hot club."

"So?"

"There's usually a cab line there," I explained. "Instead of taking time out from their shift, cabbies just urinate in their old water bottles and toss them out the window." Christy had informed me of this disturbing fact when I asked the same question.

"Ironic when you think about it," he continued. "All those cabbies stuck here, using bottles as decatheters, and now we can't even get a single one."

A pickup with a spinning yellow light led a convoy of four huge flatbed trucks, which rumbled the ground beneath our feet as they zoomed north toward the Lincoln Tunnel. Huge twisted girders were strapped on the back, and I wondered if they weren't the mammoth steel bones of the World Trade Center, which were still being excavated.

"Maybe we'll have better luck on Tenth Avenue," Bridges suggested.

I agreed and we started walking east on Nineteenth Street.

"You know there's a charming little bistro just down here called Hellfire that we could take refuge in," he said and pointed south.

"I got work in a few hours," I replied as I walked quicker. He mumbled some dour rejoinder and slowly followed. About halfway down the deserted block, past closed art galleries and warehouse spaces, under the disused elevated train trestle, I heard him periodically groaning. When I looked back I saw he was limping under the weight of his bulky shoulder bag.

"Are you okay?" But as I asked this, I noticed that he was only wearing one shiny penny loafer. The other foot was clad only in a black sock. "Where's your right shoe?"

"I must have left it in my dressing room," he replied as he hobbled up to me at the corner of Tenth Avenue. I silently relieved him of his bag and we continued walking.

"You know this bag is pretty heavy," I huffed. "You sure you don't have a pair of shoes in here?"

"Oh!" he said in an inspired tone. He took the bag from my shoulder, unzipped it, and extracted a half-empty quart of Jack Daniel's, which he unscrewed and gulped. Then, ever the gentleman, he extended the bottle to me. "Want some?"

"No, thanks," I said, and found myself chuckling. The notion that I was stranded with this sexual menace was surreal.

As we continued marching toward the Meatpacking District, the mist thickened. We walked under the looming signs of mini storage spaces, past vast empty truck bays and dark garages. All of it seemed to make us smaller and more vulnerable.

"It looked like such a beautiful vehicle," Ronnie eulogized the Lincoln.

"I suppose," I replied tiredly.

"And the fucking thing goes flat almost as soon as we get in."

"I remember." But I kept wondering how the hell a person could forget his shoe.

"You know what it's like, this whole thing?"

"No, what?"

"It's like . . . *Ow!*" Ronnie suddenly shrieked. He had stepped on something sharp and hard and jumped into a deep doorway. He cursed violently as he hobbled in ever-tightening circles of excruciating pain. I watched as the white-tiled entrance to some meatpacking plant became speckled with blood.

"Hold it," I said, seeing a long rusty nail that had been driven right up through his sole. I pulled it out as he screamed.

"Shit, you're going to need a tetanus shot."

"Fuck!" he yelled and sat on the ground, closing his eyes in focused agony.

After about five minutes of just sitting there, he opened his eyes, tapping something, and asked, "What's that?"

Behind me, Ronnie was tapping on a small black plastic box with a hole in it.

"Oh, that's a rat box." I remembered Christy telling me about them too.

"A what?"

"Unlike squirrels, who forage in the open, rats will only eat in burrows, so they put poison in there for rats to eat."

"Oh God!" He jumped to his one good foot and started hopping a few feet out in the rain before he collapsed again to the ground. I asked him if he could get up, perhaps we could slowly proceed.

"I can't," he uttered, "I need an ambulance."

I opened my bag and confirmed what I already knew. My cell phone was out of juice. I forgot to recharge it the night before, after being with asshole Baxter.

"Where's your cellular?" I asked him.

He started fumbling through his bag, and finally cursed, "Shit!" He slammed his bag against the ground. "I must have left it in my dressing room." Probably next to his right shoe.

"It's okay," I assured him.

"It's not okay!" he screamed back futilely. "We're going to get eaten by rats here!"

"Not today," I replied, and grabbing some slightly soiled Starbucks napkins from my bag, I put them inside his sock against the wound. Then, reaching into his jacket, I pulled out his wallet, removed some cash and dashed out to the small group of cars stuck at the red light at Tenth Avenue and Seventeenth Street.

"Excuse me." I tapped on the window of a Volvo driven by some debonair clown with faint blue hair. "Please help me."

"Leave me alone," the effete bozo replied, his windshield wipers flipping back and forth on high speed.

"We need help. My friend is hurt."

"Screw you, whore," he said and drove right through the red light.

"Help us, please," I said to the next vehicle, which looked like it was draped in a brightly striped bedsheet. The car was a mobile flagpole. A huge Stars and Stripes flapped from a broken fishing rod that came out of the antenna hole. An old Subaru station wagon riddled with body rust was underneath this moving icon of America.

As I pressed a twenty-dollar bill against the patriot's filthy windshield, Ron came limping out from behind.

"Holy shit, that's Stinky Mulligan!" the old driver said. The man had a pair of close, squinty green eyes that resembled martini olives and an uneven white beard that looked like it was made of scrunched yellowed toilet paper. He slowly rolled down the passenger-side window.

"Mr. Bridges stepped on a rusty nail. I'll give you twenty bucks if you take us to Saint Vincent's Hospital."

"Get in," he said, snatching the Andrew Jackson from my hand. The backseat was stuffed with old newspapers, filthy clothes and countless beer cans. I pushed them to one side and loaded us in. It appeared as though our paid benefactor lived out of his car.

"I saw all your Stinky films," the driver gushed without a trace of irony. He was referring to the series of pictures Ronnie had made twenty-five years earlier. "*Stinky Down Under* was my personal favorite," he added.

"Stinky Mulligan is an American hero," Ronnie replied, leveraging his vanity against his agony.

"He was a cur . . ." the driver slurred as he swerved in and out of adjacent lanes.

"Keep your eye on the road," I shouted, reaching up to the front and steering us straight ahead.

". . . but you always got away," the driver finished his blurry thought.

"That I did," Ronnie retorted. Acclaim assuaged his pains. Turning to me, Ronnie asked, "And which of my films was your favorite, my dear?"

I shrugged. Not one to kick someone while they were down, I didn't tell him how each of his awful movies took a little something out of me. More than aging or illness, deliberately bad art seemed to diminish my very spirit.

"I'll have my personal assistant send you the Boxed Stinky Series," he quickly filled my silence.

"Thanks."

A bumper sticker fastened to the dashboard showed the flag and next to it was written THESE COLORS DON'T RUN. It was a minor miracle that the car did. As he drove, the driver reminisced about crappy films he had seen Ronnie in years ago. The old actor held the compress to his foot, trying not to wince. Probably because of the high alcoholic content in his bloodstream, the wound was not congealing. At one point when the wind abruptly shifted, the flag on the rooftop covered the windshield of the rusty Subaru, compelling us all to scream. The car dweller stuck his head out the window to prevent from crashing.

"Your love of country," Ronnie barked, "is going to get us all killed!"

The car dweller kept his mouth shut from then on. He had to focus all his faculties to pilot us around the perilous potholes as we headed over to Seventh Avenue.

"Can you believe this?" I asked the actor. "We couldn't even get a cab."

"It's a fucking curse," Ronnie commented. "I've met two U.S. presidents, I slept with four Academy Award–winning actresses. Okay, they were supporting actresses, but I'm not counting nominees. Hell, I was the number-one box-office draw of 1973." He groaned. "It's worse than going off heroin."

"What is?"

"Fame. They give you the keys to the castle, only to take them quickly away." The depth and sincerity of his pathos at that moment far outweighed his performances in all his films combined. "You spend your whole life looking back. All-consuming nothingness is infinitely better than being a ghost forced to look back over a life of B films."

"They weren't that bad," I said, hoping to encourage him. He was just in a foul mood.

"You can't even name one of my films."

"*Stinky Takes a Dump?*" I joked. He didn't laugh. Although I didn't know any of his films, from my preadolescent years I did remember ignoring a variety of chintzy merchandising with his likeness on it: action figures, T-shirts, school lunch boxes. Where did they all go? Landfills and camp kitsch resale shops. I used to turn from talk shows when he walked on. Merv Griffin seemed to be a second home to him. I recalled flipping past tabloid pages when I saw his grinning visage. Who would guess that years later I would be stuck in a smelly old car with him in the middle of the night as he sucked from a liquor bottle and clutched his bloody foot. Unexpectedly, he started silently weeping.

"Oh, come on now!" The two qualities of success, acute popularity and sudden wealth—as I always figured it—seemed to be the secret of permanent happiness.

"I can't help it," he cried, "I'm just so miserable." He fell against me weeping. His tears slicked down my neck and back. I actually felt sorry for him. It was clear what had gone wrong. Fame had pampered him, made him soft and then abandoned him—Hollywood's saddest orphan. I held him reluctantly as we turned down Seventh Avenue. Then he started kissing my neck.

"Please stop that."

"I'm sorry but . . ." He put his right hand on my breast, staining my shirt with his liquored blood.

"Quit it," I repeated.

"The quality of mercy is unrestrained, it blesseth both the bosom and the grabber," he misquoted as he squeezed my breast. I finally swatted him across the mouth, causing one of his front teeth to pop out.

"Hey! No hitting the actor in my cab," the human detritus said as he pulled up in front of the hospital. Ronnie silently slipped the denture back in his mouth.

"I'm an actor too," I assured the driver.

"Maybe so, but I recognize him," the driver said, pointing to Ronnie, who was sucking down the last of his Jack Daniel's. I helped him and his bag out of the backseat.

"Please don't tell anyone about my denture," Ronnie appealed.

"I won't," I replied. Who would care anyway?

"Officer Stinky Mulligan on deck. Ten hut!" The driver loosely snapped him a sad salute. I later learned this referred to the movie *Stinky Joins the Navy*.

"Thank you, my valiant and chivalrous squire, I dub thee, knight," Ronnie said, making the sword-tipping gesture with his empty bottle. It was the same manner in which he had been knighted in his recent Vegas production of *Man of La Mancha*.

The driver with the dangerously large flag puttered off. I helped the limping thespian into the emergency ward, where we signed clipboards and were told to wait.

"I don't mean to be rude," I informed him after lowering him into a wheelchair, "but I'm utterly exhausted and I have to get to work soon."

"Gee, I was hoping we could go home together afterward," he said quite seriously. After the long, weary slog of the day it seemed as if so little was sloppily holding this raggedy old man together. Yet, even though I was plenty disgusted, it also amused me that, God bless him, he was still horny.

"Maybe another time," I replied, and I stepped back outside into the rain, where I grabbed a cab home. In ten minutes, I locked my door, stripped, and jumped into bed.

11

INTERMISSION

THE·NEXT·DAY·AT·WORK life went from bad—right through worse—to ridiculous. Aside from the early morning's misadventures, the cold rain had continued on through mid-day, completely drenching me as I raced to work. I sweated my butt off with two other temps, typing mailing labels and stuffing envelopes to send out a stack of announcements on SHW's "Can't Miss!" upcoming season. It was a perfect matching: films that went straight to video premiering on cable, with mail that goes straight to the garbage without being opened. At six o'clock the supervisor, Ms. Gelbert, requested me in her office where she explained that my services were no longer needed.

"What do you mean?" I said in shock.

"You missed two days of work right when we needed you most."

"I didn't enjoy being sick," I appealed. "It's not as if I got sick pay."

"We wish you the best of luck in the future." May pigeons shit in your eyes, I thought back.

When I got home that evening, I pushed the Play button on my answering machine. My message machine rewound for almost half an hour. When it finally stopped and replayed, I heard a snarling and sniveling Christy, who had finally gotten around to actually reading all the diplomatically crafted notes I made in the margins of her painful script all those months ago. She had her own note: "Where the fuck do you get off . . ." multiplied by an encyclopedia of profanities, expletives and just plain angry sounds.

Among the other droll and disappointing messages on my machine, there was one from Cynthia Pumilla, who informed me that my last upcoming scene—also in the nude—was going to be shot uptown in about a month or so, and, "Manny Greene asked me to personally thank you for looking after Ronnie Bridges. We heard about your unfortunate evening and we know what a handful he can be." The last call was the woozy, semi-intoxicated voice of Bree Silverburn asking about the progress of the production.

I laid in bed, and flipped on the TV as I prepared for my voyage into sleep. Before I could turn the TV off, a news item came on, talking about all the asbestos launched into the air by the World Trade Center collapse. I rubbed the lump I had found in my left arm and thought, Thank God it's not in my breast, but either way I knew I should have it checked out. As soon as I flipped off the TV, the phone rang. It was Edith asking how my meeting with Huey had gone the other day.

"At first he gave me all this bullshit and I thought we lost him."

"What kind of shit did he give you?"

"You know, 'I could never direct something on so demeaning a level.' So I got up and was about to walk out."

"Good for you, girl. You got to face up to him," Edith said. "He talks the talk, but he's got no bite. Sorry about the mixed metaphor."

"Exactly what is it you like about this man?" I made a final appeal to Edith's intelligence.

"He might be a difficult person, but he really is a very creative director," she replied. "More importantly everyone feels comfortable with him."

"But I'm sure I can get someone else who's not as difficult."

"Look, the reason I personally want him is because I know that we can endure a bad director, but he's got something we need more than anything else. He's incredibly connected. I know that if he directs this play, producers will come to see it, and we will have reviews. And no one else I know can get that."

Much as I hated to admit it, she had a point. Having him direct the play was the price we were going to have to pay for getting noticed. She asked me how Huey responded when he heard that we had the lost classic.

"It all changed when I mentioned that we had Lilly Bull's last play," I said. "He promised to read it, but you better be prepared if he doesn't like it."

"I know he will," she said assuredly.

"Well, I'll tell you right now, he might accept the cast and limited budget, but there is no way he's going to stick around if we put this up at Old Theater for the Smelly City or any other Off-Off-Broadway dunghole."

"The only thing to do," she replied, "is find the cheapest space that he'll work in and get a great deal."

"I got to get some sleep. I got fired today and need to find a job tomorrow." It was not a good time to be unemployed. She wished me good luck and good night.

12

CRAFTY SERVICES

EARLY · THE · NEXT · MORNING, I awoke as routine dictated, only to remember that I was unemployed. I had to call my temp agent, but since I dreaded the man, I figured I'd get a little more sleep first. Every time I closed my eyes, though, the growing sense of unemployment anxiety loomed larger. Finally clearing the morning out of my throat, I called the despicable Simon La Toya.

"I was expecting to hear from you," he said almost immediately. I explained that I had been discontinued at SHW and needed a new gig. I heard him chuckling.

"What's so funny?"

"If flirtation without intent was a crime you'd be on death row."

"Huh?"

"You only call me when you need something," he observed, "what am I to think?"

"Realize that you're running a business and you're getting a fee from my labors."

"But I'm giving you plum assignments, do you realize that?"

As I silently ran the ball of my fingers up my silky thin arms, I stumbled across my subcutaneous lump.

"If you have lunch with me tomorrow," he broke my silence, "I'll get you a great paralegal gig at MTV."

"Back in the legal department, huh?" These places were all legal departments. Production companies and studios didn't make films anymore. They made deals. Films were never really art, they were business. "Okay," I sighed, "I suppose MTV is as bad as any other."

"Oh no you don't, not till you have lunch with me."

I agreed to meet him the next day at the Union Square Diner. Then I hung up the phone, turned off the ringer and slipped back into the sleep of the unemployed.

When I woke up about an hour later, I found myself dreaming about "the tooth sculptor."

Although I didn't want Sheldon to think I was running back into his arms, I was feeling an acute need to "stretch small, mid-muscles" as Dr. Wang had put it, so I called him at his dental office. His secretary-hygienist answered.

Feigning a foreign accent I asked, "How do you say, the opposite of an extraction?"

"Is this Irene?" she suddenly asked.

"Who?"

"You can't keep calling here," she said softly.

"I'm not Irene," I assured her.

"Well, I'm sorry then," she said, "but he's very busy. What's this about?"

"Just tell him it's Hannah."

"Eight o'clock tonight at the same restaurant as last time," Sheldon said, coming right on the line.

"Fine," I replied. I could tell he had his mask on and a patient in the chair. I had to save all questions about Irene until later.

I lay down and tried to remember the last restaurant we ate in.

The last time I actually recalled eating with him, I recalled twirling pasta—an Italian cuisine. I think it was Fellini's. Soon I drifted off.

When I awoke, I made some calls, then, while watching TV, I exfoliated my face and polished my nails. Afterward I headed uptown. By eight, as I waited in front of the Italian restaurant on Columbus Avenue, I began to nervously wonder if the twirled pasta was at a noodle house when a cab pulled up and Sheldon popped out.

The waitress tightly packed us between two soft-spoken, flinching couples. Sheldon quickly began with his booming voice and windmill arms. I couldn't stop stealing glances at the two fidgety couples around us, who ate with their arms wrapped around their entrées, as if they were in prison.

When he finally paused ten minutes later, I asked him, "Who is Irene?"

"My wife."

"You mean your ex-wife."

"My soon-to-be-ex-wife, we're separated." First Franklin, now him. Everybody had a soon-to-be-ex.

"You know if we were still dating, I'd be pissed now. How come you never told me before?"

"It didn't come up."

"You're supposed to bring it up. How long have you been married?"

"Four years."

"Any children?"

"No, that was why we split. I just didn't think it was fair to bring them into a loveless marriage."

"So why is she calling you?"

"Division of property, stuff like that." After a break, he asked, "Any more questions?"

Finally we ate and walked back to his apartment building. Once on the couch, he turned the lights low, poured me a bourbon, and commenced the kissing.

"You know, you're really wonderful."

"Wonderful how?" I said, instead of how wonderful.

"Just the way you carry yourself and all."

"You mean on my legs?" His compliments seemed so broad they could apply to almost anything.

He let out such an earthquaking guffaw that I felt sorry for his neighbors, but at least we were alone.

"You're right as usual. Words are plaque that can only be flossed with action," he said, and after dashing into his kitchen, he returned with a small box wrapped and ribboned that could only have held an engagement ring. "Open it."

"It's okay," I said, handing it back to him. "I'm superstitious about gifts."

"Please open it," he said softly and earnestly. He rose and stepped up close with this look of sadness in his face that compelled me to dread that he might burst into tears, which from him would probably be a monsoon.

I opened the wrapped box as though it were a bomb. Inside, to my delight, was a small golden box of Godiva truffles. I happily took a bite of half and put the other half in his mouth.

"Just like these two halves belong together," he mumbled, holding it on his tongue, "so do we."

We kissed and rubbed and nipped for a while. He had a wonderful, in-charge style of making love that was in direct contrast to everything else he did. In a matter of minutes, I was back on his sexual conveyor belt. All I had to do was lie limp and let him press, shape and gracefully move me from one stage of recreational sex to the next.

It was like a horizontal soma dance. He led, I just huffed and puffed until smoke came out of my ears and my eyes blinked. Dr. Wang would have been proud.

We awoke early the next morning. When I came out of the shower, a westward window offered a humble slice of the kiwi-colored Hudson River and the crusty coast of eastern New Jersey.

We languished in bed, where he canceled his 10:00 and 11:15 appointments and made love to me through my lazy unemployed morning. Finally my midsection felt so loosened up I was sore, but the lump was still in my arm. I persuaded him to take me to the new "brunchenette" downstairs, the Cuspidor. I had a fruit cup, and without asking me he ordered two mimosas. Thirsty, I sucked it down quickly through the little red straw.

In a moment, he got into one of his postcoital moods that involved a great storm front of loud conversation. Though I smiled and nodded a while, when he started with the traumatizing laughter, I finally jumped up and said, "I'm getting a migraine."

"Huh?"

"You . . ." I was going to call him a big bore with a polo mallet for a laugh, but I didn't want to be mean. "You have to be a little more . . . sensitive."

"Of what?"

"Your audience."

"What audience?"

"Whomever you are talking to, dear, which in this case is me."

"Oh!" He looked down sadly. I knew that once I began criticizing him, it was just a matter of time before I turned into a full-fledged bitch, and there was no point in putting him through all that, because no matter how much he tried to alter himself, I'd always find him coming up short.

"Look, Sheldon, I know this sounds like a cliché, but I don't think you know the real me. I mean, I can be a pretty awful person."

"Not to me you're not."

"Well, remember we're only friends, right?"

"Yes, but I have to confess that when I'm with you, I mean . . . what I'm trying to say is . . ."

"Holy shit!" I jumped to my feet. I instantly realized that at that very moment I was supposed to meet with Simon La Toya, the horny temp agent. When I took a few steps I realized how drunk I was. "I've got to run."

"But Hannah . . ."

"I'll call you later."

I staggered out the door. A cab appeared to be excreting someone, so I got in, shouted my destination and about ten minutes later I was downtown at the Union Square Diner—only fifteen minutes late.

13

The Agent

I · WAS · TOO · LOW on the acting totem pole to have a film agent, but I regarded my temp agent as good practice. There were good gigs and bad gigs, just like film roles. I had to convince him to send me out for the best jobs.

I immediately spotted Simon brooding in a corner table. With dark Mediterranean features and an expensive suit, he was good-looking in a slick way. A colorful pin stood out from the lapel of his jacket. The silhouette of a tiny firefighter's helmet against the letters FDNY. As I approached, the wheeler-dealer popped to his feet, gave me a big hug and a sticky, inappropriate kiss, which I would have blocked if I were properly sober.

"Where'd you get that?" I pointed to the pin.

"I donated two grand to the fire department's nine-eleven fund, and I know what you're going to say, that their families got a lot more money than the other victims of the towers, but they were the heroes," he said frantically, "they dashed into the towers to save those inside!"

"Take it easy," I replied. "I'm not arguing with you."

"So have you got any interesting acting work lately?"

Everyone was prosecuting me with the same question: "Not lately."

"You know I'd love to see you perform sometime. If you ever land a role promise you'll tell me."

"I swear," I said, uninspired. Not even pretending to make small talk, I filled the silence by checking out the latest fashions adorned by the tall skinny waitresses, who all seemed to have their muscular midriffs showing.

"You know I have to tell you, I have a dozen other temps, wonderful workers who're unemployed since nine-eleven and they would just love to get this shift."

I smiled, silently attempting to quell the urge to tell him to give it to them.

"I know what you're thinking," he said and smiled, leaning a bit closer. Reaching over the table, he toyed with a lock of my hair. "You're thinking that I'm playing with you over this job. You're angry, aren't you?"

"If you know it makes me angerer . . ." The mimosa had slurred my speech.

Just as our waitress, who looked like a younger, taller, sexier version of me, approached, Simon asked, "Have you been drinking?"

"A mimosa," I said, desperately trying not to lose my cool.

"Can I get you anything?" asked the waitress, whose beautiful face made me self-conscious.

"Would you like something more to drink?" Simon asked.

"A coffee," I ordered.

When the waitress left, Simon moved his chair around so that he could casually drop his hand on my arm. "Are you okay?"

"Sure."

"You know I like you a lot." His fingers gently stroked my arm. "But sometimes I feel like your probation officer."

"You know what?" I said, looking at my watch. "I have an audition this afternoon."

"No you don't," he said confidently.

"Look," I whispered, "we agreed to have lunch."

"You haven't even opened your menu."

It lay on the table before me closed. When the waitress returned with my coffee, I ordered poached eggs on English muffins.

"You can get more than that," Simon pushed.

"I'm not really hungry."

"You're not sick, are you?" Again his chilly hand extended over the table up to my forehead and down my cheek. In an intentionally accidental gesture he swept his fingers along my shoulder and down my arm, coming to rest exactly on the lump, as though he knew it was there.

"What's this?" He delicately prodded it.

"Nothing." I pulled away. I wished that the mimosa hadn't been so strong.

"You know, Hannah, we're a small agency. We work hard to find our clients. It's not as easy as you might think." Again he was informing me what a great prize I was getting in exchange for this slimy interlude. It was taking the last of my self-control to keep my mouth shut.

"What exactly do you want from me?" I asked him, twisting my emergency smile on. "I mean, you get a commission off my salary and you have to send someone to do the job anyway, don't you?"

"That's all true, but I also have to feel confident that you're the best person for the job."

"What does that mean? Do I look like some kind of a half-wit?" I was still clinging to my final smile.

"Well no, but . . ."

"You force me to go to lunch with you, then come on to me while telling me how incompetent I am—in exchange for what? Some receptionist gig at fucking MTV—then you give me this can I handle the job bullshit!"

People around us were now staring and I knew I had officially blown all chances of being Miss Congeniality and winning the new assignment, but at least I gave the bastard a piece of my mind.

"I'll tell you, sweetheart," Simon jumped in, "what I say might sound like bullshit, but that's only because I was too polite to say that you blew the SHW account for us."

"What are you talking about?"

"I'm talking about how I gave you a prize job at SHW and you got fired and didn't even have the goddamn decency to tell me about it. Due to September eleventh we lost three major firms—that's half our business."

"I took two sick days. Is that a cause for dismissal?" I should have figured he'd find out about the SHW debacle.

"What are you going to do in a few years when your drinking and cock-teasing and all your other bullshit catches up with you and your clothes and attitude no longer cover for you?"

"I guess maybe then I'll sleep with you," I shot back, not feeling that I deserved this rage.

The waitress with the golden belly button stud placed the runny eggs in front of me.

"I wouldn't worry about that," he concluded. "If that growth on your arm gets any bigger you won't have to worry about your future."

In my calmest, most measured tone, I said, "In the years I've temped for you I've always done a professional job. Still, from time to time everyone gets sick. As soon as I felt ill, I promptly called them. And as soon as I felt better, I dragged myself in and worked a full day with no complaints. I'll try my best never to fall ill again, but I do have a suggestion for you. Next time you chew someone out for incompetence don't do it right after you come on to them and they don't reciprocate. You end up looking like the sleaziest scumbag in the world." With that I got up.

"All right," he said, looking slightly embarrassed. "Let's just both calm down."

"That's okay, I'm too pathetic and am probably going to die soon."

Although it was early, I grabbed a cab home, got a *New York Times*, and made a pot of Dr. Wang's magic concoction, which I brought to bed. Then I lay down, cracked open the paper, and sipped the potion. It tasted like liquid shit. As I angrily flipped through pages, I considered the fact that perhaps I had been too flirtatious to further my career. Yet nothing I ever did felt as degrading as letting Simon play with me over lunch. He had hit the nail on the head. Not only was I pathetic, I wasn't even going to be around long enough to ever be really ashamed of it. I looked at my arm bump in the mirror. A few weeks ago I thought it was just a bruise, but it had grown.

The phone rang; I let the machine have it. I heard Bree screaming that he had left messages on my machine and I didn't even have the courtesy of calling him back. It fed into my momentary bout of masochism. I picked it up and apologetically explained that I was still trying to iron out a lot of little kinks.

"Kinks! What fucking kinks? You either are going to do the play or you're not," he simplified gruffly.

"It's not that easy, we're trying to assess our resources and—"

"What the fuck is wrong here? Just call and say yes you're going to do it!" Shaken from my stale self-pathos, I remembered now what a short-tempered, over-entitled asshole he was.

"Look, Bree"—I regained several vertebrae of backbone—"do you want this play to be produced at a good theater with a serious director or do you want some traffic cop to sling it up on a high school stage, because if you want the latter, the answer is you're talking to the wrong person."

"I understand that but—"

"In the land of the grown-ups, important people take time to read things and then get back at their goddamned leisure. Now I read the play, and as I mentioned I liked it and want to do it. But I have a committee of producers and a variety of other people and they have big rent costs and a million other details to tackle. I am trying to work this out as quickly as I possibly can."

"You have one more week," the little shit said curtly. "I'm not trying to be nasty, but I too have people waiting and other options I can pursue."

"Fine," I said, instead of go fuck yourself.

My astrological chart today must've said, steer clear of men, but there were some advantages. Bree's wrath was like a cold shower followed by a demitasse of espresso. It was still early and I was still unemployed. First I flipped to the classified section of the paper. The stacked ads from clerical agencies were designed to place young nitwits near phones, faxes and Xerox machines. We were modern-day, educated migrant workers without benefits, pension plans, or a future. Where we came from or vanished off to, no one knew or cared. I circled a bunch of temp agencies. Next I flipped on my laptop, opened the file entitled "Résumé" and did a quick update, adding my recent stints at NBC and SHW, then I faxed it out at the local Kinko's. By the time the final stain of sunlight washed out in the western sky, I had contacted six temp agencies, two private firms, and yielded four appointments for the next morning. It was the first time I ever tried to undertake a permanent position.

Within the week I was a paralegal in the Midtown law firm of Morris, Lawrence and Carlyle, which another embittered temp had nicknamed Moe, Larry and Curly.

"These guys are definitely the three stooges," he explained from his receptionist desk on my first day. Taped up on the wall behind him was a poster the *New York Post* had printed of Osama bin Laden. Underneath it said, WANTED DEAD OR ALIVE FOR MASS MURDER IN NEW YORK CITY. When he saw me looking at it, he sung, to the tune of the Bon Jovi song, "Wanted, dead or alive, Osama, on a camel he rides . . ."

Considering the state of the economy I was lucky to get the spot. I worked twice as hard and made five dollars less per hour than I had at SHW, but I had a staff position with health benefits, modest job security, and without a bogus agency stealing half my earnings. I loved the fact that it was in a smaller, older building; I was able to get from my desk down the back stairs and out to the street within two minutes.

After three days on the job, I called to catch up with my coproducers. Noah had landed an extra job in the new movie version of the '60s TV show *I Dream of Jeannie*. Mike had enrolled in a scene class at HB Studio. Edith got cast in and dropped out of a racy interpretation of Racine's *Phèdre* in which she would have had to perform in the buff. She didn't mind the nudity but found the director stripped of talent. No one had heard from Belinda, and Huey Baxter still hadn't called. Thank God to both. In fact, I prayed, and soon believed that the shitty Brit director was securely involved in the Roustabout project and simply wasn't calling me ever again—Hallelujah! I started asking around, assembling a short list of possible new directors to approach. But before I started making calls, I got a plucky e-mail from across the pond:

Hannalla darling,

I was stomped and gored by the Bull play and of course loved every moment of it. (Why can't any of our angry young ladies write like that?) Please forgive my tardiness in replying, I had to pay a sudden visit to the motherland, but will be back in town in two weeks. Bottom line for me is, I would like to bring at least one name actor to the production and will have to insist that he play the role of Reggie. Also I have to approve of the theatre space, but the good news is, I am willing to forgo a salary and expense account for a generous back-end deal. I am hoping we can go to lunch and tie up all the loose strands. I have a major project in the fall that is ironclad. So, if all is acceptable, we can go into production straightaway. Looking forward to drinks with you. Shall we say Thursday night at 8, in the Bowery Bar. Great! Can you make a point to bring the option agreement from the Bull estate just so I can see the specifics of how long we'll have it up and how far we're allowed to go with it (in other words—to Broadway? Hollywood?!).
Cheers,
Huey

There wasn't a single mention of the Roustabout project. I called Edith at *Self* magazine, where she worked as a copy editor, and told her the possibly good news.

"You don't sound particularly happy," she noticed. I could hear her computer keys clicking in the background as though they were typing themselves.

"Whatever," I tried to sound upbeat. "Listen, we have to have an emergency meeting tonight, and I want you to notify everyone. And I don't want it at my house."

"Fine, Mike said we could have the next one at his place. Let me see if it's all clear with the boys for tonight. If I don't call you it's a go."

Of course, I was the one stuck with inviting Bree. He wasn't home so I left the time and place for the production meeting on his machine.

That evening after a dose of Wang's crappy tea, just as I was beginning to calm down, Cynthia Pumilla called to remind me that my second big scene was slated for Franklin's film tomorrow night. Ronnie Bridges would not be present, but I felt tense and jittery nonetheless.

That night we all showed up and waited outside Mike's apartment building. Of course he came last, coasting up to us on a collapsible shiny scooter.

"Holy guacamole!" Noah smirked. "Look who just arrived from the lollipop guild."

"Does your mommy know that you're riding that?" I asked with a smile.

"Yes, she does, and she doesn't mind a bit," he replied as he folded it up.

"They don't give you the exercise of a walk, they're slower than bikes, and they're more dangerous than riding a bus," Edith sensibly critiqued as Mike unlocked his door.

"But they're so sexy," Mike retorted. He had just returned from an advanced class at the Strasberg Institute on Fifteenth Street.

As we entered his building, Bree was still nowhere to be seen. When we all took seats, Noah was again the chairless one. He stood by the window and lit his smelly pipe.

"Okay," I began. "Here's the bottom line. Huey Baxter is interested, so if you're all still in, you've got to ante up some time and money."

"For what?" Noah asked, referring to the cash.

"Sundry expenses," I replied, "like taking him out for dinner. I'll keep track of all receipts."

"How much do you need?" Mike began.

I took out a nice leather accounting book that I had snagged from Moe, Larry and Curly's, and said that twenty bucks per person should hold things for a while. Then I added, "Oh, we also need a short list of affordable theaters to attract Baxter as the director."

"An Off-Broadway theater?" Noah asked.

"Damn right," I replied. "I only have Baxter by the tips of my fingers and he's slimy. If he even smells some dank Off-Off Broadway joint, he'll freak and dash."

"Crap," Mike replied, tightening his brow, "just the cost of renting the theater for a two-week run is going to sink us. Forget about production and publicity."

"Hold it," Noah interrupted softly, puffing his pipe next to the window. "Who wants to sleep with me first to show their gratitude?"

"Just say it," Edith blurted.

"Well, it's not secure, and it's not strictly Off-Broadway, but it has a reputation and it's a nicely renovated space," he said, smoldering his ashes and joining us slowly. "The Delphic Theater."

"Not that dive on Fourth Street?" Mike asked.

"Former dive," Noah corrected. "HPD just finished a huge renovation of its interior. I had a date with a girl at a craft table and it turned out she was booking the space. She said that it's difficult getting the word out that the space is available and right now they're actually willing to do a part rental, part door deal if they see a production that can bring some publicity to the place."

"That sounds perfect," Edith said.

"Yeah, but the Delphic really did have a reputation of being a dump," I said.

"It was closed down by the city for being structurally unsound," Mike recalled, "and Huey's going to know that."

"That was the old theater," Noah countered. "With the renovation it's a whole new space. This is what we'll do. I'll call my friend and arrange so you can bring Muhammad to the mountain. I know that if Huey sees it, it'll knock him off his jolly rogers."

"Actually, the place also has a reputation going way back," Mike noted. "If I'm not mistaken, that was where Yuri Lipshiski directed the first American production of *I Speak Before I Think*." This play was a theatrical landmark in the '50s.

"Baxter always was a big theater history buff. If you tell him that," Mike said, "he'll bite for sure."

"I'm telling you the place looks fantastic," Noah reiterated. "He'll love it."

"Oh," I said instantly, remembering bad news for Noah. "Unfortunately another one of Huey's preconditions is that he wants to cast the part of Reggie."

"My role!" Noah yelped.

"I'm sorry," I said.

"Waldo is a good role," Mike tried to comfort Noah.

"Waldo's a faggot!" he hollered back at Mike.

"Actually I'm a faggot," Mike replied, because he was gay. "Waldo is undecided."

"Miles is a macho character," Edith offered. "He's the Vietnam veteran who sleeps with Samantha."

"Shit! I liked Reggie," Noah moaned.

"I thought Reggie was perfect for you," I fueled his frustration, hoping to win his support in dumping Baxter, "and I know some excellent directors who'll agree."

Noah didn't respond.

Little theater row on Fourth Street was right down the block from Bowery Bar. It would be easy to bring Huey by the Delphic. Mike and Edith each pitched in their twenty dollars for my prior expenses at the Time Café and the upcoming Bowery Bar. Noah first argued that he shouldn't have to pay his twenty dollars as compensation for losing his dream role. Finally, though, he dropped the point, promising to bring his money next time. Fortunately no one asked about our no-show member, Bree.

14

THE ADDICT

AFTER·A·SLEEPLESS·NIGHT, I bolted out of bed, sweaty and itchy, and headed off to Moe, Larry and Curly's. On the bus ride to work, I squeezed into a handicap seat toward the front of the bus and tried to wake up. Some guy standing in front of me was reading the *Post*, with his paper rustling up against my face. I looked up to see the bottom boxed column on Page Six:

> ### A PLAYBOY WITHOUT A WORLD
> Synge's classic was slated to be put up by the Roustabout Theater starring **Rupert Everett** with **Huey Baxter**, legendary theater director . . .

As the man reading the newspaper pushed the yellow stripe for his stop, I thoughtlessly clutched the bottom corner of the page, tearing it from the paper as he dashed out.

. . . at the helm. Well surprise, surprise. It was suddenly yanked from next season's lineup when Everett declared that he never committed to the project in the first place.

"Baxter begged me to be in the play but I told him flat out that I was already booked. Apparently he just went ahead and told the Roustabout that I was on board. I regret any inconvenience, but I was previously engaged." Baxter replied that he was sorry for the misunderstanding.

So that was why we lucked out with Huey. Either Baxter made up the entire commitment or he drunkenly misheard the sexy actor. I arrived at Moe, Larry and Curly's with a smile, ready to go over my lines, only to find that another paralegal and I had been given an extended assignment of reviewing a stack of telephone book–size documents due at the Securities and Exchange Commission on behalf of a client company. So we loaded into taxis with several lawyers and scooted downtown to a legal printing firm, B.J. Dix, on Varick and King Street.

Tonight was my second film shoot on *Success!*, but at the printing firm I was unable to sneak any downtime to study my lines. My anxiety was not reduced when I checked my cell phone. An insanely paranoid Bree left a message claiming that last night's last-minute production meeting was deliberately scheduled in haste to exclude his participation: "I'm warning you—and I don't give a fuck if you take this to the police—you gave me your word, and if you try to produce that play without me I'm coming after you—I ain't kidding." Charming.

I stepped into the hallway for some privacy and cell-called him back. I could hear his television blaring in the background.

"Look, Hannah," he began, having simmered down. "I mean, I'm not one of those guys who needs to have his hand held but I gave you more than a week and—"

"Now you listen to me," I cut in. "If you want to take your ball and go home, be my guest, but the next time you freak out or leave threats on my machine, I will come after you with a rusty axe, do you understand!"

"All right, I'm sorry," he replied, "I've been on Benadryl all day and it's making me jumpy."

"We conduct things in a businesslike manner or not at all, capisce?"

"Yes," he replied.

"Apologize!"

"I am truly sorry."

"All right." I caught my breath. "I'm ready to sit down with you and talk."

"I would very much like to sit down and have a face-to-face with you as soon as humanly possible." It sounded like we were doing a drug deal.

"I'm in SoHo, I can meet you during my lunch break."

"I'll be there in ten minutes," he jumped back.

"Watch the rest of *Jerry Springer* and smoke a joint." I could hear the show in the background. "I don't get lunch until one." I told him to meet me on the northeast corner of Spring and Sixth Avenue to avoid any embarrassing situations with my colleagues, and suggested that he try to calm himself before meeting me. For the remainder of that morning a paralegal and I ruined our eyesight completing the tedious line-read of a mammoth legal document that was printed in a microscopic six-point font.

When I finally dashed down the stairs for lunch, it was one o'clock and I was seeing double. Bree showed up fifteen minutes late, his T-shirt soaked in a drug-induced sweat.

"What's the deal, Lucille?" he rhymed. If he started rapping I'd rap him. As he tensely sucked his cigarette, I could see his body was trembling. His nervous system looked badly short-circuited and in the six months or so since I last saw him at Manny Greene's party, he appeared to have lost about twenty pounds. His cheekbones were so taut they looked like they were about to tear out of his face.

"Do you eat food?"

"I'm on a diet." He smiled tensely.

"Do you sleep?"

"I'll sleep when I'm dead." That did not look too far away.

"Why don't you eat something, get some sleep, and meet me tomorrow."

"No way, man," he replied quickly. "Now that I've pinned you down, I ain't letting you go until I'm done with your ass."

"Please restrain from using sexually aggressive rhetoric," I said politely. I found it had an unsettling effect on my dreams. I pointed ahead and casually suggested, "I know a café a few blocks away."

As I strolled and he skip-walked, I felt a strange sense of pointlessness. I was once in a production of *Danny and the Deep Blue Sea* with a cokehead and it was a constantly jittery experience. I simply didn't want a speed freak in a play I was going to be in. They were invariably late, unless of course they didn't show up at all. They were either going a mile a minute, over-the-top *intense* or nodding out to the point of d-r-o-o-l-i-n-g.

Near Broome, we entered Café Café, a local dive, and I watched Bree lurching and catching himself like a character in a silent film. I got on line for a coffee, he followed.

"Hey, I heard you're from central Jersey," he said, glazed over and febrile.

"Actually," I replied, "I'm from Great Neck."

"*Great Neck!*" he screamed as if it were a remote fishing village on the Malay Peninsula. "*I'm from Little Neck!*"

The lunch crowd fell instantly quiet and everyone even from the upper mezzanine looked down to see the skanky drug addict and his latest crackwhore—moi.

"You know what?" I said, getting out of line. "I'm not hungry. We can talk out here." We stepped outside and sat on an empty bench in front of the establishment. As I was about to mention the latest developments of the play, we both heard the low-flying engines of a DC-7 passing by.

"Oh fuck!" He stood up pointing at it. It really was too low.

"Relax."

"It's going to fucking crash," he said under his breath.

We remained silent until it safely passed by.

"I swear every time I look at the Empire State Building now, I think to myself it's just a matter of time before it's gone," he said. "I mean, if the fucking al-Qaeda doesn't do it, some other fucking terrorist group will. . . ."

"Would you mind if we changed the subject?"

"I still can't get over the fact those eight cocksuckers with box cutters . . . I mean, is that a fucking joke or what? . . . I mean, can you imagine eight Japs with box cutters taking out Pearl Harbor. I mean, if I had a box cutter could I take out Penn Station?" People were looking at us as they passed, still he continued ranting, "I mean, we really dropped the fucking ball on this one. This was our fucking failure, not their victory. The Pentagon knew this scenario existed for decades. . . ."

"Okay," I said, hinting for him to wind it up.

"I mean, how much would it cost to have a separate entrance for the flight crew in the front, and another hatchway for the passengers, so they wouldn't even be able to get into the cockpit without blowing up the plane? And what kills me most of all is the fact that George W. doesn't get a single spot on him? Hell, he goes up in the fucking polls! If a fucking Democrat was in office they woulda torn him a new asshole. . . ."

"Stop it!" I finally screamed. "I can't deal with you like this."

"You're right, I'm sorry."

I took a deep breath, and started walking up Greene Street. He silently stayed with me. I think he was trying to demonstrate his self-control, as he didn't utter a word. We trudged over the cobblestoned blocks toward Houston, and neither of us said anything. The entire time I tried to hide my anxiety and disguise the fact that I didn't know what I was going to say or do with this terrifying young man. I couldn't just tell him to buzz off. His play had attracted backers and a director. On the other hand, he was whacked out of his fucking skull. I was in lockstep with him—simple as that. Silently we walked through crowds and red lights.

Eventually we passed Bleecker, Third Street, Fourth Street. From time to time, while looking out for cars, our eyes would connect and he'd smile timidly without a sound. He was content to just stay in step with someone sober. We silently, busily walked. I tried to think of something to talk about, several times clearing my throat, but nothing came out. How could I say I wanted his play without him? I considered offering him two hundred dollars, but he knew he could get much more than that. A half an hour later, we were running across Twenty-third Street. Still neither of us had uttered a syllable. Forty-five minutes after Café Café we were marching frantically through Midtown, dodging parolees from work, unemployed temps, and tourists. Every so often, as the crowd thickened, I'd lose sight of him. Then he'd abruptly turn up in front of me, behind me, or to the sides, buzzing about like a human gnat, and we'd keep walking. The only time we stopped was at Forty-second Street when a wailing fire truck cut us off. I looked over at Bree, and to my surprise I saw him and several other idiots solemnly saluting the speeding red vehicle. We were definitely living in strange times.

Somebody had to be worrying about me back at Moe, Larry and Curly's. It was nearing three and I was supposed to be back at a quarter to two. As Fifth Avenue got increasingly dense, with large groups slowly strolling six abreast, I angled between the fenders of cars and the sides of buses while trying not to go deaf from their honks or inhale their fumes. I pressed onward, dashing for lights, jumping out into the street. By the time I crossed Fifty-seventh Street, I realized the thespian-addict was nowhere in sight. For an instant I was about to shout his name when I realized that I was free of Bree! I headed over to Sixth Avenue, grabbed the F train, changed for the C at West Fourth, and I finally arrived back at the legal printing office in SoHo. Sweaty and winded, I collapsed in my chair to strange looks from my coworkers. I felt as though I had spent the afternoon in a Special Olympics marathon.

Bree didn't call me back that day. I suspected that he was still walking north. Intermittently, I'd imagine where he might be: Yonkers, Dobb's Ferry or Fishkill. Like the Energizer Bunny, he was running on mythic energy. I wondered if there was a remote chance he'd make it to Canada.

After work, I knew I needed to rest for tonight's performance in Franklin's film, but my heart and head were still racing. And I was a little worried about Franklin. He seemed to be storing up more tension every time I deflected one of his advances. The irony is that through December I was actually hoping to get involved with him, but he was too busy. Now I felt this odd anxiety, as though I were expected to sleep with him, which made me feel cheap and uncomfortable. I couldn't stop thinking about it. I just knew I was going to be a wreck by call time. If this wasn't bad enough, I started hearing these moans of ecstasy pouring out of the airshaft. Some deep-throated woman was being royally serviced.

Even though we formally broke up, I ended up calling Shel. By defanging our relationship, I felt I wasn't being dishonest to him. When I got him on the phone I seductively asked him if he wanted to fill an emergency cavity.

"Sure, hon," he said, "but why don't you meet me in my office. That's where my instruments are."

"I don't mean that kind of cavity."

"Oh . . .Oh! Oh, okay," he laughed.

As I dashed out of the cab and into his apartment, he caught me in his arms like a high-speed puck.

"Hannah, I wanted to talk to you. . . ."

"Later," I said, "I have a film shoot in less than an hour."

I pulled him into the boudoir and in a moment he was doing the only thing, with the possible exception of dentistry, that he did wonderfully. Eventually, after a violent shudder on my part, I floated through a particularly black, godless void, falling into ever-sinking stillness. Then, in the same way that my TV goes from a small dot into a bright flash of white light when I turn it on, my eyes snapped open to the stark realization that I was going to die.

The asbestos and plastics and rubbers and plate glass from the endless windows, phones, computers, drywalls and everything else that made up the millions of tons of those two gargantuan buildings crushed together had injected a carcinogenic cloud down my throat and into my arm. The lethal lump had increased in size and grown more sensitive—it must have metastasized.

In the darkness, I could feel a fleet of malignant cells spread along my breasts, drop anchor on my ovaries, and colonize my colon. Another body was growing inside my own. Cancer ran in my family so consistently it was almost a natural cause of death.

"Hey, Sheldon, does this look like cancer?" I asked, trying to shake him awake, but he only snored louder.

I jumped up and silently pulled my panties and bra on. Then I searched out other articles of clothes buried in the dark linen. As I considered the shell lying next to me—a large, handsome, financially viable hunk—I felt only this big knot of unshareable feelings, and wished he were the man he initially seemed to be.

When I finally tiptoed out of Sheldon's apartment it was a quarter to ten. I had fifteen minutes to be at Pier 61, Level 2 of Chelsea Piers.

1 5

THE SHOOT

AS · MY · TAXI raced downtown, the city that night seemed to be empty, as though it had been evacuated. Upon arrival in the little rotunda just off of Twenty-third at Chelsea Piers, I paid and headed inside the huge maze of a building to Cynthia Pumilla's office for instructions.

Bug-eyed Joey, the production larva, was waiting for me. He led me to my new dressing room.

"There have been some minor changes in the script," he said boldly, handing me the revised pages as though he were the screenwriter's son. "Nothing to worry about."

"As long as there aren't fewer lines," I warned.

"They're better lines," he was trained to say, as I counted.

In the surreal hierarchy of motion pictures, you are your screen time. Nothing more, usually less, and you struggled to gracefully extend every syllable of your papier-mâché existence. My life had been cut six lines shorter—"Fuck!"

Things ran smoother this time. My entire scene that night was to begin and end naked in a big circular bed. I had to straddle yet another middle-aged man. Fortunately it wasn't Ronnie. This one was the unethical filmmaker.

Gilda the wardrobe mistress explained that I had a choice. I could either do this scene in the nude or I could wear a sheer piece of fabric taped over my private parts.

"What does the piece cover exactly?" I said, inspecting it.

"Your vagina," she said in a heavy Brooklyn accent.

"Is the actor wearing something?"

"Yes, but you have a choice," she explained.

I wanted to ask how she knew he wouldn't object to a naked woman sitting on him, but then I realized that no heterosexual man would. I took the twelve-inch hourglass-shaped piece with sponged adhesive strips on the sides and went into a dressing cubicle. As I stripped down and stared at parts of my body in a cracked mirror, I saw the result of too many drinks and hors d'oeuvres and too few yogas and Pilates sessions. When I tried to tape the small, flesh-colored fig leaf over my groin, I saw my pubic hair slightly fuzzing out and realized that my feminine coif owed more to France than Brazil.

I put on a torn terry cloth robe and stepped out of my room looking over the bedroom set. About twenty-five to thirty techies, mainly paunchy men, were walking, sitting or standing around.

I reviewed my lines. No one seemed to notice or care who I was. Manny Greene, the executive producer, was there talking to Franklin until a severe-looking woman interrupted them with some questions.

Manny came over to me. "I wanted to personally thank you for helping poor Ronnie the other night."

"No prob," I said, smiling. Manny was a handsome man in his sixties with a solid reputation as a good indie producer and a gentleman.

"He said you turned into Wonder Woman out there."

"I what?"

"He said that neither of you had a cellular, he was bleeding to death, and you went to the stoplight, pulled some guy out of a car and drove him right to the hospital." A typical Hollywood take on an unusual evening. I set the record straight, explaining how I hired a transient with transportation.

"If anyone working for me had half the vigor and guts," he said, "I'd make them a producer."

"That's Franklin's wife, isn't it?" I changed the subject, pointing to Ms. Severity. I had seen her on my first day there, but was never introduced.

"Helen, yeah," he confirmed my suspicions. "You don't mind me watching you in this scene, do you?"

"Why would I?" I asked happily. I wanted the entire world to see how fat and ugly my body was.

"I know you go naked as a jaybird, but seeing that you can act will certainly add to my confidence in you if I go with Christy's film." Christy had introduced us several times and she told him she wanted me to play the role of the maid. But that now was unlikely to happen.

"Let me ask you something," I said, on the spur of the moment, "I recall reading that you've produced plays before."

"I've done a few, yeah, but I don't do casting," he replied, suspecting what any actress would want.

"It's not that." I smiled. "Have you ever heard of Lilly Bull?"

"The woman who tried to kill Ganghole, sure. Her play had a great run in San Francisco."

"You didn't by any chance see *Bull Session*, her collected writings? It just came out?"

"Never heard of it, why?"

"She mentions having finished a play that no one ever found— *Unlubricated*." He listened attentively. "I'm in a small theater company and one of our members stumbled across the manuscript. It's really great. It has humor, suspense . . . it's perfect for the times. Anyway he returned it to Bull's aunt, she's the literary executor."

"Is she selling the rights?" Manny asked.

"She already gave us the premiere rights as a reward for his discovering it."

"Really," he commented. "I've never heard of someone just giving away the rights."

"We actually have to pay a percentage."

"So your company is selling them?" he tried to anticipate.

"We want to do the play," I explained. "And we have a hot director."

"Who?"

"Do you know Huey Baxter?"

"I've met him somewhere or other," Manny replied. "Frankly he struck me as a jackass. He's kind of arty, isn't he?"

"Oh no." Arty is code for "makes no money."

"So how far along are you with your production?" he asked.

"We've just begun rehearsals," I lied, but I knew Huey wanted to start soon.

"Tell you what, I'm not opposed to a coproduction. If you get some decent reviews, give me a call. I'll take a look at it. If I like it, I'll see if I can bring you to a larger stage."

"If we get decent reviews we can take it to a variety of backers," I gently one-upped him. It was difficult talking business when the only thing between me and this man was a bit of terry cloth.

"So what exactly are you getting at?" he asked with the sort of smile an adult puts on when dealing with a precocious child.

"I can get you a right of first refusal for twenty thousand dollars," I said, aiming way too high.

"Wow!" he replied and laughed. "I'm impressed."

"This is Bull's final play. *Coprophagia* had a run of sold-out shows and this one is much better—fifteen thousand."

"You need cash toward your production, do you?" he asked.

"It can't hurt."

"Let me look at the script and if I love it I'll make an offer," he replied calmly.

"Lilly Bull's really hot right now. Ask anyone under thirty," I kept pushing. If I were able to get him to put up the cash, the production would be a cakewalk.

"If I like it, I'll make a generous offer."

That was fine, because everyone loved it and a generous offer from him was probably the most I could get for it. We shook hands and he stepped outside to make a cell call.

Franklin's high-powered wife chatted with some grip or boom. I courteously waited for her to finish talking then stepped forward and said, "Hi, I just wanted to introduce myself. . . ."

Without even pretending to ignore me, she rushed past, nearly knocking me down. She must have sensed something.

When the actor playing the unethical director finally arrived I was delighted to see that it was none other than Jonah Baye. As I thought of sitting naked on top of him, having my pubic hair bristle his thighs, I started hiccuping.

"You okay?" asked a rather self-important-looking lad, who watched me trying to hold my breath.

"You don't have a Xanax or Paxil, do you?"

"I have a Prozac," he offered, "but they take a few weeks to work." I popped the pill anyway, and gulped down a glass of water. Then I pulled my robe tightly around my waist.

"So what's your name again?" he asked, leaning seductively against a wall.

"Hannah," I said politely. He wasn't bad-looking.

"I'm Lorenzo," he said and shook my hand.

"So what do you do?"

"I'm the best boy."

"And someday if you eat your greens," I kidded, "you'll be the best man." Just as I was about to ask him what exactly he did best, Cynthia Pumilla appeared. She had me sign a new form and said Franklin wanted to confer with me. When I went over to him, he ended a conversation with one guy holding a clipboard and, turning to me, he asked, "Are you ready?"

"I think so."

"Here's what you are going to do," he launched into it. "When the scene begins the director is banging the hell out of you. He comes, rolls off you, and you light a cigarette thinking that you have the part."

I couldn't hear him say all this without interpreting it as sexual hostility, but I tried not to show it.

"In the script it actually says I'm on top of him," I timidly corrected.

"We'll try it both ways." And seeing my less-than-enthusiastic expression, he added, "If that's okay."

"Sure," I said, under my breath, "but I really think you're drawing my character dumber and sluttier than you have to."

"Oh, come on," he said impatiently, "you're not one of those kinds of actresses?"

"What kinds of actresses?" I caught myself.

"You know, one of those actresses who thinks they're a real person." I hoped he meant one of those actresses who thought their character was a real person.

"I know Virginia Rolaids is not a real person. I just believe that the smarter the character is, the more believable she is, and the more credible the entire story becomes."

"Thank you, Aristotle. Now take your clothes off and get on the bed." Fucking asshole. "Okay," Franklin called out, "aside from you, you and you"—he pointed to several essential crew members—"all out."

A small squad of horny men marched off, not hiding their disappointment. Franklin came right up to the edge of the bed. "Can we drop the lights to about ten watts."

"Yeah," some voice came back, "but it won't show up on film."

"Just do it," he replied, and down the lights went.

16

The Nude Scene

THE·DISCREET·TONE Franklin set made me feel much more comfortable. I was reintroduced to Jonah Baye, who instantly put me at ease. We politely shook hands and he kidded, "It'll be a pleasure to hump you. Maybe we can go for coffee sometime."

I laughed, but it was a fairly accurate statement on the irony of this profession. In all the moment-to-moment acting, you became intimate in some ways before you grew familiar. I took my robe off and tried to ignore the eyeballs rubbing up against my tits and ass.

I lay down on the bed, opened my legs and looked up at Jonah, who was wearing a kind of flesh-colored cock sock.

"Okay, guys," Franklin said to Jonah and me, "in the scene before this one, you two will have had a sexy conversation on the phone in which Jonah tells you he's got a hot script with a perfect role for Virginia Rolaids. And she believes this film is really going to make her a star." Turning to Jonah, Franklin explained, "You're not just trying to nail her, you're really trying to win her over."

"Why does he need to win me over?" I asked, since Jonah didn't seem to give a shit about his character's motivation.

"Because he wants you to convince Antonio, the producer and lover"—as played by Ronnie Bridges—"that his script should be produced."

"But the scene we're shooting is him fucking me, how does that win me over?"

Franklin gave me a nasty yet subtle expression and said, "I want this scene to be really sexy. Would you guys like to be alone a moment and go over it together?"

"Not necessary." What the hell did he think—I forgot how to screw? "Just tell me how long we're supposed to do it before we can pretend to come."

"I don't know. Not long, a minute or so," Franklin replied. I wondered if he was basing this decision on how long he took to orgasm.

"A minute and then I'll start coming and you join in," I suggested to Jonah, who nodded blankly.

"I think he should come first," Franklin replied. "I mean, you're going to get this film financed, but ostensibly you're also screwing him for the role. You're there to please him."

"Guys usually want the ego gratification of knowing they pleased the woman first," I informed him. "That's why women fake orgasms."

"Tell you what," Franklin said, "we'll try it both ways." That was what directors said to avoid a fight. Do it both ways and then they use their way. "Okay, let's get ready for our first take."

Serge, the allegedly gifted cameraman, took a few minutes setting up and lighting for the first shot. The camera perspective was right up behind Jonah's sweaty butt as it slammed into my nearly naked midsection. A makeup girl dashed some color on my legs and his ass, then sprayed us so that it appeared we had been sweatily banging each other for days.

"Start hyperventilating," Franklin said. We panted for a while, then he called, "Action!"

Jonah began frantically slamming his groin into mine, simulating screwing me for about a minute before he started loudly moaning and groaning, making a steady ascent toward climax. A moment passed and I too joined in, yelling, "Fuck me! Fuck me!"

Since there was a camera behind him, I dug my fingernails into his back a bit, causing him to yelp.

"Cut!" yelled Franklin. I apologized to Jonah. He said it was okay, he just didn't expect it.

"Do me a favor," Franklin asked. "Don't yell 'fuck me,' just groan."

"But . . ."

"We can't get an NC-17 and the ratings board has this weird scoring system that includes dirty words." In other words, he could fuck me, but I couldn't yell it.

We began the scene again from the top. My fingers, which were digging into his back, slipped down so that they gingerly scratched at his thigh, forcing every inch of him into me. As I groaned and convulsed, orgasming more dramatically than I ever did in my entire life, Serge yelled, "Shit! The film just ran out."

"Cut!"

We had a short break as the camera was reloaded. Jonah didn't have time to get up so we made the same small talk everyone did these last few months—about how difficult it was during this time of war. That led to brief yet mandatory comments about 9/11. He said that he saw the towers come down from a pier in Hoboken.

"It's amazing how far away people could see it," I commented. Sightings were reported as distant as the middle of Long Island's south shore, all along eastern New Jersey and even the southern tip of Connecticut.

"Where were you when you saw it?" he asked.

I blanked a minute and then remembered, "I was about four blocks away, and I didn't even know it was . . . All these people . . ." As sudden as a sneeze, I found tears streaming down my face. Jonah immediately hugged me as I pulled myself together.

"Okay," Franklin said, returning. He clapped his hands together. "Let's get moving here."

"Do you need a minute?" Jonah whispered.

"I'm okay."

Again we were misted by the makeup person. We started our hyperventilation aaaand . . . Action! Jonah started his grinding again, soon his climax, my climax—"Cut!" The whole time I just focused on not thinking about the World Trade Center buildings crashing to the ground, dashing terrified through the billowing smoke and dust, feeling the earth trembling as I scurried away for my life. One camera was moved above us while a second camera profiled us. More lights were brought in and, once again, "Action." More screwing, climaxing, then cut. By the third take my fig leaf was slimed with sweat and slipped off. I spent several minutes trying to put it back on but the adhesive was no longer sticking.

"If you don't mind," I said to Jonah, referring to my nudity.

"Whatever," he said tranquilly.

"Everyone has to make sacrifices," Franklin joshed tensely. Fuck off, I wanted to say. The only thing I hated more than having to degrade myself this way was him.

Yet I couldn't quit. I tried to blot out that I was a hundred percent exposed, and just focus on the job: misting, panting, grinding. This time, only the thin fabric of his sock was pressed against me, but to judge by the flaccidity of Jonah's pouch, he was just focusing on his job. There was something truly existential about the entire exercise, far more absurd than anything Beckett or Ionesco ever wrote. Part of it was because Jonah was such a professional. He was as good at pelvic slams as any WWF wrestler. Gradually submerging himself into character, he developed a few dramatic flourishes, hoisting my thighs high up in the air so that my feet were pushed up over my head. Later, he slipped his middle finger into my lips for me to suck on. But not once during our entire sexual gymnastic trial did I feel any trace of his horse. Any man with a dick, even gay, would have felt something by now, if only from the friction. I wondered for an instant if he was a eunuch. I was grateful that unlike Ron Bridges he was not taking advantage of the situation. He was quite sweet; during each break, he stopped and asked me if I was okay.

"So is this your first big film?" I asked him during one interlude, while Franklin stepped out, wondering what rung of his career he was on.

"Oh, no." He then produced an impressive résumé of Hollywood films that included some major box-office hits over the last ten years.

"Holy shit," I replied. "Did you make it through the final edits?"

"Oh yeah," he replied, "but it was usually just as a walk-on. I've been a waiter, a cabdriver. Several times I was a guy who got shot. I was blown up in *The Siege*. I was stomped on in *Godzilla*. I was shot in *Die Hard Two*." It was like an Ode to the Uncredited Actor.

"How old are you?" I unintentionally blurted out.

"Thirty-five."

"Have you ever gotten to speak?"

"A couple lines here and there. That's it."

"Can you survive on this?" I didn't just mean financially.

"Well, I get other work," he replied, and mentioned that he also got occasional Broadway and Off-Broadway jobs, but the bulk of his income came from commercials. He mentioned a New York State Lotto commercial he recently did in which he skied off a mansard roof in preparation for an Alpine vacation he hoped to afford once he got a winning ticket.

"Sure," I remembered, "that's a great one."

As quickly as I recalled it, he was a star. Well, maybe not a star. Perhaps just a small planet or a large moon, but that was still something in the acting constellation. In the role of an Off-Off-Broadway Hamlet, he was immensely talented, but in a long-running TV commercial he was recognized. He smiled, blushed and excused himself to use the bathroom. How could he not be incredibly frustrated? It was like being permanently stuck at the base camp of Mount Everest. Always being on the great peak, but never getting to summit. Yet he actually seemed quite at peace. After ten years or so he must have come to accept his place—a foil for others with barely a five-line speaking part. But at least he made it onto the screen and was able to make his rent.

Manny Greene, who I had forgotten about, emerged from the surrounding shadows and came up to me as I sat on the bed virtually nude.

"I watched your last four takes. You really have a seductive quality," he assured me. "I'm glad you're in this film, because now I know you can really act."

"Thanks so much." Being a fuck doll didn't exactly show my range, but even empty flattery was appreciated.

"I have to run," he said, "but I'm not sure if I gave you my card." He handed it to me. I slipped it between my boobs, causing him to laugh. "Call when you have the Bull script. I'm serious about that option."

I had the script, but I figured I had only one shot with him. If he saw the production, I knew he'd be more impressed and we'd get a larger investment from him.

After we did about another ten takes from every goddamned angle, so that the only conceivable missing shot was positioning a camera in my womb and shooting outward, Franklin finally called it a wrap.

As I walked with Jonah, he compared Franklin, the script and this set with other films he had been in.

"Do you think this film has a chance of making money?"

"I've no clue," he shot back. "I've been in films that had great scripts, wonderful directors, were superbly acted and they never even made it to video. I've been on other films where everything sucked or went wrong and they were hits."

"One can only hope," I replied.

He smiled and headed off to his nearby dressing room and I went to mine, which apparently was in Siberia, another small reminder of my insignificance. I dressed quickly, wanting to get home, hoping to quickly shower and then to sleep. Before I had my shirt buttoned, though, my door opened without a knock. Franklin stood there holding a single wilted rose.

"You did marvelously," he said with a smile.

"Thanks."

"I hope I didn't say anything untoward or anything."

"No . . ."

He kissed me softly on my cheek.

"Hon," I said softly, "I'm really tired."

"I'm sorry, you really were hot back there," he whispered back.

"Really? You got a thrill out of watching me getting nailed by another guy?"

"Sort of."

"Did anyone see you come in?" I asked, not wanting the entire cast and crew to think I had to part my legs to get this role.

"No," he said as he ran his fingers along the ledge of my shoulders, pausing on my right clavicle. "I don't want to seem rude, Hannah, but when we first met, how can I put this, I really thought we were going to . . . I don't know, wind up together in some way."

"Me too," I said earnestly.

"Well, that's good, because I'd hate to think that you were just leading me on," he said softly, looking quickly away.

"I don't do that," I replied, but immediately thought of Simon La Toya and his cruel accusation about my being a tease. I hugged Franklin gently. "Call me old-fashioned, but I was hoping for a real date."

"A real date?" he said, surprised. "The only problem is, with this film and all, I won't be able to go on a real date for a while."

As his cold fingers trickled down under my shirt like ice water on my back, I silently enumerated several facts: Firstly, I liked him and found him sexy. Secondly, he gave me my first big break. Thirdly, he got me my apartment, and last, he was soon going to be divorced and quite eligible, but that was only a reason to refuse him. Sleeping with him would do me little good. He was too selfish to be a good lie-down man, and making myself fully available to him would only make me look cheap.

Still, I just couldn't stop him as he kissed me and massaged parts of my body. Perhaps sensing my reluctance for full consummation, his lips and tongue slowly began their long trek southward. For the first golden moments as he exposed me, there was a great deal of excitement. Then amid the mechanical redundancy, his lips and tongue seemed to repeatedly pronounce: *I'm neglecting my own orgasm in favor of yours.* To bring the session to an end, I grabbed his head and pulled him tightly into me, and gave my best exhausted moan and shudder.

After a momentary pause, I caught my breath and thanked him.

"You were magical," I said tiredly as we both cleaned off. He excused himself, dashing back outside to his mega-wife—the producer-mother he never had and I would never be.

A few hours earlier, I had been at the dentist's house, and I couldn't imagine going home to an empty apartment, so I located my cell and called Sheldon, waking him up.

"I'm going to be there soon. Could you let me in?"

"Look," he lowered his groggy voice, "I'm sorry things didn't work out, but you got to stop calling me."

"What?"

"Who is this?" He was suddenly alert.

"Hannah."

"Aren't you in bed with me?" he asked, confused. I heard a pause and he called out, "Where are you?"

"I went to the shoot. Who did you think I was?"

"Oh, no one," he chuckled. "I was having a bad dream is all." I knew he was lying. "Come right over."

Within twenty minutes, Sheldon and I were back in the thick of it. It was a study in contrast; with the dentist I actually enjoyed having sex. But I knew that the longer I stayed, the harder it would be to leave, so, once again, I vowed that this was definitely going to be one of the very last times.

17

THE THEATER DIRECTOR

THE · NEXT · DAY at work, I felt increasingly cheapened by my sordid session with Franklin. I simply had never slept with anyone for a role, nor would I. The whole thing was wrong. It seemed coerced, and even though we didn't actually have sex, the entire act felt like payment.

When I first met the young director, he was attractive, shy and allegedly about to be divorced. I never should have gotten involved with him.

That afternoon, Noah left a message on my home machine saying that he had arranged entry into the Delphic Theater. "I'll be standing out front tonight between nine-thirty and a quarter to ten. When you guys come by, I'll let you in."

The message reminded me that tonight I had to meet Huey Baxter and sell him on the cheap theater where we were hoping to stage *Unlubricated*.

After work, I went directly to the Bowery Bar. Through all the NYU students and downtown bridge-and-tunnelers mulling on the corner of Fourth Street, I spotted Huey. He was standing on the concrete rampway with a felt red handkerchief sticking out of his white blazer pocket. He looked like a sixty-year-old lad on the way to his high school prom. Wearing dark glasses, the director was talking to some dangerously cute guy in mirrored Ray-Bans. When I closed in, I recognized him. It was the mediocre young British actor Kenneth Eltwood.

Although he was good-looking, critics agreed that he was little else. He had been in a big box-office film two years ago, *Bounce Back*, but hadn't been able to follow it up with anything. Huey greeted me and introduced me to the sexy young man. Both of them gave me simultaneous pecks on opposing cheeks.

"Kenny was just passing by," Huey said, "so I asked him to stick around for a gin and tonic. Hope you don't mind."

" 'Course not," I blurted. The maître d' led us around the bar and past the black-and-white booths out to the back. The walled-in garden was strung with white Christmas lights. Soft cha-cha music commingled with the thunderous rumbling of Third Avenue traffic.

"Huey, I have to tell you," I began, "you completely caught me by surprise. I thought you were busy with the Roustabout project." I loved knowing the truth about his Page Six lie, and silently holding it over him.

"I had to decide between doing a hack revival on the bright lights of Broadway and an original brilliant work in the shadows, and I came to the realization that history would thank me more for the latter," he replied nobly, instead of mentioning the Rupert Everett bullshit.

A waiter came over and we all ordered drinks and entrées. I didn't want any food, but Huey insisted that I order a meal, so I got the big salad.

"Turkey club for me," Kenny ordered, after Huey requested the steak.

"So, Ken," Huey said, turning to the young actor, "razzle us mere mortals with your hotshot cohorts." It was at that point I realized that I actually hadn't seen him in anything other than his one big film.

"Well, I did hear one speck of dirt," Ken said. "It's unconfirmed, mind you. They all are."

"That's the kind we like most," Huey retorted, rubbing his moisturized palms together.

"You know the film *Juxtaposition*?" The movie came out about five years earlier.

"That mindless thriller about a magician who's a spy?" Huey clarified. It was actually a gymnast who was a cop, but it obviously didn't matter.

"That's the one. Well, you know Justine Blandis Peirson, she's supposedly a real cunt." Although I didn't care for the profanity, I wanted to hear all about it. Peirson was on the cover of that month's Paris *Vogue*.

"What actress isn't?" Huey replied tiredly. I didn't say anything. If I grew indignant every time a male behaved like an asshole, I never survived lived past college.

"Do you know the director Brent Tattaway?" Ken asked.

"Actually yes, we were juxtaposed on a Pete Shaffer play, some twenty-five years ago."

"During the film, he supposedly yelled at her and she locked herself in her trailer crying inconsolably. Well, Brent broke in the door." Ken leaned closer and in a controlled tone, he completed, "Word has it she was so turned on by his violent behavior she serviced him right there."

"Beastliness," Huey summed up, "still the number-one aphrodisiac."

Huey then proceeded to relay some equally vulgar and unbelievable anecdote about an actress whom he had directed on the West End twenty years back. He explained that she had such a case of butterflies that before each performance he would send in a studly young actor to sexually exhaust her, otherwise she would suffer horrific stage fright.

"I wish I was that actor," Ken replied.

"Oh, you will be, my boy," Huey said.

The whole thing struck me as a subconscious form of verbal homosexuality. They were too guilty to just go off, smoke a fag and stuff each other in their merry old arses. They needed a woman present in order to assure themselves that they weren't queer.

"So," Kenny confided to us, "I'm in a bit of a pickle."

"How's that, mate?"

"Well, my agent got me an invite to the Second Annual VJ Music Awards on Thursday, but I've no one to bring." For the past few years, while the Grammys were being held out west, the VJ Music Awards was the newest copycat award ceremony on the block.

"Blimey," Huey said, obviously amused by Kenny's little quandary.

"You wouldn't know any duckies available, would you?" Kenny asked me pointedly.

"Let's see"—I stared idly up—"do I know any single girls who wouldn't mind going on a date with a British movie star to a star-studded, televised awards ceremony?"

"You want to be my date?" he asked simply.

"Sure," I responded without thinking.

At that moment the waiter came over with our dinners. No sooner was his dish set down than Kenny looked at his Rolex and said that it was late, he had to dash. He took one french fry from his plate and forsook the triple-decker turkey club.

"So I'll pick you up at your house at seven on Thursday," he said, putting on his sunglasses, even though it was after eight.

"Fine."

"We'll go for din din beforehand. Where do you live?"

I nervously scribbled out my name, address and telephone number on a corner of the script, tore it off and handed it to him. I was out of business cards.

"What love nest are you flying off to?" Huey inquired.

Kenny plucked another fry and explained that he had an appointment with a big-time producer for a possible summer blockbuster next year, then was gone.

We ate in relative silence. The waiter disposed of Kenny's uneaten sandwich. While Huey sawed into a small, bloodless steak, I stabbed through my leafy amazon salad and realized that I didn't even have a dress. Nor did I have makeup, shoes, the looks, nor the self-confidence to attend a glitzy gala like the VJ Music Awards.

"You know," he finally spoke, "you really have stumbled across a find."

"So you'll do it," I confirmed, taking a break from my eight-foot endive.

"Do it? Hanny, dear," he said drunkenly, "I don't know if you quite understand what you've got here." He put down his knife and fork, then folded his hands to stress the seriousness. "A play like this is not a vehicle for us. We are vehicles for it. In a thousand years, a million years, long after our bones are dust, this play will continue to be produced, and maybe then two aliens from another galaxy light-years away, while putting it up, will wonder what life-forms brought this work to the stage and the planet from whence they came."

That sounded like a yes. It also sounded like he had been watching too many episodes of *Star Trek* during his happy hour. I wiped a smudge of fat-free honey mustard dressing off my chin.

"The only important thing is what is best for the play," he went on, talking about it as though it were the heir to the English throne.

"What exactly do you think is best?"

Pulling his chair up so that he was looking me right in the eye, he said he could get a lineup of serious leading actors for the play. He knew for a fact without a doubt that Ethan Hawke and Kevin Bacon would do it.

"Or we could sling it across the pond," he said with a tune of inspiration. "Ewan McGregor! He'd be perfect for the role of Waldo." And Huey knew that Gwyneth and Uma were both looking for edgy theater roles. "They'd read for the two female leads."

"How about Kenny Eltwood?" I asked, half testing, half teasing him. "He'd make an interesting Reggie."

"Very probably so," he replied without a hint of humor.

He then explained that if I wanted to eject my amateur group we could do it the right way. Of course, I could remain attached as a principal. Then he could attract a cast of real talent and go after some big-money investors to do a proper Broadway production.

"I am telling you that this can be really big. Not just critically, but also box-office big."

"But . . ."

"Broadway is so hot for dramas right now."

"But a dozen plays have shut down on Broadway just in the past month."

"This nine-eleven slump is temporary. It'll come back. The real tragedy is the fact that Broadway has to draw on so much revival. There are no replacements for Tennessee Williams, or even Neil Simon." He rattled off a litany of classics that had been booming at the Ticketmaster in the past year or two. "This play will be an infusion of fresh young blood."

Then, as though he were reading from the banner of a Broadway play, he said, "This is the time of the drama and this is the drama of our time!"

He was repackaging and repitching my project back to me.

"Just hold it!" I finally interrupted him. "We're starting this Off-Broadway."

"But, Nana, this is so much more important than that! Millions of dollars, playing in cities around the world. I mean we can start this at a much bigger level with some real names attached."

"But that wasn't part of the deal." He lifted his empty glass, signaling a refill to a distant waiter. "And my name's Hannah!"

My cool response was obviously unexpected. Just a few years ago, I would have been jumping up and down, clapping my hands in his shower of confettied shit. But I had encountered so much fecal glitz in this biz that it just didn't wash anymore. Promises of imminent success on a mind-blasting, star-catapulting, mass-adulating level no longer moved me. In fact, I had come to resent it. I hated the deluding as much as the deluded. This was the swill they troughed out to the lower tiers in the acting pyramid. Every few months or so, you'd encounter some poor schlub who swore that he had just landed a role that will make him. Directors, acting teachers, and talent agents promising crap on a silver platter, and the city is your oyster, and "I'd like to thank the Academy . . ." Yet when I considered what I had sacrificed for Stein to get that filthy little role, I knew I was not completely clear of it. I was at that delicate stage where I was still stupid enough to pursue the dream, but I despised all the hullabaloo and pinwheels.

"All right," Huey said after a couple deep breaths. The waiter brought him a fresh glass of booze. "Let's just slow down. Did you bring the contract with you?"

"What contract?"

"The option from the Bull Estate," he said, sipping from his third or fourth drink.

"It's not an option, it's a theatrical rights agreement."

"Did you bring it?"

"Why?"

"Because I find it difficult to believe that they would permit a small Off-Broadway production when this play can get the works."

"Look, even the best plays get workshop productions. Why don't we just get this up?" Then in an effort to end our bickering, I perked up and said, "I'd like to get this to a bigger theater as much as you, but not all at once. Let me show you the space that we've got."

"It's meaningless without a recognizable cast, but let's have a look," he said and signaled the waiter for the check. I glanced at my watch; it was already 9:30. Noah was waiting.

As I paid the excessive check, Huey asked, "Did you happen to catch Kenny's last flick?"

"Sure, *Bounce Back* was fun."

"No, he did a romantic comedy." I vaguely remembered seeing something with his grinning, Photoshopped face on a video box.

"*Love dot com*?" Huey reminded me.

"Oh, right," I recalled. It was comic misunderstanding between two brilliant computer hackers who think each hates the other when they actually loved each other.

"You know I might be wrong, but I think he took a fancy to you," Huey said, throwing me a plastic bone. I smiled politely. Though it was a pleasant thought, I wasn't pathetic enough to pursue a delusion of a relationship with a hunk who was down on his luck.

"Let's get a move on," I said. "I want to show you the theater we have in mind."

As Huey and I stepped outside, the air felt as though it had been warmed by a space heater. We strolled down Fourth Street toward the little theater row between Third and Second Avenue.

"Where exactly are we going?" he asked as we approached the grungy exterior of the Delphic Theater.

"Over there," I said nervously, already sensing that this renovated showplace was not going to make his snooty grade. Even though it was clearly dilapidated, with a rusting spiral staircase and rotting wooden window frames, it was actually a beautiful old building.

"Not this," he gasped, inspecting the filthy crumbling mortar.

"Hey! Hannah!" I heard. Noah Rampoh was across the street waving at me, in front of a shiny new theater—the New York Romper Room.

"Noah!" I said in shock.

Without pause, Huey Baxter walked calmly across the street, causing a taxi to screech to a halt before him.

"The old Truck and Warehouse, eh?" Huey said as he stepped in through the door that Noah was holding open.

"They've got another play up right now," Noah explained, "but you can examine the space."

The New York Romper Room had an active schedule of plays. Its biggest success was *Condominium*—a musical about a group of Yuppies who turn a filthy ghetto into a viable community. It had made the jump and was still running on Broadway. Eager to replicate this success, NYRR had the set up for another rock musical—*Small Town, Blacked Out!*, based on the famous '80s novel.

Noah winked at me unnecessarily. I knew that there was no way in the world we were going to be able to afford this place. In fact, I didn't think they even rented the space out.

"How many instruments do they have up right now?" asked Huey, surveying the various bars of overhead lighting.

"I don't know offhand," Noah said as the director strolled around the stage.

"How long do we have it for?"

"A one-month run with a possible second month continuance," Noah said, clearly having thought that detail out.

"That's good. Much after two months and we should be taking it to a larger venue," Huey replied, then asked, "So when exactly are our dates?"

"Curtain is three months from today," Noah said with a big smile as I nodded my head in disbelief. It was all such an obvious lie.

"That's rather far off," Huey remarked, "but I suppose twelve weeks should allow us to explore every angle of the play."

Three months of being directed by this madman sounded like cruel and unusual punishment. The usual length of rehearsal time for a small production like this was about eight weeks.

"What are the dimensions of this stage?" Huey asked, looking at its length and breadth.

"I don't precisely know," Noah slowly admitted.

"You don't know the dimensions of your own theater!" Huey weighed in. I sensed distress in the pipe-sucking extra's splotchy face. Huey thought Noah was a stagehand at the Romper Room. He had completely forgotten that this young actor had suffered through his abusive workshop for an entire year in college. It was vain of Noah to think that Huey would have ever remembered him or any other student who he hadn't attempted to seduce.

"Huey, he doesn't work here. This is Noah Rampoh. He was in your undergraduate class. He's also a coproducer in Disaffected Artist Types."

"Of course," Huey replied, swatting his forehead as though a mosquito was sucking out his tiny brain. They shook hands. Noah recounted flattering details of Huey's workshop class. The older man responded with a modest smile until he finally lifted his hand, signaling Noah to shush up.

"Okay, why don't I meet with the rest of your little band," Huey concluded, and pointing to me he added, "And don't forget to bring your agreement with the Bull Estate."

"Fine."

Baxter took out his Palm Pilot and poked through it. His only available wedge of time that week was Friday night at eight o'clock. There was no question of our availability. We had to clear our schedules for the maestro.

18

THE BAD BOY

THE · NEXT · MORNING, I called everyone from work and told them
at eight o'clock on Friday at my place we were going to have a meeting with the director of their dreams. I also called Noah and got his
machine: "What the hell kind of hole have you put us in! He's going to
hit the roof when he realizes that we don't have that theater! Call me
back as soon as you get home."

Once I regained my composure, I called Bree, our resident addict.
His machine answered, "Hello, you've reached Moviefone, leave a
movie you want me to be in at the beep."

"Our first big production meeting with the director will be at my
place Friday night. . . ."

"Wait!" He picked the phone up.

"How are you doing?"

"We just met a few days ago, didn't we?" he asked.

"Yeah, for lunch." Our insane afternoon walkathon.

"Christ, I wasn't sure if I was imagining that or not. Did I do anything weird?"

"Just the usual."

"I'm sorry, I've been on medication. I felt too embarrassed to call you." Damn, I could have just neglected him forever.

"We are meeting with Huey Baxter on Friday night at my house, and he's demanding to see the agreement."

"What agreement?"

"The one you made with the Bull Estate!"

"Oh, shit, okay, I think I can do that."

"You *think* you can do that!" I hollered. "You told me you already had the agreement."

"I do! I do!"

"Bree, I have gone through heaven and hell to get this thing going."

"It's fine, I got it! There's nothing to worry about," he replied and added, "But remember our deal—you have to call Svetlana Palas."

"Huh?"

"You agreed that she'd be our stage manager."

"Fine. Tell her to call me."

"Would you do it?" Bree requested. "I just know that if I do it, I'll somehow screw it up."

That he was learning his severe limitations seemed worth encouraging so I agreed. Besides, Svetlana was exceptional. Quiet and intelligent, she had been involved in every play that went up in the entire undergraduate program while I was there. Yet the thing that I remembered most about her was her byline. In almost every issue of *The Pledge*, one of Yale's undergrad literary magazines, I'd see her short stories, sometimes even theater reviews. I was always amazed that she refused to quit stage managing and take up journalism or creative writing.

Bree gave me her number. I called her up and left all the details of the upcoming meeting on her machine.

The next couple of days were a scramble for money in order to buy a dress appropriate for Kenny's ridiculous VJ Music Awards shindig. Since I had never been to an awards ceremony before, I browsed through the magazine racks at my local supermarket to see what I was expected to wear to such an event. Looking through an issue of *Us* at a newsstand, I realized that I was absurdly out of my league. Versace, Donna Karan, Valentino and other brand dresses were handed out by designers to be worn once and then auctioned off at charity balls.

After a lunch hour of barnstorming through the racks of SoHo, I got a flash course lesson in fashion extortion: a sixteen-hundred-dollar shearling jacket with satin pockets to go with a silk Emanuel Ungaro skirt at Variazioni. Thirteen hundred bucks for a wrap dress at Prada. It was far more than I could ever afford. I finally wound up at Ina that evening, where I spent less than a quarter month's rent on a second-hand silver sequined Gucci minidress with one shoulder strap. It had been marked down from two grand.

I left work early the next day and finally dropped seventy-three dollars on a haircut. Then I went right home. Since Kenny was supposed to take me to a nice dinner first, I skipped my starvation salad. Instead I showered, dressed and waited like Cinderella for the magic hour. As the minutes beyond six o'clock ticked off, I swaggered around in my dump of an apartment wearing my only expensive glittery gown. After a while I slowly regretted the fact that I had gotten myself in this pseudoromantic fantasy.

As six-thirty headed toward seven, I began getting nervous at the possibility of meeting celebrities. While in the bathroom, I remembered that the former renter and retired actress, Thelma Derchoch, had a hodgepodge of old antidepressants in her medicine cabinet. I quickly went through them and located a half-full prescription of Valium with a lapsed expiration date. By seven-thirty, though, I resigned myself to the thought that Kenny Eltwood had forgotten our dream date and was not going to show up at all. My stomach churned and turned as I realized that I had invested all that money on a costume, haircut, and cosmetics that would never be appreciated. By eight o'clock I popped a pill. Sweating profusely, I had to use a blow-dryer on my upper extremities.

Just as I opened a bottle of wine to enjoy alone in my nice dress, the doorbell rang and I nearly had a heart attack. I bounced to my feet, flying out of the apartment, down the steps, and through the front door.

"You look great," Kenny said, standing out front in a tuxedo. He kissed me on the cheek. "How are you doing, dove?"

"Fine. Fantastic," I said, restraining my anger as we both climbed into the back of his ridiculous white stretch limo. Neither of us said a word about his being late.

A TV was on, and a small bar held a tight confinement of square liquor bottles.

"So . . . how was your day?" he asked politely.

"Great."

"What projects are you working on?"

"Excuse me?"

"What exactly are you doing?"

"In what regard?" I had spent the day Xeroxing insurance claims from April 1983.

"You're a theater producer, aren't you?" He revealed the fallacy that prompted his curiosity in me. I realized that Baxter must have amplified the hype that I had originally spun to him. In the slimy entertainment industry, everyone was elevated to their most colorful hyperbole. Instead of being a faceless, nameless wage slave, I was now a glam-rock Broadway producer. That instantly explained why Kenny had even bothered to ask me to this event. I could either tell the truth, abdicate the throne, and have him spend the evening treating me like a pathetic mercy case, or I could keep feeding the lie.

"I'm with a fairly small company."

"What's the name of your operation?"

"Disaffected Artist Types."

"I think I've heard of you." He meant the company, but he couldn't have. "What have you done?"

"Last year we did Beckett's *Endgame* and *Mourning Becomes Electra*." I listed two lies from my own professional acting résumé. "We're considering doing a Shakespeare next."

"Oh, which one?"

"*Macbeth*," I replied, because it was his shortest.

"I did the Scottish tragedy years ago," he said, immediately showing interest. Nothing in this city was free or innocent. "That's not what you want Huey to direct, is it?"

"No, we have something else for him, but we're in the middle of negotiation and I'd rather not discuss it, you understand."

"Absolutely," he replied. I wasn't sure if he was being polite or if Huey already told him about the Bull play. He didn't ask anything else. But it really didn't matter because around then the initial effects of the Valium began rolling over me like a large, warm wave.

"Oh, this is for you, sweet'ems," Eltwood said, handing me a small box. I thought it was a piece of candy, but when I opened it, there were two small pins. Tiny metallic images of a red, white and blue ribbon.

"What are they?"

"Actually there is one for each of us." He took out the colorful pins. He handed me one and pinned the other to his lapel. "They're solidarity for nine-eleven pins. Everyone's wearing them."

"Oh." As I pinned mine on to the top of my dress, Kenny took out a compact mirror, something I had never seen a man carry before, and he checked his face.

"Ready?"

I nodded yes. He threw open the car door and—whammo!

The carpet was a five-foot-wide bloodred tongue that parted the sweaty asphalt. The throngs were squeezed behind red velvet ropes. The marquee was bright, but what struck me most was the buzzing sound. It was the split-second, high-speed recoil that accompanied the spontaneous burst of a flashbulb. That seductive mechanical recoil motor snapping six photos per second was continuously humming during our entire walk from the car and past the tidal pool of photozoa.

"Ben! Where's J. Lo?" Queries were shouted out.

"Reese, are you having another kid?" I heard shouts directed to celebrities I couldn't see. More questions that informed (yet uneducated) minds wanted answers to were pelted from a cacophony of yells and screams.

Entertainment Tonight was interviewing someone who looked like Seal. Other celebrity interviews were occurring as we strolled through the lobby. I was pharmaceutically blasé about the whole thing. Valium had sanded down the hard edges of self-consciousness. With an ear-to-ear smile, I floated through my own private, giddy glamo-plasm.

Once inside, an usher with a clipboard and a headset led us to our seats. The farther down in front you were, the higher your face was carved on that great popularity totem pole. We were nine rows from the stage, right on the aisle. I was amazed how close we were—how did Kenny hook these up? Sting was seated eight seats down from us. Keith Richards, who looked even worse than in magazines, was two seats in front of us. Michael Richards, *Seinfeld*'s Kramer, sat across the aisle. He was more handsome than he seemed on TV. Tina Turner, who looked great, was talking nearby with that distinctly rough voice. James Taylor, who didn't look like himself at all, was in front of me. Sitting among these mythical figures was sort of like being in Heaven on earth.

Before the festivities began, people scurried around the aisles. Deal makers who someday might utilize Kenny came by and greeted him. He, in turn, excused himself and I watched him shake hands with those he wanted to use. Finally, the hundreds of lights went down at once. People took their seats. Hush spread and then we were asked to rise. Wu-Tang Clan or some band who looked like them played a wild hip-hop rendition of the national anthem.

A hot young comic named Roland Thames was the master of ceremonies. He made some remarks about New York coming back and patriotic shout-outs to our boys in Afghanistan. Then he made a flurry of sodomy jokes about Osama bin Laden and other related poli-social events in the news. Finally he brought the first pair of presenters—a boy rapper named Bambam and a girl rapper named Bubbles. In Ebonic phraseology they explained the importance of the award because it was "like, you know, artists like we be" commemorating other artists. Until then I always thought of artists as poor and obscure, yet all the artists here, as well as presenters, were famous and rolling in more green stuff than they could spend in a lifetime. Finally Bambam tore open the envelope. Bubbles read the name, and Bambam handed out the award. The next pair of presenters were the musician Willie Colon and Daisy Fuentes, the "voluptuous" ex–MTV VJ. They presented the Latin music award to a young Latin band.

Two large cameras above us focused on the stage and two handheld camera units virtually attacked the winners as they came out of the audience. I realized that the more I applauded and yahooed, the more frequently one of the TV cameramen would pan in my direction for a reaction shot. So I clapped wildly, until Kenny finally leaned over and gently put his hand on my arm and whispered, "Give it a rest."

I initially thought he was just embarrassed and kept applauding, but there were more awards, more bands, more jokes by Roland Thames, more categories I had never heard of, and all you could do was applaud. So about eighteen hours into that tedious, self-congratulatory orgy, my hands felt like bloody stumps at the ends of two mop sticks.

Virtually everyone there except Kenny and me had won one of those silly awards, which were nothing more than the company logo dipped in brass—how modest.

"How you holding up, ducky?" I heard at one point.

"I hope we land soon," I uttered, unable to feel anything below my waist.

"Another few songs, awards, one or two more protracted thank-yous and we're out of here."

"God, I'm hungry," I moaned.

"You should have eaten something before you came here," he commented.

Trouper that I was, instead of reminding him that he was supposed to take me to "din din," I just smiled. Soon amid more slap-on-the-back hoopla and mutual high-fives, I drifted off to sleep.

"The Rockettes want the hall back," Kenny said, shaking me. "Time to go."

As I got to my feet my lower limbs felt like a pincushion as the nerves reawoke. Slowly we headed back up the rampway and out the door with everyone else. We waited as a party of twenty hip-hop types in dark hoods and gold dentures loaded into a creme-colored SUV that stretched half a block long. Outside, only a handful of the photographers remained. Along with the adoring fans, many of the cops went home, leaving only the Mark David Chapman and John Hinckley types behind. But I could barely keep my eyes open.

"Well, that wasn't too bad, was it?" Kenny asked.

"Actually," I replied, emerging from my little Valium cocoon, "that was a good incentive to be mediocre, never to win anything."

"There's no shortage of that, hon." Kenny chuckled a bit and added the obvious: "It's all about publicity . . . to sell stuff. That's the biggest and worst part of this job. All said and done, we are all horn honkers and vanity hustlers."

"I should only be so lucky."

"Our limo's here." He opened the door and helped me inside.

A short silent drive and the car stopped in front of my apartment, where Kenny kissed me on my cheek and wished me a good night.

When I turned back to wave, he was gone. A few years ago, I would've died for a night like tonight. Now the best part was just getting home and pretending it never happened.

19

THE INGENUE

THE · NEXT · MORNING, I woke up woozy, and dressed, battling the effects of last night's Valium. I dashed into Moe, Larry and Curly's late with a terrific hangover only to have the receptionist, Shannon, holler, "There she is—the stah!"

"What?"

"You was on TV last night, hon!" Two others from the office came lunging at me.

"Oh my God!" A temp named Lara Dell tackled me and held on like a leech. "You were with that British actor. We all saw you clapping."

"It's true," said Dennis Mahaffy, the buzz-cut head of office operations. "Your eyes looked really glossy. Were you doing coke?"

"No, Visine," I said instead of Valium.

The remainder of the day the calls streamed into my cell. An asylum full of inmates called to congratulate, ranging from high school and college alumni whom I thought I had eluded long ago to a roster of relatives that included a dopey pair of West Coast cousins who asked if I could get them Kevin Bacon's autograph.

Franklin Stein left a message saying that he had heard I had a date with Kenny Eltwood and, far from jealous, he wanted to know if we "did it." I replayed the message several times, trying to discern whether he sounded jealous or aroused. When Edith and Mike called, I took the opportunity to remind them that we were all supposed to get together tonight for our first meeting with the theater director of their dreams. At the day's end, Noah finally called to give his congratulations. Before he could say anything, I screamed, "Where the hell have you been! Don't you return your messages?"

"I'm sorry, I was just—"

"What the hell was the idea of coming up with that bogus theater! Huey's not an idiot! He's going to flip when he realizes we lied!"

"Look, that night I just finished ten hours of extra-ing on that stupid fucking movie, *Underdog*, only to come home exhausted and discover that the bitch at the Delphic Theater had backed out. I saw an old friend I knew who was assisting the lighting person at the Romper Room. I gave him twenty bucks to let me look around. Now I ask you, what would have happened if you showed up and I didn't have a theater? Do you really think Huey would've stuck around another moment?"

He had a point.

"You better tell Mike and Edith about what happened so they don't blow it at tonight's meeting," I warned him.

"I already told them."

After work, I ate a joyless dinner and did laundry before the others showed up. By eight-fifteen Mike and Edith had arrived and were waiting for the entrance of the great sun god Huey Baxter. As usual Noah showed up last. Tired of being the one always standing, he brought a gift for me. Noah had found a nice French ladder-back farm chair on the street, which I'm sure would have been four hundred dollars at ABC Carpet. Edith took the liberty of putting some water on to boil, knowing that Baxter was a typical English tea drinker. Noah, though, insisted that he was a big gin lush.

"He won't be doing that tonight," Edith responded, "not during a business meeting."

"Wanna bet?" Noah shot back.

"Put them both out and we'll see which he goes for," Mike suggested. I didn't have gin. The only booze I had was Franklin's bottle of Australian wine. I uncorked it and took a taste. It tasted like antifreeze. When the doorbell rang, they all got excited, and I opened the door to see Svetlana Palas, the "attached" stage manager, taking a fresh notepad out of a bag.

"Is Bree here?" she asked nervously, looking over my shoulder instead of saying hello.

"Not yet," I replied, tensely, "but he better get his ass here soon. Huey wants to see the Bull Estate's permission statement."

Svetlana asked everyone how they were doing.

"Fine," I replied for all, "how have you been?" It had been at least a year since any of us had last seen her.

"So-so," she replied and exchanged hugs with the others.

"Have you been working?" Noah asked.

"I got gofer work on a couple of awful Broadway fiascoes."

"What's the going rate for stage managing a play for a one-month run?" I asked.

"I got seven hundred a week for my last play," she replied, but seeing the poverty on our dirty faces, she kindly asked, "What's the budget?"

"How about six hundred up front and six hundred later upon completion?" I threw my lowest ball figuring she'd haggle up.

"That's the cheapest I've ever been offered," she commented, "but I'll take it."

I tried not to act shocked, as did Edith, but of course Noah looked aghast. I thought he was about to tell Svetlana that she was getting underpaid, in which case I would've slapped him upside his oily head and made him dole out the difference.

"How the hell did you get linked up with Bree?" Edith asked, wisely changing the subject.

"I saw him passed out on the fourth floor of the New York Midtown Library about six months ago, but I hadn't seen him up close since he was in a production of *The Real Inspector Hound* that I managed in my first year."

"I remember that production," Mike commented. "He forgot his lines and ad-libbed this ridiculous monologue about the Whitewater scandal that went on until the other actor finally just walked off the stage."

"Actually," Svetlana said, "he didn't forget his lines. He had just done a hit of herbal ecstasy and he liked Clinton."

"Maybe he's on it right now," I said, and, as if we were in a play, at that very moment the doorbell rang.

"Speak of the addict," Mike quipped.

Over the intercom, I heard Huey Baxter's giggly greeting. I rang him in. A few seconds later we all heard it and collectively cringed—Huey's voice echoing up the stairwell was accompanied by the chirping of the up-until-now absent Belinda. When the door opened and with my own eyes I finally saw the two walk in, I felt my knees wobble.

"Belinda! What the hell are you doing here?" I took no pains to disguise my bitter disappointment.

"I bumped into Huey and Kenny Eltwood at a VJ Awards party last night and he told me about this hot new group that had come across some great lost property. Imagine my surprise when I realized that it was *my* group." She gave this gotcha grin.

"It's good to see you back," Noah said with a stone-carved smile.

Everyone competed to give Baxter a warm greeting. He gave Mike a pat on the back, Noah, a stern handshake, Edith he kissed on the cheek, and Belinda, whom he arrived with, he kissed on the lips probably for the tenth time that evening. I was glad to stay where I was and not risk any physical contact. To Svetlana, he simply threw a glance. In a strange way, by not having to give her any reassurance, he seemed the most intimate with her. Then, ignoring the tea, he went right for the Aussie wine.

"Okay, gang," he began, rubbing his hands together. "I'm going to spell it out for you clear as daylight. Although all of you are long on talent, and I have no doubt that all of you, someday, will be matinee idols, today is not that day. In addition, due to the horrific Trade Center tragedy, we are hoping to bring this play out during the worst season the theater has seen since Ethel Merman got hit by a truck. This is actually why I asked to cast the Reggie role, to try to get us some star glitz. We're still going to have some problems. We don't have enough of a budget for any real publicity. We really have just one thing—a brand-new, name-recognizable, kick-ass script. Ms. Bull had garnered quite a bit of buzz from the fringe press due to that one shit-eating play of hers. I'm pretty sure critics will also come to this one. So if we can dazzle them on the boards, they'll be our publicity budget."

Then he put his glass down and added, "Oh, we also have a glorious starting gate at the New York Romper Room."

Right, Edith mouthed jokingly behind his back.

"The New York Romper Room doesn't do outside rentals," Svetlana corrected automatically, not being cued in on our little lie.

"Well, applaud this young go-getter for that magic trick," Huey said, pointing to Noah, then took another gulp of wine. "He did the impossible."

Mike clapped in Noah's direction. When Svetlana looked over to me, I put my finger over my lips and she didn't press the point.

"Now," Huey resumed. "I made some calls and got my friend Juan Valasquez, who is the theater editor for the *Local Vocal*. Not only has he agreed to write up our discovery of the piece, he also confided to me a tidy tidbit that we might be able to put to our advantage." Huey leaned forward and spoke in a slightly lower register, as though a rival company might be listening. "Lucille Lexington is doing a one-woman show based on Bull's bizarre diatribe *C.O.C.K.* at the Public."

"That'll be perfect," said Belinda, instantly joining onto our hopes and dreams.

"If we can get this production up at roughly the same time, we should be able to grab some collective attention. Bull's hysterical manifesto reviewed side-by-side with this well-crafted swan song, which, in my opinion, is the only work she will be remembered for, will be perfect. The reviews will be to Lexington's detriment and our advantage."

Everyone was very excited by the prospect. When all simmered down, Huey said, "Before we start scheduling rehearsal times, I need to know who is the head chequer?"

"We have some anonymous backers," I replied, not wanting to reveal that this was a pathetic vanity production.

"Fine," he replied. "Now, before I say another word, where is that pesky production agreement?"

"Bree hasn't arrived yet, but—"

"I have it," Svetlana interrupted me. Reaching into her bag, she located a crisp manila envelope and handed it to Huey. I felt slightly nervous as he took the legal instrument out.

"Wow, this is a lot thinner than I thought it would be," he said, weighing the three-page document in his hand. "I figured it'd be the size of a phone book."

"It's just a boilerplate permission statement. It might even be a Blumberg's legal form," Svetlana said and spelled it out as he read it. "They allow for unlimited performances and a percentage of the box based on the price of tickets and size of the theater."

"Are there any restrictions in regard to theaters that are over ninety-nine seats?" Huey asked.

"No," she said, taking the document from him and flipping the page. "But there are some provisos if the production goes to that level."

"So if we took a hiatus and then opened up on Broadway we'd be restricted?" Huey asked her as if she were an entertainment lawyer.

"It says here"—she ran her finger down to a lower clause on the second page—"Paragraph 3(a): If we submit a statement of intent, we still retain our rights provided we reopen within a certain time limit. I think the grace period is three months."

I was deeply impressed that Svetlana had actually made sense of the muddled legal minutiae. During my first two years of college, before switching my major to acting, I had taken pre-law classes, and recently worked on a flurry of contracts for Moe, Larry and Curly, yet I still couldn't make heads or tails of most documents.

"Who, or what is . . ." Huey closely read the bottom line signature, "Free Silver Birds?"

"Bree Silverburn," I elucidated. "He's one of the actors in our company. He was supposed to be here tonight."

"He called me sick at the last moment," Svetlana explained, "so I swung by his place and picked up the agreement."

"Good work," Huey said, and looking about he added, "Now let's go around one last time and tell me your name and the roles you're going to play."

Noah said he was going to shape the role of Miles, the Vietnam veteran. Mike would assay the flaming queen Lenny; I explained that Bree was slated to be Waldo, the ambisexual provocateur.

"I've approached a friend who is a big casting agent," Huey stated. "He solicited several name actors for the role of Reggie."

"Really!" Noah said, startled by the thought of playing across from name talent.

Huey ignored him and said, "Now let's hear the female roles."

"We still have to discuss that," I said, hoping to stave off a catfight that could bring the production to immediate ruin.

"What's next?" Huey asked.

"Scheduling," Svetlana replied, and continued, "If everyone will please look over this schedule." She passed around pages containing Xeroxed checkerboards, listing each day of the week and dividing them into morning, afternoon and evening. "Please write out your availability."

"And please keep in mind . . .," Huey muttered under his breath, prompting Svetlana.

"And please keep in mind," she finished his remark, "that we are here to act. If you are serious about this profession, every box should be marked free."

As we silently filled out our schedules, marking when we were working, Huey announced that he had to dash. Everyone thanked and bade him good-bye. As soon as he was gone, and the filled-in schedules were handed back to Svetlana, all eyes turned to Belinda.

THE SWORN RIVAL

"WHAT·FUCKING·GALL!" Belinda came out swinging. "I started this goddamned group! I approached you people about a vanity production and you all turned me down. . . ."

"Yeah," I replied, "for *1776!* What are we, six years old?"

"You bitch!" she fired back. "You could've shown me this! You're all a bunch of backstabbing bastards!" she shot back. "Not one of you had the decency to call."

"I called you when you were away on the West Coast, and I did leave a message."

"Well I'm ba-a-ack," she said in a mocking singsong tone.

"Belinda, there are only two female roles in this play," I broke the tragic news.

"Fine, one of us will play understudy to the other two."

A terrifyingly long silence was finally interrupted by Noah, who valiantly rose to his feet and declared that he had to run.

"Me too," Mike joined in with equal parts of awkwardness and eagerness. They said good night and were out the door. It wasn't their problem and both were sharp enough to know better than to get involved.

"Belinda," Edith started timidly, "Hannah and I started this project. We already made key arrangements and we feel——"

"If I don't act in this play," I charged in, "I don't produce it. Simple as that."

"Fine," Belinda retorted succinctly, "Edith and I can produce it. Bye-bye."

I looked over to Edith and realized that I had made a mistake. She had been fighting for both of us while I selfishly just tried to protect my own role.

"Look," Belinda laid it out. "We can all fight it out and fuck up the whole production, or we can try to work it out."

"Belinda, we tried getting ahold of you, and the simple fact is that we were committed to this project first," Edith argued.

"And I could've accepted that," Belinda rebutted, calmly, almost legalistically. "If I got a message saying that you found a play and it only has two female roles, and we're going to do it——although I wouldn't have liked it, I would've swallowed it. But not one of you had the decency to mention that."

Edith looked at me, evidently under the impression that I had done this.

"I left a message asking for you to call me back. I didn't think I should just dump the information on your machine."

"You're doing this as a Disaffected Artist Types and"——she took out a business card and pointed to the top line——"it says right here, Disaffected Artist Types Productions founded by Belinda St. John." She tossed her prop-piece card dramatically into the air.

"Fine, we'll start our own company," I replied.

"Look, I only want what's fair. How about the usual procedure in which these matters are straightened out," Belinda said. She obviously had given this problem some thought. "An audition in which the director picks. The winners get the roles. The loser is the understudy."

"I still think that this is unfair, but I suppose I can live with that," Edith said, not surprisingly, since she was great in auditions.

"Me too," I felt compelled to say in a wind-knocked-out tone. But it wasn't fair. Huey liked Belinda because he could always get his ass wiped by her brown little nose, whereas he probably sensed that I thought he was a fool.

A toilet flushed and we realized that we were not alone. Svetlana was still among us. Edith and Belinda used the interruption as an opportunity to get going, but I realized that I had another problem yet to deal with.

Svetlana was about to exit with my co-rivals when I asked if she could stay. Even though Belinda had just shown up and was the founder of the group, I still regarded myself as executive producer and I wanted to speak to her alone.

After curt good-byes, the actresses headed off together to Williamsburg. Edith was on the first stop on the L, Belinda was on the second.

Alone with Svetlana, she asked, "What's up?"

"This is a little awkward," I began, "but I don't think we'll be needing your services after all."

"What!" she shrieked.

"Frankly, I agreed to bring you on as a deal with Bree, but apparently he's dropped out."

"He hasn't dropped out!" she exclaimed. "Hannah, I've worked with Huey Baxter and all the rest of you before. You know I'm a hard worker. If there's a problem . . ."

"Look, I don't mean to sound like a control freak, but I got enough headaches with everyone else here. I just don't need any unnecessary bullshit."

"What unnecessary bullshit?"

"When I say something, I don't want to be corrected."

She recoiled into silence.

"See, the strings that are binding this production together are thin and quite frayed. I don't want to go into a lot of boring details. . . ."

"Just tell me what I did wrong?" I could see tears in her eyes. It was time to bring her back to the fold.

"It's as simple as this: You have to let me decide what information goes out and what doesn't." The entire reason I fired and rehired her was because she knew far more than me about production. Therefore she had a tangible power. Additionally I feared that her primary loyalty would be to Huey and Bree.

"That's fine," she said willingly.

"If there's a problem, by all means we can talk about it and I would be very grateful for your help, but I'm the one calling the shots. Any future communiques, or sub rosa deals with Bree . . . I'm the minister of truth here and I call the head honchos until Belinda or someone else takes over."

"Fine," she said meekly.

"So tell me what you know about this goddamned play."

She exhaled deeply and explained, "I know everything you know."

"How are you involved with Bree?"

"He owed me a big favor."

"Did you save his life too?"

"No, I was the one who got him cast in *The Real Inspector Hound*. I used to go to his house and sober him up."

"Why did you do that?"

"Because I liked him and felt sorry for him. When he's not acting up or on drugs, he's actually a really sweet guy." Feeling sorrow or kindness for someone sounded fishy to me. My first suspicion was that she'd had an affair with Bree in college, but there was something asexual about Svetlana, so I didn't press.

As she assured me that all would go well, the phone rang. I let the machine get it. I was surprised to overhear the dentist mumbling on my answering machine. I caught the phrase "I was wondering if you were available tonight."

"I have to take this," I said to Svetlana and answered the phone. "Hold on for a second, please," I said professionally, then unplugged the headpiece from the phone so he couldn't hear me.

Svetlana said that she had to run anyway. She had a long ride out to Brooklyn. We agreed to talk tomorrow.

"Listen," I said as she was heading out the door, "if Bree wants to be in this play, you better tell him that I'm not going to delay rehearsal by a minute. If he misses another meeting, permission agreement or not, he's out."

"Whatever," she said calmly; apparently her loyalty to him had waned. As she left, she softly closed the door behind her. I plugged the phone back in and in a breezy, sparkling tone, I said, "So what's cooking?"

"Nothing really," Sheldon began. "I saw you and that Kenny guy on TV at the VJ Awards and you looked so beautiful I guess I just wanted to see how you were. . . ."

After a bit more banter I sensed he was lonely and wanted a little companionship. After all the times he had stepped up to the plate for me, how could I just turn him down: "Just this once, okay?"

"Fine."

Besides, with the theatrical tension and without any proper addiction to lean on, all I had was him. I hastily packed some overnight things and grabbed a cab up to him his place last time.

I didn't know if it was due to having to suck up to Huey and company or perhaps it was because of bullying Svetlana, but as soon as Sheldon opened the door, I felt incredibly powerful.

After a half an hour of heavy petting, I found him prostrating himself before me like a common slave whose only happiness is in the pleasure of serving his mistress.

Upon awaking from a shuddering orgasm, I realized one of the key reasons he was a great lover, other than his technical skills, was in the simple fact that I was able to effortlessly erase his existence.

Just as I was about to share this sad confession, and tell him why breaking up was probably the best thing for both of us, he hopped out of bed and into the shower.

I collected my clothes off the floor and placed them on fern-scented wooden hangers, then I joined him in the bathroom. He was toweling off so I showered.

He brushed his teeth and peed. Then he mindlessly flushed and I was scalded.

By the time I had brushed my teeth, flossed and climbed into bed, he was asleep. I lay quietly next to him, watching him as he slept. If I were thirty-nine years old and facing a middle-age spinsterhood, I would grab him with both hands and hold on for dear life. But as I stared at his beautiful sleeping face, I just kept thinking that somewhere out there was a Mister Righter.

Sensing the unevenness of his snoring, I wondered if he was still awake.

"Maybe we should get back together," I whispered as a test.

"All right," he joked. Fuck, he was wide-awake.

"Just kidding," I clarified nervously.

"Don't worry. I know," he confessed, then he timidly asked, "So are you and that British actor dating?"

"No, he just needed a date for the ceremony. We didn't have sex or anything."

"Whatever," he said. "You know I'm going away to the Caribbean for two weeks' vacation. Want to join me? I'll cover all the expenses."

So that was why he invited me over. He was trying to lure me back with an all-expense paid vacation to the tropics. I could think of nowhere I'd rather go, but obviously I was deep in the shit, and even if I was a heartless using bitch, I couldn't leave now.

"It's a sweet offer, but you shouldn't waste it on me. That's something for a girlfriend."

Perhaps to reassure me that he wasn't being clingy or manipulative, he yawned, and rolled away from me.

21

ROYALLY SCREWED

THAT·MONDAY·AT·WORK I got a call from Svetlana explaining that Huey had chosen the barely recognizable British actor Kenny Eltwood to fill the role of Reggie. He must have really been down on his luck.

Since Huey committed to a directing schedule, Svetlana explained that she found a great deal on a bulk of cheap rehearsal space in the basement of Saint Barnabas, an Eastern Orthodox church on West Thirty-fourth Street.

"Terrific," I replied and realized how lucky we were to have her working for us. I really had no clue how to produce a play.

"I hope you don't mind but Huey called me, and he wants to combine the audition for you, Edith and Belinda with the first read-through on Thursday."

"No, I don't mind," I replied, suddenly feeling my midsection tense up. "I just want to read for the Samantha role."

"He wants all three of you to try for both female roles."

"Great," I replied, pissed.

"Do you have the script and a pen nearby?"

"Yeah, go ahead," I said impatiently.

"He wants to hear pages fourteen to sixteen of the Lucy role. And for the Samantha role he wants pages thirty-two to thirty-three. You'll be reading across from an actor."

"Fine," I said, noting the pages.

"I know this sounds demeaning," she said apologetically, "but he also wants you all to bring your résumés to see your training and experience."

"Then I better notify everyone."

"That's my job," she said, then quickly added, "unless of course you want to."

"No, I'd appreciate it if you did."

"I just want you to know, Hannah, you don't have to worry about any question of loyalty or anything, I'll clear anything with you before speaking to Huey."

"It doesn't matter anymore," I replied. "I probably am going to lose the role."

"Don't say that," she replied. "In fact, I overheard you all talking while I was in the bathroom, and if I may make a suggestion, don't freak out if you lose to Belinda."

"What?"

"Did you know that she has gotten six roles in various student films over the past two years?"

"No."

"She got an agent when she went out to L.A."

"You're kidding!"

"No, and he promised her auditions. That means in the next few weeks, he's going to call her for pilot season."

"But pilot season's over," I pointed out. This was when Hollywood producers put together new shows to pitch to TV studios.

"She's still going back. The only reason she returned here was to visit her parents."

"I'm sure she'll be in the play," I replied.

"She's incredibly ambitious. She doesn't even like theater. And she's never worked with Huey outside of school. The first time she misses a rehearsal for some audition, he'll dump her. And you can take over."

"I wish I had your confidence."

"Also don't worry about Bree, let him go. What you said the other day was right. He's unreliable and he's not going to contest the rights to the play."

"Give the guy a chance."

"How many meetings has he missed?" When I didn't answer, she replied, "Once the play makes money we can give him a finder's fee. I'll speak to him myself and get some kind of settlement."

I couldn't believe Svetlana was such an operator. The only thing I didn't understand was how she hoped to benefit by it. Even if the play went to Broadway, she was still going to get a fixed salary. The next biggest problem on the horizon was actually locating an affordable theater. When I called everyone to relay this concern, all concurred in their own way that it was a problem, but we still had about two months before they had to worry about it.

That night, I sounded like a broken record, reciting the same five minutes of Samantha's monologue over and over, wanting it to be perfect. If any of my neighbors had overheard me through the walls, it would probably seem as though I had hit an impasse and I couldn't advance through into the next minute of my existence.

While at work the next day, I squeezed every bit of downtime calling theater companies throughout the city trying to locate a cheap proscenium. That afternoon, I got a call from Kenny Eltwood thanking me profusely. He seemed to think that I had a hand in getting him his part in the play, a misconception I didn't deny.

"Even though it only pays scale," he said, "I was dying for some theater work where I can show my true talent. I know we'll do great together."

"Actually we might not," I said and confessed that we had one girl too many in our company and had all agreed to be auditioned by Huey.

"But you're the executive producer."

"It's a repertory theater. We are all equal members. We agreed that whomever is best for the role gets it."

"Do you have an acting coach or someone to help you coax out the role?"

Coax out the role? Was this his roundabout way of asking if I had a boyfriend? I told him I didn't have a anybody.

"If you'd like to make use of me," he pitched, "I'm available for most evenings this week, and as I need to get off-book too, we can help each other run lines. Are you available tonight?"

"Sure, if you don't mind." This was actually helpful: useful feedback from a modestly accomplished actor.

"Where precisely are you?"

I gave him my address again, and to my surprise when he arrived that night he had a small gold box of Godiva chocolates that he had presumably picked up en route. The same kind Sheldon had bought for me. I wondered if they hadn't teamed up for a two-for-one sale.

I thanked him and led him into my living room/kitchen/bedroom. We each took out our script and located the first scene that I was expected to read. It was for Samantha's role. Samantha had just finished reading her short story to the otherwise male writers group. Each of the guys start criticizing her piece. Slowly the attacks turn ugly, and finally the "gay" writer, Lenny, accuses her of secretly being "a woman who hates other women."

It was a poor choice for an audition as it had four actors in the scene, so Ken had to read the three males against my one. First we just read through the lines a couple of times, gradually growing familiar with the roles. About fifteen minutes later, as I was just getting into character, Kenny said he needed to loosen up. He jumped to his feet and started shaking out his hands, arms, and head, making strange yodeling noises to warm up. Then he sat back down next to me, and we picked up our scripts. I read my first line, when he suddenly bounded back to his feet and dashed across the living room into my kitchenette, where he opened my fridge as though it were his own. Taking out the unfinished bottle of Franklin's cheap Aussie wine, he uncorked it and poured two glasses halfway and brought them over, handing me one.

"I need a touch of the vino," he explained, "and it's bad luck to drink alone."

We clicked glasses and drank, but before we could get back to rehearsal, Kenny asked, "Would you mind terribly much if we now went to the other role—Lucy."

"Okay," I replied, hoping that this might be some sophisticated technique he had learned at RADA or some exclusive acting conservatory like that.

We flipped to the Lucy role. On the surface it is a typical seduction scene. Reggie is getting her in the sack, but the subtext is of a novice seeking validation as a writer from her lover and mentor Reggie. He, on the other hand, suffers from terminal writer's block and is intensely jealous of the fact that she is young, talented and has no problem writing.

We read through the role several times and then the young Brit rose, stretched again and asked, "Would you mind if we got physical a bit. I think it might be more liberating."

"It is a seduction scene, isn't it?" I replied. As we read, Ken held the script with one hand and gently stroked me with his other, rubbing my back as he did his lines. I reciprocated in kind, stroking his arm, staring into his eyes, validating my character's deep insecurities. During the scene, Reggie (Ken) looked lovingly into Lucy's (my) eyes. He kissed Lucy (me) on her (my) mouth, but suddenly his tongue slipped in my mouth where no audience could see it.

When we broke apart, I was totally turned on. We began the scene again, starting with a deeper level of commitment. By the time we reached our erotic crescendo, Ken had his hands up my shirt in my bra. Reggie's need to sublimate his jealousy in sexual aggression and Lucy's urge to be reassured amorously kept up until we were all out of juice, but Kenny (the actor) reassured me (the person) that he'd give me as much support as I (Hannah) needed. So we rehearsed two more times before the audition.

During downtime the next day at work, instead of studying the text as I should have, I called various theaters attempting to track down leads for an affordable space. I finally found a nice little stage in the Village, the Orpheus, that was available during the exact times we needed it. The asking price was an unbelievable fifteen hundred dollars a week, forty-five hundred bucks for a three-week run. Way over our budget, but still a steal. When the theater director called me back, though, and I offered him an even four grand for the three weeks, he laughed in my face.

"What's so damn funny, I'm just asking for a five-hundred-dollar break."

"It's not fifteen hundred a week, it's that much per day," he said, putting all my hopes to rest.

That night, in rehearsal with Kenny, everything started out as usual. We quickly went through the pretense of touching on the Samantha role, which was the only part I ever wanted in the play. Then, slowly we read the Lucy role, which led to an hour of mind-blowing sex. That loosened me up a hell of a lot better than Dr. Wang's tea. Afterward, though, naked and covered with sweat, I was faced with the panicky fact that I was all out of rehearsal time.

"Shit, you've got to get out of here so I can work on Samantha."

As he pulled his pants on and buttoned his shirt, he apologized.

"It's not your fault," I replied. Great sex with a minor celebrity was always a serendipitous thing.

"It kind of is my fault. I've never done anything like this before," he said and revealed that the Samantha role got him really excited. She was such a self-righteous prig. But the Lucy role would finish him off. Where "Bitchy Samantha" created a sexual tension, "Slutty Lucy" offered a sexual release.

"You were really wonderful in both roles," he said, "it was like having an economy-class ménage à trois."

"That's me, always fucking myself over."

THE UNDERSTUDY

SAINT·BARNABAS·CHURCH was a dirty stack of old stones that looked like it lost all its worshippers and would have had to close long ago if it had to pay taxes.

The entrance to the basement was a long, dingy corridor that smelled faintly of insecticide. It had a variety of smaller doors that were always locked and two big rooms that were always open. The first room, near the entrance, accommodated some support group, probably AA. They usually broke up before we arrived. The second room, toward the rear of the basement, was about half the size, but it was still a nice big space. It was about seven hundred square feet with over-waxed linoleum floors, fluorescent lights, and a long, Formica-topped table surrounded by plastic foldout chairs. The stylelessness helped float it through the ages. Edith, Belinda and I arrived before the others, which proved awkward. We all probably hoped the same thing, to be auditioned before anyone else showed up. Of course we weren't that lucky; everyone arrived promptly at seven. Even the heretofore unseen Bree showed up on time.

Everyone shook hands with him. He appeared remarkably clean and sober. Of course Huey Baxter arrived a half an hour late with preppy-looking Kenny and fastidious Svetlana in tow. She was toting a little briefcase that contained her copy of the script and a spiral notebook filled with secrets.

"My! Everyone looks so delicious," Baxter said. He put his valise down in the chair at the head of the table.

Bree apologized for missing the first few meetings and shook Huey's limp hand.

"Ah, the script bearer—so how'd you come by it?" Huey inquired.

"Friend of my aunt's," Bree said succinctly.

"Well, if your acting is half as good as your acquisition skills, you shouldn't have any problems."

I discreetly informed Bree that due to unforeseen circumstances he had been cast in the role of Waldo. He didn't bat an eyelash about losing Reggie, his character of choice.

"Everyone here?" the director asked Svetlana.

"Yes sir," she replied, and softly asked the three of us for our résumés, which she placed on the table before Huey.

"The gentlemen are excused for about a half hour. Have some Earl Grey and come back slowly boys. We're going to audition the actresses first." Bree, Noah, and Mike stepped outside. "Ladies, you have the honor of reading across from the fabulous Kenny Eltwood. Okay, let's begin with our great executive producer, Hannah Cohn."

"We're all executive producers in this company," Belinda pointed out to diminish any partiality on his part.

"Ah, yes, four big chiefs, no little Indians," he replied absently. "Hannah first, Edith second and Belinda last. Each of you will read for both parts and then I'll give you a summary decision."

Svetlana opened her script, as did Huey, who put on reading glasses for the first time ever, and we began. Kenny read in this pathetic, too helpful manner that all but said, Because we had sex I'm trying to give you special treatment.

"Can we start again?" I asked Baxter halfway through, and turning to Ken with a stern politeness, I softly said, "Just read the lines, okay?"

"Thank you," Huey muttered in agreement.

Ken nodded and read his lines matter-of-factly without his coaxing. I wasn't too nervous and in another moment it was all over. It seemed an adequate read of the Lucy role, but it wasn't much more than that. We flipped to my coveted Samantha role and Huey realized for the first time that the scene required three actors.

"Who the hell made this selection?" he asked impatiently.

"You did," Svetlana uttered without making eye contact.

Huey rose, dashed out into the hallway, and returned a moment later with Noah, who was eating from a big bag of barbecue potato chips. He along with Svetlana and Ken read the three male roles to my Samantha. Finally I came to Sam's big speech:

> I admit it. I thought Lucy was an excellent writer. But just like the tight miniskirts and low-cut blouses she wore, she sold herself short. She lacked confidence. Every time there was a choice between a challenge or some stupid little pleaser, she'd do the cute thing. Well it was our job to be ambitious for her.

I overemphasized the "I thought Lucy . . ." line then blurred the "tight miniskirts and low-cut blouses" remark. I virtually spat out the main idea of Lucy lacking confidence, and finally understated the conclusion.

Huey sensed my disappointment and kindly asked, "Would you like to give it another go, dear?"

"Please," I said. On the second go-round I felt I hit several lines right on the head and nailed the concluding speech. Yet there was something fake about the entire reading.

"Just great," Huey replied, and looking over my résumé, he asked me several questions about training and other plays that I had been in. He seemed impressed by the fact that I was Nora in a college production of *A Doll's House*.

"Wait a second." He suddenly made a face. "That was the Ibsen directed by Vito Seven?"

"Yes," I replied excitedly.

"Well, to be absolutely truthful, I remember seeing that play and I just don't remember you in it." That was not a good sign. It made me wish I could forget ever having sex with him.

I assured him that I wasn't lying, I could produce the program.

"I have no doubt," he replied, "I also remember liking the production, and that's all that really matters, isn't it?"

No! I screamed silently and smiled awkwardly.

He thanked me and asked me to send Edith in. I saw her sitting on the floor in the hallway and told her Huey was waiting for her. She took off her jacket and I could see she was wearing a bright miniskirt and a halter top. She had actually dressed for the Lucy role. In fact, with her latest hairstyle and tacky makeup she was Lucy.

When I stepped outside for air, I nearly bumped into Belinda, who was in the doorway feverishly reciting the Samantha lines to the night sky. She had committed them to memory. When she saw me watching her, she flipped on a big smile and asked, "So how'd you do?"

I couldn't respond. I knew it was over. Edith had customized herself into Lucy and Belinda had committed herself into Samantha. If I were casting the play, that's how I would go.

I walked outside, bummed a cigarette from some guy who looked like a terrorist, and walked halfway down the street to a desolate curb cluttered with garbage. While I sucked the smoke down into my very soul, I twisted the fleshy tumorous knob on my arm, trying to pop it open. What could I do to save the situation? I couldn't just take the Bull script and walk. It was Bree's and for the first time he was here—sober and happy. I couldn't fire anyone. I didn't have the power. I couldn't beg anyone, and I wouldn't flirt with anyone. Maybe Svetlana was right, maybe Belinda would fuck up and get fired, but that seemed unlikely. The only real question was whether I would stay and remain as the understudy and producer, or put my time and resources into another project. Looking carefully at the litter on the sidewalk before me, I realized I was staring at a grouping of melted candles. A rain-streaked handwritten sign was taped to a post. It was an old street memorial. The water had blurred out the name, but the dates were still readable, "November 29, 1958–September 11, 2001."

With a renewed sense of self-delusion, I went back down the hallway of Saint Barnabas and tried to muster up some hope. Maybe my audition wasn't as bad as I thought. Maybe Edith with her perfect, overprepared mannerisms and Belinda, with her cloying good looks and sexy smile, would somehow strike Huey as gimmicky or contrived. Through the wall I could faintly hear Huey applauding Edith. He obviously remembered the plays she had starred in. Belinda didn't even notice me as she turned on her smile before the door even opened.

As soon as Edith was off to the side, she pulled on her long coat, covering up her ridiculous outfit, something she'd never otherwise wear. I could see that she was in a complete lather.

"Christ," I asked, "how did you get so worked up?"

"Oh, it's a very physical role," she remarked earnestly.

"It was just supposed to be a line read."

"Huey said do it as you see it."

She ran off to the bathroom and gave herself a quick sink-shower. After about five minutes of silently listening through the cinder-block wall I heard some giggling. Next some moans. Then I heard Huey Baxter yell something, and then silence. A moment later, Svetlana opened the door and asked, "Where's Edith?"

"Right here," Edith shrieked from around a corner as if her life depended on it. Her hair was down, and her cosmetics were wiped off—she had reverted back to her tasteful, low-key self. We both entered. Belinda was seated on the edge of the table, the hem of her dress gently swaying.

"Let me begin by saying you're all marvelously wonderful," Huey gushed. "The two female roles are rather interesting, because where one character is strong-chinned and dogmatic, the other is tremulous and frenetic. Mark my words, this is the sort of play that a pair of great actresses in the future will alternate roles." He sighed, amazed by his own brilliant observation. "My decision paradoxically is that two of you had the disadvantage of being narrowed into the peculiar slots of the two prescribed characters, where only one of you has a greater range and flexibility and could actually be suited for both the roles." He again paused and marveled at his splendid rejection, and staring directly at me, he concluded. "With that said, Hannah, you're the most versatile of the three. Therefore you have the dubious distinction of understudying for both roles. Edith you're just Lucy and Belinda you're just Samantha."

A blunt, end-of-the-world panic was followed by a kind of sober drunkenness. It felt as though I was falling while standing up. Staring over at Edith and Belinda, I could see them employing their narrow talent at restraining boundless joy. There were few moments more gratifying in this business than the instant when one was informed of getting a part. Inversely there were few moments more excruciating than losing. After working so hard at sucking down so much shit and pulling all these details together, I had lost my one great shot at success.

"Okay, people," Huey said, clapping his hands, "let's gather around and begin our first read-through."

As everyone took a seat and lifted their scripts, I fetched my coat and bag, and headed out the door.

"Hold on," Huey stopped me. "Where are you going?"

"You don't really need me tonight, do you?"

"We most certainly do," Huey replied.

"Come on," Noah called out. "We can't do this without you."

"Please, Hannah, you're the keystone of this group," Belinda acted with Oscar-caliber earnestness, relinquishing her founder power. Others pitched in their plea on how indispensable I was to the show. They didn't want to lose their number-one stagehand. The only thing worse than losing the role was being splattered with dribbly ladles of pity. To bring an end to the consolation, I plopped back down in a hardback chair and they began.

Svetlana read the stage directions and each actor did his part. I followed intermittently, the actress without the role. Huey would occasionally pause and ask them questions about their characters: "Why do you think you're saying that? What does Lucy want from Reggie in this scene? Where's Waldo's head with this line of thought? What is the easy way to deliver this exchange and what's the hard way? How do you feel about what Miles just said to you?"

From time to time, Edith or Mike would read a line, pause and ask, "Can we try it this way?" Almost before the suggestion was made Huey would politely veto it. This gave me some pleasure as I could see how impossible Huey was going to be to work with.

Now and then the great director would turn to Svetlana and tell her to take a note. When the script finally came to an end, all seemed happy except for Bree, who was manically fidgeting with his pencil, doing his clean-and-sober best at trying to hold himself together. Svetlana reviewed some details of the rehearsal schedule for everyone's edification. Then Huey made encouraging remarks and lighthearted quips before departing.

Everyone made a big deal of not making a big deal about my expulsion. I felt like I had lost in the very first round of some awful reality TV show. I smiled awkwardly, the first unavoidable casualty of the production. Even though I lived in the same direction as Edith and Belinda, I really wanted to be alone so I claimed I was heading elsewhere. After walking a few blocks, and adjusting to the solitude, I caught a cab home. In the backseat I saw a sticker of the Stars and Stripes. Upon it was emblazoned the phrase "United We Stand." In black Magic Marker, someone had scribbled under it, "Alone We Sit."

The Open Call

ONE·OF·THE·PRIMARY·REASONS I had initially undertaken the production was to lift myself out of the great depression that so many people in the city silently struggled with. Now almost as a therapy to avoid self-pity for losing my role, I dwelled on the tragedy. Without thinking, I was constantly finding my eyes pulling south, like an opposing compass needle, searching for the great absence in the lower part of Manhattan—the missing towers. Like Mike, I took to reading the obituaries in the *New York Times* that focused on minor things in the subjects' lives, usually just a handful of idiosyncratic details. It seemed so little that summed up an entire life, like getting some customized cup of coffee every morning at Starbucks. Yet as trivial or pathetic as that appeared, it did seem to be a consistent high point in my own life. From work, I called information and tried to get the address or phone number of the actress who I met that day, Patricia Harrows. No one was listed by that name in Lower Manhattan.

When I would review the events of that prior season I kept thinking how nothing really led up to it. The summer of 2001 was a nice one. I was in a good relationship with Christy, who was eagerly writing her script. I had high hopes that a new and exciting stage in my life was about to begin.

The notion that the city's most devastating tragedy was about to hit compelled me to wonder. If there really was a God, or a higher power, wouldn't He at least offer some signs? I vaguely remembered several odd and random details. I recalled reading that summer about two Pakistani girls out in the Rockaways, who were swept into the ocean by a rogue wave as they were standing in knee-deep water. I also recalled spending a weekend night in Williamsburg with Edith. She woke me up early Sunday morning, and with coffees in hand we marched off to Greenpoint where, from a safe distance, we witnessed the carefully planned implosion of two giant empty gas towers. This was only about a month or so before the World Trade Center fell. In retrospect there was something uncanny about their collapse, as if fate was cautiously practicing a tremendous evil in miniature.

Just a week earlier, I had gotten a message from Christy, but because I felt so confident about being in the Bull play, I never returned the call. She had asked if I would be interested in reading the latest incarnation of her third-world love triangle before she finally pitched it to Manny Greene. In other words, she wanted me to say I loved it, or tell the truth, and face another round of bitter, ex-lover recrimination. Still if she had considered using half my notes, there might be some reason to hope.

Throughout that first week after losing my role I kept obsessing about the disaster, breaking into tears constantly. I found it difficult dealing with people, much less calling Christy back. I later learned that many were experiencing the same depression. The post-9/11 trauma dovetailed very gracefully with my disastrous life. In an effort to find some peace, during a lunch break I bought a dozen roses and decided to lay them at Ground Zero. Grabbing the A train, I got off at Park Place. Most of the exits were still sealed, but after a lot of walking and zigzagging, I finally found myself heading down to the site with a stream of others. I was surprised by the bizarre new locale that seemed nothing like the place I had been to just six or so months earlier.

Thousands of tourists with still and video cameras were heading to the new walkway as though visiting some ancient ruin. Lining the curbs were illegal aliens selling 9/11 memorabilia galore. The entire city had been awash in the 9/11 junk since the day after the tragedy—NYPD and FDNY hats and T-shirts, pictures of the buildings before and after the planes hit, and the infamous shot of the firemen erecting the American flag amidst the rubble. I never had any illusions about what was sacred, but it was freaky how the area had converted into 9/11-ville. The only thing that was missing was a simulated ride where the tourists could sit in a miniature skyscraper and race out as it collapsed. What wasn't crassly commercial was disposal cornball: The gates of Saint Paul's Chapel, as well as the wall lining the Trade Center site, were loaded down with cards and posters and everything else people could tape to it.

"How long does it take to get to the ramp?" I asked a cop as I was looking for the end of that endless line.

"About four hours," he shot back.

"There's no priority for New Yorkers?"

"One line for all," he said smoothly.

"Suppose you were here when the buildings fell?" I said, waving my roses. "Does that give you any added priority?"

"One line for all," he repeated.

Others must have tried that one, but I wasn't really trying to pull a fast one. The real tragedy here was the way the event was already becoming a kind of cliché of patriotic sacrifice, when in many ways it was actually a very private and great tragedy for thousands of people. I ended up walking over to Broadway and retracing my steps on that day. I finally placed my roses on the ground near the Starbucks where I had bought coffee with Patricia Harrows. Then I turned around and made it back to Moe, Larry and Curly's before my lunch break ended.

As I missed more rehearsals, each of my "coproducers" called and left pleas on my machine, even Belinda. I only picked up for Edith.

"We really do need you," she said as if it made me feel better.

"I appreciate that. I'm just feeling sick right now. I think I have a head cold. I need some time off."

"Well, come back as soon as you're able," she stated. "Aside from producing, you actually have the biggest role here, learning both Lucy and Samantha's parts."

I had never been in such a pathetic situation. I wanted a legitimate excuse to leave the production, but I could only do that if I could announce some new face-saving venture. That meant I had to get into some other new production.

So my first desperate act of finding human contact as well as searching for a new project required calling crazy Christy back. As her phone rang, I decided I was just going to play it cool and pretend she called only yesterday. She picked up on the first ring.

"Hi, what's up?"

"What's up? I called you a week ago is up!"

"You're drinking a bit early, aren't you?" To judge by her anger level, she had consumed roughly half a bottle of white wine.

"Well at least I'm not going to dumb VJ Award orgies with Madonna and Guy Ritchie."

"I'm sorry if I called at a bad time." I tried reversing out.

"No, you called at the best time. Greene turned down my screenplay. Are you fucking happy?"

" 'Course not, I'm so sorry."

"Yeah, like you didn't know anything about it."

"How would I know anything?"

"He told me he saw you naked in that scumbag Stein's new film. How many times did you blow him for the role?"

"Fuck you!" I yelled back and slammed the phone down. I was always caught on the dark side of her bipolar moods.

A moment passed before the phone rang. I picked it up and heard Christy utter, "Sorry for being an asshole."

"What's wrong with you?"

"I'm just coming to terms with the fact that I'm the unluckiest person in the world."

"There's no such thing as luck, 'cause if there were, I'd be the unluckiest."

"You! You know, Manny liked most of your snappy, sellout suggestions."

"What did he say?"

"He gave me a shitload of notes in the event I wanted to do a rewrite."

"See, he wants to do the project."

"If I do his rewrites, I'll be making his film—indie *Pretty Woman*."

"Manny is not that bad," I argued.

"His fucking loss, I sent the script to three other places yesterday." She paused. We both knew that for a hundred different reasons Manny was her best bet.

"Look," I said as a final effort to be helpful, "why don't you send me the script and I'll see what I can come up with."

"What are you, a writer now?"

"I've been writing a little lately," I replied, scribbling the word "asshole" on a piece of paper.

"I'll tell you what, I'll send you the stuff, but don't give me any more of your bullshit notes, just rewrite the fucking thing yourself. If he picks it up, I'll give you the screen credit and the bulk of the script money he's giving me."

I wasn't sure if she was kidding or not. I was always amazed how sane and lucid a nutcase could be once they were backed into a corner. I said fine, if only to end the conversation pleasantly.

With Christy's project definitely out of the running, that left only one other alternative. I was left to wander through the dark forest of open auditions.

Early the next morning, I perused the back pages of *Back Stage*, the *Local Vocal* and *New York Press* for head-shot photographers. My old head shots, taken by Christy, made me look butch. Balancing quality with cost, I made appointments for a sixty-dollar hairdo and a fifty-dollar makeup session, then I paid double that sum to the head-shooter.

"Where exactly are you located?" I asked.

"Do you know Westbeth?"

This was a subsidized housing project for artist types in the West Village. Christy once explained that when Westbeth first opened back in the 1950s, vigorous young artists had indeed lived there, but over the years many had moved away or died. Now the former office building consisted largely of their ex-wives, widows, and stepchildren. When I later learned that Christy's parents applied for and failed to secure an apartment there I wondered how much of her analysis was just sour grapes.

In a small loft on the third floor, I met with some sleek ponytail. His assistant illuminated me under a thousand watts in front of a lush blue backdrop and pressed powder into my cheeks. His stiff personality made me uncomfortable enough, and his stupid pose directions made me feel completely idiotic.

"I have to tell you," I confessed through my frozen smile, "I think I'm going to look like a complete moron."

"Trust me," he said confidently. "You might not look like you when I'm done, but you'll love whoever it is you look like. My portraits get auditions."

Since I usually didn't like how I looked anyway, I acquiesced. A week later, after doling out more money for development and reproduction costs, his prophecy came true. A stack of glossy eight-by-tens looked nothing like me. Maybe that was why the stranger in the head shot looked so hot.

For about a half an hour, I fell under the spell of giving myself an Anglican screen name, and looking at fashionable monikers in various magazines, I toyed with: Morgan Mammogram, and Jocelyn Porsche. When I reached Marion Worthless, I decided to stay with my own name.

After stapling copies of my attractively exaggerated résumé to the back of the attractively exaggerated pictures, I flipped through *Back Stage*. There wasn't much to choose from: Three student films called for actresses either five years older or five years younger than me. Being in my twenties was a theatrical liability. A number of high-definition videos were being shot, but they were either C-grade horror flicks or they called for ethnic actors. Most of the remaining casting calls were for Broadway musicals being performed in the sticks: A Mary Magdalene was wanted in an Oklahoma production of *Jesus Christ Superstar*. I saw myself with six-shooters underneath my shawl. An Eliza Doolittle was being stalked in the wilds of Manitoba, and Chain Gang Productions was doing Miguel Piñero's *Short Eyes* to tour through minimum-security prisons of the Northeast. Did prisoners really want to see a prison play?

I mailed out my head shots to the Globe Theater, who were doing a nonunion production of Shakespeare's Henry trilogy up in Inwood. Another company, Screaming Naked Through the Streets Actors, situated in Garden City, New Jersey, needed "the girl" for their *Fantasticks*. Finally, though, near the last page, I spotted the real casting jewel. It was an open call for a membership to the Jean Cocteau Repertory Company. To get in would mean being cast in an entire season of plays at the respected Bouwerie Lane Theater.

The call was for nine the next morning. So after work, dinner and a little TV, I went right to sleep and awoke early at seven, a real novelty for me. When I arrived in the East Village at eight, I had little doubt that I would be ahead enough in line to audition quickly and still make it to work on time. Astoundingly, a line of young actors threaded down Bowery, around Bond and up Lafayette. As I walked to the rear of the line, I stopped counting after I passed two hundred yet-to-be-discovered stars and starlets like myself—none of whom I knew. I waited for about an hour. The line didn't budge. Finally a young actress who'd had enough and was leaving spoke to the guy in front of me, apparently an acquaintance.

"They're only seeing four hundred people, and earlier they gave out time slots for three hundred and fifty. So they're only going to see the first fifty on this line."

"You're kidding," he replied.

Though there was no chance, I waited hopelessly for another hour before some geeky, spazzy dweeb popped out like an overripe zit and announced, "Thanks. That will be all for today."

To further tease my tightly caged hopes, I got calls from both the *Fantasticks* and the Inwood Shakespeare productions offering auditions. Some polite man at the Globe Theater said I had a three o'clock appointment and auditions would be at the Shelter Studios.

"Do you want a monologue or are we going to read sides?"

"Sure, the side of a monologue will be fine," he said inexplicably. Still, the idea of trying out made me feel dizzy with hopefulness. The *Fantasticks* people said I could skip the monologue and go directly to sides.

The one Shakespeare monologue I knew by heart was Titania's soliloquy in *A Midsummer Night's Dream* when Oberon confronts her with jealousy:

These are the forgeries of jealousy:
And never, since the middle summer's spring,
Met we on hill, in dale, forest, or mead,
By paved fountain or by rushy brook,
Or on the beached margent of the sea,
To dance our ringlets to the whistling wind,
But with thy brawls thou hast disturbed our sport.
Therefore the winds, piping to us in vain,
As in revenge, have sucked up from the sea
Contagious fogs, which, falling in the land,
Hath every pelting river made so proud,
That they have overborne their continents . . .

It went on like that. Perhaps few liked the language as much as the actors reading it, but Shakespeare always gave me a buzz for about ten seconds. Beyond that I would start to fuzz out. Checking on the female roles in the three Henry the Sixth plays, the two key parts were Queen Margaret and Joan La Pucelle, or Joan of Arc, who only seemed to be in the first play. This role immediately grabbed me, particularly since she didn't appear to be in the other two plays—I remembered dozing off during an experimental production of the Henry cycle at a small theater in the far East Village.

The other play, *The Fantasticks*, I knew nothing about. That night, in a bookstore, I read the first five pages of the longest-running play in America, which had recently closed. I decided that the only thing fantastic about it was the title. I knew that many people saw and cherished this simple tale of young love, but it made my skin crawl and there was no way in hell I was going to commute to Garden City to be in it. If most plays didn't require the patience of a saint, they called for the innocence of a child and I had recently ran out of both.

That Saturday I headed over to the sixth floor of Shelter Studios in Midtown for the Shakespeare audition. A large crowd of twenty or so strapping actors, knights and spear bearers were loitering in the hallway, where most of them appeared to be struggling with the awkward Shakespearean verse. Inside the little office, packed in chairs, as though in the waiting area of a free clinic, were a dozen or so older Falstaff types, old men snoring or reading newspapers.

"Where are all the actresses?" I asked aloud, not seeing a single one.

"You're it, sweet'ems," the strappiest of the young men replied.

Angling past the hairy-eared chairs of loose-skinned geriatrics, trying not to wake them up, I made it up to the receptionist window. There, coughing into a contaminated phone, was a stone-faced old lady. When she cursed and slammed it down, I announced that I was there for my three o'clock appointment.

"Please don't give me no guff, 'cause I've had it up to here with the guff." She brought her liver-spotted hand up to the thousand little scales of flesh that made up her ancient forehead.

"I'm just saying—"

"Here, your ladyship," she shot back, handing me three Xeroxed pages that were stapled together. They were sides for the Queen Margaret scene. "Go right in and read that. Is that quick enough for you?"

"I think I'm supposed to do a three-minute monologue first," I said, "and I was hoping to try out for the Joan of Arc role."

"Darling, I know God doesn't talk to you, 'cause if he did, he'd tell you to stay home. Now take 'em and go, before I send in someone else."

BURNT AT THE STAKE

I·WALKED·DOWN·THE·DARK, unswept corridor and stopped before the large wooden door, where I took a deep breath before opening it. A room full of laughter instantly grew silent. Two men, one elderly and one late-middle-aged, were seated behind one narrow desk that looked more like a pine door without a knob. Before them stood a muscular male in a T-shirt who was holding a script. He didn't look anything like King Henry or any other gawky member of the British royalty.

The older and balder of the two seated men rose, extended his manicured hand for a friendly shake and said, "I'm Jan Wayne, I'm directing here."

"Sicilio Ballacci, the executive producer," said the rounder, shorter one.

"I'm Tony Sinclair," a thespian hunk named Tony Sinclair said.

"Hi, I'm Hannah Cohn," I introduced myself. "The receptionist said you didn't need to hear my monologue, but if you do . . ."

"Oh, you," Sicilio said, pulling out my head shot and flipping to my résumé. "We've been waiting for you."

"Well, I've been looking forward to meeting you," I tried to be pleasant.

"Look here," said the director, pointing to the résumé, "she studied Shakespeare. And also voice and movement."

"I can read the sides if you like, but I was hoping for the role of Joan La Pucelle, so it might be better if I did my prepared monologue."

"You know what," said Jan, "you don't even need to read the sides. You got the part."

"I what?"

"You got it," he repeated.

"Congratulations," said Tony the actor.

"What part do I got?"

"You said you wanted the Joan La Pucelle."

"But how do you know if I'm right for the role?"

"You're more than qualified," Sicilio said.

"I don't have to put any money into this?" I asked, suspecting a scam.

" 'Course not."

"Oh, I don't perform in the nude," I said abruptly, fearing that this was some freaky weird sex production. It just didn't jibe. No one except Julia Roberts is just handed a role.

"No nudity," the director replied. "We want families to come."

"How do you know if I'm right for the role?"

"Truth is," Sicilio spoke, "I saw you in a play."

"What exactly did you see me in?" I asked, wondering if this was a bit for *America's Wackiest Videos*.

"*Morning Became Electric*," he misread one of the credits off my résumé.

"I never did *Mourning Becomes Electra*," I confessed, "that credit was a lie!"

"You know," said Jan the director, who until now seemed to defer to Sicilio, "you're right. Why don't you do an audition."

"What exactly is going on?" I asked, suddenly panicking that I was surrounded by rapists and kidnappers.

"Take it easy. We're on the up-and-up," Sicily replied, and pulling out his wallet, he opened it up. I thought he was going to show me some review of the Globe Theater's prior work; instead he showed me a picture of a small, hairy dog. "That's my little girl. Her name is Ruby. She's a Brussels griffon."

"Have you ever directed a play?" Jan asked me.

"No, I'm an actress," I said, and deciding I'd had enough, I stood up to leave.

"Oh, boy, here we go, just like this morning," Sicilio muttered.

"Can you just give us a moment to explain," Jan said. He let out a great sigh and said, "See, Sicilio had the head shots of all the actresses. We only need four. The idea was to pair them against our boys. But he only called you and this other lady who came this morning, but she sort of freaked out and ran."

"Where is all this heading?"

"I left the head shots on the freaking train," Sicily said. "You were the only actress who I called back aside from that bitch. I was going to call them all from my downtown office, but I just called two before I headed down there and left them on the Number One."

So that was why I was the only actress, but there seemed to be more to this mystery. "Why do you have all these young guys and older men?"

"We're a joint production," Jan replied.

"I represent the young fellows here. We're all private sanitation workers," Sicilio said. "Jan handles the seniors."

Jan handed me a printed flyer that revealed the final mystery of the Globe Theater. Globe was a loose acronym standing for Garbage Laborers Of inwood & Beckenstein's Elderly Theater.

"What's Beckenstein's Elderly?" I asked.

"The Louis Beckenstein Senior Citizen Center up in Inwood," Jan filled in.

"We were doing this coproduction as a fund-raiser for the Fire

Department Nine-eleven Fund. But you know we couldn't really get any actresses, which was why we needed you."

"So you've never done a play before?"

"Sort of, I'm a retired English teacher. I put on several high school plays, *Bye Bye Birdie* and *Fiddler on the Roof*. Sicilio here drives a truck."

"You got your jobs cut out for you," I sighed.

"If you want you can help us produce or direct it. I mean, yours is the best résumé we've seen by far. And you really seem to know your way around acting."

I sat smiling nervously, wondering how the hell to get out of there.

"Whatever money we raise in ticket sales goes to the firefighters who died at the towers," said Tony the actor. I actually would've liked to help them, but these guys didn't have a clue, and I wouldn't even know where to begin.

"You can be the producer person," offered Sicilio. There it was again, that awful P word.

"Look, you need to hold a proper audition. The play requires three or four actresses, and while you're doing that you can advertise for a trained director and a real producer." I tried to let them down gently. "My first piece of advice is that you find something a little less challenging. These Henry plays are like scaling Mount Everest. Why don't you find something more contemporary, like an Arthur Miller play."

"That's what I said, something new," Jan replied, "but Sicilio felt we should look for some big play to stick everyone in."

"Guilty as charged," he said, waving his fat arms in the air. "Look, this one was the biggest and I just figured there'd be something for everyone."

"I suggested that maybe we should do *The Angel in America*, 'cause it's contemporary," Jan replied.

"There you go," I said, trying to be encouraging. But since he wasn't even clear about the title, I sensed that he was in for a surprise about the themes. Checking my watch, I really didn't have time to update them on the history of theater, or the million little tortures in getting a production up.

"We all lost friends," Sicilio went on. "We had to do something."

"I'm sympathetic, I really am. But this isn't something you can just do casually. There's a lot to it. And I honestly wouldn't know how to do it, even if I could."

Sensing that I was about to cry, Jan mercifully walked me down the corridor.

"Maybe a vaudeville, or talent show?" I suggested, and stopped short of saying a striptease, it was too *Full Monty*. He thanked me and I was gone.

I arrived back home and watched TV for about fifteen minutes before I finally turned it on. Then I grabbed a copy of Shakespeare's collected hits off my shelf.

Standing before the mirror I recited the entire Titania passage that I was unable to do during the audition. I knew that I would never say the words on a stage. Nowadays audiences lacked the poetic appreciation and patience for any speeches that truly plumbed the depths of feelings and expression.

As I thoughtlessly scratched my arm, I rubbed the lump, and I decided at that moment that I had to get it looked at immediately. I grabbed the subway and in a half an hour was heading down the slippery streets of Chinatown. I waited for twenty minutes before I was able to tell the great Asian medicine man that I had an emergency. He mercifully took time from another patient for me. I explained to him that something awful happened to me on September 11.

He looked bewildered.

"I was a few blocks from here when the towers fell and I got caught in that fucking cloud of dust." I didn't mean to curse. "I inhaled all that smoke and dust that they're now saying was toxic, understand?"

"Yeah, you have a breathing problem?" he asked.

"No, but a while ago I discovered this." I showed him the lump on the back of my upper arm. He looked, then put a finger above it without touching me as though to feel its warmth.

"What do you think? Is it a malignancy?"

"I think you miscarry."

"Miscarry?!"

He nodded firmly.

"You mean I lost a . . . a baby?"

"No, no . . . miscarry." He was obviously mistranslating some diffi-cult idea.

"Misery?"

"No, miscarry." He stood fast.

"Malignancy?"

"No."

"Is it cancer?" I tried to give him words. "Am I going to die?"

"No, drink the hot blackness!" Was he referring to coffee?

"No, lie-down man. Make life good." Wang could start a therapeu-tic cathouse. He must have the most sexed-up patients in the city. He walked me out to his corridor of drawers and he prepared me a new tonic of dry twigs and leaves that I would have to strain into my latest tea.

When I got home I discovered some good news in my mailbox. The landlord's bank had cashed the two rent checks that I had written in my name. Now if he just cashed my April check I would be the new official renter of my illegal sublet.

I also found Christy's script in the mail and read it along with Manny's commonsense notes. She had addressed most of my sugges-tions without blending them into the screenplay, making them into lumpy last-minute insertions. The sad part was that she really did have a story there. In fairness, a few scenes of the script were not bad, and she had several superb observations of class friction, but these moments were like interesting islands in a sea of morass. I really didn't have a clue about how to write or fix her work. Still, I sat down with a mug of Dr. Wang's shit mix and jotted down ideas.

At the end of a long depressing week alone, I decided that I felt too tired to even bottom out. Little did I suspect that someone else was bottoming out for me. About two and a half weeks after my slide off *Unlubricated*, my phone woke me up. I had fallen asleep in the middle of the "Don't Watch" Wednesday lineup.

"Hi, babe, this is Bree."

"Bree? What is it?" I mumbled. It was eleven P.M.

"Hey, hey eleven could you do me a favor, man . . ." He slipped into silence and in my drowsiness, I slipped back asleep.

"Hey, man," he awoke me again—it was midnight. We had both slept with the phones on our faces for about an hour. "Who's this, please?"

"This is me," the male voice said, "who's this?"

"Bree, is that you?" I asked groggily.

"Yeah, Hannah! Is that you?" He had forgotten that I was on the phone. "Hey, we were sleeping together."

"Yeah." I was still asleep. "I got to run."

"Could you do me a favor?"

"What do you want?" I sat up feeling aggravated.

"I did some shit and I don't think I'm going to feel too well tomorrow."

"Well, I'm not in the production any longer, call Svetlana." I was about to hang up when he yelled, "Wait! Wait a sec. . . ."

"What is it?"

"It took me like an hour just to dial your number."

"All right," I said to be rid of him, "I'll call Svetlana and tell her you're going to be sick tomorrow."

"Careful of that one." He laughed weirdly.

"What one?" For a while I heard only labored breathing.

"I feel really . . . sick."

"Look, I'm sorry but I'm not your mother." I flipped off the TV.

"I did some Lethal Weapon. I got it on Second Street and I . . . I'm shaking and flashing. . . . Can you get me to a hospital?"

"I saved your life once before, remember?" I said angrily. "Call someone else."

"And I got you this play!" he shot back.

"I lost the part to Belinda, call her!"

"If you come over right now and help me get to the hospital, I'll tell you something that you'll thank me for later."

"I'll be more thankful if I don't have to get you," I replied wearily.

"Just this once please . . ." he beseeched.

"Do you only remember my number when you're high or something! I'm not your friend. Bother someone else!" I hung up the phone and went back to sleep.

THE STAGE MANAGER

THE·NEXT·DAY while working busily with a roomful of lawyers at Moe, Larry and Curly's, my cell chimed. Everyone looked at me contemptuously as I flipped off my cell phone. Later, during lunch, I checked the incoming number; it was Svetlana Palas. I remembered Bree's midnight request, so I phoned her back. She wasn't in. I left her a message that Bree was strung out and wouldn't be at rehearsal that night.

Svetlana called me back that afternoon.

"I just wanted to tell you that Belinda just got a call from her agent."

"Fascinating," I said tiredly.

"Mark my words, unless you start coming in, you're not going to get her part."

"Has she missed any rehearsals?"

"Her agent is going to ring her for more auditions. If you just have a little faith, I guarantee I'll get you back in the play."

"Okay," I said, deciding I had nothing else to lose. "What do I have to do?"

"Come to rehearsal tonight." I didn't say anything. "Also . . . I need a little help."

"Aha!" I said aloud and chuckled. "Why do I always have this awful feeling that I am just being strung along and used."

"It's a healthy fear," she conceded, "but you have to trust me."

"Suppose I come in and do all this work and trust you and nothing comes of it?"

"I'll give you my salary—six hundred bucks. All yours," she replied.

It wasn't enough, not nearly enough for all the time and humiliation, but what else did I have? Though I didn't want, and wouldn't take her meager salary, the offer somehow eased my bruised pride.

After work, I went to a Korean salad bar and prepared my fat-free tasteless salad. It was all I ever ate anymore. The only real variety to my dinners was in the selection of awful no-fat dressings. Usually it was just vinegar, but tonight I decided to treat myself by squeezing a lemon on the vinegar. The only alternative to blandness was bitterness. While munching lettuce, all alone in the seats that usually absorbed the lunchtime crowd, I flipped through Christy's rusty script, and tried to figure out how writers wrote. I thought up some witty dialogue but it didn't relate to any of the characters or stories. Finally, in frustration, I looked around and spotted the other diner in the seated area. She was an older woman eating all alone, staring out a window as though she was in an Edward Hopper painting. Feeling instant despair that I was glimpsing myself in twenty years, I picked up the script and dashed out to the basement of Saint Barnabas. I was about a half an hour early and found Mike reading a copy of *Variety*.

"Damn," he said, "and I was hoping we got rid of you!" I had missed almost three weeks of rehearsal.

"Odd as it sounds, I decided that I hadn't quite had all my teeth kicked down my throat."

"I understand entirely. I really come here every night to see if Huey can fully stick his Bruno Magli shoe up my butt."

"What's it like being directed by the best?"

"He doesn't direct, he reads the *New York Times*."

"Probably to see if he's mentioned in it."

"Well, look who's here," Kenny interrupted, walking in. He kissed my cheek. "I told that bastard Baxter that your ability went far beyond that paltry audition."

"That's very sweet of you," I said in my best Audrey Hepburn.

"He's a Baxtard," Mike joked.

"It's really all my fault, isn't it?" Ken asked. "I distracted you from rehearsal and I can't tell you how sorry I am for that."

"Hey, it was fun distraction. Besides, Edith and Belinda are both great."

"Word has it," I heard behind me, "that someone came down with the kissing disease." Baxter had entered.

"That's me, a case of mono," I replied.

"A bi with mono," Mike piped in.

"So are you in or out?" the director followed up.

"In," I replied in an emphatically defeated tone.

"There are no small roles. . . ." Huey recited the loser's quotation.

"Please," I interrupted him, "there are a lot of small roles, and I'd be lucky to land just one."

Noah and Belinda showed up together. Edith arrived moments later. Uncharacteristically, Svetlana came last. She escorted a cute young man named Aldo, whom she quickly introduced to Huey and to the rest of us as her assistant. Since Bree was sick, Aldo was going to read the Waldo role. While Huey was in the W.C., Svetlana took me to one side.

"I'll go over Lucy and Samantha's blocking with you later if you like." She was so delicately polite.

"Fine," I tried to be upbeat.

"You know," she said quietly, "you did the right thing by not helping Bree."

"What do you mean?"

"He called you last night and asked you to come over, didn't he?"

"I suppose so."

"You did the right thing," Svetlana assured. "He's had far too many enablers and crutches. That's how he's fallen to where he is now."

"Where is he now?"

"He's home, but he called me and for the first time in a while, he's vowing to go back to NA."

"What are we working on today?" Huey shouted from across the room at Svetlana. Bladder light and zipped up, the maestro was tapping his baton on the podium.

"The beginning of act two," Svetlana replied upon checking the rehearsal schedule. Immediately she set to work, positioning several chairs and a table to simulate the set. Next she strategically placed certain hand-prop pieces that she had brought with her.

"How are you doing?" Edith came over to me, touching my arm.

"Fine." I kept the smile in the air.

"You're still in the production, aren't you?" Belinda asked, content to be a supporting character to Edith's principal sympathizer.

"Sure, I'm your understudy, remember?" I said, trying not to sound too sarcastic.

"Let's get into position for the beginning of act two," Svetlana announced, softly slapping her palms together, treating the cast like the retarded children that they were.

Everyone assumed their places. Huey took his chair and, opening the *New York Times*, he told them to begin. Except for Edith, all still held their scripts in hand, which they would intermittently glimpse at. I listened as they worked their lines against each other until Kenny—in the character of Reggie—had his epiphany, "Waldo's written a fucking novel!"

"Hold it," Huey interrupted, still staring at the newspaper as if bored. He finally said, "Just go through your blocking from cue to cue beginning with the second act."

Kenny took position on the couch, where his character was asleep when the scene began. Noah started speaking the lines.

"Hey, stupid!" Huey hollered to him. "I said blocking only from cue to cue."

Noah apologized and they silently went through the movement of the characters as Svetlana checked it against her choreographed script.

Finally, Kenny's Reggie went to the location that was supposed to be the bathroom.

"Okay," Huey said to him. "When you exit the loo your character is changed through the entire second act, isn't he? All with that first line. Yet you're muttering it all the way back there, aren't you? Therefore, in the course of the act, I want you to work your way to the front of the stage slowly, so by the time you get to that line you're front and center, where you can speak that line very loud and clearly."

"But by this point in the play I'm drunk," Ken responded.

"Ah, but booze in the theater world is not for bonding or pleasantry or anything short of cruel candor. That magical elixir has an embitter-ing effect on you—you're a nasty drunk, aren't you?"

"I think so," Kenny replied. Huey had the cast go through the sec-ond act slowly again, this time emphasizing not so much character motivation as spectacle and audibility. Though they all did as told, he kept careful focus just on Kenny's character. When his neglect of all the others became painfully obvious, he gave one dull pointer to Belinda: "You're being feministic when you should be feminine and vice versa."

"But I am arguing with Lenny, who's gay," she countered.

"So what are the two of you?" he asked her.

"Actually, I think—"

"You're a pair of bitches!" He gave her the answer he wanted. "Only he's a queen and you're just a woman."

Unlike Kenny, I could see that Belinda did not take well to Huey's autocratic input. She didn't like being forcibly directed, particularly when she felt she was right.

After she begrudgingly went through the newly directed scene exerting as little energy as possible, Huey said, "Much better." Then he called a fifteen-minute break.

Edith went to the phone, Belinda to the bathroom. Noah approached Huey, begging for critical crumbs. "Any notes would really help."

"The only note I have for you is quit pestering me," Huey replied.

MACHINATIONS

AS·I·WAS·HEADING to the ladies' to splash some water on my face, Ken grabbed my sleeve and led me down the hallway toward the men's room.

"The whole thing is immensely unfair," he uttered.

"What is?"

"The fact that you initiated this play," he replied. "Your co-actors should have some loyalty to you."

"They are loyal to each other—to the company and to the play getting up."

"Didn't you get them the script?"

"Yes, but . . ."

"Didn't you get them Huey Baxter?"

"I suppose."

"And he brought them me," Kenny concluded, as if he were the last stop on the Success Express. "What exactly did they do for you?"

"This doesn't make me feel any better," I replied.

"Take the play elsewhere."

"Bree has the rights," I explained, even though I thought it was public knowledge by now.

"I know, but he listens to you."

"No one listens to me," I assured him.

"Sure he does. He came to you with the script, didn't he?" Ken said and leaned close. "Now here's what you should do. Tell him you can get a much larger production and I guarantee you'll have your choice of female roles and——"

Suddenly Huey stepped outside; he made inadvertent eye contact with Kenny then turned on heel and went right back in. Kenny excused himself and went to the bathroom.

With that exchanged glance, my brains started connecting the dots and filling in colorful theories. When Huey first heard I had the script, he desperately wanted to control the production and I prevented him. When Huey met Belinda at a party he must've known that getting her back into the show would drive me out and put a wedge between me and the rest of the company. Huey was also manipulative enough to convince Kenny to sex me up during those crucial days that I should have been rehearsing. Then he selected Belinda and Edith for the two roles, forcing me out of the group. Now the great conniver was using Kenny to try to make me believe that the real betrayal came from my fellow actors.

That would also explain why he was giving the half-wit Brit more direction than anyone else. Eltwood was the only actor who would remain in his new, stolen production.

For a moment——as I reviewed these possibilities——I realized this man had cut me out of my life. He had to be stopped. At that instant, I truly felt like I was infused with the paranoid spirit of the late Lilly Bull.

I went back inside and saw him sitting with his back to me, talking to Mike. Before I could lift the large cinder-block doorstop with both hands and bring it down on Huey's thick, combed-over skull, Svetlana grabbed me.

"Focus! You're here for a role," she whispered in a strangely assertive voice that sounded like Lady Macbeth on Ritalin.

"What exactly do you want from me?" I exclaimed, sensing that she was using me somehow.

"I need help to get this play up. These people are useless."

"What do you mean they're useless?"

"Whenever I ask them about finding a theater or hiring carpenters or any of it, they scratch their heads like they got lice, and point to each other. They haven't got a clue. They think this whole production is just going to mount itself."

"Svetlana, while in college Belinda did all the real production work, I have no idea how to produce a play."

"I've done a million of them. I just need help. We'll do it together. Relax. Start studying the Samantha role. I guarantee you'll get back in the play. Trust me." There was another awful word. But there were more schemes and cross purposes in this little vanity production than in most of Shakespeare's intrigues. Either Svetlana was totally deluded or she had a secret compartment in her large ring from which she dispensed poison.

When I got home that night, I picked Christy's script from my desk, flipped through Manny's notes and wished I knew how to shape the work into Manny Greene's vision of an indie moneymaker.

I considered trying to convince Christy to let Manny hire a cowriter but I knew how difficult she'd be to work with. Christy might let me take a crack at writing the script but she wouldn't let anyone else touch it. If I had the cash I would hire a ghostwriter to rewrite it. Unfortunately, I was broke. A great shame, as this really would be a career catapult.

A brief sleep, a long day at paralegaling and then back to the waterbug-filled basement of Saint Barnabas, where as the cast rehearsed I silently prayed that one of the actresses would unexpectedly drop dead.

The next day upon arrival, I was surprised to see Bree curled on the tabletop fast asleep like an inebriated cat. He was the first one there. I wondered if he hadn't arrived earlier for AA, which had just ended in the adjacent room. But this seemed highly unlikely as he looked miserable. When Huey and the other actors finally showed up, he jumped to his feet, and didn't say anything to me. Presumably in his narcotic stupor Bree had forgotten that I rejected his late-night phone pleas for help. As soon as Svetlana walked in, they began from the top of act two.

Bree was clearly the weakest runner in this relay race of ensemble acting, but his one stroke of luck was the fact that he had lost the part he originally wanted as Reggie. By default, Bree had gotten Waldo. The role he had stumbled upon was a confused, drugged-out, psychologically tortured insomniac, and it was perfect camouflage. If he performed any of the other roles, his flaws would have been spotted immediately.

Unable to commit anything to memory, Bree sluggishly read from his worn-out, bent-up script. Looking over his shoulder, I could see he had highlighted his lines over and over in bright yellow Magic Marker and underlined them multiple times in red pen. He seemed to be punishing the words into his memory, by repeatedly marking up his text. His margins were heavily annotated. Next to one dramatic line, I read: "SAY IT SADLY ASSHOLE!"

The steady strain of microscopic self-scrutiny was compelling him to unwind. I had seen it all before. It wasn't the work per se, but the anxiety of failing, of dropping a line or a cue. And the only break from anxiety for an addict were his drugs. During rehearsal that day, whenever he screwed up, Huey would softly rustle his newspaper. Nothing more.

Despite my effort to resist, I truly found myself feeling for Bree. At the age of twenty-four, he was burned with serious addictions, yet he still clung to this noble dream of being an actor. Clearly, though, his hold was slipping.

Over the next few days at rehearsals, Svetlana's assistant, Aldo, also showed up. He had a copy of the script that he read along with everyone else. It wasn't until I looked over his shoulder the following week and saw that he had underlined the Waldo part that I realized his real purpose there. Like me, he was waiting for his chance. But where I constantly fidgeted, knowing in my heart of hearts that I'd never get up on the boards, he seemed a lot more confident. Like a polite grim reaper he was just biding his time, waiting to collect the fallen role.

Since I always felt like a third wheel coming to the rehearsals, I'd chronically arrive a bit late. That way I didn't have to talk to anyone except Svetlana. During that week, I begrudgingly felt a quiet thrill in watching the play come to life—the actors were clearly getting more comfortable in their roles. Even Baxter's hash-slinging direction began looking good. However, the splendor of creation only added to my pain of not being a part of it. To avoid any patronizing kindness, I'd sneak out just before the sessions were over so I wouldn't have to hear any consoling tones.

On Thursday of the following week, I arrived a bit early to catch Huey and Noah alone.

"So," Huey asked tensely, "when exactly are we going to begin rehearsing at the theater?"

"I'm going to have to get back to you on that one," Noah replied cordially. At that very moment I knew that he had said the wrong thing. If Noah had provided some confident lie, then Huey would have shut up, particularly since Svetlana wasn't there to retain any details. However, the great English prima don invariably saw ignorance as something to probe.

"What exactly are the dimensions of the stage?" Huey tested Noah, who silently shrugged. "How many light instruments are there? What are the acoustics like?" and finally, "When exactly can I look at the space?"

Noah looked across the room at me with muted terror in his eyes. At that instant I felt glad to be out of this doomed loop. I finally heard the professional extra sputter, "I think the others are probably more in the know than I am."

"'More in the know'?" Huey repeated thunderously. "That's not even a proper phrase!"

As Edith and Mike entered together, Huey Baxter battered them with the same questions, only this time he was infuriated. Edith stared blankly at the far wall, as though someone had unplugged her. Mike's eyes lit up with the word *Help*. Just then Belinda tumbled in.

"Belinda, dear!" Huey charged at her. "What are the fucking dimensions of the NYRR?"

"I'm not sure," she uttered in fear and turned around to the chorus of contorted faces. Her voice lilted into a peep and she asked, "Hannah?"

"Don't ask me," I said delicately. "I'm just the understudy."

"Where the hell is Svetlana?" the director roared in frustration.

"She's coming late today," I volunteered. It was revenge of the understudy and I loved it.

Turning to Noah, Huey marched up to him, and digging a fat finger into his barreled chest, he overenunciated, "I am not rehearsing a fucking syllable today until I get those fucking dimensions! And an exact date!"

Noah tiredly fished a quarter out of his pocket and went to a pay telephone in the corridor. After ten incredibly strained minutes, in which Huey stared into the Arts Section of the *New York Times*, I snuck out and found Noah holding the phone to his ear, probably contemplating suicide.

"What the fuck are you doing?" I whispered.

"What can I do!" he hissed back. "I tried calling the theater but no one's there!"

I took a piece of paper and pen from my bag and drew a large rectangle, then I scribbled fictional dimensions. Throughout the large rectangle, I wrote a series of numbers referring to the various lighting instruments:

At the bottom of the page I wrote:

Different lights and their locations:

1. (5) beamlights 2. (2) fresnels 3. (3) floods 4. (1) profile 5. (1) P.C.

When I could think of nothing more to add, I handed it to Noah and said, "Give this to Huey. And tell him we'll have the space in three weeks, pronto!"

Noah raced back inside and handed Huey the sacred diagram, just as Svetlana and Aldo strolled in the door.

"Finally!" Huey yelled out, looking the page over. "All right, I'm going to call them later to make sure this isn't bullshit. But for now let's get started."

Deciding to exploit his pissy mood, Huey skipped ahead from what he was scheduled to direct to the final passionate denouement of the play when the group discovers that Waldo, who seemed to be permanently stuck on tilt, had secretly written a two-thousand-page epic.

The group of frustrated writers react furiously, each for their own private reason. But Kenny Eltwood's character, Reggie, who up until now was the most understanding of the blocked writers in the group, provides the volcanic eruption for everyone. He destroys the diskette containing Waldo's unexamined masterpiece and then physically attacks the frail writer, played by Bree.

The only problem was that Bree, and he alone, was still not off-book. This was where the play moved at a terrifying pace and the young addict was visibly being dragged by the rapid-fire exchanges with the others. In fact, he was trembling and sweating while the other actors were clearly growing fed up.

Huey, however, was unusually restrained. Even while looking at the actors, he'd have the newspaper open across his lap. Each time Bree dropped a line or forgot a note, Huey grew a little more tense, crinkling his *New York Times* audibly to show his displeasure.

Before Bree could attempt his big monologue, Svetlana whispered to Baxter that there were only twenty minutes left to today's session.

"Tomorrow, Bree, I want you to perform this scene off-book, no fucking around—yes?"

Bree nodded fearfully, grateful for his momentary reprieve. Within minutes, everyone grabbed their belongings, and equally relieved, all silently headed home.

27

Dragged Through It

HUEY'S TRUEST GIFT wasn't directing but mind-fucking. Perhaps this was the quintessence of the craft. I had no doubt that Baxter could convince young computer geeks to castrate themselves and join him in an invisible spaceship, or that he could persuade a community to give up their lives for him in a fortified Texas compound. He balanced egomaniacal charm with pathological terror. When the first failed, he slowly summoned the second.

At that moment I came up with my own plan: If I could get Bree and his permission agreement, I could take the play to Manny Greene and attempt to have him produce it under the proviso that I play Samantha. Bree was the wild card, yet fortunately he was most inclined to find Huey unbearable.

I called him around eleven o'clock that night. He picked up before the first ring and shrieked incomprehensibly into the mouthpiece.

"Relax, Bree, it's me. How are you doing?"

"What the fuck do you think I'm doing! I'm studying my fucking lines!"

"Just inhale, exhale and relax."

He did so and said, "If you only knew."

"Don't overdo it," I advised. "You'll be too frazzled for tomorrow."

"If you only knew," he repeated weirdly, "if I could only tell you the real truth behind all this," he said weirdly.

"What is the real truth?" I asked.

"The real truth is tomorrow is going to be the scariest fucking day of my awful fucking life."

"It doesn't have to be," I assured him.

"I'm not dropping out of the play," he shot back.

"That wasn't my suggestion."

"What's your suggestion?"

"That you and I *vamos*—I know a big producer. We can take this to someone else and get a decent director."

"No fucking way."

"Why not?" I asked. "You and I are both being cut from this group, and we're the ones who started it. Think about it."

"You're an understudy and I'm not being cut," he replied.

"But suppose you are?"

"I can't."

"Look, the agreement is in your name. I'll wait until you go through a good detox program, then we can go to Manny Greene and—"

"I got to get back to studying my lines!"

"But—"

"I *can't*!" he screamed.

I slammed the phone down angrily, and deciding I didn't want to get further pissed, I unplugged it and put a pillow on the answering machine. His behavior made no sense. Nothing did. After a troubled sleep, I awoke the next morning and listened to two messages on my machine from the night before. The first message was from Cynthia Pumilla, who informed me that in two days they were shooting my final nude scene. She specified that this was the movie-within-the-movie sequence—a tasteful lesbian seduction. Making Stein's film had turned into some strange form of Dante's *Inferno* where I felt I was doomed to play out all the lascivious acts I had ever committed while trying to make it in this godforsaken industry.

The second message was from my supervisor at Moe, Larry and Curly's. They wanted me to help at another law firm in Midtown. Feeling tired and demoralized, I took a shower and dressed with the radio on. While listening to the news, I heard another terrorist alert warning had been issued by the attorney general. I never could figure out the color level. Still, the subways were perfect targets for anthrax, and tall buildings were still available for kamikaze planes. Unfortunately I had to take the shuttle to what would probably be a tall building in Midtown.

When I arrived at the reported address, I stood and stared up in trepidation. I was supposed to work at over seven hundred feet above sea level, on the seventy-third floor of a wavy, shiny new skyscraper on Sixth Avenue. It looked like a huge, mirrored bowling pin just waiting to be knocked down. I just couldn't bring myself to step into the lobby.

I kept remembering how very few people above the floors where the planes hit—the ninetieth floor in Tower One, and the sixtieth floor in Tower Two—made it out alive. Initially this boggled my mind; why didn't people just walk down the stairs and exit the buildings? Subsequently I had read how only one of the three stairways in the south tower was passable from above the floor of the impact; only a couple people made it down. Even if you could see through the pitch black, and hold your breath in the thick smoke, and find your way along the maze of corridors and stairs as water rushed behind you, even if you could hastily move down that obstacle course of fifty-plus floors—this alone being a difficult feat for most—who could've guessed that those twin colossi were going to crash down? Not me. Sitting at your desk and waiting for help seemed smarter and safer.

I stood outside on the street and wondered how I was going to make it through that day. Finally I grabbed a cab back home. In the medicine cabinet, I located Thelma Derchoch's tranquilizers. I grabbed them and in a cab back to the shiny bowling pin, I snapped one of her pills in half and swallowed it. Then I put on my screensaver smile, walked through the immaculate lobby, signed in and rode the elevator to the seventy-third floor. I spent the day trying not to screw things up, just functioning on autopilot. The hours passed slowly and woozily. By five o'clock I raced out of the building so quickly papers twirled in the air.

That night, I dragged myself down to the hellish depths of Saint Barnabas a half an hour late. Everyone was silently engrossed in the latest crisis. Huey was trying to direct the final dramatic confrontation between Kenny and Bree. The young actor, though, was not in the best of shape. I could see that he was already sweating. Boldly, he wasn't holding his script.

The first run-through started slowly and though Bree twisted and only mangled some of his lines, he was actually working from memory. Huey ordered another run-through, this time giving him more notes. Again Bree dropped and tortured yet more lines, but he was hanging on for dear life.

"Pick up the pace," Huey said, opening his trademark newspaper. The actors ran their lines until Bree would get stuck. Sometimes Svetlana would cue him, or he'd just improvise and keep going. Slowly his shirt soaked through with perspiration. Smoke seemed to come from his ears, and he kept slipping back to a slower cadence.

"I said pace!" Huey shouted, just as Bree slowly seemed to be getting into it. The director looked out over the Metro Section. "Try it again."

Again the actors began the scene. It was actually sort of touching. No one really wanted to work with Bree, but now they couldn't abandon him in his time of need. I watched both Edith and Mike, stealing nervous glances to make sure Huey wasn't watching as they mouthed lines and slightly nudged him along in the blocking. Even Kenny, who was supposed to be having a violent confrontation with him, had lightened up. Finally, Huey glimpsed up.

"What is this! The Special Olympics of acting?" he shrieked, tearing his newspaper in half. Stepping up to Kenny, he asked, "Do you think you're doing him a bloody favor? What are you going to do when you're on the stage in a few weeks?"

"I just thought he could ease into it gradually," Kenny said quietly.

"Step aside," Huey said, deciding to try his own brand of tough-love directing. He was going to take Kenny's place as Reggie and do the scene the way it had to be done. The director told Bree, "We're taking it from the top and going to go to the end. If either of us fucks up, just improvise, okay, kid?"

Bree held his index finger in the air for a moment, and closing his eyes, he seemed to retreat to some strong, comfortable place deep inside himself.

Looking over Svetlana's shoulder at the script, I perused the final part of the lengthy scene:

REGGIE: Where does a little pimple like you come off writing all those pages? Whenever it was your turn to read (*mocks WALDO's voice*) Sorry pals, I didn't write nothing today.

WALDO: It's therapy, asshole.

REGGIE: Making money is great therapy.

WALDO: That is a private journal. My psychiatrist recommended I keep it to control my depression.

REGGIE: Did he fuck you too?

WALDO: Fuck you!

(*REGGIE punches him in the face and jumps on top of him.*)

REGGIE: Admit it! That's why you've been acting so weird all night, isn't it! (*WALDO struggles, as REGGIE pins him down.*) Say it! Say it! You got AIDS!

It was a powerful end. Bree took several quick breaths, which seemed to tie him to the mast, then to Baxter he said, "Okay, ready."

The piece started at a tense point and moved steadily higher. Baxter set the pace and Bree clung on, counterpunching his lines along the way. I was surprised that Huey had committed all Kenny's lines to memory, but when it was evident that Bree was rising to the occasion, the director took it up a notch, improvising, and inserting verbal jabs that targeted Bree personally. For a couple lines, Bree gave witty repartee. Then he started getting jumbled, stuttering, trying to recover into the script. But Huey wasn't letting him back in. Instead he kept mocking the way he blathered. As the end approached, Huey, still in the character of Reggie, grabbed the thin thespian and started shaking him. During what should have been the crescendo, Huey actually shoved him, knocking Bree to the ground.

"Hey!" Edith rose, intervening, but it didn't matter. The scene was done.

The poor guy rose, rubbing his back where he landed.

"Bree!" Huey pronounced with a sneer, "an appropriate name for a big cheese."

"I just don't feel well today," he sputtered back.

"Oh, you're not well, my young friend. But I'm going to tell you what you should do to get well." Huey marched up to him. "I want you to go to whoever the fuck told you you could act, and slug him as hard as you can." He lowered his voice, almost sympathetically, " 'Cause he abused you, boy. The man gave you false hopes and cruel dreams."

"What an asshole," Bree muttered.

Huey whispered something, compelling Bree to shout, "No! You can't."

"I just did."

"Well, I'm not going," Bree said frantically.

"Then you'll all be needing a new director, because we both can't be in this play," Huey said loud and clear.

"Fine," Bree said twitchingly, then yelled, "I have the rights!"

"Bree!" Svetlana screamed at him. It was one of the few times I had heard her shout.

Bree staggered out into the hallway, trying to catch his breath and hold back his tears. I raced out after him and before he dashed up the stairs, I called out, "We can go elsewhere! Don't you understand?"

"*No we can't! This is it!*"

The Awful Truth

A · MOMENT · AFTER Bree dashed off, I was about to exit when I felt four gentle fingers press squarely on my lower back.

"Could you stick around?" Edith said. "We're having a meeting after Huey leaves." For a moment I considered the ridiculous possibility of dressing in drag and assuming Bree's now-vacant role.

"Ladies and gentlemen," Huey said as we reentered, "I am going back to merry old England for three glorious days. There are two pressing items that need to be ironed out before my triumphant return. We need a new and brilliant Waldo, and in order to start polishing this production, we have to get into the New York Romper Room. Study your lines, and I'll see you in a few days." With his poison sacs empty and his fangs retracted, he slithered out the door with Kenny and Svetlana skipping in his wake. The rest of us remained silent until Mike said, "I can't believe he hit Bree."

"It looked a lot worse than it was," Edith said.

"I don't think he should have the right to fire Bree," Noah said, surprising me that he was willing to stand up to the bully. Then I sensed he probably feared that his head was next on the chopping block.

"It's all done now," Belinda said, displaying her profound sense of humility. "The only thing we have to worry about is finding an adequate theater space."

It felt good not having to be the one to lead the questions, let alone come up with the answers.

"Huey is going to kill us when he discovers that we lied about NYRR," Edith said, "and Svetlana has been trying to get us to find a new space."

"This never should have happened," Mike replied, looking directly at Noah. He vocalized what we all felt. It was blame time and Noah never should have given Huey the illusion that we had a theater.

"We all have to work around the clock to try to find something," Belinda said with alarming gusto, having done almost nothing else for the entire production since her reappearance and pushing me out of my role.

"You think so," Noah said sarcastically.

"Yeah, I want us all to meet at my place tomorrow," Belinda declared with an unprecedented take-charge attitude.

"Nothing personal, but I'm too old to go to Williamsburg," Mike said. "Let's meet at my place."

We all compromised on a time—three o'clock on Saturday.

I walked out the door last with Edith as she said, "This whole thing is turning into a big goddamned mess, I see that now." Under thick, cloudy skies, we silently parted.

Around midnight, the rain started falling. Lightning split the sky. Feeling safe in my warm bed, not having to worry about this fiasco, I drifted off to sleep. When the phone rang, I let the machine get it. In a semi–dream state, to the background of a driving rain, I could faintly hear Bree weeping: "I need help . . . and that bastard. That fucking bastard . . . and that cunt! They forced me out! And the whole thing was my idea in the first place! That's why I couldn't . . ."

I got up, turned down the volume of my answering machine and lay back in bed until it ran its three-minute length and clicked off. Then a moment later, as I tried to resubmerge into sleep, it clicked on again, and three minutes later, off. Back on again. In my sleepiness, I lost track of whether he was talking or not. The rain was coming down in sheets, pattering on my windows. With a thunderhead directly above my building, the lightning exploded like artillery shells. I finally turned the volume of my answering machine up for a second, to hear the son of a bitch weeping, "Svetlana betrayed me. . . . She was the one . . ."

I picked and hung the phone up on him and decided to turn my machine off, but I accidentally hit the Play button instead. That's when I heard Bree's recorded lament, "She didn't just con me—she conned us all! I'm telling you, she's fucking brilliant! She got a copy of the galleys of that book and saw that *Unlubricated* was a lost play by that Bull dyke and she just wrote it out, draft after draft. I was the one who came up with the rest of it, but . . ."

The phone rang again. I snatched it off the cradle.

"Bree?"

"Yes," he said, startled, expecting my machine.

"Where are you?"

"Home, but—"

"Give me your address." He did—Little Italy.

"I'm on my way."

I pulled a coat over my pj's, yanked my shoes on and dashed down the stairs. There was an unbelievable storm outside. The downpour was so severe when I got to the street it felt as though I were underwater in a pool filled with bubbles. As I sloshed around looking for a taxicab, it was almost difficult to breathe through all the water. When I finally got one on Ninth Avenue, we submarined south and east to Bree's place on Mott and Spring.

The lock on his front door was broken, as were all the doorbells. I dashed right up the worn marble slab steps to his front door, which was ajar. Bree was holding a liquor bottle, sitting against a wall in the middle of an unfurnished studio apartment that was completely strewn with garbage. Old newspapers, food wrappers, clothes, and other clutter littered the floor. The young man had never picked up so much as a sock. I could see him shaking. His face was streaked with dried tracks of tears.

"Are you telling me," I launched right into it, "that *Unlubricated* was not written by Lilly Bull!" I dripped all over the top layer of his debris.

He nodded and took a swig from a half-empty bottle of Absolut.

"This whole thing is one big con job!"

"I thought you were Barbara Suffolk at that fucking party," he explained.

"What are you saying?"

"That night at Stein's party, I thought instead of just pitching it, if she thought she was eavesdropping on me, I figured she might be interested and . . ." He sniffled and wiped the last of his tears away.

"You . . . conned . . . me!"

How the fuck did I get myself in the middle of this bullshit! But gradually, as though I were looking down at myself, exhausted, soaked and cold, in a filthy apartment in Little Italy in the middle of the night, realizing I had been hoodwinked by an addict to produce a play, and to be pushed out of my role by a company who brought in a madman to direct them, the complete absurdity of it all came pushing through. I started giggling and soon I couldn't stop. It was absolutely, insanely hilarious. The laughter flowed into Bree. He too started laughing.

"I didn't even know you were at the fucking party," he said through gasps, "and when Suffolk finally passed on it, I just figured you were the only one interested. . . ."

Suddenly a closed door flew open and some crazy-looking bushman leaped out, totally naked. "I am trying to fucking sleep!" he screamed. His curly afro and beard were as long and spiky as the wig around his pubis. "All night I had to hear him crying! Now you!" The bushman pointed at me.

"Sorry, we'll keep it down," Bree said, and the naked, long-haired freak turned around and slammed his door behind him.

"What was that?"

"Jerry, my roommate," Bree replied.

I laughed some more, as did he.

"You know, the sad part is, it's a great play," I finally said. "I just can't believe someone so diabolical would be capable of writing something so sharp and compassionate."

"She's not diabolical!" Bree shouted. "I mean, she wrote it, but it was my idea to get you to produce it." Now the picture was complete. It took two half-wits to create a fuckup of this magnitude.

"Some of this is also my fault," I said. Even though I was targeted for this con, who else would have acted on it? "You were talking on your cell phone, I had no right listening in."

"Hell, I don't even have a cell phone, I was talking into my wallet." He pulled it out and pressed it to his face.

"After Barbara Suffolk turned you down, why didn't you go to a real producer?"

"For starters, you really are a producer. I watched you in college, and I never saw someone take so little and make it go so far." I wasn't sure if I was being complimented or insulted.

"Also," he resumed, "we kind of got cold feet and saw you as insurance. I mean, if this whole thing came apart, anyone else would've called the police. We needed someone who wouldn't sue or have us put away."

I was already leaning against the wall of his filthy living room, so it was a short slide down to the floor next to him. He handed me the bottle. Although vodka backwash was not my drink of choice, I took a long, deep swig. This was the funniest thing I had ever experienced—even if I was the butt of the joke. And it all worked out perfectly up to a very precise point, which was my next question: "How exactly did you get a theatrical agreement from the Bull Estate?"

"I didn't. Svetlana wrote it up," he confessed, confirming my suspicion. He added, "And now that fucking bitch wants me out."

"Now this is where I'm confused. She's just the stage manager. You got the bogus permission statement in your name." I took another swig. "I mean, tonight, instead of allowing yourself to be dumped by her, why didn't you just take my offer? We could've cut her and everyone else loose, and taken the play to Manny Greene."

"Because Svetlana and I made a deal."

"What deal?"

"She knew someone might replace her as stage manager and I knew someone might dump me, so we agreed that if either of us got cut, the show would go on as long as the other remained in it. We agreed not to fuck it up for each other. This was our agreement. And now fucking Huey wants me out."

In other words, honor among thieves.

"Do you think she deliberately cut you out?"

"No," he said, begrudgingly, "but she could've stood up for me. She could've agreed to pull the plug on the production."

"Is that what you agreed to?"

"No."

"So she's sticking to your original agreement?"

"Yeah, but there's more to it. Huey is such a scumbag. He approached me from the beginning and offered me money and everything else to take possession of the play. He said I wasn't making the grade as an actor, but if I agreed to go with a new production he'd make it easy for me. Otherwise he was going to treat me like everyone else."

"So what'd you tell him?"

"I told him I would, but I couldn't do it to you."

"To me?" I replied. "Why? Who the hell am I?"

"I said . . . I told him . . . I said we were lovers in college."

"Lovers?!" It just got better and better.

"I needed someone to defer to," he explained. Now I knew why Ken and Huey kept trying to squeeze the consent out of me.

"I could've fucked Svetlana over and gone with him, but I didn't," he explained.

"He probably would've brought Svetlana along with him anyway," I pointed out.

"No, I asked him if he would and he said he had someone else in mind."

I silently nodded my head at the festering mess of it all. Then I rose in my wet shoes and soaking overcoat, and headed out before the roaches and mice could consume me. The storm had subsided. Looking downtown, I saw the two powerful beacons of light that were commemorating the missing towers. The square beams went right up like two elevator shafts to the heavens. After I hailed a cab back up to Hell's Kitchen, after the hot shower, and ten minutes of exfoliating, I threw back three fingers of NyQuil with a Valium chaser, and went back to sleep.

THEATER ROW

I · AWOKE · LATE Saturday morning with congested sinuses, a low-grade fever and a general fatigue. The freezing rain, the stress and recent sleeplessness had conspired into a healthy case of influenza. I just lay in bed numbly, wondering exactly how I was going to break the awful news of the phony play to everyone. In addition to this, tonight I was supposed to do my final scene in Stein's film. I took three vitamin Cs, two Motrins, one echinacea with goldenseal, and washed it down with the last mug of Dr. Wang's bitter mix.

Looking in the bottom of the cup, I saw the exoskeleton of a large insect, and realized with horror that a cockroach must have crawled into the mix. I was about to put my finger to the back of my throat, but then seeing several other insect segments, I realized that this multilegged creature was a deliberate ingredient in Wang's age-old mix.

I steamed in a hot shower, trying to visualize how I was going to tell the others that the Lilly Bull vehicle was a fraud. We were all supposed to meet at Mike's place at three P.M. for the great theater hunt. I rehearsed it aloud, "The play was a phony, the production is off, sorry." Beneath my regret, though, was a slight sadistic pleasure that came with having been cut out of the show. On the other hand, if I was still in the play, I probably would've thrown Bree out the window of his filthy apartment last night.

All the hopes and dreams of success and recognition for five young actors were about to go down the drain along with the thousands of investment dollars they couldn't afford, the countless hours of humiliation and suffering at the ruthless hands of Huey Baxter, and time they could've spent on fruitful endeavors. The only thing to do was break it to them gently.

That led to the next question: punishment against Bree and Svetlana. Bree was right, I didn't have the heart to call the police on them, but what they had done was beyond awful.

At precisely that point my doorbell rang. I called down over the intercom to hear Svetlana's distinct voice say, "I just spoke to Bree and I was hoping we could talk."

It was like having a quiet next-door neighbor who turned out to be a serial killer. I was forced to reconsider all the details I remembered about her. Svetlana was a tall girl with a stiff back, broad shoulders and plain features. Her long flat hair and honest eyes stood out when I looked at her. Those direct eyes and her usually expressionless face conspired with her calm monotonous voice to inspire trust.

When she entered my apartment and closed the door behind her, I couldn't contain myself. "How dare you! How could you do such a thing?"

"I didn't," she replied rigidly, "Bree did."

"Give me a break. That half-wit can't even get up in the morning. You wrote the play and you knew all this was happening."

"I've been writing plays since I was a girl. . . ."

"Whose plays?"

"Mine."

"Yeah, right. Have you been doing bogus rights statements too?"

"It was just too difficult to get them produced."

"Difficult maybe, but it's not impossible. And you actually wrote a wonderful play. Hell, I think *Unlubricated* is better than anything Bull ever wrote."

"I wrote a better play before this one. It was a full-length drama about the Clinton administration, covering everything from Whitewater to the Monica Lewinsky scandal and his impeachment. I sent that to every theater listed in *Dramatists Sourcebook*, every festival, every contest from Alaska to Hawaii. I submitted it to over two hundred companies. Afterward I was so pissed I destroyed it."

"I'm sorry to hear that but—"

"Some people have all the luck at getting produced, some get publicity, and some poor bastards are just good writers."

"Lilly Bull had a horrible life," I replied. "She was confined to a mental institution, she whored herself and died in poverty—that's not lucky." Svetlana let out a sigh as I concluded, "Despite that, though, doesn't it bother you that even if this whole escapade worked, someone else would have gotten your credit?"

"I didn't do this for money, and I'd hate to be famous."

"What do you think is going to happen when the Bullonus Estate is confronted with their first check and they're told one of Lilly's plays has been produced?"

"Initially they'll probably have a fit because they weren't notified. But once they read it and see that it's a good play, particularly after they get the first royalty check—because the principal beneficiary to the estate, Estelle, is broke—they'll validate the ownership and just take the cash."

"Or maybe, once it became a hit, you'd suddenly stand up and claim you wrote it," I suggested. That would be how I'd play it if it were my scam.

"That wouldn't work," she replied, suggesting that she had given thought to the idea. "Critics and theatergoers would be so disgusted they'd either attack it or ignore it."

"I'm not so sure."

"Think about it," she replied. "If you heard someone had pulled a number like this, exploiting a poor dead writer, would you go see the play? Even if it was the greatest work ever written, I'd boycott it on principle." I wasn't sure if she was right, but I knew that she sincerely believed it.

"And it'd fuck up your name for life—you know that?"

"Of course."

"What about future plays you might write?" I argued. "I mean, you're young. Do you think you can keep finding undiscovered masterpieces by dead playwrights? I'm sure there's a whole body of works you can produce."

"I sold my laptop," she said, as though the machine were the true culprit.

"Do you really think you can keep a talent like this bottled up in you?"

"I swear I'll never do it again." And to lock in her promise, she added, "If I ever write another word, I'll cut my fingers off."

I just stared at her in shock until a single tear finally broke free and streamed down her cheek. This was one weird situation. Though I had been conned, what did she gain from it?

If her play won an Obie, or if it went to Broadway and then was made into a movie, Svetlana wouldn't see a cent of money, not a single congratulations. All the credit would go to Lilly Bull. What was the point? The most she could hope for would be her salary as a stage manager. I tried explaining all this to her, in hope that she'd see reason and confess to the group by herself, without my intervention. But none of it mattered. She still wanted to keep the production going.

"Look, Svetlana, even if I don't say anything, even if I betray all my friends, there's no guarantee of what will happen once we put this up. We'll have gambled thousands of dollars on a production and the estate will initially order an injunction until they review things, or worse, they might sue us all."

"I planned on getting permission for the play before it goes up," she revealed.

"How? The Bullonus Estate is going to check the manuscript and discover that it's not authentic."

"Let me worry about that," she replied.

"Even if I did trust you, what about Bree?"

"Don't worry about it," she said. "I took care of him."

"What do you mean?"

"He's been paid off," she said coldly. "I guarantee he's nothing to worry about."

"Look," I returned to my original indignation, "I'm pissed that you suckered me into it."

"Hannah, this production could happen. It will happen. I can get the permission and it will go up. It'll get great notices and you will just be robbing yourself and your friends of a major opportunity." She leaned close and touched my hand. "This is an opportunity that comes about once in a lifetime. Are you aware of that?"

"You're not listening to me—they're going to spot this as a phony."

"I'll tell you what," she finally said. "Give me a few weeks, just a few weeks. By then if I don't get permission from the Bullonus family I'll pull the plug myself. It's a fair gamble," she added in a whisper, as though they were my own thoughts. "After all, if this play hits, all the actors will get great reviews."

"Why don't you make your offer to the group?" I countered.

"No!" she shot back. "I can't. They're not like you."

"What do you mean, not like me?"

"They're actors!"

"What are you talking about?" I replied. "I'm an actor too."

"I mean . . . they're naive. You never would've picked an idiot like Huey for this production. That's what I mean." She didn't need to say anything else.

"Look," I explained, "I can't allow them to take that gamble without letting them know what they're getting into. I mean, we're reaching a point where we are going to put down a deposit on a theater and I'm not even talking about costumes, props, sets . . ."

"All right, here it is," she counter-offered. "If we don't get the permission, I will compensate them out of my own pocket. I have the money. I didn't tell you this but my father is a successful import-exporter. I'll get a loan from him."

I nodded my head in regret. She didn't know what she was getting into. A father was ten times worse than a loan shark because even after you paid him, he collected I-told-you-sos until his dying day.

"I'm sorry," I finally responded. "Feebleminded as they are, and as much as they've let me down, these people are my friends. They trust me and it's unfair to place them at risk."

"Listen to me," she appealed desperately, "just give me a few weeks and in addition to covering your expense, if it all fails, I'll give you five thousand dollars regardless of what happens. Simple as that!" It would only be enough to unmax one of my credit cards.

"You're already guaranteeing your salary if I don't get a role," I reminded her, even though I never intended to collect.

As if that statement somehow undermined her sincerity, she opened her checkbook on my desk, took out a pen, and proceeded to scribble out a check.

"Svetlana, please stop this now," I said, exasperated as I retreated toward my desk. "You are an extremely talented writer and it truly saddens me to say this, but I just can't. . . ."

She slumped forward silently, catching herself on my desk for support. Below her extended hand was the latest incarnation of Christy's creaky screenplay. This was where my own private little greed suddenly surged. I looked at her holding the half-written check, hopeless.

"All right, here's the deal. Keep your money. I'll give you some time to get the permission agreement. If you don't get it, you take all the blame, and cover everyone's losses. But in return I want you to rewrite this as best as you can." I pulled Christy's script up and handed it to her.

"A film script?" She read the title page in shock.

"Yeah, the story is already there. It just needs some doctoring. . . ."

"But"—she looked at me bewildered—"rewrite a film script?" The concept didn't seem to sink in. It was as though she was from the seventeenth century.

"Yeah, just make it conform to these notes," I said, sliding Manny Greene's pages out from under the text.

"But . . . I've never done a film script."

"It has got to be easier than a play. You can have car chases and sex in airplanes and stuff like that."

"But I've never had to make anything conform to anything else before."

"Look, this is my final offer. Take it or leave it."

"Suppose I come up with a better idea than is in the notes?" she asked. "Then what am I supposed to do?"

"Work within the basic characterizations and themes. And don't forget that this is a film. It should be visual, easy to follow and sappy as possible. Also," I quickly tagged on, "since I don't believe you're going to get permission, and I have no intention of throwing away thousands of my own money, you'll have to cover my percentage of the production."

She looked at me dumbfounded, so I added, "But I'll make sure you get all your money back if the play goes up and makes any money."

"Okay," she agreed tiredly, "but I'll still need your full commitment in coproducing it. I need help and you're the only person I can trust."

"What the hell," I replied tiredly.

She hugged me, kissed me, grabbed the screenplay and dashed out. I sat there feverishly tingling at the prospect of having a hot script for Christy while wondering what more I was getting myself into.

30

THE PRODUCER

AFTER SVETLANA LEFT, I realized that my sense of moxie was uncharacteristic even for me. It came from a strange light-headedness—nothing felt real. When I passed my hand before my eyes, it blurred as if the hand had a meteoric tail. When I touched my sweaty forehead, I discovered that I was burning up. When I laid back down in bed, I seemed to slip into a strange new reality just below this one: I lived in a world of kindness and love where everyone was on the same level so there was no competition, no envy, jealousy or greed. The downside was, though no one was a failure, no one was really successful either.

Upon waking hours later, I realized I was twenty minutes late for Belinda's big theater scavenger hunt. Although I still felt miserable, I dressed and caught the train down to Mike's place. As I entered, Svetlana was already in mid-discussion. Seated next to her was Bree's replacement, Aldo Finegold. Everyone said hello as I entered and Svetlana resumed speaking: ". . . in addition to the fact that Huey wants him out, Bree's missed more rehearsals than anyone else and was still unable to get off-book."

"I just don't like the fact that he made the decision without first consulting us," Noah argued against Bree's expulsion.

"But he was right to do it," Edith took Svetlana's argument. "He was bringing the play down."

"Getting back to the main point, no one objects to Aldo?"

After a brief silence, the resolution seemed to pass. Although Bree was never a part of our group, none of them even remembered that he was allegedly the one who had the rights statement in his name. I didn't rock the boat. I was too busy trying to stay awake, wiping my runny nose and sweaty brow.

Belinda rose next. To our general amazement we learned that she had made full use of the Internet and the phone book, compiling a comprehensive list of every decent, mid-range theater that was available in Manhattan with ninety-nine seats or less. She divided the list into four parts and each of us were expected to call roughly twelve theaters apiece and try to haggle for a three-to-four-week mini-contract beginning in two to three weeks. We figured that our maximum budget would be three grand a month, which was embarrassingly little.

"Can't you pitch this to your producer friend now?" Edith asked me. All eyes turned pleadingly toward me.

"He specifically said we have to put it up and get good reviews first," I replied. Unlike the rest of them I knew Manny Greene would spot that the estate agreement was a fraud. The group talked about other problems for another ten minutes, then we disbanded.

In the hallway, Svetlana hijacked me, making yet another request. "If you just show your producer friend the play, it'll take him a few weeks to decide if he likes it, right?"

"Svetlana," I said through a stuffed nose and a head full of pus, "you're already pushing it."

"I know, and normally I would never ask so much, but in three weeks I'll either have the permission or I won't. And if your producer likes it, we'll have enough money to pay for the theater and it'll all be legitimate." I sighed tiredly. "I mean, I'm really not asking this for me," she added. It was a persuasive remark; I knew everyone was hurting for cash.

I told her I'd think about it. No promises.

Perhaps to throw me a bone, she said she had already began reading the Christy script.

When I got home I found that the dentist had left a message. "If you can't join me for dinner, send me a signed eight-by-ten glossy, because I forgot what you look like. A little joke. Ha ha, ha."

He seemed to also forget that I had broken up with him ages ago. That night I was supposed to perform in Stein's flick, but I couldn't even take a nap because I had to root around for available theaters. Among the stages on my list, I had to call all the prosceniums and black boxes on Little Theater Row along West Forty-second, including the Samuel Beckett Theater and the Harold Clurman, which I discovered had just been torn down.

Since it was a weekend night, the only theaters that even answered the phone were the ones that had shows up. The box-office clerks usually had no idea of the theater's upcoming season, but in this case, since our production dates were less than a month away, most of them knew that their spaces were unavailable. The most common answer was to call back during business hours. When I countered that I needed emergency contact numbers as I required a booking right now, I got some additional numbers, usually to uncaring phone machines. After about two dozen calls over two hours, I dozed off for three hours.

It was seven P.M. when I poured out of bed and trickled along the floor to the kitchen. I blended an envelope of onion soup with a packet of TheraFlu. It tasted strangely Middle Eastern. Then I dressed as best as I could and swallowed some more Cs and echinacea. I packed slippers and a bathrobe, and just as I was about to turn off the light and leave, I noticed my copy of *Unlubricated* sitting on my night table.

What the hell, I thought, and grabbed it. If Svetlana could actually secure the rights, maybe Manny Greene would take out an option just from reading the script. I tiredly plodded down the shaky stairs past the unpainted walls of my old building. On my way out the front door, I noticed something in my mailbox. Among the junk mail to Thelma or "Resident," there was a handwritten letter to me. Ripping it open with an optimistic joy that someone knew I was alive, I discovered that it was a letter from the landlord. In addition to my April's rent check, there was a sloppily written letter:

Hannah Cohn, whoever you are,
You arent no Thelma Derchoch. Wheres she? Im returning your rent to you as its no good to me. Please move out by the end of the month or Ill kick you out myself.
My name is Thomas Hallin and Im the Landlord.

There it was—the final semiliterate wooden stake through my vampire heart. I was being evicted from my coffin. If this wasn't bad enough, instead of going back upstairs to bed, I had to do this final scene in Franklin's film—a gratuitous lesbian flirtation that only a male would write. Push all this out of your head, I kept thinking as my cab headed up Eighth Avenue over to a new film set in an Upper West Side brownstone.

On Eighty-eighth Street between Amsterdam and Columbus all the parking spots were swallowed up by a mobile army of large trucks and dusty Winnebagos. I introduced myself to a production assistant and asked if he knew my assistant, Joey, who I thoughtlessly described as having "bugged-out eyes."

"No, but maybe I can help," he replied and got on the walkie-talkie. After a quick series of radioed questions, he directed me to my Winnebago on the northwest side of the block. There, taped to a door, I read my character's name, Virginia, on a piece of paper. But then I realized I had to get my costume on first, so I located Gilda the wardrobe person, who had a perpetual cigarette dangling between her lips. She checked her clipboard and handed me two boxes, one big, another small. I opened the large one and saw a black Lulu wig pinned onto a small Styrofoam half skull. The smaller box had pink platform shoes. She also gave me two hangers, one with tight black slacks, another with a gauzy white shirt that tied across the midriff.

"Gerty is the hair person. She's on the set. She'll help you put that on."

"You don't know when they're shooting my scene?" I dared to ask.

She repeated the question into her walkie-talkie. Everyone seemed to have one except me. I slouched back in a chair as they bantered back and forth until finally Gilda announced, "Go to your trailer and they'll send someone to get you."

I thanked her and dragged myself back to my Winnebago. Thankfully it had a narrow fold-out cot. I flung myself on it, dropping down into an immediate sleep. An unclear slot of time later, someone was knocking on my door. "Ms. Cohen, you're wanted on the set!"

"That's Cohn," I yelled back tiredly. My last name was always being stretched one syllable too far. I rose, dressed, pulled my slippers on and dragged myself outside. A freezing mist felt good on my feverish skin and sobered me up as I crossed the street to the brownstone. I passed a crew of thirty or so utility belters, people whose names you suffered through in the closing credits of the film if you didn't leave the theater in a timely fashion. A craft table was opened out front, filled with wet cold cuts, soggy bagels and other moist snacks and beverages. Inside the brownstone I was directed to the second floor, the set, a big, queen-size bed. Sitting on it was a queen-size redhead, my thespian lover. Her over-upholstered white breasts pushed out of her blouse like a pair of pink silken throw pillows. She introduced herself as Jane, no last name. She was a nice face, a voluptuous body and not much else. As lights were screwed and focused in place, and cables and electricity and instruments were rerouted, Jane and I chatted.

"I hope it doesn't take too long for the check to come," she said. Then, inspecting her loosely concealed breasts, she volunteered, "I'm planning on getting a boob job."

"Your boobs are great," I replied, wiping my permanently runny nose. If her knockers were any bigger they'd block the sunset in Queens.

"Like Venice," she kidded, "they sink an inch a year. I need a lift."

"I'm getting my ears and tail clipped," I joked back. Either she wasn't amused or didn't get it.

For a while we talked about different operations and which

celebrity had what done, then Jane decided that her energy level was low, so she slipped off to the craft table downstairs. This table of gourmet food, prepared for the principals, was much better than the soggy crap outside. I joined her and we both had chocolate walnut brownies and flavored coffee.

The caffeine and sugar didn't stimulate me, so I found a place to curl up, and, to the pinging sound of a GameBoy that some techie was playing, I drifted to sleep.

Eventually, a P.A. came over and much to my surprise he announced the scene was finally lit. Franklin was looking for me. I returned to the big bed, where Jane was flipping through *Jane* magazine while Franklin and his Latin cinematographer were chatting.

"Did anyone do your wig?" were the first words Franklin said. Considering that the last time I saw him we had become more than friends, I was kind of hoping he'd at least say hi.

In a moment, Gerty was brushing, pinning and clipping a long, silly hair extension on my head. Afterward she kindly knotted the scarf around my neck.

"Let's start with the girls over here," Serge said, pointing at one of the squares on the storyboard. "Have them meet and move onto the center of the sofa and then conclude the scene here." He pointed to another square on the board. "All in a single sweeping shot."

"I know we wrote it that way, but I was thinking it might be easier if . . ." Franklin gave his two cents, and they went back and forth as I drifted off to sleep on the bed.

"Hey! Get up!" Jane was shaking me. Lights were hanging over and around us. A large camera was placed on a tripod before us like a machine gun. It was like going from zero to a hundred in a second. Wide-awake and frantic, Franklin ran me through the scene. I had to approach Jane and make silly remarks ("I could eat you in a single bite"). She had to respond in kind ("So what's keeping you, dollface?"). Then we were supposed to kiss . . . "Cut!" It was supposed to be a snippet from a porn film—no exposition, no subtlety, only idiocy.

"Actually," I interrupted Franklin, "I hate to say this, but I have a cold, and I don't think Jane wants to catch it."

"Fine, just move toward her like you're about to kiss her, then we'll cut."

The only half blessing to my benumbed brain was that the fever removed all self-consciousness.

First was from this angle and with these notes, and that was six takes. Next was just on her face, four takes. The third shot just focused two cameras and a thousand lights on Jane's lunar breasts. Finally, miraculously, the torture was over.

Because every detail of my body was thoroughly controlled and manipulated by Franklin Stein's direction, what I was doing could hardly be called acting. All the slowly acquired method techniques designed to tap and utilize powerful childhood memories, all the late nights we stayed up contemplating the nuances of truly great performances, all the tools we acquired to scrutinize text and investigate character motivations—all of it was pointless.

It would just be a matter of time before all of us would be replaced by computer-generated images, leaving actors the hardest part of the job—as Kenny pointed out—talk shows, award ceremonies, and other publicity stunts.

When we were done, I pulled on my robe and dashed downstairs, where I literally ran smack into Manny Greene.

"Glad to see you," he replied, rubbing his chest where I had walked into him.

"Do you have a moment, there's something I wanted to talk about with you."

"I have to settle a minor union dispute," he said. "Where are you going to be in five minutes?"

"Winnebago number six across the street. My character's name is Virginia."

"See you there."

31

COMPROMISING POSITIONS

I·EXITED·THE·BUILDING, crossed the street in the soft rain, and headed down the block to my trailer, when I heard, "Hey, hold up." It was Franklin, leaning out of some equipment truck, giving instructions to a utility belt.

With a runny nose and fever, I was in no mood to wait in a cold rain. Franklin silently followed me to my trailer. Once we got inside, he stood behind me, where he surprised me with a small gold box.

"You're kidding," I said. It was the same fucking box of chocolates that both Sheldon and Kenny Eltwood had presented to me. I was too tired to laugh.

"The landlord returned my rent check," I shared what was uppermost on my mind as he rubbed his hands around my shoulders, massaging the intricate braid of knotted muscles in my neck. I tried to continue speaking without losing my train of thought. "He wants me to vacate immediately."

"I'm so sorry, honey," he said sympathetically. His hands slowly migrated south down my back.

"It's my own fault," I replied tiredly. "I shouldn't have put my name on the checks."

"You put your name on the checks?" he asked. His hands stopped mid-massage and I felt like an idiot. He seemed to give an exhale of forgiveness and then said, "I'm sure we'll find you another place."

With that comment, his hands seemed liberated from any guile, and moved around cupping my breasts. Before I could shrug him off, the trailer door swung open. Manny Greene stared at Franklin a moment. The hot young director broke free and started laughing awkwardly.

"I can come back," Manny offered as I pulled my robe around me.

"No, no." I didn't want Manny to think I was involved with Franklin. More importantly I wanted to pitch *Unlubricated* now, because soon I would be healthy again and would lose all my light-headed gracefulness.

"I was just leaving," Franklin said and walked out.

With my fever and my nearly naked rain-and-sweat-soaked body, I felt too tired to be embarrassed, even though I must've looked like a tramp with Franklin.

Manny took a seat across from me and asked, "What's up?"

"Well, I don't know if you remember the last time we talked . . .," I began.

"About the Bull play."

"Right," I replied as I fumbled through my belongings for my copy of the script. "I was hoping you could look it over and decide if you want to take out that option before we go into previews."

As I leaned over and handed the play to him, I was aware of him looking down the front of my robe.

A long pause ended with him asking, "You're not having an affair with Franklin, are you?"

There wasn't a hint of judgment in his tone, so I answered honestly, "It's more like a flirtation that's gotten out of hand."

"It's none of my business," he remarked, "but I just heard that he reconciled with Helen and is moving back in with her."

"You're kidding!" I said. Too tired to feel either like an idiot or a cheap slut, I added, "He didn't tell me a thing."

"Weren't you involved with Christy?"

"Yeah, we broke up several months ago," I said earnestly. "We're still dear friends."

"You're a very attractive young woman," he remarked. "And the interesting thing is that so much of your beauty—your strength—really comes from your character."

"What exactly does that mean?"

"It means . . ." he looked to the ground, searching for words, "you have an intelligence that comes right from . . . I don't know, a pragmatism maybe. You can get things done, and you seem to see things clearer than most." He leaned in so that he was inches from me. He lowered his voice to a level of intimacy. "I can see your willpower, your determination to overcome any obstacle. I think you're going to go far, aren't you?"

Of course I was, but that was beside the point. A man like Manny Greene couldn't just say, "Fuck me and you'll get the part." He wouldn't make himself that vulnerable. Greene was offering just a tiny cheese wedge of an opportunity: You had sex with Christy and you got a shot at her film. You probably screwed Franklin and you got this demeaning role. With me you'll go far.

There I was, at that watershed, crossroads, make-or-break moment: to be sleeping with this man, or not to be? That was the question. Though I was sick and exhausted, I carefully measured the question against the only real criterion I ever really addressed: Might I sleep with this person anyway? Franklin and Christy were both young and sexy. But with Manny the answer quickly came back as no. He was older than anyone I had ever slept with. Even though Hollywood films always teamed young females with older males, guys his age invariably reminded me of my father. Unlike most girls who had that Daddy attraction, I had a Daddy disgust. But I was attracted to influence, and no one I had ever slept with exuded nearly as much power in my chosen profession as Manny Greene. Just getting into this degrading situation was an enviable achievement. Although they'd never admit it, I knew that many actresses would trade in their Equity card to be able to have sex with someone who could get them into SAG and make their career. But if I did get intimate with him, would I spend the rest of my life feeling shame or self-loathing?

A handshake, I decided, was all I could safely compromise of myself. So standing up, I shook his hand.

"Thanks," I said.

He smiled and took *Unlubricated*. Then he looked at me with those benevolent dictator eyes of his, smiled, rose, and walked out with the career I always wanted.

That night I went home, slipped into a coma and died. Early the next afternoon I was resurrected by an exuberant Edith, who had located an affordable theater—the Leopold Samyoff Theater in Chelsea. For some reason the place rang a bell but I couldn't remember why. It was a ninety-nine-seat house that had been converted from an old synagogue. Edith explained that an upcoming production of *The Hellmaker* had suddenly canceled when the writer-director, B. Henry Hilton, had abruptly dropped dead. The rental cost was usually two grand a week, with a big discount if rented for a solid month—only four grand. With Hilton's production gone, the leaseholders were panicky about losing the whole month of revenue. No other production would rent the space on such short notice, which meant the theater company would have to pay the rent out of their own shallow pocket. Edith slowly and carefully begged them down to thirty-two hundred dollars for an entire month run. It was eight hundred dollars less than their usual fee, but it was two hundred more than our agreed-upon maximum. If this wasn't bad enough, she had to cough up two grand before the sun set, or the deal was canceled.

All of us were to meet within the hour at Joe Junior's, a greasy spoon on the corner of East Sixteenth Street, to scrape together the whopping deposit. The balance had to be paid upon possession of the theater. I drank a gallon of coffee and stood in a cold shower, letting my skin get wrinkled. I toweled off and pulled on some clothes. After two trains, long waits for each, I was the last of the gang to be seated in a worn Naugahyde booth in the East Side diner. Since Svetlana was technically only the stage manager and not a partner she was not even notified. Except for sneezy me, there was a general mood of relief.

"The only problem is," I explained in a nasal-impacted pitch, "there's no way Huey's going to go for it."

"He'll go for it if it's all he's got," Mike retorted.

"No, he won't," I replied, knowing how arrogant the prick was.

"You're not just saying that because you don't want to pony up the cash?" Noah asked, probably still nervous that his neck might still be in the noose for pulling the original NYRR scam.

"Look, if it's because you're no longer in the cast . . . ," Belinda said.

"Give me a fucking break!"

"For that very reason," Edith said with her standard air of fairness, "I don't think she should have to pay the same amount as the rest of us."

"It's not the money," I said, finding myself with the distinction of being the group's devil's advocate.

"So what is it?" asked Belinda, crawling out of her nook of guilt.

"All I'm saying is that we should first approach Huey and tell him we lost the Romper Room but we got this one. Clear it with him first and then we put the money down. That way there's no risk." It was a simple and practical matter.

"But if we don't put down the deposit by today," Mike replied, "they'll withdraw it."

"Bullshit," I countered, "they're over a barrel and are anxious to close." Turning to Edith, I said, "Say no to their offer and see if they don't call you tomorrow with a better offer."

"For God's sake, Hannah!" Edith shot back. "You want to risk everything to save a couple hundred dollars?"

"I'm not after the couple hundred, I just don't want Huey to leave us holding the bag."

"If we give him a choice," replied Noah, "he'll definitely walk. . . ."

"But this way he doesn't have a choice," Belinda finished Noah's thought because neither of them could come up with a single complete idea.

"Yes, Belinda, he does have a choice," I explained, "he can walk anyway and we'll all be out two grand. Huey is out for Huey. From the onset he's been trying to dump you all and take this production elsewhere."

"You're kidding," Edith said.

"Someone should really shoot the son of a bitch," said Noah.

"I appreciate what you're saying," Mike said, "but I still feel because we're so close to completion that he'll go for it."

"Right," Noah added, "and because we're almost done, if he doesn't go for it, we can put up the play without him."

"And he knows that this is merely a stopover for us to get reviews," Edith added, "and then we shoot over to a bigger house."

Maybe they had a point. He now needed us a bit more than we needed him.

I had read somewhere that up until about a hundred and fifty years ago, writers used to direct their own works. The cult of directors had swelled immensely in this century, probably due to the invention of motion-picture film, when the entertainment industry became producer-centered. Directors usually didn't write the work, they usually didn't act in it, and rarely did they produce it, but their power had somehow eclipsed every other profession of the theater, except perhaps of the star.

Checkbooks were cracked open. My share came to four hundred dollars, for which Svetlana had promised compensation. Edith and Belinda then cabbed back to the Samyoff, where the deal was cut. In roughly two weeks' time we would be the proud owners of a month-long theater lease. I went back home and jumped into bed. When I awoke hours later, I found that Edith had left a message on my machine, saying that we would be able to spend some time at the space a week from Thursday. That was the final performance date of its present play, *Our Town*. The very next day, the show before ours was set to load in. She felt we should just bring Baxter to the space that night and break the news that way.

In the spirit of getting things done, each member of the company was assigned a task. Over the upcoming week, we had to call and find the best and cheapest techie for different aspects of the play. Mike located a designer, who put together a miniature of our set. Edith suggested a costumer, but since we were doing a contemporary play, we decided just to each pick from our own wardrobes and let Baxter decide. Noah got a lighting designer, who would map out the instruments with Huey and talk about filters and gels. Because we were short on funds and the play really didn't require it, we skipped a sound designer.

The only glaring detail that we couldn't afford was a publicist.

32

THE CONSUMMATE ACTOR

THAT EVENING, after we secured the theater, I tried to slumber, but I kept having these panicky dreams that I was falling. They prevented me from falling asleep. I realized the dentist must've returned from his vacation so I broke down and called him.

"What's up?" he asked.

"I was just wondering how the Caribbean was?"

"Dreamy."

"This is a little difficult for me, but I was wondering . . ."

"Just say it."

I explained that I was having panicky dreams and asked if we could just sleep together—no sex.

"Sure."

When I walked into his place, I saw that he had taken the splashy New York paintings off his walls. He had even removed all the little trinkets and figurines that he liked and I had found annoying.

True to his word, he just held me in his tanned arms as I slept like a baby. The next day when he quietly got up, I awoke as well.

"You can stay and sleep," he said, knotting his tie.

"No, I should get home." I got up and slowly started dressing.

While watching him dress and getting ready for work, I sensed something wrong. He didn't seem to be his usual effusive self. Behind his sofa, the paintings were stacked against the wall.

"Why are your canvases back there?"

"No reason."

"There's always a reason."

"I just sensed that you didn't care for them." That was probably why he had removed all the tchotchkes.

"That's no reason to take them down. I mean, everyone's entitled to their own taste."

He shrugged and we went downstairs together. He headed off to work and I grabbed a subway.

When I got home, I called in sick and slept all day, but my presence was required at rehearsal that night. An annoying ride downtown, and I was at Saint Barnabas with a cup of coffee and a pocketful of symptom suppressors. Huey listed all the indignities that he had to suffer in passing through security on the plane ride home, which included the removal and inspection of his prized Bruno Magli shoes.

"So what's the name of the understudy again?" he asked.

"Aldo," Mike said.

"And where is young Aldo?" he asked, looking around at the rest of us.

"Oh," Svetlana said, a little flustered, "I fired him."

"You what!" Belinda shot back, unable to believe her ears. With a cutthroat smile, she inquired, "Who the fuck gave you permission to fire anyone?"

"I did," I said, always glad to undermine Belinda.

"Who the fuck gave you permission?" Huey asked.

"Unless you all fire me, the last I heard I'm still a producer and understudy here." What a tangled web.

"So why exactly did you fire him?" Noah asked. Amid silence and stares, I put my index finger up. "Give me a moment. Svetlana, can I speak to you?" We stepped outside. "Why the fuck did you fire Aldo?"

"Because we can do better."

"Better? Aldo knew all his lines, he took direction. He was fine."

"But the play deserves better. And if this production needs anything, we need recognizable talent." The play was giving her an acutely swollen head. Although I was pissed at putting myself in this situation, it was difficult not siding with her, the anonymous playwright, who had sacrificed so much to get her play up. I chuckled and figured out how I was going to handle this. Going back into the rehearsal space, before the jury of eyes, I simply transplanted my assessment of Huey into Aldo's mouth. "He said you were an incompetent, pretentious, pompous ass, and we found that intolerable."

"God help I should ever run into that little shit," Huey responded, content with the dismissal. No one else contested it. "Now, the other matter I believe we were supposed to iron out is when will I see the Romper Room?"

"Next Thursday at eight," Belinda said eagerly, cutting off the rest of us.

"Fine," Huey replied, and turning to Svetlana, he said, "And by the way, if you expect me to pull another name actor, like Kenny, out of my ass, you're gravely mistaken. You two"—he looked over at me—"are in charge of finding a suitable replacement for Frodo."

"Aldo," Noah corrected.

"Whoever," Huey replied.

"Fine," Svetlana responded. I nodded. That night, we went through rehearsal with her reading the role formerly occupied first by Bree and then Aldo.

Svetlana had already contacted Breakdown Services, a listing of auditions that went out to all agents. By the end of the week, she was sifting through mountains of head shots, then she scheduled three-minute monologue appointments.

After all the work, she narrowed it down to two contenders. The first was the handsome son of a major theater actor from the '60s who was competent, but that was all. The second nominee was Wilson Dove, a young and extremely handsome soap opera actor from *Siblings and Spouses*. He had a TV quotient, meaning he had appeared in several TV shows. The only problem was, by his own admission, he had little theatrical experience and admitted that he needed a lot of time to prepare for the role.

That night, I convinced Svetlana to let me call someone who was a quick study, a good actor and had appeared on TV. The next morning, I tracked down the only man who had ever had sex with me without ever having of an erection, Jonah Baye.

"Are you interested in being in an original play by Lilly Bull? Directed by Huey Baxter and starring Kenneth Eltwood."

"Are you going to be in it?"

"Yeah, but I don't take my clothes off."

"Oh, well, all right," he joked.

"Listen, you got to do me one favor. Don't say a word about the film, particularly that weird scene we did."

"Somehow I sensed you were going to ask me that."

He came in early the next day and did a cold reading that blew all the competition out of the water.

"Do you think he can get up to speed quickly?" Svetlana asked me softly.

"He did the best Hamlet I ever saw on stage, and he was the understudy." Later I asked him, "How soon can you be off-book?"

He looked over the play and said he could be ready within the week. The next day, he came in for his first reading with script in hand and listened carefully to Huey about blocking and motivation.

What an asshole, he mouthed to me. After his second rehearsal, Jonah was off-book and he knew his blocking. Huey, who only stopped reading during scenes when the acting was either very good or very bad, never even made it to Section A. Jonah was superb.

"You did a commercial for Sprint?" Noah questioned.

"Actually, it was the New York Lottery," he replied.

"You can't get me a discount on tickets, can you?" Noah dopily asked.

By the fourth rehearsal, he started earning envy points from

Kenny and Noah and turned the Waldo part into the most moving role in the play.

Still feeling shaky, I made a walk-in appointment to see Dr. Wang the next day during my lunch break. I got off the train at Grand Street and made my way to where no tourists dared to go, past ancient Asians playing mah-jongg, through throngs of old tongs war survivors, to the ever-narrowing doctor's office under the shade of the rusty Manhattan Bridge. While waiting for him to finish with another patient, I read some of the ingredient labels in the drawer-lined corridor: Crocodile for Woman, Snake Penis, Healthy Brain Pills, Hacked-Off Deer Antlers (with fur), Black Deer Tails, and, my favorite, Armadillo Counter Poison Pill. As one of his clerks was restocking some newly arrived ingredients. I asked, "Are there any bugs in the tea?"

"Ya! Bug, ya!"

"How do you remember where everything is?"

"Iz wol, it's wol . . ."

"It's what?"

"Iz worl . . .ld!" he struggled to pronounce the *d* and made a circular motion with a slightly palsied hand.

"The world?" I clarified.

"Oh, yeah." He pointed to the top shelf. "That the sky: bird feathers, old raindrops." Then he kicked the bottom shelf. "This is rock from earth belly." He slid open the drawer. It looked like dried lava pulverized into dust.

Wang finally waved me in. As soon as we were alone, he looked deep into my tired eyes, listened to my labored breaths, and then scrutinized the back of my limp right hand. He started talking softly in his pidgin English, and some words jutted out of his unintelligible sentences: "healthy . . . happy . . . good . . . joy."

To make matters worse, his volume gradually diminished. And just when I thought I was going to drift off, I heard the phrase "out of bawance."

"I'm out of balance?"

"Oh, yeah," he replied.

"What kind of balance?"

"Bawance between . . ." He said a foreign word as he weighed an invisible weight in one hand, "and," then said another equally foreign word, weighing another unseen gravity in the other hand.

"How can I get balance back?"

He shrugged.

"Do I lie with a man, is that it?"

"What?" He looked stunned.

"Am I supposed to have sex with a guy?" I asked as plain as I could make it.

"Why you say this?" he asked with an owl-eyed expression.

"Lie down with man," I repeated.

"No! No." Then he proceeded to slowly perform a three-part squat thrust. Upon crouched knees he said, "lik." The second part, with arms extended, he said, "don," and the last part bouncing back upright, he said, "mag."

At that moment I realized that I had been taking the wrong prescription. Instead of getting regularly laid, he wanted me to do squat thrusts.

"You have someone?" he asked.

Again I was unsure, but this time I didn't want to take any chances. "What do you mean, someone?"

"You got brother or sister?"

"I'm a single child," I explained.

"But the child bringers—the parents!" he suddenly exclaimed. "You see parents. Spend time on them, yes."

"I don't talk with them too much. We have issues," I explained. He prodded the most bruised part of my life. After releasing a sigh, he finally led me back out to the corridor of drawers that contained all the herbal shavings of the world. He scribbled down his prescription and gave it to his assistant.

"Good day," he said politely and slipped back into his office. I stood with his assistant, who proceeded to pull open the various shelves between heaven and earth and shovel out a small portion from each. He weighed a delicate amount in his hand scale and divided it into four paper plates. Seaweed, straw, leaves, and large dehydrated beetle corpses—I was grateful they weren't waterbugs. Finally he scurried up a long ladder to the very top shelf, where he removed a tiny rock. I watched him place it in a marble bowl and grind it into a fine gray dust. I could only imagine that this must have been a fragment of an asteroid.

"This soup, you drink," the assistant said.

In the past it was always a strained tea, but I didn't want to quibble.

I grabbed the bag, paid him and headed out. As I retreated west through the fashionable SoHo and then through gay Chelsea, I thought about Mom and Dad. It wasn't that I disliked them. I appreciated their concern. They wanted the best for me. In other words, they wanted to live my life for me. And there was nothing wrong with their lives, but after a cozy lifetime in the suburbs, where exactly do you go from there?

"Just consider all you're taking for granted and all you're going to be losing out on," Mom used to argue, referring to the wealth and luxury, and all the rewards they had accumulated. My reply was that for most, these comforts were fine, but for a select few, the struggle was the reward. Before I had actually tested those beliefs, I was confident that I was in that select group. I honestly didn't know that it would be this difficult. Now, ironically, one of the primary reasons I didn't give up was because I just couldn't give them—particularly my father—that victory.

At nine-thirty that evening, we were all supposed to surprise Huey with the theater transplant: NYRR was gone. Shazam!—The Samyoff Theater was our magical new space.

Unsure why this strange name rattled around in my head, I looked up Leopold Samyoff on the Internet. The namesake of the theater was one of the group of progressive men and women who, back in the '30s, went to Moscow, shook hands with Stanislavski, drank vodka with Meyerhold, then returned with the great secrets of method acting. The group also started the Comrades Theater, in which they produced plays of social realism designed to show the plight of strikers and working-class men. Later they appeared one by one before the House Un-American Activities Committee, where they were each held in contempt and fined a hundred dollars apiece. They did some early TV work in its "Golden Age," and ended up starting acting schools in the '60s. Initially, they attracted certain smart, young movie stars, but later their work consisted largely of abusing foreign and suburban acting students for a lot of money. Samyoff's acting school was closed in the late '70s when accusations were made that some of his radical acting techniques were sexually abusive. The former house of worship, now a tiny theater on the western edge of town, was all that remained of him. And I still didn't know why I knew his name.

The artistic manager, a meek, emaciated fellow in his sixties named Jed, was outside chatting with Belinda and the others when I arrived. We could see a modern-day, all-Asian performance of *Our Town* taking its final bows.

Jed had refused to allow us to view the space any earlier, citing that if we tripped over the set, the theater would be liable, but *Our Town* had no set—that was its major innovation. We all waited until the last of six patrons filed out. Svetlana slipped me a four-hundred-dollar check, covering my share of the rental. Jonah showed up late, but so did Kenny and Huey, both slightly intoxicated.

"What the hell are we doing in this windswept rat hole overlooking New Jersey?" Huey asked as he trudged through the auditorium and up the four steps to the stage.

"Huey," Svetlana heroically spoke on everyone's behalf, "this is where *Unlubricated* is going to open."

"Over my dead body," Huey fired back, looking Noah squarely in the eye as though he had imparted the news. "The NYRR is twice the theater this place is, and even that place is a bloody dump."

"Technically," Belinda pitched in, "this stage is bigger."

"I compromised myself directing amateurs and forgoing a salary. I am not going to compromise the theater. We agreed to the NYRR."

"Huey, we lost the Romper Room," Noah said, martyring himself to the cause.

The great egotistical director turned away, walked slowly upstage, and seemed to struggle with the idea before it was untimely torn from him, "*Fuck!*"

His lengthy concentration of silence forced us all to wonder the same thought: Would Huey leave or remain? Slowly he turned around, facing us.

"I was conned!" he said accurately, to no response. "If I was a more principled man I would just leave here and never look back."

"Can I tell you what happened?" Noah asked, never missing an opportunity for abuse.

"You can't tell me a fucking thing. Let's bloody get on with it then." Everyone seemed to sigh.

First Edith and Noah talked a bit about the various people we had hired. Then they set up dates they could come in to talk with Huey.

"So what are the dimensions of this god-awful stage?"

Mike located Jed, the artistic manager, who rapidly replied to each of Huey's questions about the space. Just to be on the safe side, Svetlana and Edith moved around with a tape, measuring parts of the theater, while Noah and Huey had Jed bring them into the booth to inspect the light board and sound equipment and test the instruments and amplifiers.

While interrogating the stage manager as though he were a prisoner of war, Huey learned that a new play, *Sinister Ministers*, was loading in early tomorrow morning, so he proclaimed he wanted a quick run-through of *Unlubricated* straightaway. Chop chop.

"Right this minute?" asked the tired manager, who had no intention of remaining there another moment.

"Bloody right!" Huey shot back. The artistic director nodded his head and sighed. Then, taking Svetlana aside for a minute, he made arrangements to leave the theater in her care.

Everyone except me took their places at the top of the show and began the run-through. Svetlana sat in the audience with the script open in her lap, softly correcting the actors as they missed their cues, lines, or movements. On the whole, the play looked pretty decent and I kept ping-ponging between two thoughts: I wish I were in it and Thank God I'm not. When and if it was ever discovered that Bull didn't write a word of it, I knew the cast was going to go berserk.

Huey stopped the show several times, reblocking certain moments to fit the space. Svetlana meticulously noted these amendments in her big book. Late that night, everyone eventually dragged themselves home to bed. The next evening we were all herded back in the dusty basement of Saint Barnabas for rehearsal. During a break, Huey suddenly turned to Noah and asked, "Who is the publicist for your company?"

In a perfect déjà vu of his former idiocy, Noah shrugged. He had learned nothing about bullshitting himself out of a situation.

"Are you a complete moron!" Huey shrieked.

"He's afraid of you," I stepped in, tired of Baxter's petty tyranny.

"I asked a reasonable question," Huey said, "and expect a reasonable answer."

"We have no publicist," I said for the group.

"Well why didn't he just say so?" Huey replied. When I explained that we had put together the budget without taking a publicist into account and were now strapped for cash, Huey said he knew a very good publicist who would work for "peanuts." He gave me the phone number.

So we all de-shelled another twelve hundred peanuts for a discount publicist named Ricky Sykes who doubled as a still photographer.

Except for me, since I wasn't actually in the play, they all met him at his studio with head shots and résumés. Noah delivered mine.

Mike later described to me how Ricky positioned everyone around a long, golden corduroy sofa and had them posing for wacky shots that became part of the press kit. He also wrote a snappy and catchy little release entitled "*Unlubricated* From the Grave."

Edith called me Sunday night and told me that Belinda had been sneezing and coughing the entire time.

"She might've been allergic to the guy's Persian," she added, "but she may have the flu."

33

CRUEL HOPES

SVETLANA·PHONED·ME later that night and said that Belinda would be out the next day and that I would read in her place.

Though I would've loved to be in a hot up-and-coming play, I wasn't confident that this fraud would miraculously legitimize itself. Either way, there was still more than enough time for Belinda to get deathly ill and fully recover.

"Have you gotten permission from the estate?" I asked Svetlana.

"Not yet but—"

"Look, Belinda will be fine. You can get anyone to read for her, don't ask me."

"You're the understudy. It'll be a great opportunity to get the blocking down. And it'll look odd if you don't show," she argued. "Besides, I wanted to go over the film script with you. Show you what I've done."

The next day in rehearsal I realized just how jittery everyone was at the approaching curtain date. Baxter, too, was testier than usual, twice yelling at me. Jonah alone seemed calm, and during a short break, he came up to me and gave me a small bouquet of flowers.

"This is for getting me the role," he said. "I am really enjoying the play."

"No problem," I replied, feeling incredible guilt that I had pulled him into this fiasco. Before leaving that night, Svetlana took me aside and showed me twenty pages of the new screenplay. As I started reading it, she said, "I've taken some uncivil liberties."

"Like what?"

"For one I gave Jesusita a secret lover."

"That's good," I said. The Guatemalan maid could use a lover of her own. It also allowed the character to have a confidante to show her vulnerability.

"Oh, listen," Svetlana said as I read through the dialogue. "Belinda is probably going to be sick for a few days."

"I can't deal with Screwy Huey for that long," I replied.

"Please, he knows you're just filling in for Belinda. He's been going easy on you."

"That was easy?"

"I'm calling her parents to get an update."

"Look, I'm really sorry about Belinda, but—"

"Listen, I've been working around the clock on that screenplay and it's going to be a great film," she said, pushing it too far.

"Three days. I'll do it for three days," I said flatly. "After that *I'm* going to come down with the flu."

She seemed tacitly grateful. After rehearsal, I felt tense all over.

In the darkness of my apartment I could only see my home machine blinking, like a beacon of hope. It was from Sheldon: "I guess I was a little lonely and was just wondering how you were sleeping?"

I really didn't want to call him back, because it just wasn't fair to like part of a person and reject the rest. But I was so tuned into my own frustrations that I finally picked up the damn phone. For a moment I tried not to dial, but of course I finally did.

When he said hello, I didn't know what to say for a moment, but finally I told him that he didn't say a word about his Caribbean getaway. When he started listing the temperature of the water, the cost of the hotel room and the SPF number of his sunscreen, I interrupted by saying, "You know this friendship is going to blow up in our faces if we keep hooking up."

"You called me."

"I know, and you should have just hung up on me."

"Look, I might seem like an idiot, but I've been on both sides of the drill, and I know exactly how it is. You don't have to feel guilty."

I wasn't sure if we were using each other equally or if I was using him more, but that didn't seem too far different from most relationships. So I went over. Outside the apartment, an attractive woman who looked like a taller, less fashionable Belinda asked me if I had the time. I checked my watch and told her. Instead of thanking me or leaving, she just stood and stared for a few long seconds, getting a good look at me. Finally, abruptly, she smiled and walked off.

Upstairs, Sheldon greeted me at the door with a half-filled snifter with cognac. The music was on low. Lights were soft. I took a stiff drink and kept bouncing between the thoughts that I was here because I was weak and I was doing nothing wrong.

"So how was your day?"

"Well, when you consider that most of the world lives in poverty and ignorance, I guess I'm doing great."

He smiled and, taking a deep breath, he led me to a mirror in his room, where he showed me a photo he had cut out of a magazine. It was a picture of me with Kenny Eltwood at the VJ Awards.

"Oh God."

"You look great together."

"Please, that guy was such a creep."

I feared that he was about to launch into some long goofy-ass response, but then he seemed to catch himself.

Just as I was about to ask him what he was going to say, he started kissing me softly on the neck, delicately flicking his tongue around my ear, causing me to lose a couple of minutes.

"What were you . . . ," I finally asked.

He leaned in, kissing my lips as his hands rubbed my stressed-out spine and lower back. The seduction was so graceful and deft, I never remembered exactly when we went from the back massage to the kaleidoscopic sex. It all just seemed part of the same benevolent act. Afterward, I awoke with a sigh.

"You okay?" he asked gently.

"I just feel like I'm using you because this relationship can't go anywhere," I finally confessed.

"First of all, I can't tell you how much you give me, and secondly, I'm not sure if any relationship really ever goes anywhere."

At the time, I thought perhaps he had a point. Maybe I should stop fighting it. A loveless relationship might be better than none at all.

The long days of stand-in rehearsal passed with all the ease of a painfully oozing yeast infection. The only thing I learned from Huey was that ugliness was contagious. After spending so much time with the man, I found myself less patient than usual. I also realized Svetlana's gift—she seemed to make herself invisible to all the anger around her. Additionally, she had a great sense of timing. She waited till the last seconds of rehearsal to break the unfortunate news to everyone that Bree Silverburn had OD'd.

"He didn't die," she quickly added, "but he was found unconscious by his roommate. He's in a mild coma." I didn't know there were "mild" comas.

"Poor guy," Edith said, stroking her own arm.

"Well, I saw that coming a mile away," dopey Noah replied.

"That doesn't affect our permission to do the play, does it?" Huey asked, not even pretending to care.

Svetlana assured him it did not. But I couldn't take my eyes off of her. The one saving grace of most addicts was that they didn't have enough money to crash and burn. They were lucky when they could afford to indulge their little habits, one pill or syringe at a time. I couldn't help but wonder if Svetlana's little payoff hadn't caused Bree's overdose.

Wordlessly, I tugged on my coat and slipped into the cold night air while everyone was still chatting about Bree. Svetlana followed me out without her coat or bag.

"Belinda's still sick." She leaped right into it.

"If she drops out, call me."

"I'm calling you!"

"This is bullshit!"

"I'm doing the best I can," she replied, rubbing her chilly arms.

"Did you help Bree the best you could?"

"What are you talking about?"

"Screw it," I said. This was a cruel world where the weak fell by the wayside. I was no less guilty than Svetlana. Picking my battles carefully, instead of mentioning Bree, I said, "I don't like the fact that everyone is being led down this rosy path and they're going to all get screwed—it makes me feel shitty." That was bothering me most.

"We should have a definite answer very soon," she replied. "And by the way, I should also have your screenplay in a few days."

"Lucky me."

"So whose name is going to be on this script anyway," she asked as I hastened away from her, "yours or Christy's?" She made it evident that she wasn't the only person perpetrating some kind of literary fraud.

"Look, I'm holding up my end of the bargain," I said as I searched for my MetroCard, "but it doesn't mean I have to like it."

"Hannah, I'm trying to tell you something important and you're not hearing me," she said, pulling her freezing arms into her shirt to keep warm. "Belinda is not getting better. Her role is yours."

"She's only been out a week," I replied. "I'm sure she'll get well over the weekend." I refused to allow myself to be disappointed by believing I would be in this play.

"Her parents checked her in to Lenox Hill Hospital," she explained. "They think she could have encephalitis."

"Encephalitis!" This was why Svetlana had followed me out without a coat.

"They're not sure yet. What they do know is she has double pneumonia and the long and short is, she's out of the production." A truck zoomed by with its horns blaring. "I haven't told anyone else yet, but if you want the role you've got it."

Even though I had only a loose grasp of her lines and blocking, that didn't bother me as much as the fact that the play I was supposed to perform in was a fraudulent play.

"Look, Hannah, you're the only one that knows the truth, so if you want out, that's fine too, but I need to know now if I have got to replace you."

"Let me sleep on it," I replied and dashed across the street to catch the subway home.

34

THE REWRITE

I·AWOKE·THAT·MORNING sweaty from a deeply disturbing dream: I was slowly, sadistically strangling a child. I quickly realized it was a guilt dream. I initially thought it was Sheldon I was throttling, then I remembered that the child was a girl. I felt somehow responsible for what had happened to Belinda. I called Svetlana and found out that she was in the ICU section of Lenox Hill Hospital on East Seventy-seventh Street. Bed number 336. I didn't have to be at work until ten A.M., so I walked over to the hospital. When I reached Forty-fifth and Sixth, a loud roar split the sky. Everyone nervously looked up to see two F-14 fighter jets flying in tight formation crisscrossing the city. For crafts so loud, they were surprisingly small, like two airborne sports cars. The pilots must have been fantasizing that it was 8 A.M., September 11, when they could've made a difference. Now they were just annoying. After another half hour I was out in front of the hospital. Just like all hospitals in Manhattan, there was still a wall of photos showing some of the missing from 9/11.

I dashed past the memorials, into the building, and up to her room.

Four other patients were lying in the semiprivate area that was divided by track partitions.

Even sick and unconscious, Belinda looked sexy. She had an antibiotic drip hanging over her. An uneaten plate of eggs and toast was sitting on her tray waiting to be bussed. With the tips of her curls wet, she was clearly febrile. The beeping of one of the monitors punctuated the hushed conversations and muted television shows. I didn't want to wake her, but I hoped to speak to her before leaving. I stood there until she peeked out.

"What's this, last rights?" she muttered.

"I'm sorry," I told her and quickly explained. "I wanted the part of Samantha, but believe me, I don't want it anymore."

"Doesn't matter," she said softly.

"I wish you were well. You know that, don't you?" I asked. I slid my fingers from the stainless steel sidebar onto her hot hand. "Despite everything I always liked you. Remember our first year in college, we were best buddies, weren't we?"

"Please don't . . ."

"I always thought . . . I always thought you were prettier and a better actress than me."

"I'm not going to die and then you're going to feel like an idiot," she labored to say.

"I know, but I feel crappy. I wanted you to get hit by a truck at the beginning, but now I really don't want the role." I stopped just short of telling her why, just in case she chose to inform the others.

"So don't do it."

"I can't not do it." She understood and I just stood there feeling foolish.

"If it makes you feel any better," she said, sucking air as if through a straw, "I did it."

"Did what?"

"Gave Brandopey a blow job."

I always suspected. Brandopey was the nickname I had given my visceral, over–method acting boyfriend in college.

It no longer bothered me or even mattered. She smiled, all tapped out, and closed her eyes. The white room was so bright, I was able to study Belinda's face. If she were to die, she'd leave a beautiful corpse. She looked as if she got daily facials. Her skin was so tonally perfect, her features so delicate. She really did deserve to be a star, but she never would be because she was always so damn precious. She lived on such a pedestal and wouldn't ever get off of it. Although she'd done all the ugly, dirty, awful things I had done, she didn't do them intelligently. I slipped my hand up my arm and located it, my little bump, the living talisman that reminded me of what most people forget—that we would all someday die. I stumbled to exit.

"Break a leg," she said through closed eyes.

"I'll break them both." It felt like the closing scene of *Stage Door*. She was the talented one who lost the role and I was the young and undeserving Katharine Hepburn.

As I boarded the big elevator and headed down to the lobby, I considered some of the lucky few and how they were able to break into the business. If only we were born into it like Gwyneth or Drew. If our parents had only slipped us into the pipeline as child actors and we made that rare transition to adult stars like Jodie or Kirsten. Or if we just had incredible strokes of casting luck, then we too could be celebrities—queens of the living. Our day-to-day annoyances, fights with cabdrivers, and petty gestures, like thoughtlessly generous tips, would all be grist for the gossip mill. Our unmade, unposed-for faces would be in magazines. We would be household names, merchandised into T-shirts and assorted trinkets. Our political causes would get attention because of our cameo appearances. We could become objects of adoration and contempt by schoolgirls and drag queens because of roles that writers wrote, directors walked us through, and wardrobers and makeup people and publicists and plastic surgeons and the vast army of the invisible had a hand in. We'd get the praise, but they could watch us on Oscar night as we made our blathering, incoherent acceptance speeches, and they could say to their friends, "I helped sew a thread on her robe. . . ."

The elevator door suddenly opened and I stepped into the waiting room of the emergency ward of Lenox Hill, where I walked past the neglectedly sick and medically uninsured, out beyond the wall of "missing" 9/11 victims. I took a deep breath and dashed downtown to my desk at Moe, Larry and Curly's.

Throughout my shift, I tried to learn Belinda's lines for the rehearsal. The process of memorization always seemed strangely religious. Lines were like prayers that you had to run over and over. (None of Brando's many indulgences struck me as awful until I heard that his script was fed to him over an earpiece.) Slowly as the words went beyond rote recitation and gained greater meaning, they had to be interpreted, and in rehearsal they were developed and structured still further. One of the marks of a truly great stage actor was their refusal to rest on a single interpretation. Olivier was famous for his constant rephrasing of words and movements, which perpetually kept his fellow actors on their toes.

Initially I'd try to get a basic sense of the script, but gradually I'd focus on the cues, and, after my lengthier lines, just the conjunctions. They joined the boxcars of lengthy sentences. I was always amazed by the fact that in Elizabethan theater, in the days before Xerox machines when everything had to be copied by hand, each actor was only given a script with just their lines, and the cues of the actors who in turn cued them.

As I kept trying to read the lines, and consider the larger themes of the play, I was distracted by the endless clerks and paper shufflers around me. Although they were absolutely correct in their fervor to work, I kept wondering how people could do it.

I didn't mean to sound condescending and I was probably just naive, but inasmuch as I recurrently thought about the thousands of victims of the WTC I kept pondering the value of life. More specifically, I considered how the vast majority of people in this world seem to surrender to rigid routines, the rote recitations. They were like lazy actors going through the motions. How could they not want more out of their lives?

At some point, everyone must have had some dream, a desire for something greater. How could they trade their one and only gift of existence just to live in a small stall of an apartment, see boring TV shows, silly films, and wear new clothes? If there was ever a point to death, it was to give life value, to do something with the meager time we had remaining.

When I noticed one secretary fixing her hair, frightful that someone might catch even a single strand out of place, I felt I had some kind of answer. Billions of people had and will continue to forfeit any attempt at grandeur just to keep from being embarrassed in front of others. After work, I headed over to the basement of Saint Barnabas to try my hand at creating art, certain that it would involve embarrassment.

Svetlana broke the news that everyone more or less suspected, Belinda was sick and wouldn't get well in time.

"Hannah is going to fill her role," she concluded.

"I wonder if she was bitten by one of those West Nile mosquitoes," Noah speculated.

"I read that they might've been sent here by Saddam Hussein as germ warfare," Mike said.

"Poor Belinda," Edith said.

Ken, whom I suspected of sleeping with Belinda, came over and congratulated me.

"First we lose Peter Pan," Huey said, referring to Bree, "now we have Tinkerbell and only a short time to bring her up to speed with the rest of us." The great director sighed and nodded his head dismally. Yet another indignation for the self-crowned king of Ivy League scene development

I was replacing the second original actor and we had a short time before curtain. It wasn't that bad. When I took my script out, Huey widened his eyes and asked, "What exactly is that?"

"I'm seventy percent off-book," I said casually, refusing to submit to his bullshit.

"I'll expect a hundred percent by tomorrow."

Everyone got into position at the opening of the first act. Belinda had played the Samantha role with what he referred to as "a sensual vitality"; Huey had directed her not to repress her natural sexuality. Even though her interpretation brought an erotic charm to the play, I felt her character lost authority through the performance, as the Samantha role needed too much validation from others. Belinda's interpretation failed by the end of the play—when her character suddenly tried to regain that power. I decided to act against her type. Five minutes into the script, though, I altered my character's blocking just a bit in keeping with the renewed interpretation.

Huey rose, put his legendary newspaper down, picked up a chair and tossed it into the air, hollering, "Just what the fuck are you doing?"

"Acting," I tiredly responded.

"You're not doing my role that way," he proclaimed.

"Look, I'm not Belinda and I'm not here to imitate her." Catching Noah out of the side of my vision, I could see him holding his head and nodding forlornly.

"Where the hell do you get off . . .," Huey began, but he caught himself. "All right. You weren't here when we developed this so I'll give you the benefit of an explanation. There are two types of woman, aren't there—virgins and whores. They are a paradox, because the virgin doesn't let us in, but we love and respect her, and the whore gives us access, doesn't she? So men open up to her. We might even trust her, but she does this for all men, so we have little respect for her. Your character is a whore. Access, trust, but no respect. *So play it that way!*"

Without intending to, I chuckled at his textbook oversimplifications. All it really showed was that Baxter had no understanding of people in general, and women in particular. In an effort to be diplomatic, I politely said, "I don't think it's that simple. If you have to reduce her to these two qualities I'd say she has certain elements of both qualities."

"How dare you!" he furiously replied. "You think you can just stroll over our production that we all worked on so hard, and just reshape it!"

Five minutes later, he was still screaming. Yet the only thing that bothered me were the expressions of the others. It was evident that he was going to keep raging against me until I backed down. So as his voice started growing hoarse, Edith tried soothing him. Others just waited, looking miserable. I rose from my position on the couch and went over to Svetlana.

"What's the status regarding the rights of this play?" I asked softly.

"McClellun and Associates, the law firm that represents the estate, sent it to Estelle Bullonus, the aunt in charge. She has yet to read it and accept our offer."

"Holy shit, she's represented by a law firm?"

"I think they're working on commission."

"What exactly did you tell them?"

"That one member of our company discovered her missing master-piece and we're hoping to be able to put it up as a reward."

"Who did you say found it, and where?"

"That while in San Francisco, Bree Silverburn came across a stack of pages in a Dumpster near the Salinas Valley Hotel and this manu-script was among them."

"Why didn't you take the opportunity to make yourself recipient of the permission?"

"Bree agreed to it and frankly I'm chicken."

"Did you specify that we have put thousands of dollars and hours into rehearsal and have already sent out publicity photos and are des-perately awaiting her response?"

" 'Course not," she replied calmly.

"Suppose they decide to claim the work is hers but they just dump us and sell the property to someone else? 'Cause that's what I would do."

Instead of responding, she got up and joined the others in trying to calm Huey down. It pissed me off that the lawyers for the estate hadn't immediately spotted the work as a fraud. It just prolonged the agony of hope. On the other hand, if the lawyers were fooled by this sudden entry into the rather spare Bull canon, maybe Estelle Bullonus would be as well.

"So what exactly did you request?" I asked Svetlana when she broke away from Baxter.

"We stated that in lieu of a recovery fee, we were hoping we could do the first production of this play and we'd pay twenty-five percent of each night's box-office receipt to the estate."

"Is that a standard cut?"

"I'm not sure if there is a standard cut. I think every deal is negotiated differently. I just tried to be generous. If the box falls below a certain minimum amount there's some default fee. The lawyer I spoke to advised that a large percentage was the best way to go. Try to get a quick approval and have them take back-end profits, thereby they share the risk and we don't have to pay out of our pockets."

"Did you tell them anything about our company?"

"Just that the esteemed Huey would be directing it," she said, looking at Baxter, who now appeared to be baying like a wolf.

"What about the question of taking the production to a larger stage?" I asked. That's where all the real money was.

"In the cover letter we said we had a producer who would like to bring it to Broadway should it receive favorable notices," she said, then looking over at Huey, she added, "Would you please placate him?"

Baby Huey's larynx was now completely destroyed, so I got up and said, "Okay, how do you want Samantha?"

In mime and whispers, he spent the next three hours draining out any lifeblood I might've brought to the performance, then he embalmed me with his own bland preservative of the role. He essentially tried to Belinda-fy me. He even had me imitate details of her speech pattern and gestures. I played along completely because it didn't matter. When the show went up, I was going to do exactly as I liked and there would be nothing he'd be able to do about it.

The next morning, I felt an immense sorrow for Bree Silverburn, now having some sense of the abuse he must have suffered at the sticky hands of Baby Huey. As I sipped a cup of coffee, I called Bree at home, intending to leave a sympathetic message. I was surprised when he picked up.

"I figured you'd still be in the hospital." Last I heard he was in a mild coma.

"I wanted to stay, but I couldn't afford it. They checked me out the day after I woke up." Suddenly someone knocked at my door. I sure wasn't expecting anyone, and feared it might be the illiterate landlord.

"I'm really sorry about what happened," I whispered as I took the phone into my bathroom.

"Me too." He sounded refreshingly sober.

"I don't know if you heard, but Belinda got sick and dropped out. Now I'm in her role." I finished my coffee.

"I heard. Congratulations. I wanted to say something when she first nudged you out, but frankly I was too scared." Three loud knocks rapped against my door, compelling Bree to ask, "Do you have to get that?"

"No," I whispered, adding, "The one who surprised me most is Svetlana, I had no idea she was so . . . ambitious."

"You know, the more I think about her the more amazing I think she is. And as far as I'm concerned she's perfectly entitled."

"I thought you hated her for dropping you from the show."

"She told me she did it for my sake and whether she was lying or not, she was right."

"How about the money she gave you?" I whispered above more knocks.

"What money?"

"Thelma, open the door! Someone's trying to steal your apartment!" yelled a voice from the hallway. He was too late, Thelma was history.

"Svetlana said something about paying you off not to squeal to anyone. I figured that's how you were able to OD."

"Not at all. In fact, before I overdosed, she actually put a five-hundred-dollar deposit down for me to go into High On Life, a private detox clinic in Yonkers. Three days in, then it's outpatient treatment."

"Did you go?" I sat in the dry bathtub and slid down below the curled faux marble edge.

"No, I was too pissed. That's why I got so high." He chuckled. "Now, with no pressure from the play and no money for drugs, I'm ready. There's a slot available in a few days."

"Aren't you worried that she's securing rights for a fraudulent play in your name?" Whoever was out in the hall started pounding again.

"Hey, it's the least I can do," Bree said. "I mean, if they decide the play is a phony they're not going to sue me, they'll just say so. No harm done. Besides, I didn't sign anything, I can always claim I was bamboozled. And if it does go up, Svetlana won't make a cent. Ultimately I think she wrote a great play and she's only screwing herself by not taking credit for it."

"I told her the same thing," I replied.

Over the phone, I heard Bree's alarm clock go off. He said he had to take some medication. I told him to stay in touch. He promised that he would come and see the play.

"Good luck with the detox."

"We only get one life and we owe it to ourselves to protect it." It sounded like some of that twelve-step stuff was seeping through. Good for him.

When he hung up, I got up and looked at my lump in the mirror. It might've been shrinking but I wasn't sure. I called Dr. Wang for another appointment. The phone rang and rang, but no one picked up. It didn't matter, I was late for work. I listened at my door but couldn't hear anyone in the hall. Slowly I peeked out. It looked clear, so I snuck down the stairs and out the door.

That night at rehearsal, Baby Huey repeatedly reviewed my big scene in which I criticize Edith's character, Lucy, for being a sellout both in her fiction and her way of dealing with men. After about thirty minutes of repeating the scene, the director rose and said, "Something about this isn't really working."

"What?" I asked indifferently, as if a fly was buzzing too loud.

"Belinda had this levity and . . . you just sink like a stone."

"I'm really trying to float."

"I know you are, but it's coming across as phony." He gave me this ugly fey expression I never saw before. His personality had transformed since the start of this play. He was turning into a big tearful pansy.

"You want me to try it again?" I asked, hoping to stem what I thought was going to be Huey's latest tirade.

"No, let's try it differently. Do it with more defiance." So I began the scene again.

Nuance by nuance, gesture by gesture, through vocal and facial direction and modulations, Huey altered the Belinda interpretation that he had battered into me. In the course of the next several rehearsals, he slowly steered me back toward most of the adjustments that I had originally made. Of course he never gave me credit, or for that matter even acknowledged his revision of my role.

During that ego-crushing week, I tried my damnedest to let go of the stress, but I still felt a growing anxiety tearing away at my sleep. I believed the only thing giving me any strength was Dr. Wang's herbal calmative. Also I probed the lump and it seemed to be growing softer. I sensed that the asteroid dust was burning it up. Soon, though, I was all out of the mystery juice. Every morning, I'd try to call the good doctor for a refill. Unfortunately he never answered the phone.

Finally, after one night of lying wide-awake, I got up early, put on some clothes and took the F train down to East Broadway. As I walked past the tremendous stone foundations of the Manhattan Bridge, above the fray of cars and foreign voices, I heard an insane wailing. It sounded like someone was hurt, and though I shouldn't have, I followed it. About fifty feet below the center of the bridge, where train tracks passed overhead, I saw the back of a little old lady bent on her knees, weeping loudly. Over her shoulder I saw smoke rising and I realized she was tending a small fire that was burning on the pavement. As I came closer, I could hear that she was saying something in Chinese; it sounded like a prayer. I watched as she fed items into the flames—photos, letters, as well as dollar bills. I sensed she was destroying all earthly traces of someone she loved one, something that was done in other cultures.

As she continued crying, I found tears coming from my own eyes as I quietly crept away. When I finally arrived at Wang's office, what I saw made little sense. His shop was locked, and along the corner of the door a big white sticker in red lettering proclaimed CLOSED BY ORDER OF THE NEW YORK DEPARTMENT OF HEALTH. Looking through his glass window, I saw that all the drawers of distilled earth were pulled out and spilled into a big pile. Nearby I passed another acupuncturist's office. I went in and tried asking if they knew about Dr. Wang.

"Sorry, I don't know the man," the younger, taller Asian healer replied.

On my way out, I noticed that this guy had a sign that read LICENSED ACUPUNCTURIST, O.M.D. Except for his HAPPY HAPPY! sign, Wang had never displayed any diplomas.

By the time I got to work, I was freaking out. Why would he be closed down? I called the city's Department of Health. After four more phone calls and countless time on hold, I found out that Wang was an impostor. A Ms. Lee explained that the man had no credentials, and upon getting five summonses to appear in court, and finally a bench warrant, he was arrested and brought downtown. He posted bail, cleared out, and hasn't been heard from since.

"But he was my doctor!" I nervously explained. "He made me feel . . . happy."

"How you feel is no indication of your health," she replied mechanically. She recommended I see an accredited acupuncturist.

I couldn't believe it. I was a natural skeptic, but I had faith in this small semiliterate man. I truly believed in his tenuous link to something arcane and mystical. He was my one-man HMO. The idea that he was a fraud left me deeply shaken. I almost wished that I never knew the truth. Maybe it meant nothing, but no doctor had ever made me feel nearly as confident.

As Patricia Harrows, my 9/11 companion, said, life compensates in strange ways. That night at rehearsal for the first time almost ever, being directed by Baxter wasn't excruciating. I was fully off-book, and I knew the blocking. My character had found a comfortable niche between my initial interpretation and Belinda's rendering of the role. Everyone else was fairly at ease. Mike and Edith had purchased several used furniture items—set pieces for the play. Huey had calmed down and, during the rehearsal, he was nearly able to get through his entire newspaper without looking up.

To top it all off, that night, before going home, Svetlana presented me with the finished draft of *Love Hurts*, "by Hannah Cohn," her reworked version of Christy Saffers's screenplay.

Early that week we were set to have dress and tech rehearsals. Our first preview was slated for Wednesday night. In our press releases we combined our press night with the premiere. The only problem was, we still hadn't gotten permission from the Bullonus Estate.

Because my mailbox was usually filled with clothing catalogues and other mailing-list junk addressed to Thelma Derchoch, I was used to opening the box infrequently, only to clear it out. After rehearsal that night, probably because I felt optimistic from Svetlana's screenplay, I did the charitable thing and unlocked the poor little mailbox. While shuffling through introductory health club and cell phone offers, I saw the puke-green postcard addressed to Jane Doe from the Landlord-Tenant Court. It was dated two weeks ago, just after the last time I cleared out the little box. In Spanish and English it ordered me to appear in court eight days ago. Life was only getting better. I still hadn't received an eviction notice though, so I figured that with a little luck I could still get my case back on the judge's docket. I had faced eviction once before and learned that if you played your cards right you could usually get continuances and extensions for up to two months.

That night, combined effects of eviction and pre-show jitters blended like amphetamines and alcohol in my system. It compelled me to break my umpteenth self-imposed vow never to see the dentist again. I called him.

Upon his machine's beep, I yelled for him to pick up.

"Hi."

"Are you busy? I was hoping to come over."

"Umm . . . a half an hour?" he asked softly.

"See you then." We had streamlined the process nicely.

An hour later, as I was about to walk into his apartment, I heard, "Excuse me."

I turned to see a cute blond woman getting out of a parked car. It was the young lady who had asked me the time when I last came by.

"You don't know me," she said, "but my name is Irene."

"Oh." I suddenly felt incredible discomfort—she was Sheldon's soon-to-be-ex-wife. "I don't know if I should be talking to you."

"You have nothing to worry about," she said calmly. "I guess I just wanted to tell you good luck."

"Good luck with what?"

"Well, I don't know if Sheldon told you, but I've been trying to get back together with him. He's obviously in love with you, so I just want you to know you got a great guy."

"Hold on," I said. "I didn't know . . . I mean . . ."

"Don't feel bad. It's not your fault," she said and simply added, "What can you do, you love him and he loves you."

"But I don't love him."

"You . . . What do you mean?"

"I mean, we actually broke up a while ago."

"I don't understand. Aren't you going upstairs?"

"Yes, but . . . we were just . . ."

"I know he loves you," she said. "He says your name every time I speak to him. I saw a photo of you on his wall."

"What can I tell you? I like him a lot. I just don't love him."

She nodded her head in confusion. "How can you not love him? He's handsome, he's smart. He's funny and kind and generous . . ."

"That's all true," I said, even though I didn't quite agree with her inventory. "But I feel what I feel. I mean, I enjoy his company."

"Well, that just sucks, lady!" she shot back, angry. "Love isn't frivolous. People suffer. It's not something to trifle with."

"I'm not trifling with him. I never lied to him," I repeated. "In fact, I think he feels the same way about me. He told me he fully understands . . ."

"Haven't you ever been with someone who you loved and they didn't love you back, where you'll just do or say anything to spend just another minute with them?" Tears started coming to her eyes. "You're cruel. You don't deserve him."

"Look, I didn't know that someone else loved him," I said earnestly, and not knowing what else to say, I suggested, "If you love him, you should have him."

"Well, it doesn't work that way, does it?" she replied, fighting back tears. "You can't just pass him over to me."

"No, I guess not."

"Do whatever the hell you want. I should keep my nose out of . . . Just please don't tell him that we talked. He'd never forgive me."

"I wouldn't say a word," I assured her.

I went upstairs, where Sheldon greeted me at the door. For the first time, with my blinders removed and all my suspicions confirmed, I saw the boundless hope in his eyes and realized the agony that lay ahead.

"We have to talk," I began succinctly.

"Sure."

"Well . . . I don't know how to say this, so . . . I met someone else."

"What?"

"I met someone."

"That British actor?" he asked jealously.

"No way. Actually another girl." I deliberately said a female so that he wouldn't feel his masculinity was being threatened.

"Who?"

"Just some girl."

"Can I ask her name?"

"Belinda, she's another actress," I replied. "What does it matter?"

"I just want to know what the hell it takes to win your love?" He was clearly pissed.

"Do you know my last relationship, my girlfriend, Christy, dumped me. I know what unrequited love is like. I'm sorry for hurting you."

"Well, I'm glad you finally met someone who gave you the resolve to leave me."

"I'm sorry," I said again. I opened the door and he closed it behind me. There was nothing left to say, and I knew he would never call me again.

Outside, I looked around to see if the wife was still camped out in her car. She was gone and another car was in the spot. Despite the fact that I probably did the right thing, I really liked Sheldon. Aside from being a great lover, he had always been nicer to me than any other guy.

As I headed down Central Park West, I imagined what Sheldon must've been feeling at that moment and felt miserable. New York cab-drivers seemed to sense when people are despondent. One pulled up and I surrendered myself. In a few minutes, we came to a red light on Fifty-ninth, the fare came to $4.65. I instantly realized that I only had a five-dollar bill and a MetroCard with an unknown sum on it. In haste while dashing uptown, I had only grabbed my keys.

"Driver," I said into the Plexiglas. In the rearview, I saw an excerpt of an overworked face, with tired, red eyes. "I have a bit of a problem. I only brought five dollars and I got to get downtown." I paused a moment and added, "If you take me to Hell's Kitchen and trust me to dash upstairs and get more money, I'll give you the fare and a really nice tip."

He pulled his vehicle over, sighed and asked, "Tell you what, do you have an ATM card? I can take you to an ATM machine."

"Unfortunately I don't."

"Lady, I'd like nothing better than to take you home," the driver responded, "but the last forty-seven people who I trusted with going upstairs never came back down."

I understood, got out, and trudged to the subway at Columbus Circle. It turned out that I had one swipe left on my MetroCard, proof that God was merciful, but not generous. I waited twenty minutes, feeling crappier by the moment. The real reason we had to break up wasn't because of the wife, but because I was growing complacent. It would've just been a matter of time before I left him for someone else. Also, to paraphrase the words of Billy Joel, Sheldon was changing to try to please me. He had taken down his paintings and trinkets, sensing that I didn't like them. What was worse was the fact that he was restraining his goofy, unmodulated self, and that really was sad.

When the train finally screeched into the station, I took a seat and ignored a generous selection of New York's poor and homeless staring at me as I tried not to drip tears on the filthy linoleum floor.

When I finally arrived at home, I thought to myself that when I left here a little while ago I was facing homelessness. Now I was facing homelessness without what I very loosely came to think of as a default boyfriend. And not having any asteroids or bugs to boil into a consoling soup, I picked up the screenplay of *Love Hurts*, curled up in bed and started reading it. It was still basically the same story, the dilemma of a Guatemalan maid and her young, rich Yuppie sponsors from an intelligent, fast-paced and sexy viewpoint.

Svetlana had made the young prosperous couple who employed the girl absolutely engaging. They start out from a position of high morality, nearly adopting the young Latina as one of their own. They are enmeshed in her plight, which gracefully becomes empathetic love. Slowly, starting with the man, then with his wife, that pure love sours into base lust. Since the young married couple want to have an honest relationship with each other, they propose a ménage à trois with the young immigrant woman. She is slightly bewildered by this sophisticated concept of three-way, nonreproductive lovemaking, but wholeheartedly trusting them, she puts her innocent, brown self in their randy, white hands.

The rest of the story shows how that initial love and sensitivity that each of them has morphs into something darker and greedier. The woman tries to replace the third world maid's "marianismo" (the silent suffering, female version of Latin machismo) with modern ideals of sexual feminism. Simultaneously, the man attempts to make her a private old-world concubine. The dialogue crackled with wit and irony. Several times I laughed aloud, and although I thought I was all cried out from the Sheldon breakup, tears came to my eyes twice. I couldn't slow down my pace of reading it, and at the same time I didn't want it to end. Although it was longer in pages, it seemed to be a lot shorter than a full-length script. I had to backtrack and check that it had three acts. When I finished it, I wanted to call Christy immediately and tell her that I had a perfect script, but I knew she'd want me to come right over. Then I wanted to call Svetlana and thank her, but it was too late. She was undoubtedly asleep. Despite all the awful things that had happened just that evening, I was giddy. I felt hopeful that I might actually be in a film that would be a critical hit.

The next day at work, I made a copy of the film script. During my lunch break I hightailed it over to Christy's apartment. I rang the door for about ten minutes before I heard Christy's screeching voice, "Who the fuck is it!"

"Me, open up."

"Come back later."

"Buzz me right now. I have something to give you!"

The buzzer sounded and I rode the elevator up to her place. When I got to her door, I found it open. It was about one in the afternoon, and she was still in bed. Much to my surprise—even though she had mentioned him—lying naked next to her was indeed something resembling a male.

She didn't introduce us, but I recognized him—Pete, a skinny grab-bag grad student who had been buzzing around Christy since she taught a postproduction workshop at SVA last year.

"So what do you got for me?" Christy muttered without small talk.

"Your hot new script, I finished it this morning." I took it out of my bag.

"Put it on the cabinet," she said from under the sheets, "I'll read it when I get up."

I put it down, and as I was heading out through the kitchen, I saw something that made me smile. A photograph of the two of us hugging when we were still in love last summer. A lifetime ago.

35

THE KID IS CUT FROM THE PICTURE

SATURDAY · WAS · WARDROBE · DAY. We were supposed to meet
at Mike's at one in the afternoon to go over our selection of costumes.

I had gone through my closet and considered what Samantha might
wear to her writers' workshop. Casual, loose-fitting, subtle colors.
Button-down and pullover shirts. Nothing new or showy. Slacks, jeans,
no dresses, not if she was supposed to spend an evening with a group
of guys she wasn't interested in. Except for Noah, who was extra-ing,
everyone brought in clothes and the afternoon went fairly smoothly.
Huey made his choices and Svetlana took notes while we all chatted
about how this time next week the play would be up. But unbeknownst
to everyone we still didn't have permission. When the lighting person
showed up to talk with Huey about the various setups and cues, I
slipped out.

When I got home that afternoon, I had a message on my machine
from Christy: "Frankly, I was looking forward to giving you some of the
same shit you gave me, but I'm reading your script and it's really, really
good. I am surprised the way you—" My machine had cut her off.

I called her back. She went right into what she liked. "There are several points that need to be fixed up a bit, but I had no idea you were so talented."

"What exactly did you like about the script?" I asked proudly. I didn't write it, but I did extort the script out of the writer.

"You brought out exactly what I wanted to say. And the character of Ernesto was brilliant." That was Jesusita's new lover.

"Everyone deserves someone they can open up to," I said as Christy gushed on. The only reason I didn't tell her that Svetlana wrote it was because I wanted her to give me the Jesusita role.

Christy said she couldn't wait to show the new script to Manny Greene. We both said good-bye and I hung up. Then all was still in my apartment. I found myself thinking of Sheldon.

I felt guilty about how I'd treated him, and thought about calling him up and telling him about the real me, and all the awful things I had stupidly done: I was scamming my own friends by putting up a fraudulent play. And I had essentially extorted a talented writer to rewrite a screenplay for a female director, only so I could get a starring role in her film. Oh, and while with him, I had also had sex with Kenny and Franklin, but technically we'd broken up long ago, and he seemed to sense that I was involved with others. The real problem was the fact that I hadn't stuck to my original plan. My temporary fix for acute loneliness, my December-January affair, had, by delay, hatched into a using relationship.

I decided that I had to shake the mood by going for a walk. It was a nice, warm, sunny afternoon.

Strolling down crowded Eighth Avenue, in no time at all I crossed Fourteenth Street. Then heading westward, I stumbled along the cobblestones that had been shoved up by the root system of the trees that lined Jackson Square. Sparrows gave themselves dust baths in the dry dirt under the green benches. When I reached Greenwich Avenue, I looked up and suddenly wondered what was missing. Of course, it was the towers. When I first moved to New York and finally developed some architectural sensibility, I had decided I didn't like them: two large sheer blocks dominating the sky, what was there to like? They were as goofy and imposing as a pair of giant tourists. Now I missed them intensely. As the arguments began about what to build in their place, I found myself siding more and more with those who felt they should be resurrected exactly as before. Then we could tear them down ourselves and build something else there, but—I hated the fact that someone other than New Yorkers—particularly some bearded, trust-funded baby—had ultimately decided the fate of our skyline.

I caught the subway back home, where I turned on the TV and dined on a pint of low-fat Ben & Jerry's frozen yogurt. When a commercial came on for the play *Rent*, I suddenly remembered my impending eviction. On Monday I had to go to Landlord-Tenant Court and try to get the eviction postponed as long as possible. Under the marquee of this disconcerting thought, I somehow fell asleep.

On Monday morning I was awakened by the ring of the phone. I let the machine get it and listened as the exuberant message bubbled out: "I got it! I got it! It was FedExed this morning!"

With no idea who it could be, I picked up and groggily asked, "Who got what?"

"It's Svetlana! I got the permission statement."

"You are fucking kidding me!" She had fooled the Bullonus Estate with all their goddamned lawyers!

"I'm holding it in my hand."

"Hallelujah! We're going up!" I yelled.

"We are going up and we're staying up," she screamed and I screamed back. I was so excited that holding the phone to my ear, I actually bounced ecstatically around my apartment. I couldn't believe it! The play was actually going up. All that work and money would be for something after all. And now we could sell Manny Greene the whole bill of goods.

"You know the worst part of it," Svetlana said as the conversation started winding down, "we can't even tell anyone about this."

"Speaking of which," I said, not meaning to sound distrustful, "do you mind if I look over the permission statement?"

" 'Course not. Call the lawyer and verify it if you like," she replied calmly. "I'll bring it with me to rehearsal tonight."

When I hung up the phone, I thought about it and realized I should have had more confidence that it would go through—just like Svetlana had said. Even if Estelle Bullonus, the executrix, spotted it as a fraud, it was a win-win situation for her. It put money in her pocketbook and elevated Lilly Bull's overall literary prestige.

But I had no time to celebrate. I called in to work and gave them a stock excuse as to why I'd be late: an unforeseen plumbing crisis. Then I dressed hastily, took my notice of judgment and headed down to 110 Centre Street, where I had to pass through a metal detector. Since September 11 they had added additional security and a lot more flags. If a terrorist showed up, they could beat him to death with the Stars and Stripes. At the information desk, I was directed to the assigned courtroom upstairs—several rows of pews where depressed tenants and hopeful landlords, or lawyers representing them, sat and haggled. Beyond a rail in the front half of the room behind her elevated wooden desk, in black robes, sat an Asian variation of Judge Judy. I got to the rear of a small group of nattily dressed people that were petitioning the court for one indulgence or another.

A black, middle-aged court officer in a sharp, dark blue uniform finally asked what I was waiting for. I politely explained that I had missed a court hearing for eviction. He asked me the name of the landlord. When I told him he checked a long ledger book; I was amazed that the system hadn't been upgraded to computers. I watched him open a second ledger and run his finger down what looked to be a long list of handwritten names. He returned to me, handed me back my official notification postcard, and said, "It's already gone out."

"What does that mean? What happens now?"

"It's out of our hands. The city marshal happens now."

"So you're saying . . ."

"I'm saying you better pack, girl."

"Are they going to evict me today, or a week from today?"

"If they filed it immediately you probably should have been evicted already."

"How much notice do I have before they can take over the place?"

"Seventy-two hours from posting."

I thanked him for his bleak tidings and numbly rolled out of the building and into a nearby subway hole. I had to get to work. Twenty minutes later, when I popped out of the train sweaty and anxious, I contemplated calling the landlord to see if he would negotiate: I'd offer him three hundred dollars more a month in rent in exchange for getting the lease in my name. After all, he was restricted by the rent stabilization board from renting it too high and Thelma was gone. He had to rent the apartment to someone. Once at my desk, though, I was inundated by a barrage of menial chores.

After work I barely had time to grab a salad and then dash over to the Samyoff Theater, which as of that day was ours. We were scheduled to do our first full-dress rehearsal that night. As I entered, Svetlana handed me a pile of invitation cards and flyers that low-budget publicist Ricky Sykes had printed up. We were all supposed to distribute them in our area and hand them out to friends, as if grassroots invitations to our play could undo years of TV, VCRs, and movies, and bring the masses back to the theater. Ricky had also made a poster from one of the group photos, which he wild-posted around the city. Of course, Belinda was on it instead of me.

The rehearsal that evening went flawlessly. Huey, who hated me, actually complimented my performance. I knew I could do a lot better, though. While we did a complete run-through of the play, Bob, the lighting person, slipped gels into lights, and fine-tuned the many instruments.

In the dressing room, I asked Edith if I could possibly spend a night at her place.

"Who?"

"Me?"

"When?"

"Soon."

"You know I've been dating this guy."

"The copy editor at *Us*," I remembered.

"Yeah." She looked at me, exasperated. I couldn't blame her. Edith had just had her sexual awakening and she still felt self-conscious about her friends hearing her screaming, "Fuck me!" But if I did find myself unexpectedly evicted I might need an emergency crash pad.

"It's just for one night," I said tiredly.

"I already let you spend the night once," she said, looking off.

"I know, last summer. But I might have an emergency brewing."

"What kind of emergency?"

"Well, there's a pyromaniac who lives downstairs and I'm afraid that he might burn the place down." It merited a lot more sympathy than to recount how I had botched several opportunities in Landlord-Tenant Court.

"All right," she conceded, rocking her head from side to side, and rolling her eyes, "if your place burns down give me a call."

As I climbed the steps to my apartment that night, I braced myself for the seventy-two-hour notice on my battered wooden door. It wasn't there. I wondered if the landlord was playing with me, but then I realized that he was just lazy. After all, he had waited for the last possible month before even taking me to court. I should have answered the door when he was knocking. I could have tried to deal with him then and there. Hopefully he'd bang on my door again to serve the summons. I laid down in bed and recited the Samantha lines over and over in my head until I drifted off to sleep.

The next day, looking through a copy of *Local Vocal*, I got some leads on new dwellings: a toxic box in Tribeca for $995; a beach umbrella with three others in Williamsburg, $790; a mud puddle in Bushwick for $850; a tree burrow in Inwood for $1,050.

Flipping through the middle pages, under the "Pick of the Week," I saw:

Lilly Bull, Gary Ganghole's near executioner, left a short if vulgar bibliography with *C.O.C.K.* and *Coprophagia*. The buzz says that her final play, *Unlubricated,* was a breakthrough. It is her most structured and complex work by far. The legendary English director Huey Baxter, who has been on furlough teaching for a number of years, has come back with a vengeance. He's set to direct this guttersong and it's promising to be one of the big hits of the downtown season. How the unknown Disaffected Artist Types managed to snag this gem is still a mystery, but catch it at the Samyoff before it goes uptown.

During our tech rehearsal that night, everyone brought in the last collective payment of the production before the curtain went up. Since Svetlana had been paying my share, I had lost track of exactly how much everyone had invested. That night everyone's final check was for a whopping $2,400. Edith and Mike, who had done the math, stated that each person had invested $5,321. The entire play had been produced for a little more than $21,000. Except for Edith, who had saved scrupulously all her life and was now simply broke, everyone else was overdrawn, overborrowed and maxed out.

At work, I handed out invites to everyone at Moe, Larry and Curly's, and, when asked, I politely explained that there were no freebies. If you loved me it was $12 per ticket and time to prove it. I also went through my Rolodex and invited every person, e-mail address, and answering machine I could to come see the play. The one final call I had trouble making was to my parents.

Although I really didn't want to see them, I knew they'd be deeply hurt if they found out I was in a play and they weren't invited. All my life I bugged them, annoyed them, and generally pissed them off—particularly the paterfamilias—but I never deliberately hurt them. So I waited until six o'clock, when I knew they'd be out at their country club playing mixed doubles, then took a deep breath and left a message on their machine in a 78-RPM voice: "Hi, all, I'm in a play at the Leopold Samyoff Theater on Twenty-third and Eleventh, opening on

Friday at eight. Come if you want, but if you don't I understand. Good-bye. . . ." Phone down, big inhale.

Tonight was the final dress rehearsal—a preview with a test audience consisting largely of our poorest friends, who couldn't even afford the twelve dollars. Mike invited about twenty-five fellow students who he had studied with at HB and the Neighborhood Playhouse. At exactly seven o'clock the curtain went up. A few lines were transposed. Some of the blocking got jumbled. Svetlana screwed up several lighting cues, and the props weren't all where they should have been. Despite that, we could feel the audience glued to us right up to the end. When we took our final bow an hour and a half later, the applause exploded as if it had been ignited by a single fuse. I didn't remember the last time I felt so good. One woman I'd never met before said my character really brought an edge to the show.

Afterward everyone was going out for drinks, but I was pooped so I headed home. As I tiredly climbed upstairs, I saw it. The eviction was taped to my door: "By the Order of the City Marshal, you have seventy-two hours to vacate the premises, at which time it will be reclaimed . . ." Checking the date and calculating the time, it meant I had to be out that Friday at noon.

On my way out the next morning, I opened my mailbox and discovered a mysterious manila envelope with my address scribbled on the outside. Just as quickly I realized it was a copy of *Self* magazine that Edith had sent me for reasons unknown. I slipped it under my arm and was about to leave when I spotted a sign that said IN CASE OF EMERGENCY CALL THE LANDLORD AT . . . His number was listed. I copied it down. When I arrived at work, I called him.

"Hi, I'm the woman living in Thelma Derchoch's apartment," I introduced.

"No more of your monkey business," he said. "You have to go now."

"I know, I was just hoping that maybe we could negotiate—"

"Monkey business—no!"

"I was just hoping—"

"I already rented the place away." He had a slow way of talking that suggested an accent but might just have been brain damage.

"I could pay more than whoever it is you rented it to."

"No, leave." He hung up.

I flipped on the Internet and located a roommating service called OutInTheCold.com. On the site I found a stinking rat hole in the Bronx, where for $600 per month they could squeeze in one more rodent. It was five minutes from Yankee Stadium, which wasn't a good thing, and with the aid of the 2, 4 and 5 trains it was only about a half an hour from the known world. I could move in Friday, which was perfect. The only question and problem was moving the few sticks of furniture that I had purchased, but they weren't exactly antiques so I wasn't sweating it. I reserved a rental car for tomorrow to haul my few items up to the Bronx. Then I told my supervisor that I would be out the next day, performing in the premiere of a play.

"Break an egg."

That evening was supposed to be our tech-through. This was when the play just ran from cue to cue—light cues, word cues, and action cues. But thanks to final revelations from Huey, a variety of last-minute alterations were made. While the director was blathering, Noah took me aside and whispered, "Don't ride the trains for the next two weeks."

"What?"

"Someone told me that a friend of hers drove into a gas station upstate, and this Arab guy couldn't pay for his tank of gas, so she gave him a couple bucks. In gratitude he told her to stay out of the subways for the next two weeks."

"You're kidding!"

"Hell no, terrorists are going to anthrax the tunnels."

"If this is true why don't you or your friend call the FBI?"

"Hey, if you want to, be my guest, but I'm not going to be put on a sodium-pentothal drip and chain-interrogated for the next three months."

"Hey, stupid," Huey shouted to him, "you just blew your cue."

Three hours later, the British helmsman was done. As I was heading uptown, starving and tired, I checked my voice mail and heard a frantic message from Christy Saffers, "Call me immediately. I got some big news! I have to speak to you at once."

I cell-called her from the crosstown bus.

"Can you come over right now?" she asked.

"It's eleven o'clock," I said tiredly. "Can't you tell me on the phone?"

"This is big news. It's regarding the film."

Noah freaked me out of riding the subways, so I transferred to the downtown bus on Seventh Avenue. At night when they don't have to stop at every block and there's no traffic, buses zoom like rocket-propelled breadboxes, so I got off on Varick in just a few minutes. As I walked across lower SoHo, hungry and tired, I bought a granola bar and was still chewing it when I pressed her doorbell. She rang me up.

As soon as I entered, I saw pencil-dick Pete, her Intro-to-Men 101, sitting at the corner desk frantically scribbling something.

"So how the hell are you, hon?" Christy said excitedly and surprised me with a hug and kiss.

"Fine," I replied tiredly, smelling alcohol on her breath.

"Let's sit down. I got something big to tell."

We sat on her Ligne Roset couch.

She offered me some merlot. I passed.

"There's good news and bad news," she said, leaning toward me intimately. "The great news is Manny absolutely loves the screenplay. He says it has it all. It's an intelligent downtown story, but it has enough action, sex and romance to play well in the sticks. He says he couldn't have hoped for better."

"And you told him you wrote it," I said, anticipating the bad news.

"Well, yeah," she replied. "But that's not the bad news."

"As long as I get to act in it," I said, staking my claim.

"And that's the problem," she slowed her pace and lowered her volume. "See, he showed it around to some places and he just found out this evening, which is when he told me, and that's why I'm telling you now. . . ."

"What the hell are you saying?" She hit my panic button.

"Manny says he thinks he can get a coproduction with two other bigger companies."

"Great, so what's the problem?" I asked, trying to get out of there and home to bed.

"The problem is he says he can only get the coproductions if we get Salma Hayek, or maybe even Penelope Cruz. And he thinks there's a good chance." Those names were deal makers, the actresses that attracted investors, box-office bucks, and critical notices. It was like being whacked over the head with a polo mallet.

"But there is some good news," Christy jumped in. "Manny is offering you something else."

"Another role?"

"Maybe," she said, smiling. He had no role and she knew it.

"Let's save the bullshit. You're saying I'm screwed."

"Look, I'm really sorry. But this is business. I will give you half the money I'm getting paid to write it," she replied. Now I knew why she greeted me so warmly.

"You were going to give me that anyway. You promised me a starring role," I shot back. "If you're using my screenplay I want all the writing money and a cowriting credit."

"Out of the question," she replied. "I'm the writer. Now a copy of this script with my name on it is already in Manny's office. You can dispute it, but there's little else you can do. Take this deal or leave it."

"Actually, you're wrong," I replied, and thinking fast I pulled the manila envelope from *Self* magazine out of my bag. I waved it at her and said, "I knew you were going to pull something like this, so I mailed the script to myself two weeks ago. It's postmarked. You want to argue this before a judge, this is my exhibit A."

"I'll take that," said spindly Pete, who had been silently listening to the entire event.

"Don't . . . ," Christy said to him.

He snatched the envelope from my hands. Just as quickly, I kneed him swiftly in the groin. When he fell to the ground, I grabbed the envelope back. I couldn't believe he had the nerve to jump in like that.

"You fucking bitch," said Christy's man-boy, struggling to his feet.

"Sit your fucking ass back down before I toss you out the window!" Christy screamed at him. Then, turning to me, she said, "All right. All right, just take it easy. I'll give you the cowriting credit, but I still am only going half on the writing fee. Be reasonable, Hannah, I did locate the story, option it, and write the original draft. That is still the back-bone of the screenplay."

"I made it bankable, and you're still getting a directing fee."

"It's a single lump fee," she clarified, then contemplating it for another moment, she said, "All right, I'll take two-thirds, you can have a third."

"Backstabbing bitch," I muttered, instead of shaking her hand. I couldn't believe that I once loved her.

"So we have a deal?"

"You were doing a lot better with women," I said, staring at grimacing Pete. Then, grabbing my things, I stormed out the door and down the filthy stairs. For every film ever made, someone always got screwed; this time the roulette wheel stopped squarely on me.

I hailed a cab and tried not to punch out its windows as it soared like a meteor uptown toward the last night in my apartment. I stopped in front of my building, paid, got out, and nearly tripped over a pile of garbage that had been haphazardly stacked out front near the cans. Looking carefully at one item, a ladder-back chair, I realized it was the one Noah gave me.

36

THE WANDERER

RACING·UP·THE·STAIRS I pulled out my keys. That was when I
noticed the shiny new cylinder replacing my old lock. Frantically I
tried shoving my key into it. I had already accepted the loss of my
apartment, but I didn't think I'd lose my belongings as well. I distinctly
remembered that the eviction was not supposed to take effect until
tomorrow at noon.

I went back downstairs and discovered my twin mattress leaning
sideways with my satin sheet still on it. In the time it took me to go
upstairs and then return, someone had taken Noah's chair. The dining
room table and chairs must have been snatched earlier. It felt as if all
my things had been tossed into a blender. Some things were recovered
but most were destroyed or gone. All the electrical appliances were
missing: my portable TV, the phone, the clock radio. Some of my books
were there. I found some old love letters from Christy, some photo-
graphs. Most of my clothes were gone—including my entire VJ Music
Awards ensemble. I never got to auction them off for charity. I pulled
together what little I could, then I headed back into the doorway. First

I considered calling the police and trying to rectify the situation, but the notice itself, which had been in the apartment, was now gone. Cops didn't like adjudicating. They would just say it was a matter for the courts. The room I cyber-rented in the Bronx was not open until tomorrow. I took out my cellular and called the emergency crash pad, Edith's home. Her answering machine caught it, and I yelled for her to pick up, but to no avail.

I called back and left a message: "Remember I told you about the pyromaniac downstairs? Well, he burnt me to the ground. Please call my cell as soon as you get home."

At that moment and only for that moment, I deeply regretted breaking up with Sheldon. After sex, the next best thing I did at his house was sleep. I knew Mike was staying with his lover, and Noah's place was a pot-reeking frat house somewhere up in Harlem. I really didn't feel I knew Jonah well enough and I sensed that Kenny would only provide a convenient lie as to why he couldn't help. I squeezed my salvaged belongings into a big ball and headed east toward Eighth Avenue at Forty-fifth, where I spotted an all-night diner. I ordered a lemon meringue pie, which sat in front of me uneaten like a large Styrofoam flotilla that prevented the waiters from kicking me out. I thought about going back to Christy's place, but the idea was simply unacceptable. It would be letting her off the hook. I tried to remember where in Williamsburg Edith lived, but those streets of low-slung buildings were all a blur. Even if I knew where she lived, chances were she wasn't even home. Intermittently I called her, sometimes hanging up, sometimes pleading for her to pick up. I considered heading off to Penn Station and going to Great Neck, but the idea of showing my parents what a mess I was in was excruciating, particularly if they were going to see me in the play tomorrow night. At two in the morning, I finally called Svetlana, who lived with her rich parents in some town house out on Ocean Parkway in Brooklyn. She was my last hope before dropping ninety dollars that I didn't have on a cruddy hotel room.

"Hello?" She spoke in a groggy whisper.

"Hi, Svetlana, this is Hannah."

"What's going on?" I could tell I had woken her.

"Well, I was supposed to move tomorrow 'cause I was getting evicted," I introduced the situation slowly.

"Can you call me about it tomorrow?" she asked.

"No," I jumped ahead, "see, when I came home from rehearsal tonight I discovered I had been evicted. Edith was supposed to put me up."

"Well, she isn't here," Svetlana replied tiredly.

"I know." It was too late, and she was too tired to deduce anything. "I need a place to spend the night and was hoping you could put me up."

"That's impossible," she said softly.

"Why is it impossible?" I asked. "If I can't stay at your place I'm not going to get any sleep tonight and if I don't get any sleep I'm going to be horrible in the play tomorrow night."

"Hannah, I just don't have the room."

"I thought you said your family was wealthy."

"They were wealthy, but their money is tied up right now and—"

"Come on, Svetlana. It's two in the morning and I'm standing in an all-night diner with all my worldly possessions and . . . and you're my last call."

I heard only silence, which compelled me to realize how pathetic I was. If people were measured by their friends, what did that say about me?

"All you can sleep on is an old couch," she finally relented.

"That's fine."

She gave me her address along with intricate train-to-bus directions, which I politely pretended to write down. I thanked her, hailed a cab and sailed toward Brooklyn. While we were over the bridge, I looked back at the lights and towers of the Manhattan skyline. The city that night looked like a stage with infinite lights flickering uncued on endless levels of tracks.

"Lady, we here," the driver grunted, waking me up in the backseat. The digital red meter said $21.65. I must have slept right through it. I gave him twenty-five and walked into the lobby of a ghastly, tall brick apartment building that conjured up images of neglected old age. Going through the list of names and buzzers, I spotted the name Palas 12D and rang it. I was buzzed in quickly.

Up the elevator to the twelfth floor, through the narrow and dim corridors with a wallpaper pattern that looked vaguely like a million tiny skulls, I finally saw Svetlana leaning forlornly from a doorway looking like she was posing for a Diane Arbus photo. She led me into a large dark room. Although she didn't turn on the lights, I saw no pictures on the walls. No knickknacks were around anywhere. The few pieces of furniture looked tired yet functional. She pointed to a hard, wirehaired wool sofa with a disgusting plaid design. I thanked her and she wordlessly retreated behind the only other door, where she presumably collapsed on her bed. The phosphorescent hands of a small windup clock said 3:30 A.M.

I took off my jacket, and along with my ball of pseudodesigner clothes and my Taiwan knockoff of a handbag, I tossed them on something that in the darkness looked like a large white shelf. I proceeded to strip down and place the remainder of my clothes on the little shelf near me. But as I was undoing my shoes, I saw my coat flinch.

I carefully picked it up and underneath I saw a tiny, silver-haired lady, purring fast asleep. She looked no bigger than four feet tall. I carefully removed my things, which I had casually tossed upon her. I lay down on my sofa and drifted quickly off to sleep.

I awoke to the sensation of something slipping between my toes. Opening my eyes, I saw the little lady, who I had accidentally buried, wearing her little camisole, smiling down at me like a shrunken angel. She had fit her bony little index finger between my big and second toes. The small alarm clock said 5:45. I had slept for only two hours.

"I'm ready for breakfast," she said in a reedy little-bird voice.

"You are, huh?"

"Yes, please," she requested.

"Well, I'm not the one who gives it to you," I replied, pulling the covers over my face. I felt her delicate little fingernail scratch the sole of my foot.

"Please don't do that," I stated softly. "I'm trying to get some sleep."

"I've got to eat," she announced indignantly.

"Tell Svetlana. She's in there." I pointed to the door.

"Okay," she replied, and I pulled the covers back over my head. Again I felt her scratch at my heel.

"All right," I said, clearly pissed. "That's quite enough."

"But I'm hungry," she whined like a little girl.

"All right," I groaned and hopped out of bed.

"Oh my, you're in your skivvies," she said, referring to my bra and panties.

I pulled on my pants and tugged on my shirt. "Where's the damn kitchen?"

"This way," she said and led me down a small foyer that I hadn't noticed before. Once at the end, I could see why she needed me. A wooden, accordion-style drying rack was stretched sideways across the floor, forbidding her passage. I tiredly angled over it into the kitchen.

"What do you want to eat?"

"I usually get my Wheaties at this time," she divulged. She looked at her wrist as though she was wearing a watch.

I went through the shelves but all I could locate was a box of Frosted Flakes. In the fridge I found some milk.

"Also my 'nana," she said, pointing to a bowl of fruit. "For potassium."

I poured the cereal into a bowl, put in the milk, and sliced up a greenish banana.

"Sugar," she called out from behind the little barricade, where she was patiently waiting. I rooted around until I found a jar of sugar and carefully I candied up the entire bowl. Then I worked my way back over the barricade, cautious not to break my neck, and past her. She followed me back into the living room, where I placed the breakfast on a dining table.

"I could also do with a cup of coffee," she said.

"No coffee," I replied tersely. "Eat your flakes now. I got to get some sleep." I jumped back into bed, pulled the covers up, and tried to snatch a few more hours of shut-eye.

"If you want a bowl you can help yourself to some," the old lady offered politely. I pulled the pillow over my head. "I need this cereal to keep regular," she went on.

"Please, lady," I groaned with exhaustion. "I really need to sleep."

For a while all was silent. Then, just as I was going under, I felt a tug at my blanket and heard, "So what's your name anyhow?"

Shit! I lost it.

"Now listen to me, lady! You wanted cereal and I gave it to you. Now it's six twenty-two in the morning. Everyone's asleep. I have to sleep too, understand?"

"I just wanted to know your name," she innocently repeated.

"My fucking name is Hannah. Now please leave me alone!" Why the hell didn't I go to a hotel!

"There's just no need for that kind of language." If I had just left my belongings on her face, accidentally obstructing her airways last night, we both would have been happier now.

"I was just trying to be polite," she stated. For a while she didn't say a word, then I heard it—the TV, she had turned it on to the *Today* show. Matt and Katie were talking to family members who had lost loved ones in the World Trade Center. Opening one eye, I watched what I had seen more times that year than anything else. An amateur video captured the jet that had roared from across the Hudson and smacked into the south tower. You could see the fireball and the smoke coming out of the front. I remembered reading how it was estimated that the terrorists had spent a little over a hundred thousand dollars on expenses. In return they took a little under three thousand lives, destroyed the World Trade Center, which alone was worth tens of billions of dollars, and slowed down a national and world economy, costing the majority of a trillion dollars. They ran a short montage of videos showing the towers burning and collapsing over and over. Each time they did, I felt myself shudder. Finally I jumped to my feet and flicked off the TV.

"I was watching that," she said.

"Try reading something," I said tersely and jumped back into bed. The TV suddenly flicked back on, louder than before. I got another view of the second plane careening into the south tower at six hundred miles an hour.

"*Goddamn it!*" I screamed at the top of my lungs. In a moment Svetlana appeared at the door in a long nightshirt.

"Grandma, are you bothering Hannah?"

"I was just watching the television."

"Come on, Hannah, you can sleep with me," she said. Inside was a tiny room with a small desk and manual typewriter under a high loft bed. She climbed up and I followed. It was a thin tightrope of a mattress. And at that altitude a cloud of steamy humidity gathered and kept me from quickly going under. For what seemed like hours, I struggled not to fidget or fall. Finally, in a semiconscious state, I threw my arm and leg around Svetlana to hold on. I tried to evict all thoughts, but I kept seeing the images of the impacting planes.

Like a steam whistle at a lumber mill, a loud shriek compelled me to flip over and fall five feet down, landing on my face and the right side of my body.

"I knew it, you're a lesbian!" called the shrill voice. But I couldn't get up. My face and body were stinging with pain.

"Mom, Hannah was just sleeping," Svetlana said to a middle-aged version of herself who was standing in the doorway.

"Am I bleeding?" I asked, garbled. Svetlana climbed down the ladder and helped me off the floor.

"I don't like this one bit!" the lesbophobic mama shouted.

"Come on." Svetlana led me to the bathroom. "You have a tiny gash above your eye."

"Oh no."

"It's not deep. It won't scar."

"I think I broke my jaw," I said, holding my mouth. "The entire right side of my face is in pain."

"You split your lip a bit." She looked carefully and touched it gingerly. "You're going to have some bruises."

"I have to perform tonight," I said tiredly, achingly.

"It'll be all right," Svetlana replied. "We can cover it up with makeup."

"Why couldn't she sleep on the sofa in the living room?" the mother shoved into the bathroom and asked Svetlana.

"Because that—" I restrained several expletives, "that old lady kept waking me up!"

"I don't know who you are!" the mother shot back, "but I want you out of my house!"

"Mom, she's just very tired. Please just relax," Svetlana tried to calm her down.

"I wake up and find you in bed with another woman."

"Hannah had nowhere to sleep."

"Why don't you have a boyfriend?" her mother asked. "Why aren't you dating men?"

"Because they're all either goofballs or scumbags!" I informed her as I achingly pulled on my pants.

"My God!" the mother shrieked.

"Not that women are any better," I muttered as I struggled to pull my shirt over my swollen right arm.

Svetlana apologized to me while I grabbed my knotted belongings. Her mother marched off fuming. I told her I'd be fine, and was sorry for intruding on her like this. If for a moment I thought it was going to turn out this way I obviously would've checked into a cheap hotel.

"I'll see you tonight," she replied and closed the door behind me. I pushed for the elevator. A minute passed, then another, soon five, ten minutes ticked by. As I held my finger against the elevator bell, I found myself focusing on little, far-off things, the way you do when you're exhausted. I could hear a distant engine growing louder. The montage of the planes smacking into the buildings replayed in my angry head. I felt myself sweating profusely. I really wanted out of that fucking building. That was when I heard this sudden thud from above. Looking at the window in the hallway, I detected a slight rattling. The building was shaking. Something was wrong.

"Hey, release the fucking elevator!" I yelled down the stairs.

I didn't hear a sound. I thought I smelled smoke. Then I heard another huge boom and that was it. I tossed my bundled clothes over my shoulder and moved quickly down the steps, gliding one hand along the banister.

By the time I reached the third floor, my heart was beating in my throat, and even though my head was throbbing and I was hyperventilating, I couldn't stop. The landings were divided into three, three-foot intervals. By the second floor, I hopped down the last two landings. Hitting the lobby with a thud, I fell on my already sore right thigh.

When I pulled myself up and started walking, I felt a stabbing pain in my hip. I had bruised myself. I limped out the apartment building trying to catch my breath. Once I got outside, I looked up at the roof. The structure appeared to be fine. After a moment, when I calmed down, I realized that I had suffered another panic attack.

Walking slowly down Ocean Parkway in the sun, I felt achy, filthy, and brain-dead. With all my worldly belongings slung over my shoulder, I felt like a sweaty medieval vagrant. I was vaguely looking for a subway—where to, I didn't know. Instead I spotted two benches with a concrete chessboard pedestal between them. I put my stuff on the chessboard and lowered my head on it. I curled up to fend off the cold, and in a moment, I dozed off.

When I awoke, a large, circular man was sitting on the opposite seat of the chessboard staring right at me with a mile-wide smile.

"Lovely day today."

"What time is it?"

"Noon?" I had slept for about three hours. "How are you doing, young lady?"

"Huh?"

"What brings you our way?"

"Technically I was here first," I pointed out.

"We're here every day." He spoke as though I had wandered onto the closed set of his talk show—an unsuspecting guest. I got up and slowly exited the soundstage of his mind. I walked along the boulevard lined with benches until I was far from him. Then I curled up on an available bench, and rested my head on my belongings. Though I was tired, even I knew that the panic I had just experienced was classic trauma. I quietly cried and just wondered when life would return to normal.

Finally I heard someone say, "An actress, eh?" When I opened my bruised eyes the puffy circular man was sitting right next to me. He was reading one of my little invitation cards to *Unlubricated* that must have slipped out of my bundle.

"I used to act," he said as though I might be interested.

I closed my eyes, which he must have interpreted as a come-on since he said, "You look sweet."

I turned around and tried to ignore him.

"And you got a nice body, you know that?"

I wondered, if I were dead, how long into decomposition he would continue talking to my corpse.

"Could you please just leave me alone?" I finally asked and closed my eyes.

"Oh, sure, I'm sorry. I'm just saying you look fine and if you're an actress, I'd love to see you work."

"Sure, come to the play." I handed him an invite in a final effort to be rid of him.

"What's your name anyhow?" He extended his greasy hand toward me. "I'm Ainsworth Jones."

I got up, grabbed my small globe of personal effects and asked him if he knew where the nearest subway was. Two blocks this way, three blocks that way. I nodded.

"Why do you have to leave?" he asked in a sort of bewildered concern.

"It's curtain time," I said instead of beating him with my bundle. I limped in circles, asking directions until I finally stumbled across a subway station. Dying of anthrax couldn't be worse than living here, I decided. Before slipping down into the concrete wormhole, I checked for messages on my cellular—there were none. I called Edith again, no answer. Then down I went and sat on a blue wooden bench, which felt so incredibly comfortable that I slipped into sleep for about fifteen minutes until the Manhattan-bound train clamored into the station. Upon slowly stumbling on board, one of the train doors pushed me to the right, the other shoved me to the left and both bit down, holding me in their teeth. The conductor opened the door for a second, allowing me to fall forward, but then the doors quickly closed on my bundle of clothes. For a second time the conductor opened and I pulled in. I took a seat, holding my clothes on my lap, thinking how in New York you always felt a little chewed up. Again going through a marvelous tunnel of sleep, I reemerged into the pain of consciousness when the train screeched to a sudden halt and I tumbled upon that filthy floor. Eureka! I was in Manhattan.

37

A LONG NIGHT'S JOURNEY INTO DAY

AS · I · WEDGED · MY · ASS back between the other full-thighed riders onto that slippery gray subway pew, I looked at my bruised face in the dirty reflection of the opposing subway window. My right cheek and lip were swollen black with a slight bloody glaze. I couldn't take it anymore. I got off the train at Forty-second Street, located a pay phone and decided to call my last-resort numbers: First I'd call Noah, then Christy, and, if she wasn't in, I'd surrender to my hateful parents, where I'd have to suffer a lifetime of gloating about the time I showed up tired, bruised and homeless. If conscience didn't make cowards of us all, parents would gladly do the job.

I called Noah. His machine picked up and I had to listen as he gave a long dramatic monologue from Shepard or Mamet or some other stupid-ass, macho-male playwright—beep.

"Noah, it's Hannah, are you there?"

"Yeah," he picked up immediately.

"You got to do me a favor."

"I'm broke."

"I never thought I'd say this, but I desperately need a place to sleep."

"Right now?"

"Yeah, just for a couple of hours until the performance."

"Mi casa es su casa, but I'm warning you, Hannah, you won't like mi casa."

"Look, I'm feverish, I got a pounding headache and if I don't get some shut-eye soon my skull's going to explode."

"Just don't say I didn't warn you," he cautioned and imparted his address up at One hundred Fifty-sixth Street and Broadway in Harlem. Before taking the great passage north, I carefully considered calling Christy. Her place was so wonderful—so sunny, flowing with fresh air, tasteful furniture, she even had a view. I never slept as well as when I slept on her bed. The mattress was like a cloud, the sheets were gloriously soft.

The only problem was that backstabbing bitch Christy.

It was better to sleep quietly with the roaches. I got on the A train. After about forty-five minutes of riding and walking, I finally found myself knocking on that desolate door in the Latin enclave of Upper Manhattan. When Noah opened, I asked him if he had any aspirin.

"What the fuck happened to you?" he asked, looking at my black-and-blue face.

"Oh, I fell out of bed. My fucking head is killing me."

"I think there's some aspirin in the bathroom cabinet. Second door on the left." He lived in a railroad flat with three overweight bachelors who didn't curtail their single-guy image by doing faggy chores like cleaning the urine-glazed toilet, or even bothering to put the toilet paper on the spool. When I opened the medicine chest, out tumbled an avalanche of old prescriptions. Several thoroughly coiled ointment tubes probably treated jock itches from sweaty summers past, and finally I saw a brown, heavy-duty bottle of Bayer. I unscrewed it, swallowed three pills, then washed them down with rusty tap water.

"Are you okay?" Noah came into the bathroom.

"No, I'm sick and exhausted and have to get some sleep if I'm going to be onstage tonight."

"It's one o'clock," Noah corrected, "to get to the theater by six-thirty you have to leave here by five-thirty. If you're lucky you have about three and a half hours of shut-eye."

He led me to the last door on the left at the end of the long hallway. To his credit, his place wasn't as bad as Bree's, but it was still every bit as detestable as I had imagined it. A torn poster of Pacino's *Scarface* was sloppily taped to the unevenly painted wall. A stack of old and torn porn magazines was conveniently at the side of his bed. If I wasn't the first female to land on this dark moon, I was most certainly the first member of the fair sex to wind up in his icky bed. Tragically, I was grateful to be there.

"I have to go to work," he explained as he put on a baggy suit jacket, the last detail of an old three-piece suit. "I'm in the latest wacky Robin Williams flick."

"What is it?"

"A musical comedy about the riots in Tompkins Square Park during the eighties."

"What are you supposed to be?" I asked as I tiredly pulled my clothes off.

"A revolutionary hobo," he said, staring at me.

His choice of the word "hobo" underscored the problem with mainstream films, where the homeless were usually quaint, eccentric and adorable. In Hollywood, reality never really had a chance.

Noah suddenly realized he was late.

"Lock the front door behind you when you leave," he said, leaving the keys. I thanked him and he left. All his furniture had an even spacing of cigarette burns, a kind of leopard-spot motif. The sheets on his bed, once cotton white, had a brown tint, but that was okay. The mattress sagged in the middle, but I didn't mind. People get too caught up in petty details. I closed my eyes and tried to believe that all the little itchy sensations that tingled about my body weren't the delicate legs of waterbugs, or the tiny claws of mice.

Through the large, old windows with sunlight pouring in, echoed the noisy engines of daytime. I turned back to my left, and tried to sleep, but was unable. My brain, kept jerking around like a fish on a hook.

After a while, I realized that my heart was racing too. My breathing was labored.

Opening my eyes, I held my hand out in front of my face and realized that it was visibly shaking. Why the fuck was my hand shaking? I was calm when I lay down. I closed my eyes and tried not to worry about it, but I felt the sweat articulately trickling down my brow and along my neck. My heart was racing even faster. I jumped to my feet and found that I was barely able to stand. Something was terribly wrong. Sitting at the edge of the bed, feeling my heart struggling in my chest, I wondered how many people knew when they were really about to die. Danger is frequently elusive. How often do we invalidate our own fears when they should be heeded? At that moment, feeling sharp spasming in my chest, I thought that if my heart's intensifying contractions should suddenly stop, I'd be no more. After a few minutes when the sensation failed to subside, I was convinced I was having some kind of coronary episode.

Slowly I rose to my feet, and, running my hand along the wall for support, I returned to the bathroom and opened the medicine cabinet. I took out the big Bayer bottle. Unscrewing the top, I shook out some of the aspirins into my palm. Upon inspection, I gasped. Nearly all the pills in the container were different. There were thin pills with lines down the middle, large orange pills, various types of capsules, some containing a clear gel, others with a granulated powder. One or two of the pills actually had the word "Bayer" imprinted on them.

I suddenly feared that I had taken some weird kind of designer drug that only a moron like Noah would use. Hunching over the toilet, I slipped my index finger down the back of my throat and tried regurgitating. Not much came up, and since it had been about twenty minutes since I took the pills, I was convinced that the fatal ingredients were already racing around in my exhausted system. Unsure of what to do, I knocked on the other doors to see if any of Noah's creepy roommates were about. They weren't. Hastily I dressed and left his cursed apartment, locking the door behind me. Downstairs I spent ten minutes looking for a cab before a livery service car finally pulled up.

"Where you going, hon?" asked a Haitian immigrant driver.

"Where's the nearest hospital?"

"Columbia Press-me-near-to-ya is up north. Santa Luke's is that-way." He pointed over his broad shoulder.

I got in the back and told him to take me to Saint Luke's. Ten minutes and seven dollars later, I entered the emergency room entrance. The waiting area had no shortage of business. Thank God the health insurance lobby successfully blocked Clinton's fiendish attempt at nationalized health insurance. I stopped a nurse and frantically appealed, "I just swallowed some poison and—"

"Are you pregnant?"

"No, but—"

"Are you on any medication?"

"No, but—"

"Do you have a handgun or any weapons?"

"No, but—"

"Were you ever hospitalized before?"

"My parents sent me to psychiatric counseling camp but—"

"Come this way," she said. Her rapid fire of questions was dizzying. She notified a doctor on duty who was in the process of bandaging someone's ankle.

He came over with a wheelchair and told me to have a seat. When I explained to him that was unnecessary, he insisted, so I did, and he wheeled me into a treatment room.

"What kind of poison is it?"

"Well, I don't really know if it was poison. I just swallowed it down without even looking." I took out the big bottle of Bayer and showed the many pills to him. "There were a bunch of different pills inside."

"How many did you take?"

"Three."

"Really?" He looked at me doubtfully.

"I think so," I said, wondering if I could possibly have swallowed a fourth by mistake.

"Why did you take them?"

"I had this throbbing headache."

"What caused the headache?"

"Just everything." I threw my mind back to where my life started becoming impossible. "First I got into a big fight with my former partner and . . . I had this throbbing headache."

"Why didn't you just take two aspirin?"

"I thought I was."

"You said you took three pills, usually people just take two pills."

"I had a really bad headache and my hip was hurting."

He looked at me suspiciously. "Tell me about this fight."

"Oh, it was nothing. The bitch tried to rip me off. . . ." I tiredly remembered the screenplay fiasco.

"We're going to have to give you charcoal activate."

"What's that?"

"It cleans you out."

"How long will it take?"

"You'll have to be in observation for a while."

"Observation?"

"I think they hold you for seventy-two hours, ask the shrink when he gets here."

"A shrink? I don't need a shrink."

"Look, the nurse tells me there's a girl here who attempted suicide. Now you're telling me that you accidentally swallowed some pills. . . ."

"What! I didn't attempt suicide!"

"Did your domestic partner do that to you?"

"Do what?"

He pointed to my face. "It looks like she slapped you around pretty badly."

"Hell no!" He thought the fight was physical.

"Then why did you swallow a bunch of unmarked pills?"

"Wait a second, you got this whole thing wrong."

"You know it's really not for me to figure out. Just tell the psychiatrist."

"There's no way I'm waiting around to be evaluated." Due to my parents, I had a deep aversion to psycho-authorities.

"Look, we can do this the easy way or the hard way."

"All right, let's both just calm down," I said tiredly. I had accidentally slipped myself into a Chinese fingercuff and the harder I pulled the more stuck I became. I knew in a case like this, the best way out was by relaxing. If he perceived me as belligerent he would have me jacketed and then I'd be fucked for good.

"You wouldn't mind if I took a little nap?" I asked sedately. I yawned, laid down, and closed my eyes.

"Fine," he said and added that he was going to get me charcoaled, then he exited. I waited a moment, checked the corridor and dashed out.

I hastily limped over from Amsterdam to Broadway, and, after fifteen minutes, I caught the Number One train downtown to Fifty-ninth–Columbus Circle, then I waited ten minutes and changed for the A to West Fourth, where I grabbed the F, two stops to Second Avenue. I walked up to Seventh and Avenue A as fast as I could. The southeast section of Tompkins Square Park was sealed off as a mobile army of film people took possession with their trucks and walkie-talkie nerve web. Crowds of homeless and mentally impaired East Villagers had been cleared out so that Hollywood could make a touching tale about them. Most were lingering about, trying to steal food off the craft services table, or get a glimpse of the irrepressible Robin Williams.

"Can I help you?" asked some P.A. scum as I pushed through a barrier.

"Yeah, I'm in this production."

"Hold it, lady." He grabbed my arm. "Who are you with?"

"I don't have to tell you!" I yelled back.

"Yes, you do." He resisted with equal force.

"It's okay. She's with us," I heard some guy say. It was Lorenzo the best boy. He was standing with a group of Teamsters who had tried to gape at me during my nude scene in *Success!* I thanked him. As he walked me through the encamped area, I asked him where the extras converged.

"Extras Holding is over there." He pointed to a small walkway. I headed over and saw an army of Emmett Kellys and Charlie Chaplins, talking, reading, chatting, and eating.

"Noah! Noah Rampoh!" I called out.

"Noah's there!" One of the faux homeless pointed him out to me.

On a park bench, under a copy of Uta Hagen's *Respect for Acting* that balanced on his bristled face, I saw Noah sleeping.

"Hey, asshole!" I smacked his thigh.

"What!" He bounced up, sending the book flying.

"What the hell kind of pills are these!" I said, throwing the bottle of Bayer onto his chest.

"What! Oh!" He opened them. "Oh shit!"

"What the hell are they?" I screamed. "My heart's been beating like a windup toy for the last two hours."

"Oh, sorry. They're mainly harmless, over-the-counter crap." He poured a bunch into his palm and then singled them out. "These are aspirin. That's echinacea. These are probably what you took." He held up one for me to read. On it was imprinted No-Doz.

"*Asshole!*" I whacked the back of his outstretched hand so that the pills in it bounced into his face.

"I'm really sorry, Hannah, we put them all in one big bottle because they were all getting loose in boxes and we had roaches crawling around on them."

"I've got to get some sleep!" I shrieked.

"Just listen to me," he said softly. "Why don't you just lie down on a bench here and breathe slowly and relax."

"No, I'm going back up to your place and—"

"You don't have time. It's already five and we have to be there in an hour and a half. By the time you go up there and come back down it'll be too late. Lie down here. Take my bench. I'll wake you up when I'm done and we can share a cab across town."

"Fucking hell—okay," I conceded. What else could I do? He let me lie down on his jacket and put the Hagen book over my face as a light screen. The nap was more of a meditation on nothingness than a sleep. Periodically, though, I'd hear some loud noise and jump. Once when a truck backfired I bolted up, catapulting the book across the walkway. I had only to reclaim it and lie back down, where I eventually drifted off to a wonderful blackness.

38

OPENING NIGHT

"HON," · **NOAH** · **WHISPERED** · **SOFTLY.** "It's time to go. I'll get us a cab."

I rose slowly and groggily. Noah steered the way. I hobbled with him down to Seventh Street and over to First Avenue, where we hailed a cab.

"Are you limping?" he asked as a taxi screeched to a halt.

"Just a mild bruise," I explained as we squeezed into the vehicle.

He gave our destination to the driver: "Twenty-second and Eleventh Avenue."

As I leaned my head against the seat of the vehicle and ignored the celebrity advisory to buckle up, I peeked up through the back window and had a gutter-eye view of New York. I saw the old and new buildings and narrow streets as we streaked between the apartments and town houses of Gramercy Park and then passed the old warehouses of Chelsea.

I thought about the idea of acting onstage for the next two hours. I knew it would require a lot of energy.

"I don't know if I can do this," I thought aloud.

"You've got to," Noah said earnestly. "You're all we got—you're the understudy."

"What happens when the spare tire is also flat?" I tiredly kidded. It was the same question that the driver had asked so long ago when I was stuck with Ron Bridges in his car on the West Side Highway.

In a minute, Noah paid the fare and hustled me into the theater. We were late and only had forty-five minutes before showtime. There was a large dressing room in the back with six chairs lined up in front of six mirrors. But off to one side was a single smaller dressing room with a sofa—for the star. Svetlana led me into it as though I were blind, then she dashed off to fetch my wardrobe.

"What the hell happened to you?" was how Edith greeted me. I wasn't sure if she was talking about my face, my limp, or my clothes.

"Does anyone have any coffee?" I asked.

"I just touched mine, but it's black," said Jonah, who had just entered.

"Fine." It was a medium-size cup from Starbucks, which I chugged down in a slow, uninterrupted gulp. The part of my brain that allowed graceful improvisation was frozen and it had to be quickly thawed out.

"You poor girl." Jonah noticed the bruises and cuts for the first time. "What happened?"

"I fell."

"From how high?" he asked, carefully examining my cheeks, lips and forehead.

"About five feet," Svetlana filled in.

"Does this hurt?" He gingerly touched around my skull.

"Yes."

"You should go to the hospital and see if you have a fracture. You could have a concussion."

"We need her for the play," Noah said, dashing around like a puppy.

"I'm really okay," I assured him. When I dragged myself across the room, Jonah gave a bewildered expression.

"I think I can hide the limp if I . . ." I labored to walk normally, but through my smile, he detected pain.

"Maybe we should cancel."

"Not while I'm alive," I said. "I've gone through too much for this."

"Listen." Jonah came in close so that only I could hear him. "I've been doing this for years. I had to inhale carbon monoxide for *Hamlet*. And once, with a serious fever, I did the role of Jamie in *Long Day's Journey into Night* for an audience of two. I could feel myself burning up. Afterward, I collapsed, and when they took my temperature it was a hundred and three. But I was never actually in pain. I've never been in a play that's worth all the strange sacrifices that you're making."

"But I might never get another chance."

"This one role is not going to make your career."

"You don't know that."

"If you should feel dizzy or weak at any point, just lie down, understand? This is all bullshit and it's simply not worth jeopardizing your health for."

"Okay." I was touched by his concern.

"Afterward," he said, "I'll drive you home."

"You really do look like you just went ten rounds with Mike Tyson," Noah said, intent on dampening my spirits.

"She'll be fine," Svetlana said, coming out of nowhere with a makeup kit the size of a heavy-duty toolbox. Before she got very far at applying my foundation, Kenny came in and said the box-office girl had just arrived. Svetlana dashed off to quickly explain the job to her.

"What the hell happened to you?" Eltwood asked, seeing me for the first time.

"Bad face day," was the best I could think of.

Svetlana returned in about five minutes and began cosmeticizing me back to normal. I only wished that she could apply mascara internally to cover over how I felt.

"I'm sorry about Grandma waking you up and all," she said softly as she tried to hide my scabs and bruises. "She's not really senile, just lonely and annoying."

"You should have warned me."

"I wanted to, but . . ." She didn't finish the sentence, and through the tangled wires of my burnt-out brain, I suddenly realized why she didn't. She had lied, giving me the impression that she came from money. That was her way of guaranteeing the financing of the play if we should get shut down before opening. Babysitting an impoverished grandma did not fit the rich-girl profile.

"Don't worry about it," I tried comforting her. "It all worked out."

"Do you think you'll be able to do this?" she asked tenderly, as if I had a choice.

"Yeah."

She helped me dress and then we looked out on the curtained set. I could hear rock music playing and the audience streaming in. All the members of the cast had assembled backstage. Kenny talked with Edith, who looked amusingly sexed up. Noah and Mike were giggling like hell at something, probably me. When I entered, all stopped and showed polite concern.

"Are you okay?" Mike asked, holding me up.

"I'll be fine."

"Hey!" Huey entered, dressed to the Ts and light on his toes. "There's a full house out there! Juan Valasquez from *Local Vocal* and Robert Whitcomb from *The Observation Post* are right in front."

"It's going to be wonderful," Noah assured him.

Huey smiled, nodded and then, looking at me for the first time, he saw all the caked makeup and shrieked, "What the bloody hell! You look like the Phantom of the fucking Opera!"

"I got banged up."

"What happened?"

"I got hit by a floor," I said.

Edith, who had been reading one of the Playbills, said, "I count fifteen misspellings, six grammatical errors and three typos in my brief bio alone."

"Hey, I need eighteen beer bottles here and I only have twelve," Noah said, inspecting the prop table.

"I hope we're using real truffles for my scene?" Mike asked, checking his box of chocolates. One by one, Svetlana addressed all the complaints and finally started her countdown. At three minutes to curtain, lights and music went down onstage. Kenny took his position in the darkness. Lights came up and Ken (as Reggie) led Noah (as Miles) and me (as Samantha) into his living room set.

For a split second that felt like forever, I simply stared numbly at the audience before Reggie repeated his line and I was kick-started into acting.

I had read of actors who had performed while intoxicated. Some had actually done it with greater gusto, but acting while sleep deprived, I felt like a drunken acrobat crawling across a dramatic tightrope. I focused so hard on not missing my lines and blocking that I was barely acting. The sharp ache in my hip was like an invisible antagonist I was constantly working against—the only problem was, I couldn't hide the limp. A jittery line reader to the others was really the best I could offer. Nonetheless the show was working. We got our laughs when they were called for, and a silent interest as the drama built.

During a cut-away scene in the script, I was able to study people in the house. Manny Greene was seated front and center. When I looked to his right, I couldn't believe who I saw. It was that circular sleazoid who pestered me on the park bench on Ocean Parkway. Next to him was some woman who looked sadly familiar in the darkness, but I didn't know why. Not far behind, I spotted my parents, and slowly the lines passed and the minutes ticked away.

I was definitely the weakest link in the acting chain. I dropped and rephrased lines, but worse than that I had nearly forgotten all of Huey's desperate last-minute alterations. Although his final notes were subtle—facing downstage instead of left when saying this line, sitting instead of kneeling here, picking up a prop here and putting it down there—overall, my character had a tentative fuzziness. When I wasn't correcting myself, I kept blinking out, having trouble keeping my eyes open. I was experiencing what I later learned was called micro-sleep.

Yet I wasn't the only one having problems. Whoever was at the lighting board dimmed us during a crucial scene. At a later interlude he brought the lights up too soon.

There were also problems when Reggie was seducing Lucy. It was the same scene Kenny and I had rehearsed that led to our brief thespian fling. Even though the Lucy character was eager for sex, Edith was not. When Kenny started kissing her neck while moving his hand up along her ribs, she was visibly uncomfortable. Finally she broke character and brushed his British paw off her breast. I suspected her new copy editor boyfriend was in the audience. During intermission, when we retreated into the dressing room, Edith cursed and threatened Kenny if he ever touched her again.

"What the fuck is wrong with you people?" Huey screamed at us like a losing team during halftime. "You were terrific in the last rehearsal. What happened?"

"Are we doing that poorly?" Mike asked for all of us.

"No," he ineffectively backpedaled, trying not to demoralize us, "you're just not doing as well as you can. And there are reviewers out there! Put more energy into the scenes. It's like you're all sleepwalking!"

"It's a little difficult to concentrate when someone's molesting you," Edith said, touching up her makeup.

"I'm sure you'll all be wonderful," Huey said insincerely, then turning to me, he added, "except you. What calamity did you crawl out from under? I mean it hurts just looking at you. And are you actually limping?"

"Give her a fucking break," Jonah yelled at him. "She shouldn't even be on a stage considering the condition that she's in."

"She hasn't really slept in thirty-six hours," Mike explained.

"And she took No-Doz," Noah added.

"Why the fuck was she taking No-Doz?" Huey asked. Noah shrugged instead of confessing that he had accidentally doped me. I was barely able to blot the sweat and runny makeup off of my face.

"Just listen to me," Huey shifted gears. "You're grabbing your lines too tight. You have to relax!"

"I'm actually afraid I'm going to doze off," I explained.

"Well, believe me, you're actually generating a lot of suspense. It looks like you're going to have a heart attack at any moment!"

"Huey, this isn't the time to criticize," Svetlana said, amazingly. It was the first time I ever heard her not side with him.

I dozed off to sleep as she gingerly retouched my face. Everyone had already taken their places when she shook me. I leapt to my feet. She pushed me out into the darkness as if into a boxing ring. I resumed my position. Lights flared up and act two began. For the first five minutes or so, it actually seemed to be going well. Soon I had a two-hander with Mike (Lenny), and remembering Huey's advice, I loosened up and felt more relaxed in the role. But, while sitting back calmly, the unthinkable happened.

Ken (as Reggie) said a line to me, and—I was later told—I softly snored in response. Jonah, who was nearest, reached over and gave me a gentle nudge.

"What the . . . oh . . ." I sat up, blinking at the audience without a clue as to where we were in the play. A sudden roar of laughter came back at me. A headache that had been growing throughout the entire day had now reached epic proportions.

"I'm sorry," I asked Reggie tiredly, "you were saying?"

He repeated the line and I responded and the play sped ahead to its denouement. Reggie punches Waldo, he exits, I take off after him. Then Lenny and Miles remain a while with Reggie, who does his final summation before they exit as well.

As soon as I was offstage, I dashed into the bathroom, locked the door, and contemplated suicide. When I heard the first applause I gritted my teeth and realized I still couldn't kill myself. I dashed out and joined the cast for a collective bow. When I leaned forward it felt as if sharp, hard rocks had tumbled from the back of my head into the soft front lobes of my brain. I finally retreated to the large private dressing room, where the headache completely paralyzed me.

"Did you really fall asleep in the middle of the play?" Mike asked aloud.

"Just for a second," I said, holding my skull.

"In all the years on the stage," Ken fumed as he wiped sweat off his face, "I have never seen a spectacle like that!"

"You know," Noah joined in, "if you find this job boring there are a lot of actresses who can keep wide-awake."

"It's a miracle she even made it," Jonah retorted. I was grateful for his kindness.

Edith was so angry she wouldn't even look at me. I knew that to her I had committed blasphemy, not just to our little company but to the entire damn religion of acting. Just as they were getting tired of attacking me, Huey entered.

"I am so glad to see you in pain," he began.

"I'm sorry, okay?" I said to one and all.

"You're a traitor!" he replied, then turning to the rest of the cast, he said, "Here she is—the woman who fucked up all our chances of being taken seriously and getting a decent review."

"Sorry," I replied in case they hadn't heard me the first few times.

"You fell asleep, and everyone saw it!" he said as though I didn't notice. "I came seconds away from marching up onstage and smacking you wide-awake."

"I'm sorry," I replied. I didn't know what was keeping my head from exploding.

"Is this your idea of revenge upon us?" he pressed his attack.

"Give her a break," Svetlana finally interrupted. "She got evicted last night."

"Please, I heard all about it. She spent the night popping uppers," Huey deliberately misconstrued it.

"Why the hell didn't you call me last night?" Edith finally asked. "My apartment was empty. I spent the night at Brian's house."

"You were the first person I called! Don't you check your messages?" I couldn't open my eyes.

"I haven't been home yet," she said.

"I left a dozen messages on your machine. Everything would've been fine now if you just once checked it." I sobbed into the breach of darkness that was the outer world. "I told you there might be an emergency."

Fortunately, several friends of the cast were waiting outside, so

Huey, Ken and the rest had to stop shitting on me and leave. Tiredly I dressed as Svetlana went about the process of preparing the set for tomorrow's performance. Jonah said he was going to wait up and drive me home, wherever that was. Everyone cleared out and I enjoyed the solitude for a moment before I heard another knock at the door.

"Come in."

Standing behind me was the sad woman I spotted in the audience. Up close and in clear light, I suddenly remembered who she was—Patricia Harrows, the former actress who I met when the skyscrapers fell.

"Oh my God!" I got up and hugged her. "I tried locating you."

"I couldn't believe it was you," she replied with a big hug. "I felt so bad for abandoning you."

"That's silly, you did nothing of the sort."

"How did you happen to come here?" she asked.

"My company rented the space. How'd you wind up seeing the play?"

"Jed, the artistic director here, is my husband. I see all the plays here," she explained. She must have been the reason I remembered the name of the Samyoff Theater. "I'm the artistic director of a theater downtown, I could've gotten you a big break down there if you called me first."

"Listen, we should talk, but my head is pounding," I said, unable to keep my eyes open.

"You were great," she said.

"I fell asleep," I replied, embarrassed.

"Did you really! I wasn't sure if you were kidding or not! Either way, it was hilarious. The other character who was talking to you was such a bore. You stole the show by doing that. You really did. I couldn't take my eyes off you!"

She gave me her business card, and I scribbled out my phone number. Just as she said good-bye, the door pushed open and again some roly-poly in a white shirt and black tie rushed in.

"Anyone know if any of the producers of this play are still here?" The guy was huffing and puffing as though he had been blowing up balloons all day. Concerned about me being alone with this stranger, Jonah followed him inside.

"Yeah, catch your breath," I instructed him. "I'm the producer."

"Thank God I caught you," he said, holding a valise in one hand and a folded white document stapled to a legal blue back. "This is a court injunction . . . from the law firm of McClellun and Associates." He placed the document in my hand. As I unfolded it, he added, "I'm sorry." Then he dashed out before I could open it.

"Svetlana!" I called out.

"Would you like me to take a look at that?" Jonah offered. He explained that he had worked as a paralegal for years in the area of entertainment law. I handed the document to him.

"It's a cease-and-desist order," he explained as Svetlana entered.

"What's going on?" she asked.

"I don't know, I think we're being evicted from the premises," I speculated, still in a landlord-tenant state of mind.

"That's impossible!" she remarked. "The artistic director was just here. We paid half the deposit! They can't do this!"

"It's not the landlord," Jonah said, still reading the document. "McClellun and Associates represents literary estates. This is from the Estate of Lilly Bullonus."

"What?" I asked, baffled.

"I never got permission," Svetlana cut to the finale.

"What!" My skull finally blew off. Svetlana just stared silently into oblivion. "What did you say?"

"I just figured that they'd never know," she uttered.

Instead of screaming or yelling, Jonah resumed reading the document.

"I'm so sorry," she repeated. It was almost nice hearing someone else say it.

"We're fucked!" I screamed.

"There's something really weird about this," Jonah said, still reading the document. "They're not referring to the play, just the use of her name. They don't seem to recognize the play as one of her works."

I closed my eyes and waited for a chasm to open and swallow the entire theater—but that would be too merciful. Perhaps there was mercy in Jonah being there; after all, he had invested no money and the least amount of time. Regardless of everything, he simply seemed bewildered.

"I'm so sorry," I said. "I don't know how I can make it up to you."

"All I'm going to ask is that I don't have to see that awful Huey character again," he said. "That will be compensation enough."

SHOWSTOPPER

FOR·ALL·THE·TIME and money everyone had painstakingly invested, I thought it would be nice to give them one night of deluded glory before blasting their already damaged dreams asunder. For my part, Jonah dropped me off at the nearest subway and I dragged my exhausted ass up to my new home—16938 Gunhill Road, the rat hole I rented sight unseen over the Internet. The train ride was so long I was sure I was going to eventually start seeing farm animals. Finally I got off and walked. On what had to be the grimiest, loudest block in the five boroughs, I located the crummiest building. I rang the bell and was buzzed in. Up several painful flights, I soon knocked upon a battered door.

" 'S open," I heard a distant cry.

It was 11:30 at night when I finally stepped into a kitchen-sink drama and met my new roomies: a single mother, Gia, her two kids, Lucy and Angel, Gia's sister, Lourdes, and her gruesome, tattooed boyfriend, Tex, who made me wish that Lourdes was single too. For the most part in undergarments, they were crowded around a portable black-and-white TV in a tight living room: my new adoptive family.

After introductions, Gia brought me over to the dining room table, where she held baby Lucy in her lap and said, "That was why I had to leave my husband."

"What was?" I asked without a clue. She softly touched her face. When I made a curious expression and felt the dull pain of my own bruises, I realized she thought I had been beaten.

"Yep, the price of love," I said, too exhausted to explain that I was not the victim of domestic abuse. I wrote a check covering first and last month's rent and was shown to the second door on the left. To paraphrase the old joke, my room was so small I had to go outside to change my mind about renting it. Since I didn't even bother to go to Noah's to pick up my bundled belongings, I slept sprawled out on the floor. The stereophonic delight of hearing both babies from my right wall and Tex's explosive flatulence from the other had not been included in the Web site sales brochure. Still, after the past twenty-four hours, even on the splintery floor, I slept through most of it. Early the next morning I started making calls to the cast: an emergency meeting at noon.

"What's the problem now?" they all separately asked, each in their own fractured vernacular and still bitter with me from the night before.

"Too complicated to tell," I said before hanging up. When I called Svetlana and told her that we were going to break it to them at noon, she started weeping.

"What am I going to do?" she asked.

"Frankly, I can't believe you did something this fucking dumb!"

"I just figured no one would notice it."

"How could you think that?"

"When Bull was alive no one noticed her," she blurted through tears. Another unappreciated irony.

"We'll share the blame."

"You don't mind?" she responded through sniffles.

" 'Course I mind! I would never do something this stupid."

"I'm sorry."

"Did you even try pitching the play to the estate?"

"No," she whispered. "I didn't want to alert them."

"Alert them! We sent press releases halfway around the world! I mean do you know how much money everyone invested?"

"Yes," she cried, "about five thousand dollars apiece."

"They were conned! You conned them!" I yelled.

She wept and grew panicky. "Suppose they call the police on me. I'm broke, I can't pay anyone back!"

"I don't know! Let me think this over."

This was the exact reason that I was the designated pigeon for this shell game: I was the fool who wouldn't prosecute. But, led by the heartless Huey, would they? I searched my brain considering some no-fault way to present this.

All that came to mind was containment, not letting everyone know exactly how extensive this debacle was. If they knew that Svetlana wrote the play they'd be far more infuriated and unforgiving than if they learned that for some reason the estate had reneged on its offer because of some technicality. I tried to recall if any of them had examined the original contract. I vaguely remembered Svetlana briefly showing it to Huey at the first meeting. He didn't look at it very closely. Svetlana had paraphrased it for him. I considered the possibility of drawing up another fictitious contract and adding some confusing clause that would allow the estate to suddenly exit.

Then I remembered that the original false contract was signed by the expelled addict, Bree Silverburn. He was always a flake. Based on my last conversation with him, he was still devoted to Svetlana. So I considered a way to lay the bulk of the blame at Bree's feet saying something like he sold the rights to a third party. After all, why shouldn't he? He technically had the rights, and we cut him out. He had threatened to withdraw them. What did he owe us? That seemed to be the best way out: Blame the invisible wheel of cheese and let him take the fall. He was out of the loop anyway, off at some rehab camp.

I called Svetlana back and timidly asked, "I know this sounds awful but . . ." I suddenly felt too embarrassed to say it.

"What?" she pressed.

"I know this is despicable, but it's the only thing I can think of."

"What is? Just say it."

"I thought maybe we could pin the whole thing on Bree."

"That's a great idea," she immediately jumped on board. There was nothing like desperation to reveal how pathetic most people were.

"Is Bree still in detox?"

"No, he's back in town."

"Shit! We only have about an hour before our meeting, and I have to bail out of this roach motel. Listen, Bree likes you. Call him and work it out so that when Huey or someone calls, he doesn't shift the whole thing back onto us."

"Okay," she agreed.

"And do it!" I yelled. "Because I'll call him afterward to make sure you did it."

"I wouldn't lie to you," she replied, then paused a moment and added, "again."

She told me she would call me right back after the Bree call. I used the time to wash off. The bathroom reeked of infant shit. The kitchen was covered with filth and roaches. Although the two sisters were quite sweet and lived under obvious adversity, they were not fastidious. I simply couldn't remain in the northern borough.

While Gia was feeding her kids, I sat across from her and said, "Gia, I've got a bit of a problem and I hope you can understand."

"What is it, hon?" She was so grateful to have someone helping with the rent.

"I gamble," I said, surprising myself with my own spontaneity. "I'm a compulsive gambler."

"There are support groups for that," she replied as she spooned some Gerber's into her kids, taking spoonfuls for herself between the two children.

"I attend meetings, but that's not the point. The point is, that check I gave you is bad."

"So pay in cash."

I wondered for a moment if my share was carrying the entire rent.

"I don't have enough money to cover this place."

"What exactly are you saying?" She stopped the feeding.

"I'd like to pay for the night I've stayed here but I've got to move back in with my parents."

"Fine," she said calmly and resumed her duties.

"Would fifty dollars cover the expenses of last night?" I asked. It was a generous offer.

"Sure," she said blandly.

"Would you mind if I got my check back?" I asked.

"I'll give you your check back," she said, never changing her disposition, "but you don't have to bullshit me."

"What do you mean?"

"If you were a gambler, you wouldn't give a shit about a check. You spent the night and you don't like living here. Maybe 'cause of me or my sister or whatever—it don't matter. You never even bothered to check the place out. You're entitled to not like it. Just don't bullshit me because that insults me."

I was physically unable to blush so I just didn't respond. She gave me the check and took the fifty dollars. I grabbed my jacket and was gone. At a corner bodega, I bought a fifty-cent cup of coffee, which was the best cup I ever drank. I passed a large metal sign, which under old graffiti read DRESS UP YOUR NEIGHBORHOOD CONTEST, 1988. It sounded like a record as to the last time the sidewalk was swept. My cellular rang—it was Svetlana.

"Bree didn't like it, and he said that he wasn't permitted to lie."

"Wasn't permitted?"

"Yeah, he's taking his twelve steps really seriously."

"Shit!"

"But he made me a deal. He said if we paid the cost of having his phone number changed, he won't answer his phone until they do. That way he wouldn't have to dispute the lie."

"I guess that's better than nothing. Don't forget when we see them, we have to be just as pissed as the rest of them."

She said she'd meet me at the Samyoff Theater with everyone else.

Although the Bronx is the only one of New York's five boroughs connected to the continental U.S.A., that morning I felt like I was in another galaxy. The sky was all wrong—there was far too much of it. The buildings were suspiciously squat, and the people looked retro without the attitude. With the elevated trains roaring by, even the time was off. It seemed like the '40s. I finished my coffee and grabbed the D train for the long subway slide down south. I finally emerged on Planet Earth around Twenty-third Street.

The crosstown bus seemed to orbit the globe from west to east; nothing came the other way as I walked along Twenty-third. When I finally arrived at the edge of the world, I was at the Leopold Samyoff. Every member of the cast was already waiting there, including the dreaded Huey and excepting Svetlana. They all wore long, dark coats, standing out front in a circle like a coven of druids. I walked past them, entering, and they followed.

"Why the fuck are we here this early?" the director asked, standing near the door, smoking a cigarette and holding a paper cup of tea.

"If this is about your wardrobe," Noah said, swinging my gypsy bundle of clothes at me, "I brought it."

"I just hope she got a good sleep last night," Ken kidded.

"Something awful happened and——" I took a deep suck of air and tried to think of a painless, pithy line. "The show is closed."

"What!" Edith squawked.

"The hell it is!" Mike said.

"I got a call from Bree," I wheeled in the great lie. "He says that he has the permission in his name and he's notifying the estate that he has no affiliation with this production."

I considered mentioning that he had already brought a cease-and-desist order against us, but decided not to because they would have asked to see it and discovered the true fraud.

"This is what we'll do," Huey said, "we'll contact the estate and get our own permission."

"I already tried that," I explained. "The lawyer for the estate said

Bree Silverburn has the rights to do the initial production. It's already been contracted."

"Well," Huey said, "much as I'd hate to lose him, if we have to eject Jonah to save the whale, so be it. Let's get Bree back in the production."

"Wait a second," Ken butted in. "It's noon on a Saturday, when were you first notified that we had to close down the production?"

"This morning," I said, so as not to be accused of hoarding information overnight. "Bree called me and actually he gave me his lawyer's number."

Svetlana quietly entered the theater.

"Hold it," Huey said, turning to her. "I distinctly remember asking you about this when that dope fiend left the production. You said that you worked out some kind of secondary permission with Bree."

"I did," she lied. "We had a verbal agreement that he completely denies now."

Just to put Huey on the defense I added, "Maybe you should have consulted me before you kicked him off the project."

Baxter gave me a nasty look.

"Well, I'll call the son of a bitch myself," Edith replied.

"Me too!" Noah said.

"Be my guest," I said, gladly offering my cellular phone. I even dialed the number to establish credibility. The phone rang and kept ringing. I held it up so they could hear. After enough rings, I summed it up for them: "I don't think he's in town."

"My God, we're fucked," Noah said to my relief, blazing the path to stoic defeat and painful acceptance.

"I can't believe it's over. Just like that," Mike said.

"We invested all our time and money for what!" Edith screamed.

"It's awful," I established my own outraged credentials. "But what can we do?"

"Tell you what we're going to do," Huey announced. "We're going to perform the show tonight and let this drug fiend try to shut us down. In fact, you know what I'm going to do, I'll call Juan Valasquez at the *Local Vocal*. This will be great publicity! I'll have Sykes deliver photos of Bree to run with the article. We'll notify the Volunteer Lawyers for the Arts. The ACLU too."

"That would be the wrong thing to do," I said sternly.

"Trust me, this is the only way to deal with little shits," Huey remarked confidently. "You flush them down before they stink up the joint."

"Perhaps, but before you get us into some huge legal battle, please remember that this is our production, and before we get in over our heads, I think we should privately discuss it."

"I think Huey's absolutely right," Edith said. "I've never heard of a play being shut down. It's outrageous—let's call the press!"

"If they want to make this into something political, that's fine," Ken said.

"Did you see *Cradle Will Rock*?" Mike asked. It was a historical film by Tim Robbins about the heroic efforts of actors who prevail over theatrical censorship in the '30s. "Maybe someday they'll do a film about us!"

Actors always loved the higher cause.

"The problem is, they won't close us down," Svetlana joined in. "What they'll do is sue us."

"Let them," Noah replied. "Disaffected Artist Types isn't even incorporated."

"Exactly," Svetlana said, "so they'll go after everyone individually."

"She's absolutely right," I concurred, feeling a glimmer of hope that we had the upper hand. "They'll garner wages, freeze bank accounts, and confiscate assets. All of that shit."

"Let's go for it," Noah said. "They're already doing that because of my student loan."

"I'm nervously on board," Mike said.

"I'm in," Edith said, and so, of course, was Ken. Although he was technically hired by us producers, so he could arguably escape libel.

"Well, I'm not in," I finally applied the brakes.

"What?" Edith said.

"I'm sorry but I'm not in," I replied, and as earnestly as I could I added, "I plan to have a life after this and I'm just a little scared."

"How did I know you'd fold first," Huey squeezed.

"Hey," Mike spoke up, "she's absolutely entitled to not be in the production."

"I'm shocked. Despite yesterday's fiasco, I thought you were committed to theater," Edith remarked, then caught herself, "but I'm not blaming you."

"So we'll get someone else," Noah said.

"Oh, I know half a dozen actresses that will leap at the opportunity," Mike said. "They'll have to do it script in hand for a few performances, but so be it."

"Oh, God," Huey said, "you know who I talked to just the other day, and she was actually interested in the play? I mean I think I might even be able to get her."

"Who?"

"Madison Mosley." She was a popular downtown indie film actress.

As the rest of them chatted and planned, I sighed and headed toward the rear of the theater, where Svetlana sat looking despondently.

"What the fuck are we going to do?" she asked in a slow and dire whisper.

"I'm thinking," I said, but I was all out of ideas. All I knew for certain was that I couldn't let them leave here believing this play was going up tonight.

"All right," I called out, selecting the only strategy I could think of. "I'll tell you what we can do. The man has the rights to put up the play first. I'll go over there and if he's home, I'll just try to compromise with him."

"How?" Edith asked.

"I'll offer him money."

"I thought you said he's out of town," Edith said.

"Maybe he's not," I said, hoping to delay them by any means necessary.

"That's not a bad idea," Huey said.

"No, it's not fair she should do it alone," Mike spoke up. "We should all go over there. Right now. Pile into two cabs and just confront him."

"Let's get the son of a bitch!" Noah exclaimed. The others concurred.

Svetlana and I both let out an audible "we're fucked" sigh.

"Look, if he is home and we all just show up," I said, trying to keep them from leaving, "it's going to scare him off!"

"That's what we want," Huey shot back.

"I'm going to get some cabs," Noah said, and dashed out into the northbound lanes of the West Side Highway.

"Wait a second!" Svetlana yelled as everyone started heading out.

"Let me just speak to him alone," I pleaded, not budging. "I mean this whole thing started out with him and me. Let me reason with him."

"Sorry," Mike said as he joined everyone else outside. "We invested way too much money in this."

"That's true but when you consider . . .," I tried to rebut as he walked out. I grabbed my coat and dashed outside to find everyone piling into two cabs.

"What's the address?" Edith yelled from the first cab, along with Huey, Ken and Mike.

"Oh, I forgot it!" I replied.

"One Thirty-four Mott Street," Noah said, holding up his crumpled contact sheet.

"Hold it a second!" I said, but off they sped. Noah, Svetlana and I followed.

"What the fuck are we going to do?" Svetlana asked in a tizzy.

"I haven't . . . I don't . . ." The situation had completely gotten away from me. I opened my phone to warn Bree, but realized he wasn't picking up.

"We're just going to talk to him," calmed Noah, always three steps behind.

We shot down the West Side Highway, cut across Houston, slashing through SoHo into the heel of NoLita. I prayed Bree was out.

"We are in such deep shit," Svetlana said.

"This is nothing to worry about," Noah tried to calm her.

"Just don't panic," I coached her. "Let me handle it."

"We all will," said the well-meaning Noah.

"This is my fault," Svetlana started going batty, "it's all my fault."

"It happened. Just cool it," I told her.

"But it's my fault."

"It's not your fault," Noah said. His innocence was like a bad joke that was just going too far. As our taxi came into view of Bree's building, I saw the cab in front of us halt. All bounded out. Edith pushed open the broken front door of his dilapidated apartment building. Everyone from the first cab followed her inside. Our taxi came to a halt. I tossed a ten-dollar bill to the front seat and along with Svetlana, followed. Of course, Noah, who never overtipped in his life, waited around for the change so the driver wouldn't get a penny more than fifteen percent.

As we entered the stairwell we could see Huey's fat ass turning a landing up the steps and a second later heard Mike banging on Bree's door.

"Hold on now," I called out, "there's more to this than meets the eye."

My last prayer was duly ignored as we heard Bree open his door.

"Where the fuck do you get off trying to close us down!" Edith yelled.

"What!"

"Why don't you just overdose!" Mike said diplomatically. "You disgusting little drughead."

"Oh, no, this wasn't supposed . . .," he tried explaining and looked to Svetlana and me as we huffed up the steps.

Without his permission, everyone had bustled into his apartment, which was surprisingly straightened up. As Edith and Mike yelled at him, Noah finally showed up, rushing past everyone else, screaming, "I begged, borrowed and stole to get this production up and you ain't going to stop it. No way!"

"I'm not stopping it!" Bree shouted back.

Noah punched him right in the face, misunderstanding that he wasn't trying to stop the production. When Bree went down, Noah jumped on top of him, hitting him as the rest of us scrambled to break them up.

"*Stop it!!*" Svetlana screamed. "I did it! It's all my fault!"

Edith and Mike, who were struggling with Noah, instantly stopped. All looked over to her.

"I read in Lilly Bull's memoirs that she had written a play called *Unlubricated* and that the work was never found," Svetlana explained through tears. "I wrote it based on her notes."

That lapse of several minutes was the length of time it took for the slowest of the group to fully understand a great fraud had been perpetrated upon them.

"But I saw a permission statement," Huey remembered clearly.

"I wrote that too," she said. "It was all my fault."

"I can't believe it," said Huey, amazed.

"Fucking bitch!" Ken cursed quietly.

"It's always the stage manager," I joked.

"Svetlana, we invested thousands of dollars," Mike said angrily. "How could you do this to us?"

"My friends and relatives were all coming in from out of town," Edith shouted.

Five rays of anger projected by everyone seemed to merge into a single beam of pain aimed right into Svetlana's spinal cord. She sat looking off in a sort of twitching paralysis, as though she had been stung by a school of jellyfish.

"Can we have her arrested?" Ken finally asked the group.

"For what? Writing a play without a license?" I asked.

"She can't get away with this!" Noah said.

"Look, we can all work this out," I tried calming them.

"I turned down a BBC radio production of *Plato's The Cave* for this!" Kenny yelled.

"Look, I had a role in this too," I confessed to lighten some of her cringing guilt. "I knew we didn't have permission, but I figured that they wouldn't care. Just give me some time to sit down and we'll all come to some resolution."

"What the fuck are you talking about?" somebody asked. We had reached a pointlessness of no return. I no longer had to answer and no one else cared.

"You know, I had my doubts about this one," Huey said, pointing to Bree. "But you!" He looked right at me. "I knew you were crafty from the start, but I never suspected you were such a Judas."

"Give me a fucking break, the only reason you ever got into this play is because that little con you pulled at the Roustabout Theater fell through!"

"What little con?" he shot back.

"Bullshitting them that you had Rupert Everett agreed to do the Synge play—it was in the newspaper."

"You contemptible Semite!" he exclaimed. "I strongly advise you to get yourself a solicitor." It was the most euphonic anti-Semitic slur I had ever suffered.

When he walked out, the others followed. They left as they came—a disgruntled mob. Bree went to the bathroom and washed the blood out of his nose and checked his split lip.

"Well, I see you cleaned your house," I said, always looking for that silver lining.

"After Jerry moved out, I had no more excuses. It's one of the things I have to do for NA," he said from the bathroom.

Out in the living room, Svetlana remained softly sobbing on the couch in a near catatonic state. I sat next to her.

"I'm so sorry," she said through tears.

"Are you sorry you wrote a wonderful play, or are you sorry you did everything you could to put it up?" The time for recrimination was over.

"I'm sorry I lied to you."

"If you didn't, I wouldn't have put it up," I replied and put my arm around her.

After I again apologized to Bree, Svetlana and I walked to the train. She headed to Brooklyn, I went the other way to Penn Station. It was over.

40

CURTAIN RISER

THE·LONG·ISLAND·RAIL·ROAD to Great Neck usually leaves twenty after the hour on weekends and holidays. I had just missed one. I bought a one-way ticket. A moderate wait left me roaming around the long, narrow underground walkway. National Guard troops stationed near the stairs and exits reminded me that we were still a nation at war and in mourning. A bomb-sniffing chocolate Lab looked adorable but I sensed I wasn't supposed to pet it. I stopped by the southeasterly wall filled with missing posters of those killed at the Trade Center. After seeing so many of their faces from so many other memorials throughout the city, I almost felt that I knew some of them: the husband from Baldwin whose children would never climb up his shoulders; the daughter whose parents would wait forever in Manhasset; the son in the football jersey who looked like he was probably a college intern.

Soon the gate was announced. A long train ride and then a local bus down Middle Neck Road to the last stop, where the neighborhood bulged into the Long Island Sound. From there it was a ten-minute walk with Dominican housekeepers and cooks. My family's house in

King's Point was at the very end of the road. Since I last came out here the area had become busy with nouveau-riche construction. Hardworking Persian immigrants were pouring into Great Neck and all points north. One can make a fortune overnight, but acquiring culture takes a lifetime. In its place there are only bold clichés of wealth, "trademarks of elegance." BMWs, Mercedes-Benzes and sporty Ferraris slipped around the curvy roadways. The newly erected houses were architectural omelets, part Frank Lloyd Wright modernism and part Monticello classic with perhaps a slight dash of the Taj Mahal.

Up the long, windy driveway, around the manicured lawn, I preferred the soft pasture of lush grass to the hard stone steps. About a hundred feet beyond our huge pool that no one ever swam in were the blue waters of the Long Island Sound. The unfeeling monolith sat in his bathing suit and Hawaiian shirt reading the *Wall Street Journal*. I quietly took a chair behind him, hoping he might not notice me.

"Hi, kid," he said, looking up. Dad had his unlit cigar clamped in his mouth. His huge black Ray-Ban glasses that revealed what losers we all are were pointed right at me.

"Hey yourself," I coughed out. A dragonfly had landed upside down on the hot pavement and was desperately trying to right itself.

"I don't mean to sound anything other than joyous," he said, "but why exactly are you here?"

"Isn't it Passover?"

"It came early this year," he kidded back.

As I sat down, I was careful to show him my left side so he couldn't see my bruises.

"You know there's one gift I think I acquired as a businessman," he said, admiring himself. "I know when someone is holding on by their fingernails. It helps me know how low I can go in buying." When I thoughtlessly turned to him, he grimaced and asked, "Who hit you?"

"It was an accident," I said and chuckled. "You're not going to believe this, but I fell out of a very high bed."

He saw my bedraggled look and gypsy bundle of sample sale and designer clothes.

"As usual, I don't have a clue what it's like being you, but your mother and I saw you in that play yesterday. She was going to call you, but I thought, if you have nothing good to say . . ."

"I didn't have anywhere to sleep the night before," I said, not wanting to recount it all.

"Maybe you should have spent that night here," he said.

"So how've you been?" I changed the subject.

He didn't respond. I could see that he was staring southeasterly. From our patio, looking over the Long Island Narrows, you used to clearly make out three skyscrapers that rose from Manhattan in the distance. Now I could see only one—the Empire State Building. My father had slaved behind a desk for years in the Twin Towers. I knew that he had suffered when they collapsed, and it was never easy for him to talk about his feelings.

"Someone from college approached me," I tried to explain my predicament. "Said he came across this weird little play. It was funny, touching, original. . . . The woman who wrote it was allegedly a homeless prostitute, but that's another story. . . . I had these investors who were friends from college. . . . Anyway I thought if we could just get this whole thing together . . . If I could just . . . fit the pieces . . . money, a cast of friends as the investors, a hot property, a celebrity director, the pieces were all there . . . I mean, you try to do something good, something that might be original and profitable . . . I mean . . . I didn't do it for fame or money or anything. . . ."

"Well, why did you do it?" he asked.

"Just to shake the depression really. I'm not saying there wasn't anything in it for me but I thought my friends would . . ." I caught myself for only a second before I let loose: "You know what friends are? They're people who turn on you when you stumble. They kick you and stomp you. . . . You know what a boyfriend is? He's a nice, sweet guy who you just don't feel anything for." I caught myself and just breathed.

"Why don't you go upstairs?" he finally said softly. "Take a shower and get some sleep."

Silently, I went into the house and did exactly that. My mother woke me early that evening and asked how long I was planning on staying. "I just want to know if I should buy some more food."

"Buy food."

I spent the next day reclining in my large, sunlit bedroom just trying to unthink. In all fairness, they were never kinder. For several moments, I think they were actually worried. I probably wasn't myself, just trying to adjust to the darkness that was no longer life: No apartment I lied to get. No sad, misprescribed boyfriend I kept breaking up with, no fraudulent play we had all worked so hard to put up. No ethnic role I wasn't right for in Christy's film. What had it all come to?

My mother put a chicken salad sandwich and a mug of herbal tea on a coffee table near me, but I wasn't hungry. I was gorging on self-pity.

"You know your father donated three thousand dollars to a nine-eleven charity and it turned out to be a fraud," she said, trying to start conversation.

"He should call the D.A.'s office."

She asked if she could get me anything else. I shook my head. I felt like I was in some Swiss sanitarium taking the cure.

When I looked at the books and magazines on the coffee table, I realized most of them were about the World Trade Center tragedy. When I asked Mom what all this was about, she said he read everything.

"Don't bring it up," she whispered, "but he even went to some of the firefighters' funerals."

That night, I sat up in bed with the lamp on, tired yet unable to sleep. Mom came in the room and made the unprecedented move of hugging me.

"What the hell is this?" she asked, touching the lump on my arm.

"Nothing," I told her. "I had a doctor look at it."

"What doctor?" She put on her glasses.

"Wang, an acupuncturist." Then I remembered that he wasn't really a doctor, at least not licensed.

"We'll just have Dr. Burke take a look."

I agreed and that was that. Years ago when my parents decided I was too brilliant for my own good, Ma took the advice of another kind of doctor, a psychiatrist who suggested I join a kind of summer camp for the rich and precocious. No pills or bars on the window. Just a lot of psychobabble and post-adolescent sex.

The week before the camp ended, my parents came and sat on one side of a table while I sat at the other. It was like an informal trial. I remember my father stating that I was more than he had bargained for.

"I sometimes wonder if she's our daughter," he had explained. "She has completely different values and tastes."

He hadn't said anything horrific. The fact that he needed to talk to me through a child psychiatrist set the tone for our entire relationship.

The next morning, before I was out of bed, Mom shoehorned me in for an afternoon appointment. I felt as though I were a child. Dr. Burke touched the lump and asked if it hurt.

"No," my mother answered for me, "she said some Chinese man looked at it, but I thought it would be better to let you check it out."

It was evident I could no longer take care of myself.

"Well," he said, "it's probably just a soft tissue tumor, but . . ." He took a needle biopsy that stung like a bitch. "We'll know for sure by tomorrow."

When I got home, I called the Three Stooges law firm to explain that I had a tragic mishap. I suffered a mild concussion and unfortunately wouldn't be coming back. The supervisor wished me well and promised to send the balance of my paycheck to my Long Island address.

When I noticed my cellular, I realized that since leaving the city two days ago I had left my phone off. I checked my messages found several calls from some guy with a slight accent asking me to call him back. Also I had three messages from Svetlana, each one more frantic than the last. I called her immediately. It turned out my school buddies had retained a litigator who had filed a civil suit naming Svetlana and myself as the defendants.

"How much money do they want?"

"Twenty thousand dollars in real damages and another fifty thousand in punitive damages."

It really didn't matter. Neither of us had that kind of money. All it really meant was that we'd be sued and would have to file bankruptcy and now I positively, definitely wouldn't have a credit card. Unfortunately it didn't stop there. Late on Tuesday night, just after I had spent the evening awake in bed, my cell phone rang. When I picked it up, I was greeted with the question: "Did you fucking see the *Local Vocal*?!"

"You mean tomorrow's?" I asked, fairly certain it was Christy.

" 'Course I mean tomorrow—you didn't read it, did you?"

"What does it say?" I asked, bracing myself for a less-than-favorable review.

"Congratulations—you've made the cover!"

"You're kidding!"

"Well, it's actually a photo of you alone standing on one side of a scale for justice and a group of idiots sitting on a sofa on the other side of the scale. The headline says PLAYED FOR SUCKERS! by Juan Valasquez.

"Read it to me."

" 'Hitler's diaries, Howard Hughes's autobiography, JFK's love letters to Marilyn and now Lilly Bull's swan song *Unlubricated*. These will be listed as the great frauds of the past twenty-five years. In the last case, it took three people to paint, hang and finance this fake *Mona Lisa*. It all began when a young woman named Svetlana Palas, who happens to be a talented young unknown writer, read Lilly Bull's last published work. For those who don't remember, Bull was the infamous writer and attempted assassin of downtown musician Gary Ganghole. Palas evidently read *Bull Session*, her final work, specifically the notes of a full-length play that Bull entitled *Unlubricated*.

" 'Whether Bull actually wrote the play is arguable. No one has ever admitted to having read the work, but apparently friends claimed at the time that they did see Lilly carrying around a finished manuscript. She died soon afterward, and among other things that were lost to posterity was this alleged masterpiece, *Unlubricated* . . . until roughly two months ago, when a young actress-turned-producer named Hannah Cohn approached her former Yale buddies, members of a small acting company called Disaffected Artist Types.

" ' "She conned us into believing they had uncovered this lost work," actor/coproducer Noah Rampoh said. "She even attempted to sell it to indie film producer Manny Greene." ' "

"Son of a bitch," I muttered. "Do me a favor and skip ahead."

"Fine," Christy said, and continued, " ' "We're not a wealthy group of investors," actress/coproducer Edith Rothchild said after being scammed of thousands. "We all had day jobs while we were in rehearsal."

" 'Rothchild explained that after convincing everyone to pool their modest savings, they had attracted a skilled British director, Huey Baxter, into staging the work.

" 'The three young actors spent the past two months in pre-production, locating a stage, building props, and rehearsing. In fact, it wasn't until their premiere that a process server from the Bull Estate delivered a cease-and-desist order against the production. Only then did the rest of the company learn the awful truth . . .' "Christy paused. Apparently she was getting bored with the article. "Blah, blah, blah. . . . And they're planning to sue you."

"Can you skip ahead to what he thought of the play?" I asked. The only detail missing was that I didn't know the work was a fraud until it was too late.

" 'The great irony of *Unlubricated* is that it's too good. While watching it, I thought it was clearly better than anything Ms. Bull had ever written. For the first time, while watching this play, I actually thought that Ms. Bull's death was a genuine loss to American theater. She conjured up a recognizable cast of eccentric artistic types, distilling them down to their raw essence, exploring their darker sides, the grudging jealousy and violent envy, when they are faced with a nimble soul who they briefly believe is a great talent. "Bull" effectively dramatized the stew of human passions that boils out from the cauldron of creativity, along with the inevitable bitterness and frustration that rises to the top. . . .' "

Christy read on to say that the play was quite intelligent and lively. The actors ranged from "overly pompous," which was attributed to Noah Rampoh, to "delicately moving," thanks to Jonah Baye, with Baxter's direction being "flawless—"

"Valasquez would say that, he and Baxter good friends," I interrupted. "What did he say about me?"

"'Perhaps guilt makes a good primer as Ms. Cohn's acting was truly stimulating. I don't recall seeing a performance so weighed in the moment without it seeming artificial or pretentious. She brought the sober, yet vulnerable female edge that a roomful of drunken males desperately needed. . . .'"

I did feel a surge of pride, but it didn't exculpate me. The review wouldn't even have been on the cover if it wasn't to humiliate me. And even if it was simply a good review, those few critical sentences were hardly worth all the pain, anger, humiliation and sacrifice.

"'One character,'" Christy read on "'a world-class bore named Reggie, was played a little too convincingly by the mundane British actor Kenny Eltwood. During one pivotal scene while all were at the mercy of his endless bloviations, Cohn's Samantha seemed to drift delicately to sleep, which sent the empathetic audience into its biggest laugh of the night. . . . It seems a shame, with such a good play and clear promise, that Ms. Cohn should have to resort to fraud.'"

"He liked you," Christy interrupted her reading.

"Yeah, too bad I'm the biggest swindler in theater history."

"Wow," she exclaimed admirably.

I told Christy I had to get off the phone to go hang myself.

"So you didn't write the film script either, did you?" She finally added one plus one.

"No, Svetlana did."

"Amazing," she said. "I really don't know you at all."

"Hannah Cohn, criminal mastermind," I replied and she hung up. Now all the world knew the truly despicable person I was. No sooner did I hang up the phone than I saw a way to contain the legal damage. I called Christy back.

"Is Manny still buying the script?" I asked.

"I suppose, but do you really think you deserve the credit for it?"

"I never wanted it. Give it to Svetlana. I also want her to get the check. But she needs it as soon as possible because she's getting sued, and she's freaking out. And unlike me she doesn't handle guilt well. I'd hate to have a suicide on my hands."

Christy said she'd speak to Manny immediately and get back to me. Within a half an hour, she called back saying it was settled. I should call Manny the next morning at work. She gave me his number.

Slowly, as people read the free downtown paper, the calls came in—a lot more calls than the televised VJ Awards date, from people I met briefly at acting parties, talked with into the late-night hours, those I worked with at various temp jobs, who I chatted with day in, day out for months and then never saw again, those I flirted with at parties and bars—all to whom, at some point, for no memorable reason, I had thoughtlessly given my cell number. Now I was locked in that cell. They called and either in a slightly mischievous tone, or slightly embarrassed and bewildered, they asked if I had really pulled such a crazy-assed scam. I said yes to the ones I didn't like and told the truth to the few others. Finally, around ten, I had had enough and switched off the modern inconvenience.

As I wandered around the many rooms of the house, I realized my father wasn't home. When I asked my mother where he was, she explained that he went to a grief counseling group two days a week.

I sat before their new flat-screen plasma TV and watched a million cable channels until I finally dozed off. My mother woke me up the next day to inform me that the doctor had called and said the lump on my arm was a fibroadenoma.

"It's malignant?"

"He said it'll probably be absorbed into the body."

"And then it'll spread?"

"It'll be absorbed," she repeated. "He said it was soft tissue, it was nothing. He said to stop drinking coffee and other caffeinated drinks."

"But . . ." I just knew I had cancer.

"You're going to live," my mother said. "Dinner's at seven."

I had to sit down and take a deep stabilizing breath.

"Are you okay?" my mother asked, reminding me of her presence.

"I have something to tell you."

"What?"

"First I want to say thanks for all you've done, I thought coming here was going to be a lot tougher."

"You're just like a daughter to us," she joked, then gave me a hug and dove into the kitchen for cover. She was unprepared for intimacy. We were both out of practice. I decided to tell her about the little scandal later. I got my phone, went to my room, and before even brushing my teeth I called Manny Greene, still pissed that he had dumped me from Christy's film.

"I have to hand it to you," Manny said as soon as his secretary put me through. "I have millions of ways to get cash for a production, but what you did takes the apple crumb."

"Thanks," I said, "how soon can I get the check?"

"This was the bill of goods you were going to option to me, wasn't it?"

"Don't believe me, but I really didn't know that Svetlana wrote the play until later," I said, seeing no point in resisting.

He let out a bellyache of a laugh and said, "Bravo, I got to hand it to you."

"Why don't you hand me the check instead?"

"It'll take a while to work out the contract, but Christy said it's going to this Svetlana girl."

"Yeah."

"Okay, figure it'll be ready in a month."

"Is there any way you can advance it sooner. She's about to be sued for this whole scam—we both are."

"How much are you being sued for?"

"About thirty thousand in real, compensatory damages and another zillion in punitive."

"Well, she's entitled to roughly thirty-three thousand for the screenplay—I'll give the amount in real damages provided she forgoes on a thousand dollars or so on the cost of expediting it."

"Even the Mafia doesn't take that much in interest. I'll let you have two hundred off or I'll borrow it all from Mommy and Daddy until the check arrives." He didn't know that even if they did cough up the cash, I would never take it.

"Make it five hundred."

"Three hundred."

"Fine," he said. "Tomorrow's really hectic. I start interviewing people for a job here. Let's see . . ." I could hear flipping, presumably from pages of an appointment book. "I've got ten minutes at ten."

"Fine."

"Can you bring this Svetlana character? I'd love to meet her."

"Sure," I replied, "see you then." All done, and I didn't have to sleep with him.

In the suburbs there is really nothing to do other than call the city, or wait until it's time to visit the city, which it wasn't. I called Mike because I knew he'd be the natural leader along with Edith, and I sensed that I would get a smidgen more mercy from him.

"Hi, Mike," I said boldly.

"I truly never thought you'd be capable of something as low as this." He launched right into it.

"I guess you wouldn't believe me if I told you that the whole thing was a misunderstanding wrapped in a screwup."

"I don't really give a shit. We're all out about six grand apiece—that's all I give a shit."

"And you know that if you bring this to court, you'll find that I'm penniless and so is Svetlana."

"At least we'll have the satisfaction of knowing. . . ."

"You'll have more satisfaction if you all got your six grand back."

"What are you saying?"

"If you guys all agree to drop the suit, I'll get you your money back."

"When? How?"

"Tomorrow."

"Fine."

"Not fine," I said. "I want a sworn affidavit signed by everyone in the group including Screwy Huey that states you'll all drop the suit and any and all claims. And I want a sentence that emphasizes that we're not accepting any guilt."

"Huey won't be easy but if you get the money, I'll get the statement."

"Fine," I replied and hung up. Next I called Svetlana. She immediately freaked out: "I called you twenty-five times! What? Are you avoiding me now? Leaving me to take this all by myself! All right, it was my fuckup but—"

"*Relax!*" I screamed. "I didn't retrieve any of my messages. I got every nut in the city calling me."

"They've got a cover story on us in *LocalVocal*," she charged right in. "All my friends and family saw it—they're calling us con artists."

"I know, I know," I interrupted her. "I've been called a bit worse than that."

"And this lawsuit is just killing me. My mother has me down on the title of our family apartment. She's pulling her hair out by its roots that we're going to be out in the street!" The poor girl was frantic.

"There's nothing to worry about," I said calmly. "It's all over!"

"What the hell do you mean, it's over?"

"I mean they're dropping their suit."

"What?"

"I'm paying them off."

"With what?"

"The money you earned for me writing the screenplay."

"What?"

"What don't you understand? I'm paying them back all the cash that they invested in the production and in exchange they are dropping the suit and not assigning any blame."

"Hannah, this isn't some kind of joke, is it?"

"You have to meet me at Manny Greene's office tomorrow morning to sign the contract for the script and pick up the check. He's giving it to us early in exchange for three hundred bucks."

"Amazing," she concluded, as though the whole thing were a miracle. I gave her the address of Manny Greene's production company.

"You'll probably be getting a bit more money as well. There's about five grand above the thirty thousand for profit."

"Why don't we split it?" she offered.

"The only reason I wanted the screenplay in my name was to act in the film, and I got cut out. You earned the money, along with Christy and whoever else they hire, you'll get a cowriting credit."

She thanked me profusely and said there would be other plays for me to act in.

Later that day, I got a return call from Mike saying that they all approved of the deal.

"Huey initially said no. We all had to beg him. Then Noah started getting violent, punching a lamp. I think Huey remembered that he had hit Bree, because that's when he finally cowered and said he'd settle for a thousand dollars, which we all agreed to pay out of our end."

We chose a rendezvous point. I was just going to meet with Mike alone, because I didn't have the energy to run the entire gambit again. We picked the Starbucks on Ninth and Second Avenue at eleven o'clock, an hour after my appointment to pick up the check from Manny Greene. Even though it was only noon, I crawled back into bed, exhausted, and fell right back asleep.

41

THE NEW SKYLINE

AWAKENED·BY·AN·EXPLOSIVE·SLAM of the front door a couple of minutes later, I heard my mother scream, "She's your daughter too!" At least two people share the blame for every fuck-up in this world.

I pulled the comforter over my head. Someone must have spotted my head shot on the cover of the *Local Vocal* and informed them about their crazy little girl. In another moment there was a knock on my door. I didn't so much as breathe, but if it didn't work with the landlord, it wasn't going to work with my parents. Another knock, then Mom opened it.

"I'm sorry I said that," she said. She didn't even pretend that I didn't hear her.

"No," I replied, "I should've warned you yesterday."

"Hannah." She sat on the bed and pulled the blanket off me. "This is your home. We're not here to shame you. I know it might be difficult to believe it at times, but we love you. We really do. We think you're brilliant and beautiful. . . ."

"We've been through this." I knew exactly where she was heading.

"You show up here bruised and homeless. The next day your face is on the cover of . . . You've been accused of defrauding people out of money."

"I didn't defraud anyone. We're paying them all back tomorrow."

"Just tell me you're not doing drugs."

"Of course not!" I exclaimed, but I could hardly blame her for asking.

"What pains me, what pains us both, is if you were just some pretty little twit, like the kid next door—this wouldn't be an issue. We'd be glad that you're happy and leave it at that. But you graduated top of your class. You could do a million different things and be successful at them. That's what bothers us most."

She kissed me on my cheek then went back downstairs.

Although the fact that they never supported me hurt, it was still kind of a breakthrough that she was able to even talk about this. In the past, what wasn't relegated to resentful silence simmered through a high-priced therapist who I thought of as a parental translator.

Later that evening, I heard the front door close and figured they had headed out. I pulled on a robe and slippers and headed downstairs to bid farewell to another wasted day. I sat on the patio in a deck chair and stared into the night sky. A shadow seemed to cut a squiggly line across the bright moon so that it looked like a yin and yang circle without the dots. The night was still, I felt safely alone.

"I really tried to do something good," I muttered aloud.

"What was that?" I heard behind me. Sitting in a pool of darkness pulling the newspaper off his lap was Dad, apparently just waking from a snooze.

"I didn't know you were there," I replied, startled by his presence.

"You said something about doing good?" he asked, stretching his arms in a yawn.

"Oh, nothing you haven't heard."

"Come on. Bore me," he pressed.

"I was just thinking that the worst part of this for me was the fact that all my friends thought I betrayed them. I mean, they were my friends, and regardless of whatever wrong I did, I would have paid them back every cent even if it took a lifetime."

"Did you tell them that?"

"Yeah, the last time I saw them. I told them we'd work things out." I thought about it. "I mean, I was fooled as much as them. I should have known better, but I never evaded responsibility."

"Earlier, you said you did this because you were depressed." He pulled his chair closer. "What exactly were you depressed about?"

I wanted to mention that I was a few blocks away when the towers fell down. And that this past fall and winter had been difficult for me, as they had been for so many others. I wanted to tell him that I thought that keeping busy was good therapy, but I didn't know how. Instead I just said, "I got conned."

"But wasn't there some point when you figured out that this whole thing was bullshit, and you still didn't tell them?"

"Yes and no. It's kind of involved, I was in a strange place."

"A strange place where—Poughkeepsie?" he mocked.

"Did Mom tell you about the tumor in my arm?"

"Yeah."

"I know this sounds odd, but I half thought I was dying of cancer."

"Well, believe it or not, I can actually understand that. I've been acting out of anguish myself a bit lately."

"And, if the play went up and we got away with it, I would've been doing them all a big favor." I had never fucked up this badly and I felt nauseous just thinking about it.

After a long pause, Dad asked, "Have you ever wondered why Eric doesn't speak to me?" Eric was his younger brother.

"I thought you weren't speaking to him."

"No, every year I call him and invite him for the holidays. He won't get on the phone."

"I didn't know."

"Twenty-five years ago, when my father died, I was put in charge of the entire estate. I was thirty-two, Eric was twenty-one. We were left a quarter million, which was quite a sum for that time. Eric wanted to invest in some stock tip, but I put the money into a great parcel of real estate."

"Why didn't you just split up the money?"

"That's what we got into a fight over. He wanted to split up the sum, but I had the right to oversee the money until he turned thirty. Dad thought he was irresponsible."

"So you lost all his money for him."

He chuckled. "That would have made sense, wouldn't it? Actually, I made him a millionaire twice over. We resold the property for a mint. I mean, if he invested in what he wanted he would have made some pocket change, but nowhere near the return I made for him. He got more than tenfold. The reason he stopped speaking to me was because he had the right to invest his money any way he saw fit."

"But you did what was best."

"Ah, but this is the curse of being too smart. I might've done what was best, but I didn't do what was right. He had the right to lose his money and I took that away. Life isn't about making the best choices, it's simply about making choices. If you really think that someone's making a mistake, you still have to step back and let them do it. It's one of the most difficult lessons. Eric was an adult. More importantly he was my only brother. Whether he was smart or dumb, I should have given him that money. If I was really smart I would've protected our relationship."

After a momentary silence, I told him, "I just figured that if the play went up and got great reviews and made us all stars, and then they found out it was a fraud, they would've been grateful I hadn't told them."

"Maybe so," he said, "but you still would've been wrong."

I didn't need him to say that. Still, I appreciated the time he gave me. My conscience felt lighter.

"So are you okay?" I asked.

"Oh yeah," he replied, solid as always. "It's difficult to explain why this World Trade Center thing has taken so much out of me but . . ." He waved it off.

"I understand. You spent so much time there," I tried to help him. "It's difficult not to think that you would've been in your office."

"Nonsense," he kidded, "I'm Jewish. We all got the e-mail." He was referring to the ridiculous anti-Semitic rumor that Jews were warned in advance of 9/11 and told to not go to work that day.

"You know," I told him, "I'd rather you didn't tell Mom, but . . . I was down there that morning."

"Down where?"

"I got out of the train on Broadway and Vesey, but quicker than I knew what was happening, I was evacuated."

"You're kidding."

"I was on Centre Street near Worth when the first one came down. I got covered in that cloud of dust and papers. . . . I mean, I was fine. Nothing happened to me. I shouldn't have even been down there. But I don't think a day has gone by when I don't envision those people scrambling down all those dark smoke-filled stair-wells."

"Most were probably just waiting up there for the firemen," he said, perhaps trying to give me some peace of mind.

"Some of them must've realized that it was about to come down. I mean, they couldn't've just all been sitting blissfully in there. Aside from the smoke and flames, they said that you could hear the interior of the building slowly giving way before the final collapse."

"The tressels," he replied. I knew he had seen the same documentary about the engineering design of the building that I had.

"Others must have thought about their children and just thought, Fuck it, and got the nerve to break free of the rest and tried dashing down all those flights as the building was coming apart, just running to get out."

"I keep wondering how many of them would've made it if they could've put helicopters on the roof," he said.

"And we didn't even lose any family members," I reminded him, feeling as though I didn't even have the right to obsess this much.

There was a brief lapse, then he said, "When I was a young man, not much older than you, I started working in and around Wall Street. I remember when those goddamned buildings first went up. Two rusty towers that kept going higher and higher. When they finished them, my firm got an office in there. Well you know, when I retired two years ago, I'd look over and see them. They were like a memorial to all those years. I would've definitely been killed if I were still working there. All the people and friends . . . I can still see the space." He pointed to the exact spot in the skyline. "That emptiness is where I spent my life."

Suddenly he lunged forward and clung to me like a child who was drowning. Initially I could feel him weeping against me, something I never saw and was afraid to see now. He held me so hard I thought he was going to break a rib, but I hugged him even harder, intent on not letting go until he did. Finally, after a long time, we heard Mom's car come up the driveway. When she shouted my name, he softly released me.

"Thank you," he whispered, and I went inside.

42

Deux Ex Machina

THE · NEXT · DAY I spent about two hours manically dressing. It wasn't until just before I had to leave that I realized what I was doing—I was costuming as the accused. I was trying to look perfect because I knew that I was going to be scrutinized. My mother drove me silently to the LIRR as though to my execution. When another driver cut her off, she flipped him the finger.

"Wow, I never saw you do that," I said. Such honesty was uncharacteristically refreshing.

"Most people are idiots. You shouldn't worry about what they think." I knew she was trying to be supportive. I wanted to kiss her, but I didn't think she was ready.

"This is shaping into a really great stay," I said, earnestly, compelling her to turn away embarrassed. I just made my train.

As the train passed through northwestern Queens, passed the marshes of Douglaston, Flushing—the new Chinatown—passed the old World's Fair globe, and Shea Stadium, I wondered what lay ahead.

At Penn Station, I grabbed the IRT and headed over to Manny Greene's production office on Forty-fifth and Seventh Avenue. The waiting room was small but cozy. Svetlana wasn't there yet, but the magazines were all fairly current so I didn't mind. He was still with his nine-thirty. I went to the bathroom, checked my makeup, and tried not to puke or cry. When I came out Svetlana was standing in the hall-way fidgeting.

"Hannah!" I led her inside, where she immediately started pacing.

"Heel," I instructed her.

She took a seat. She really did bring out the mother in me. I sat next to her.

With her goody-goody suit, she too had all the signs of overdres-sia nervosa, putting on clothes that made her look beyond saintly. Her large checkered handbag was the only goofy exception. We both folded our hands on our laps and twiddled our thumbs, trying our best not to swindle or con anyone. When another well-dressed woman came in and took a seat with us, Svetlana started getting fidg-ety again.

"Is there anything I need to know or say?" she whispered very softly.

"Just bat your beautiful lashes, and he'll give you a check."

"That's it?"

"Then give me the check, so I can pay off the scoundrels and get the charges dropped."

Manny's door finally opened fifteen minutes later and an attractive woman in her forties carrying a maroon briefcase and wearing phe-nomenal shoes exited. In another minute, Manny came out. He gave me a hug. When I introduced him to Svetlana, he took her hand in both his palms and said, "Your screenplay is brilliant."

"Thanks."

"You have another interview at ten-fifteen," his secretary reminded him. He checked his wristwatch, thanked her, and showed us into a large office. Lining his walls were framed posters of films he had pro-duced over the years.

"How many scripts have you written before?" he asked Svetlana.

"Never scripts, just plays," she said, then corrected herself, "except for this one."

"It really pulled me in. The characters came to life. The dialogue was as crisp as an apple. It was witty with great observations—I really felt as though I were looking through a window at these people. And the plot came so naturally I didn't even see it."

"Thank you," she said. The big smile looked strange on her Mona Lisa face.

"People think that just 'cause they talk, they can write," Manny went on. "It's like assuming that just 'cause you can run for a bus you can do a marathon." Although I knew she would never have laughed at a remark like that, she giggled politely.

Manny flipped through several documents on his desk and finally located what he was looking for.

"Okay," he said, then intercommed his secretary to come in and be a witness. When she entered, he placed the multipage document before Svetlana, and flipping through it, he said, "Peruse and sign here and here and here."

She did so without reading it.

"You know, if you're interested, I might have another project for you," he said as he searched through his top desk drawer. He took out a large three-ring binder consisting of checks. As he began filling one in, I asked him if he could do us a favor.

"Why am I always worried when you ask me that?" he kidded.

"All we were hoping is that you can put"—I checked the figure—"twenty-six thousand three hundred and sixty dollars in one check and sign it over to Mike Mildone and put the balance of nine thousand dollars in a separate check addressed to Svetlana."

"Who is this Mike Mildone?" he asked.

"We're paying back the company for the money they lost with *Unlubricated*," Svetlana explained.

"Oh, the article in the *Local Vocal*," Manny recalled, and as he started cutting the two checks he said, "I've never had to pay a backer for money lost, but then again, I always told them whom the writer was."

Manny tore the checks out of his book and handed them to Svetlana. She gave me the one for Mike and put the other in her large checkered handbag. When Manny rose, we both followed. As he walked us to the door, Svetlana thanked him profusely for everything. He in turn said he would call her about a new project he had just purchased.

"I've never gotten paid for writing anything," Svetlana confessed.

"Well then, I'd say your time has come," he declared as he held his office door open. Before I could exit, he asked, "Would you mind if I spoke to you alone a moment?"

"Sure," I said and stayed as Svetlana took a seat in the reception area next to the responsible, well-dressed lady. She opened her checkered bag and discreetly stared at her new check. It more than compensated her for the money she had put into the production.

"You know I've tried to keep track of you," he began. "I mean, excuse me if I'm a bit bold here, but you had some hanky-panky with both Franklin and Christy. Maybe you loved her, but you certainly got something from both of them. You also found Christy a good writer who would work for scale wages, while at the same time putting up a play with Huey Baxter and Kenny Eltwood without having to part with a cent—all quite impressive."

"Thanks," I replied, "but I'm completely screwed. My reputation in this business is ruined."

"That's ridiculous. Show business is filled with sleazebags, charlatans, and impostors of all kinds—it's perfect for you."

"But according to Christy you dumped me from the film before you even saw me fall asleep onstage," I fired back, unable to contain my anger about that.

"It had nothing to do with your acting. It's all about money and you know that. The script was so good that I knew I could get a much wider distribution, but that meant I'd have to get triple the original budget and for that I'd need either a Penelope Cruz or a Salma Hayek. Didn't Christy tell you that I wanted to speak to you?"

"Yeah, but she said it wasn't about a part."

"Actually, I got the biggest part for you. Have a seat." I sat down with this awful feeling that I was about to get swindled somehow. "I think you'd make a great producer. You're a little young, and it's a twenty-four-hour, high-energy job, but I think you'd be perfect for it." The P word was just waiting for me.

"I appreciate that, but I want to be an actress."

"You know I've seen audition halls filled with actors who can do more or less the same part. You are the first person I've seen since Ms. Pumilla who I really think can produce."

"Well, I appreciate that, but you know nothing about me."

"I've seen you produce that play while you were acting in it, and performing in Stein's film, as well as writing up Christy's script." He nodded in disbelief. "I mean, ask my secretary, I've nicknamed you Supergirl."

"Wow . . ." I was completely flabbergasted.

"If you're interested in working on a trial basis I'm willing to give you a shot."

"But I've never formally done production."

"Cynthia will walk you through it. She's still under contract for another six months. What she doesn't teach you, I'll show you myself."

"I'd need some time to think about it."

"I'm behind schedule on a winter project and I needed someone a week ago." I stood there thinking about it.

"The starting salary is thirty thousand over four payments," he said, "but you get a big bonus with each film you complete. Ten grand up front." These figures crashed like asteroids through my impoverished skull.

Ten grand wasn't just ten grand, it was a rocket-fueled space shuttle out of what was promising to be a lengthy orbit in the Long Island nebula. And this job was the best face-saving situation fate was ever going to bestow. I had given everything to being an actress and it only took more and more out of me. The joy of doing it was constantly out-weighed by all my herculean effort to get there. Gone were the youth-ful ideals and grand notions about art leading to even greater things. The cult of celebrity, the fetish of glitz, were effectively overthrown. To me, actors were now vulgar self-promoters. Glamour was tomor-row's camp. If there was some light at the end of this tunnel I couldn't see it. More importantly I no longer had faith in it. On one hand I had no experience, on the other hand, I would have loved to give it a shot.

"I'll give the job my best," I replied, trying not to sound foolish.

Manny asked if I could report tomorrow. I could, but checking my watch, I was late in meeting with Mike. Both Svetlana and I grabbed a cab downtown. When we arrived, we found all four of them occupying the filthy couch in the rear of Starbucks—Noah, Mike, Edith and even Belinda were angrily holding medium lattes. She had recuperated enough to recoup the limited three grand that she too had invested.

"So this was why you were so reluctant for us to rent the Samyoff?" Belinda dug right in.

"I'm glad to see you're back to your old shitty self," I replied.

"Both of you, cut it out!" Edith intervened. The meeting didn't last much longer. Svetlana and I admitted that there was greed, ambition, hope and lapses, but this was essentially an error of come-dies.

After Belinda, who seemed to think we were somehow responsi-ble for her near-fatal illness, Noah was the angriest. The play was sup-posed to rescue him from extra-dom. Edith was also profoundly dis-appointed; Mike, though, seemed to be growing philosophical. None of them forgave us. Svetlana gave Mike the check and he handed over a statement dropping fault and legal action.

None of them even noticed that I had tagged four hundred dollars above the amount they collectively asked for. This way they each made a hundred dollars on their original investment, a better rate of return than any savings account.

After three weeks of commuting to the Island, I finally stumbled across a good apartment deal. It was another old studio among the many new overpriced developments shooting up in Hell's Kitchen. It wasn't nearly as nice or cheap as Thelma Derchoch's place, but it was still a bargain and a short walk to work.

As a line producer I was near the bottom of the production pyramid, but it was a start. Manny always said that if I found any interesting projects I could bring them to him, and we could talk.

Throughout the remainder of the year, Cynthia was a great teacher, showing me the day-to-day business. It was essentially an administrative job, scheduling, troubleshooting, and making sure that different supervisors got what they needed to do the best they could. Manny was right. Problem solving was my forte. In fact, Cynthia secretly offered me a whopping raise to join her at her new company, Swinging From the Rafters Films, but I was under contract and didn't intend to double-cross Mr. Greene.

For my parents my working as a producer was a mitigated victory. They were glad I was out of acting, but saddened that I was definitely not entering a more stable profession. At least, they said, I was behind a desk figuratively speaking, which was where I belonged. With this conditional peace, I started returning home on a more regular basis and we delicately built a previously nonexistent friendship.

A few months into my working at Manny's, I was introduced to the hot producer Barbara Suffolk, who said she remembered me from the article in the *Local Vocal*.

When I reminded her that Bree Silverburn said he initially pitched the project to her, she said, "Oh, sure, I remember getting the script. I thought it was too good to be Bull, and I called the Bullonus Estate."

The entire mess could have been avoided if, like her, I had made a simple phone call and checked that the work was a fraud. That also explained why the Bullonus Estate was so quick to react when they saw that the play was being produced. They had gotten a heads-up by Suffolk.

When Franklin's film *Success!* finally came out, Manny asked if I'd come to the premiere as his date, but I feigned illness. I felt just too embarrassed. Although the reviews were fairly positive and my little role got a healthy amount of notices (mainly from New York reviewers who remembered the *Unlubricated* fiasco), I squirmed like hell at my big debut. All the production people that I had worked with during the recent months and who knew me as a businesswoman were now going to see me in the slutty buff on the big screen. I couldn't bear to see their reactions in person. Over the ensuing weeks, my parents called up to say that all their friends and relatives had seen the film. That was all they said; the shame and humiliation had to be inferred.

"You know," I said to my father, "I didn't do it to spite you."

"It'd be better if you did. Then at least you'd be doing something effective." It took me a moment to realize he was making a joke.

Success! ended up making twenty-two million dollars in domestic sales and a couple million more in video and overseas, which weren't bad figures, but they weren't enough to get the instant funding Manny needed for Christy's project. He kept trying to raise the budget but for one reason or another, he was unable. Maybe it was simply the fact that 90 percent of all projects that go up never come down. For me it was sort of a sacred film—I really did think Christy was talented and deserved the break, so I would talk up the work every chance I got.

One day, when Christy heard from another producer how much I had pushed her project, she called me up to thank me. In that conversation, we got to other things, and for the first time, I finally felt like we could be friends again.

"I broke up with you because my career stalled and I thought you were going behind my back with Franklin. I took it all out on you."

"Except for Steven Spielberg, Tom Hanks and a couple others," I said, "I think everyone in this business feels that their career is stalled."

"Yeah, but I heard how hard you've been trying and . . . It's weird about relationships. Anyways, I just should've treated you better." It was sweet of her to say.

Although Svetlana never quit her day job of stage managing, Manny hired her to rewrite a romance and doctor a ghost story. Neither of them have gone into production, but she did complete another play that had a showcase production at Manhattan Supper Club's Young Playwright Project.

One evening, while attending a Bring Theater to the Schools benefit, I spotted Patricia Harrows, my 9/11 friend. She had just been elevated to the board of the THERE theater in Tribeca.

"You know, I meant to tell you that what you did was really admirable," she replied.

"Well, you're the only one who thought so," I said, "everyone else was about to sue us."

"I meant on September eleventh. I ran off and you stayed and helped that guy."

"I didn't do anything," I said. I had totally forgotten about that.

"I also think you got a bad rap on that play."

"So you heard."

"I read that article in the *Local Vocal*, along with everyone else," she said with a smile. "I meant to call you."

"What a mess that was," I replied, and gave her my version of what had happened, including the financial compensation to the cast.

"That's what it takes to get a play up."

"You saw the only showing of *Unlubricated*," I told her with a smile.

"Damn shame. It was a great play and you had the cover of *Local Vocal*. That kind of publicity you can't buy." She thought a moment. "You know, if the play were to go up now, I'm sure you'd get noticed."

"I'm out of the theater game."

"You wouldn't be interested in a coproduction?" she asked.

"What do you have in mind?"

By the end of the week we agreed to a joint venture. I was even able to have Manny invest a modest amount for publicity in exchange for an option should it go to a bigger stage. Then I called everyone up and repitched it to them, highlighting the fact that they wouldn't have to invest a cent. Mike was already committed to a student film in Toronto, Kenny Eltwood was unreachable and Jonah was in a Broadway rock musical. I thought about reprising my Samantha role, but now as a producer, getting respected and well paid, I just couldn't go back. I simply didn't have the time. I called Belinda and told her I had no hard feelings and offered her the part if she wanted to be in it, explaining that we were also going to get a new director.

"But Huey was also a victim!" she protested, ever loyal to the asshole.

"This is my show," I said in my best Joan Crawford.

Noah got to play Reggie, the role he originally wanted, and sober Bree actually did a wonderful Miles. This time the play went up with Svetlana Palas's name on the marquee. The whole credit legally read "inspired by the notes of Lilly Bull." At the cast party after the first show, we all went out for drinks. Mike and Jonah showed up. One by one, Belinda included, we made our peace.

Unlubricated got three great reviews. Under the tiny banner "Two Acts of Contrition," Juan Valasquez printed a polite update stating how I had finally and honestly produced the work. The play ran for three weeks to respectfully full houses and it actually earned a tidy profit. The real glory was for Svetlana, who finally got her fifteen seconds of well-deserved fame.

During the evening of the last performance, I came by during closing to see my father in the exiting crowd.

"What are you doing here? Where's Mom?"

"I liked the play, so I thought I'd see it a second time. It's good, and you produced it."

It was as close as he'd ever come to saying he was proud of me, and that felt just fine. As I walked him down Church Street to his car, I saw his eyes searching south for the missing towers. I asked him how he was doing. He said he was fine, he had come to accept that in some sense what had happened was inevitable.

"Why inevitable?"

"You have to expect at least one enduring tragedy in a city of endless triumphs."

ACKNOWLEDGMENTS

Thanks to:
Joelle Yudin
Peter Trauberman
St. Mark's Bookshop
Dan Mandel
Brian Lipson
Marty Lorber (in memoriam)
Nora Ingalls
Larry Coppersmith
Heather Burke

▓ Perennial

Books by Arthur Nersesian:

CHINESE TAKEOUT
A Novel
ISBN 0-06-054882-7 (paperback)

Nersesian aptly paints the picture of an artist trying to stay true to his art—and himself—while falling in love with an addict-poet, navigating among fellow artists, and living, breathing, and bleeding art in a constantly evolving New York.

"Not since Henry Miller has a writer so successfully captured the trials and tribulations of a struggling artist." —*Library Journal* (starred review)

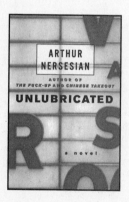

UNLUBRICATED
A Novel
ISBN 0-06-073411-6 (paperback)

After witnessing the fall of the Twin Towers, struggling actress Hannah comes across a lost play by a downtown New York icon and becomes the show's de facto producer. As she tries to resurrect the life-altering play, her life becomes a nonstop whirlwind of behind-the-scenes maneuvering and outrageous backstage personalities. Wedged firmly in the toughest months New York has ever endured, *Unlubricated* is a dynamic tale of self-discovery on the road to being discovered.

"Nersesian . . . has become, though he may not relish the comparison, the poor man's Bret Easton Ellis."
—*Toronto Star*
